Tara Pammi can't remember a moment when she wasn't lost in a book—especially a romance, which was much more exciting than a mathematics textbook at school. Years later, Tara's wild imagination and love for the written word revealed what she really wanted to do. Now she pairs alpha males who think they know everything with strong women who knock that theory *and* them off their feet!

Clare Connelly was raised in small-town Australia among a family of avid readers. She spent much of her childhood up a tree, Mills & Boon book in hand. Clare is married to her own real-life hero and they live in a bungalow near the sea with their two children. She is frequently found staring into space—a surefire sign that she is in the world of her characters. She has a penchant for French food and ice-cold champagne, and Mills & Boon novels continue to be her favourite ever books. Writing for Modern Romance is a long-held dream. Clare can be contacted via clareconnelly.com or at her Facebook page.

Also by Tara Pammi

Married for the Sheikh's Duty
Bought with the Italian's Ring
Blackmailed by the Greek's Vows

The Drakon Royals miniseries

Crowned for the Drakon Legacy
The Drakon Baby Bargain
His Drakon Runaway Bride

Also by Clare Connelly

Bought for the Billionaire's Revenge
Innocent in the Billionaire's Bed
Her Wedding Night Surrender

Discover more at millsandboon.co.uk.

SHEIKH'S BABY
OF REVENGE

TARA PAMMI

BOUND BY THE
BILLIONAIRE'S
VOWS

CLARE CONNELLY

MILLS & BOON

First Published in Great Britain 2018
by Mills & Boon, an imprint of HarperCollins*Publishers*
1 London Bridge Street, London, SE1 9GF

Sheikh's Baby of Revenge © 2018 by Harlequin Books S.A.

Special thanks and acknowledgement are given to Tara Pammi
for her contribution to the Bound to the Desert King series.

Bound by the Billionaire's Vows © 2018 by Clare Connelly

ISBN: 978-0-263-93545-5

MIX
Paper from
responsible sources
FSC™ C007454

Printed and bound in Spain
by CPI, Barcelona

SHEIKH'S BABY OF REVENGE

TARA PAMMI

CHAPTER ONE

"I'm Adir Al-Zabah, Your Highness, Sheikh of the Dawab and Peshani tribes."

He had no respect for the old king, for a man who subjugated and forced a woman—a weaker being—to bend to his will.

But Adir added a half bow to his greeting. Savage though he might be in comparison to the royal siblings Princes Zufar and Malak and Princess Galila, he knew customs and traditions.

Adir Al-Zabah stared at King Tariq of Khalia, watching like a hawk that soared the vast expanse of his desert abode, waiting for a flicker of recognition in the sorrow-filled eyes.

It was sorrow he recognized, wretched and absolute—something he had spied in his own reflection since he had heard the news of Queen Namani's death.

The genuine quality of it shocked him—one glimpse into King Tariq's eyes was enough to understand that he had loved his wife.

Any sympathy Adir might have felt died under the resentment festering in his veins. He himself had not even been granted the right to mourn her publicly, the opportunity to honor her with the last rites.

He'd been denied the chance to set eyes on her even once in his life.

His last blood connection, gone in the flicker of a sunset. There would be no more letters telling him he was cherished, reminding him of the place he had left unclaimed for so long.

He was finally, completely alone in the world.

And all because of this king.

While King Tariq stared back at him with confusion clouding his eyes, one of the princes moved forward, blocking the sight of the old king's bowed form, as if to shield the pitiful sight of his father from Adir's eyes.

"I'm Crown Prince Zufar. If you have come to pay your final respects to Queen Namani, to pledge your allegiance to King Tariq—" Zufar's words were filled with a resentment that mirrored Adir's own, making Adir frown "—then consider it acknowledged."

Adir gritted his teeth. "I am the ruling Sheikh of the Dawab and Peshani tribes. We're independent tribes, Your Highness." He injected every ounce of mockery he felt into that address. "I do not acknowledge your or your king's authority over our tribes. Our way of living knows no liege."

Something almost like admiration glinted in Prince Zufar's eyes. Gone in the blink of an eye, it left Adir to wonder if he had only imagined it. Was he that desperate for a familial connection?

"This is a private time of mourning for the royal family. If you're not here to pay your respects, why did you request an audience with my father?"

Having to go through this man who had everything Adir had been denied grated like the rub of sand on an open wound. "It is the king's company I requested. Not yours."

Satisfaction glinted in Zufar's eyes, satisfaction that he had the right to deny Adir this. Or anything he could ask for. "My father is…*swimming* in his grief over his queen's death."

His queen's death, not my mother's death, thought Adir. The crown prince's words were revealing.

There was no…grief in the prince's eyes for his mother's death, unlike in his father's. No tenderness when he spoke of her. "He has not been in his right mind for several…months now."

Adir tilted his head in the direction of Prince Malak and Princess Galila. He didn't want to feel pity, he didn't want to consider the fragility of their feelings so soon after their mother's death. And yet he found himself doing just that. "You would have me open a cupboard full of skeletons in front of your younger siblings?" he added silkily.

Zufar paled under his dark, olive skin. Not that his arrogance dimmed even a bit. "Threats will get you nowhere, Sheikh Adir."

"So be it. I'm your… I'm Queen Namani's son."

The statement he had repeated so many times to himself, in his own head, now reverberated in the chilling silence that ensued. A soft gasp emerged from the princess's mouth while Prince Malak scowled.

The antagonism in Zufar's eyes multiplied a thousand fold, roped with disbelief and a flash of fleeting pain.

Adir shifted his feet to gain a glimpse of King Tariq. His shoulders bowed, the old man stared at Adir searchingly. As if he could find a glimpse of his beloved wife, Adir realized with a frown. "Namani's son? But—"

"Do not deny it, Your Highness. The truth shines in your eyes."

Accusation painted every tense line of Zufar's body. "Father?"

But King Tariq couldn't shift his gaze from Adir. "You're Namani's son? The child she—"

"The newborn you banished to the vagaries of the desert, yes. The child you separated from its mother."

"You're our brother?" Princess Galila interjected. "But why—"

"Namani…she had an affair…" King Tariq stuttered.

"She fell in love with another man and was punished for it." Adir didn't pull his punches.

The king's face crumpled.

"And what is it that you want, on the eve of her death, Sheikh Adir?" Prince Zufar said coldly.

"I want what my mother wanted for me."

"How would you know what Queen Namani…what she wanted for you if you've never met her?" Princess Galila asked, her tone feather-soft.

"She was forced to give me up but she did not abandon me."

Prince Malak who had been calmly watching the proceedings until now moved to stand beside his father. "What do you mean, she did not abandon you?" A caustic laugh fell from his mouth. "What is it that the queen gave you that makes you talk of her as if you knew her?"

His gaze swept over the royal siblings and Adir frowned. He was missing something. They did not pounce to defend their mother's memory. No other interest showed on their faces except the shadow of fear about what he would ask.

"I did know her. Somehow, she found a way to keep in touch with me. She wrote me over the years, encouraged me to rise in the world. Told me how much she…

cared for me. Told me what my place is in this world. It is proof enough," Adir replied, choosing his words with cutting precision. "Every year on my birthday, she wrote letters and made sure they reached me. Letters telling me who I was."

"She wrote to you? The queen?"

"By her own hand."

"What do you want, Sheikh Adir? Why are you here?"

Adir faced Prince Zufar, determination running in his veins. "I want the king's acknowledgment that I'm Queen Namani's son. I want the world to know that I'm royal-born. I want my rightful place in Khalia's lineage."

"No." Zufar's tone rang out before Adir had barely finished. "All it will cause is a scandal."

He glanced at his father's form, his faraway gaze. Despite himself, Adir felt a stirring of pity for the old king. It was clear that he mourned his queen with all his heart.

"My father will become a laughingstock of the entire country if your origins come out. She—" He broke off. "I will not let her selfish actions scandalize our family now, even after she's gone. As if she hasn't caused us enough harm. If you're the great sheikh your tribes claim you to be, you'll understand that I have to put Khalia first. There is no place for you here, Sheikh Adir."

"I would like to hear it from the king."

"My decision *is* the king's decision. I will not bring scandal to our house by declaring to the world what my mother has done."

"And if I refuse to follow your dictates?"

"Be careful, Sheikh Adir. You're threatening the crown prince."

"Are you worried that I will want to rule Khalia, Prince Zufar? That I will ask for a slice of your immense fortune? Because if so, then let me tell you, I have no intention of taking anything from you. I have no use for your wealth. All I want is recognition."

"And you will not have it, not as long as I'm alive. You are nothing but my mother's dirty secret, a stain on our family."

The words came at Adir like invisible punches, all the more lethal for the truth in them that he had always tried to fight.

He was her dirty secret, banished to the desert without a second thought. "Watch your words, Prince Zufar. They carry heavy consequences."

"Have you not wondered why she asked you to claim your right only after she was gone? Why she wrote to *you* but never confided in *us* that we have a brother?"

"She was protecting you and the reputation of the royal family. She was—"

"Queen Namani—" Prince Zufar's words came through gritted teeth "—was a selfish woman who thought of nothing and no one but herself. Writing to you, I am sure, was nothing more than indulging in childish sulking. Behaving without considering the consequences…to you, to her or to any of us. It was cruel to lure you here when she knew nothing could come of it."

"And if I spill the truth anyway?" Adir hated the bitterness in his tone, cringed inwardly at the fear in the king's eyes. For years, he had watched his mother's family from afar. His mother's words about how spoiled they were, how undeserving of all the respect and privilege that were their due, had festered in his blood. "If I tell the world anyway?"

"I will not react to your threats, Sheikh Adir. The shame, if you spill it, will be yours and hers alone. Not ours. Leave now. Or I will have the guards throw you out as if you were nothing but a vulture circling at a time of mourning. If you had been anything but her bastard, you would have had better taste than to threaten my father at such a time of grief."

In the flickering shadows of the darkness, punctured only by gaslights flickering here and there, the view from the window out of which she meant to jump looked like absolute nothingness to Amira Ghalib.

Emptiness with no relief in sight. An abyss with no bottom.

Like her life had been for the past twenty-six years. Like the prospect of marrying Prince Zufar, like her future as Queen of Khalia.

She snorted and smiled into the darkness.

Ya Allah, she was getting morbidly morose. But then that was what five days of being her father's prisoner and a punch to the jaw had done to her.

Of pretending to her friend Galila that she had been clumsy again, that she had walked straight into a pillar. Of once again being the object of indifference to her betrothed. Of being nothing but a means to an end to her power-obsessed father.

She had even less freedom here at the palace of Khalia than her own home, and her house on the best day was a cage. Here, all eyes were on her.

But future queen or not, she needed escape. Just for a few hours.

Having failed to locate the flashlight she'd been looking for—her father's watchdog had probably confiscated it from her suite—Amira looked through the window again. She remembered that there was a short ledge there, a rectangular protrusion to cover the window on the lower floor. Big enough for her to land on with both feet.

From there, it would be another sideways jump to the next ledge.

From there, another jump onto the curved stairway on the other side, the stairway that was unused even by servants and staff. And she would be free of the guard outside her suite, free of her father and free of her obligations.

She could walk to the stables, bribe the teenage boy there and go for a ride on the mare she had befriended the other day. She could just wander down the exquisitely manicured gardens the late Queen Namani had famously tended herself.

For a few hours, she could do whatever she wanted. *There is a ledge there*, she repeated to herself.

All she had to do was hold her breath and jump.

Heart pounding, she climbed over the windowsill. Her legs dangled as she peered into the darkness, letting her eyes and ears adjust to the sounds and sights of the night. A horse's whinny, the soft tinkle of water from the famed fountain in courtyard, the tap-tap of soles on the tiled walkway reached her ears.

Night-blooming jasmine filled her nostrils.

Already, she felt calmer. It was a lovely night to escape.

She smiled and jumped.

"You could have killed yourself. At best. At worst, broken all the bones in your body."

Any breath that might have been left in her lungs

after she'd landed wonkily on her knees whooshed out of Amira's lungs.

She froze, the low, gravelly voice from the dark corner of the stairway sending shivers down her spine. Fear and something else swamped her. She blinked and peered through the quiet to see a shadowy outline.

Catlike eyes, amber-hued, stared back at her. Moonlight came in patches through the archway, outlining the man. He was blurry because she had forgotten her glasses.

But she could still make out broad shoulders that tapered to lean hips and powerful thighs. She searched for his face. Square jaw, sharp blade of a nose, high forehead.

Her gaze went back to his eyes. Eyes that were staring at her with unhidden curiosity.

Was he a royal guard? Another spy her obsessed father had set on her? Or worse, a guest of the palace?

No, anything would be better than her father's spy. She would even prefer to brave her betrothed and explain herself than to face her father.

And if it was her father's spy...

As if even her flesh remembered, a shaft of pain pulsed up her jawline and she flinched.

She could swear his scowl deepened the darkness as the man emerged from the shadows. "Are you hurt?"

"No. I'm...fine." She dusted her palms on her thighs and winced. The skin of her palms had been pierced when she had tried to break her fall with them.

"You're not a natural liar, *ya habibiti.*"

The upper-class aristocratic accent—similar yet different from her own or from the prince's—caught her interest. With his perfect diction and the natural command in his very stillness, he could be a visiting royal—

the last person she needed to be seen with. Or to have recognize her, come tomorrow.

He took another step toward her.

Still on her knees, Amira scooted back. Pains and aches forgotten, all she wanted was to get away from the…interesting stranger.

Whether he noticed her retreat or not, his long strides continued to eat up the distance between them. "Let me see if you're hurt. You landed so hard you could have broken something."

Another scoot back. At this rate, her knees were going to get skinned. "I did not…break anything."

"Let me be the judge of that."

Her normally placid temper simmered. "Since I have a degree in nursing, I think I can judge whether I broke something or not." She hissed a breath out. "Please… just leave. I'll be on my way in a couple of minutes."

"You don't have to fear me."

She was panicked, yes, but strangely, there was no fear in it.

She took a deep breath. Sandalwood, combined with something utterly masculine, filled her lungs as he reached her, settling into a strange tightness in her lower belly.

Arrested by her body's reaction—neither flight nor fight but more of a languid uncoiling low in her belly— she looked up at him.

Straight white teeth flashed at her when he smiled. "You intend to stay there?"

She nodded, aware of how stupid she must look, mooning over him and yet unable to stop.

"I'm perfectly fine with having a conversation on the…dirty floor," he said matter-of-factly. And before she could comprehend, he sank down on his knees with a fluid grace that was reminiscent of a jungle predator.

The traveling moon chose that exact moment to cast a bright, silvery glow through the archway, illuminating the planes of his face.

Breath arrested, Amira stared.

Deep-set amber eyes glinted with humor, and even that couldn't stop her appraisal. As if hand-chiseled by a master sculptor, he was breathtakingly handsome.

There was almost something royal about those features, something familiar yet painfully elusive.

She could see a high forehead, the sharp blade of a nose, weather-beaten skin that glinted dark gold— which told her he spent quite a lot of time in the harsh sun—and a defined jawline that invited her fingers' touch. Breathing shallowly, she fisted her hands in the folds of her gown.

His lashes flicked down to where she hid her hands and then up, that glimmer of humor deepening in his eyes.

"Tilt your head forward so that I may better look at you," he said in a low voice, no less commanding for its softness.

Years of obedience browbeaten into her, Amira dutifully did. Only when his gaze moved over every inch of her face with a penetrating intensity did she realize what she had done.

Color filled her cheeks. Instead of moving back, instead of lowering her eyes as she had been taught again and again by her father, she used the moment to study him some more.

A sharp hiss from his mouth jerked her gaze to his. In the flash of a breath, the humor disappeared, replaced by a dark vein of anger. His amber eyes glowed.

He lifted his hand to her face and Amira instantly cringed back. The softening of his expression told her what she had done. Shame filling her, she looked down at her palms. Hard concrete at her knees pulled her back to reality.

It was high time she was on her way. He was tying her insides into strange knots.

"May I touch you?"

His husky question jerked her gaze to his face again.

She thought she saw him swallow and that was strange.

"I promise I mean you no harm."

His eyes were deep pools, devoid of the barest expression, and yet there was an intrinsic trust deep in her belly that he would keep his word. That this was a man who didn't raise his hands against the weaker sex or people dependent on his mercies, for any reason. Not the least of which would be to establish his own superiority or to enforce his will.

Yet power seemed to emanate from his very pores. He would command any room he entered. And as to his will—she would bet any man or woman would surrender to it easily. With pleasure, in the latter case.

Slowly, she nodded. Something in her leaped quietly—anticipation, she realized. With every cell in her being, she wanted to feel this man's touch, however fleetingly.

She thought he would pull her to her feet. Instead, his fingers landed on her jaw with such gentleness that hot tears prickled behind her eyelids.

"These are fingerprints marring your lovely cheek." The words were devoid of emotion, feeling. Contained violence shimmered in his stillness. He was *furious* at the sight of the bruise on her jaw.

That simple concern on her behalf sent sorrow spiraling through her.

She closed her eyes, loathe to betray her weakness in front of him. She had never shed a single tear, even when her father's palm once landed on her jaw with such force that her head had jerked back, leaving her with neck pain for weeks. But now…she felt like stretched glass.

As she stoppered the emotion flowing through her, she felt other things. It was as if her senses were slowly opening up. His huge body gave out warmth on the chilly night, enveloping her like her childhood blanket—a reminder of her mother.

The scent of him—the more she breathed it, the more she wanted to—a tantalizing mixture of sandalwood and horse and pure man.

His fingers turned her jaw to the moonlight so that the bruise, which she hadn't covered after washing off her makeup, was visible. The pad of his thumb traced it and she flinched. More from the heat his touch generated than from pain.

A sharp curse flew from his mouth. "Forgive me, I promised not to cause you harm."

"You didn't," she said automatically.

He raised a brow. "No?"

"Our skin has thousands and thousands of nerve centers that react to external stimuli, did you know? Your palm is rough against my skin and also, I'm barely ever touched by anyone other than my father—and not in such a leisurely, soft way, either—so I feel a flash burn where your skin touches mine—" when his brows rose, she hurried to explain "—not like fire burns us, more pleasurable than that, and I believe that's why I flinched. Because even pleasure, especially when it's unexpected and unfamiliar to the recipient, causes flinching."

The utter silence that ensued sent blood pooling up her neck and into her cheekbones. She clamped her palms over her mouth. No wonder her father got aggravated whenever she opened her mouth.

A slow smile dawned in his eyes, causing lines at the ends of his eyes and adorable creases in his cheeks. His teeth flashed at her again and that smile made him a thousand times more gorgeous.

"I state facts and run my mouth endlessly when I'm anxious or agitated or upset or sad or angry. My father thinks I do it to ignore his dictates and to insult him."

"And when you're happy?"

She smiled. "You're very smart, aren't you? You know, people think intelligence is…" She cleared her throat and she blushed fiercely again. "I do it when I'm happy, too, yes. Pretty much all the time, now that you make me think about it."

His smile turned into laughter. It boomed out of him. Low, gravelly, utterly sensuous, but also a little rough and strange. As if he didn't do it much.

Amira wanted to roll around in that smile. She wanted to be the one who caused his serious face to smile and laugh again and again. She wanted to spend an eternity with this exciting stranger who made her feel safe. She wanted to…

"I have to leave."

He sobered up. And frowned. "So I can take your word that you're not hurt?" He flicked another glance at her jaw. "Other than your jaw?"

"I misjudged the distance between the last ledge and the stairs, but I'm not hurt."

He nodded. "And what is so irresistible that you took such a dangerous route…? What is your name?"

Zara, Humeira, Alisha, Farhat…

"You're thinking up fake names."

She blinked. Like a hawk, he watched with predatory intensity. And something else… Possessiveness, perhaps.

She swallowed. "I would get into trouble if word gets out that I escaped my room or that I was wandering the palace without guard or that I spent all this time in the dark with a stranger…a lot of trouble."

"No one will know," he said. "I will get you back to your room unharmed and undiscovered."

And all the while he tempted her, he watched her. As if he found her endlessly fascinating. "I don't know if I can trust you," she said.

His fingers pushed back a strand of hair that brushed her jaw. Featherlight and tender, his touch knocked down the little sense remaining in her skull. "I think you do trust me. Which is why you have lingered here so long already. All you need to do is take the final step, *ya habibiti*. We're strangers passing a few moments together in a long life."

Another rough-padded finger lifted her chin until she was gazing into his eyes. His nostrils flared, the set of his jaw resolute. "I would have your real name."

If he had commanded her, Amira would have prevailed. But beneath that request was a thread of longing that resonated in her soul. What could such a commanding man want that he was ever denied?

He was harshly beautiful, like the rugged landscape of the desert, and yet he looked at her with such pure need.

The last of her good sense and diffidence melted.

Innocent she might be when it came to men but she already felt like she knew him.

He wouldn't hurt her.

"Amira...my name is Amira."

Fire awakened in his eyes. They both knew she had given him more than just her name in that moment.

He tilted his head—a regal nod for granting him the privilege of her real name. Warmth filled her chest. "I'm Adir."

"*Salaam-alaikum*, Adir."

"*Walaikum-as-salaam*, Amira."

He took her hand in his, completely engulfing hers. Sensations shimmered through her, flowing like a river from where their hands touched to spread all over her body. And then he was softly tugging her to him. Raising their clasped hands, he placed a soft kiss to the tender skin at her wrist.

It was a chaste kiss—nothing more than a buss from those lips to her skin. And yet her pulse skittered under his mouth. "Meeting you has made an awful night a thousand times better."

The way he held her gaze, the banked fire in it...she wanted to answer it with her own fervor. For one night, she just wanted to be Amira and not a power-obsessed man's daughter, nor the fiancée of a mostly indifferent prince. She wanted to sink into Adir's arms and let him carry her away.

"You know, when you smile, you get two dimples. Did you know that dimples are caused when a facial muscle called *zygomaticus major* is shorter than normal? Sometimes, they're also caused by excessive fat on your face. Although, in your case, it's definitely not excessive fat, because you look hard as those rock structures we see in...in..."

His smile dawned as slow and bright like the sun over the horizon.

Amira buried her face in her hands and groaned loudly.

"So you're informing me that my facial structure is flawed, yes?"

She tried to tug her hand from his. He didn't let her. "Oh, please, you know you're flawless."

That seemed to take him aback. Didn't he look at himself in mirror? Did he not have women flocking to him for a glimpse of that wicked smile?

Still smiling, he pulled her to her feet. "You're...like a desert storm, Amira."

"I'm not sure if that's a compliment."

His eyes gleamed in the darkness. "Do you want a compliment, *ya habibiti*?"

"Yes, please."

Again that pure laughter—a reward for her boldness. "You're precious. Now, do me the honor of letting me check you."

When she straightened all the way, he patted her down in an impersonal manner. As if he was used to her antics and had done it a thousand times before. As if he cherished his right to indulge her.

A hard knot made its place in Amira's throat.

His hands rested on her shoulders. The sheer breadth of him took her breath away anew.

"So what was it this time?"

Caught staring at him once again, Amira frowned. "What was what?"

"What caused you to divulge all those important facts about dimples to me? Was I making you sad, perhaps? Upset? Angry?"

"You're shamelessly goading me into admitting

something I shouldn't. Isn't it enough that I made a fool of myself?"

"Please, *ya habibiti.*"

She raised a brow, stalling for time. "Why do I have the feeling you never say that word?"

He shrugged. "A couple of times in the last decade."

She sighed. It wasn't as if he didn't know. "I'm attracted to you. I could steal all kinds of romance novels from the library and read about all the feelings that hit a woman when she finds a man attractive, but it's not even close to what I feel. You could be forgiven for thinking it was all cooked up to sell books, this whole chemistry thing. And yet…it's new and it's strange and it's utterly scary and it's…"

Heartbreaking and painful.

Despair swamped her so fully and so suddenly that she pulled away from him. Looking up, she fought for composure.

Stars glittered in the sky above, winking at her. The fragrant night with its whispers and taunts seemed like a punishment now. It promised something she could never have.

Warmth coated with his scent reached her back. She tensed as he stilled behind her. Her pulse zigzagged all over at the closeness. He didn't even touch her.

"Come away with me, Amira. Just for a few hours. I promise you again I would never harm you."

"It's wrong."

"Why?"

"I'm not free to be attracted to you like this. I'm not free to indulge in this…this late-night stolen moment with you. And not just because my father would skin me alive if he found out." Longing curled through her and she tried to shut it away. "I'm a betrothed woman."

There was that contained energy within him again. Like walking too close to fire. "Is it your fiancé that…" the words choked in his throat "…that hurt you?"

"No. He…is a perfect gentleman who barely even looks at me. If you ask him what color my eyes are, I'm sure he wouldn't know."

"Then who is it?"

"My father. He…his temper gets away with him."

Whatever it was that made him cover the last step between them, she didn't care. His arms enveloped her on either side and unlocked her tight grip on the sill.

The graze of his hard chest against her back ripped open a longing inside of her. One, two, three…four seconds before she fell into his embrace. Sensations beat upon her. He was so shockingly hard all over—his abdomen against her back, his thighs resting against the back of hers, his muscular arms wound tightly around her own… He didn't press the part of him that she wanted to feel most, to her wicked shame.

And yet, she felt consumed by him.

She closed her eyes and leaned back into him. The scent of him filled her every breath. His heart thundered against her back. She rubbed her thumb over the back of his hand, curious for the feel of him.

His skin was rough and tanned, his fingers long and square-nailed. A dark emerald jewel sat on his ring finger and Amira traced it, too, carving it into memory.

It was the first time in her life that she had been held like this by a man. It was both exhilarating and comforting—just like the man himself.

"Is that why those shadows linger in your beautiful eyes? Because you love this man you are to marry but he does not love you in return?"

"Love? I would settle for acknowledgment as a person. My father is King Tariq's closest friend. I have been betrothed to Prince Zufar for most of my life." A bitter laugh escaped from her mouth. "I'm to be the future Queen of Khalia, Adir.

"I've been trained, educated, groomed, molded to within an inch of my life to complement Prince Zufar in every way. My life has never been my own. My will can never be mine. My dreams and desires…are not mine."

CHAPTER TWO

SHOCK BARRELING AT him with the might of a sandstorm, Adir struggled to hold himself still. She was Zufar's betrothed… The future Queen of Khalia!

The realization drummed in tune with his heartbeat even as desire filled every inch of his body. "You're shivering," he whispered, moving his hands up and down her arms.

Thoughts came and went through his head like sand held in a palm. His fingers must have tightened over her shoulders for she let out a soft gasp.

Adir gentled his grip, but for reasons he couldn't fathom, he didn't want to let her go.

The bones at her shoulders jutted under his palms as he tried to soothe her. And himself.

Desire for her, he understood. She was beautiful, brave, smart, funny.

But this fierce possessiveness that coursed through his blood… It stemmed from something else.

That she was his half brother's most precious possession perhaps? Now in his hands?

"I should walk away." Her words were a whisper in the night—a plea, a demand on herself. Yet she didn't move from the cradle of his arms. "From you. From this moment. It only tells me how much I cannot have.

This…" she brought his arms up to her face, burying it in his palms. The soft buss of her kiss against his skin burned him "…only pains me. Only reminds me of how much I never had. And never will have."

"Shh… I only want to hold you, Amira," he said, even as his mind raced. "Whatever you need, it is here, now, with me."

Turning, she burrowed into him. Her arms wrapped around his waist, her face hidden in his chest. The scent of her hair filled his own breath. He wrapped thick strands of her hair around his fingers, coiling and un-coiling, not unlike his own thoughts.

She was so damn innocent and trusting. Such a gift. A gift Zufar didn't deserve. A gift Zufar didn't even value, for why else would she crave a stranger's company so much?

A gift that had unwittingly fallen into Adir's hands.

He raised her chin until she was looking into his eyes. The transparent desire he saw there banished any doubts he might have had. Feral possessiveness filled him and he touched his mouth to hers in a soft press that sent lust punching through him.

She was so beautiful and young and soft.

So easy to seduce.

If anything inside of him revolted at the idea, Adir suppressed it with a ruthlessness learned through years of surviving the harshest desert conditions.

Shocked at first, she stilled underneath his kiss. But it was already there, the heat he had felt between them, a small spark waiting to be ignited.

Adir ran his hands over her back, soothing the tremors, learning her curves, all the while gently nibbling at her lips.

Honey and heat, she was the most perfect thing he

had ever tasted. An urgency he had never known before filled his blood, pounding at him to push her against the wall behind them. To lock her body against his hungry one. To thrust his tongue into her mouth while he entered her heat in the same way…to make her his, here, in this moment, to stamp his…

No!

A small voice inside him whispered. Whatever his reasons for doing this, he wanted to make it good for her, too. And that meant he couldn't let his libido run rampant.

"Adir?" she whispered, blinking owlishly. Making him smile. "Why did you stop?"

"I wanted to make it good for you."

"It is good. It is so… I didn't know a simple kiss could be so animalistic. So powerful."

For an innocent, sheltered beauty, how could she be saying the one thing that fired his blood? He dug his teeth into her lower lip. And licked it when she moaned. "Between the right couple, a kiss can be a lot more."

"So, it is this good for you, too?"

"You have quite the scientific mind, don't you?"

She shrugged, studying him with those big eyes. "I wondered."

He rubbed his nose against hers, a gesture of tenderness that shocked even him. It was only a prelude, he reminded himself. She had been his for the taking from the moment she had glanced up at him and sighed that feminine sigh.

What was wrong with blending into her fantasy a little? Giving her what she wanted? "You wondered what, Amira?"

"If it felt the same to you. I… I have never shared such a passionate kiss with any man."

"Not even your fiancé?" The question slipped past his lips.

"No. The most he has ever done is hold my hand. At public ceremonies." She blinked and he knew he would never forget that earnest expression in those wide eyes. The transparent desire. "Coming back to us… You've obviously been with a lot of women."

He couldn't remember a time he had enjoyed a conversation with a woman as much as he enjoyed having sex. But then, when had he had the inclination or time to have a proper relationship?

For him, women were for sex. To sate his body's needs. And only when he was on his overseas visits because he could not disrespect any of his own tribes by taking a daughter or a sister or another's wife as a lover.

Not when all the power rested in his hands.

"Why obviously? And are you asking?" he teased.

"No," came her resounding answer. "I think it is tacky and I really don't wish real life to interrupt this… dream. The only reason I brought it up is because it makes me curious if it feels just as powerful and passionate for a man who is sexually experienced and has had a variety of partners, in contrast to a woman who has lied to her own best friend when she told her that her fiancé had done more than kiss her because she feels too pathetic to admit that he barely even looks at her."

This time, her admission, instead of giving that high again, made his chest contract in a strange sensation. No…chemistry was a strange thing, and he didn't need to understand it. It was a tool tonight and he was using it. As he had always done—to carve his own path in life. To rise from orphan to sheikh of warring tribes.

To be the man who had done the impossible.

He brought her palm to his chest where his heart was

thundering. Down his chest to the flat plane of his abdomen and farther down.

Eyes wide like a dark oasis on a moonlight, she gasped when her hand reached his groin. He covered her hand with his and let her feel the shape and hardness of him. It was a bad idea that made him grit his teeth when she explored him with that innate curiosity, her breath hitching in and out in the dark silence.

He leaned his forehead against hers, locking her wrist. "I have been like that from the moment I touched you. That kiss between us, Amira, is no common thing. It is a spark waiting to burn and I can't breathe for wanting to set it alight."

An incandescent joy lit up her face, and in that smile, he felt like a king.

Clasping her cheeks with his palms, he kissed her gently. He licked at the seam of her lips. Again and again. He sank his fingers into the thick mass of her hair and pulled her toward him until she was a perfect fit for him. He licked a damp trail from her neck to her jaw, dropping soft little butterfly kisses over her cheek, her nose, her eyelids, her temple. Everywhere but the sweet offering that was her mouth.

He did it again and again, until it felt like he had been waiting an eternity to taste her. Until every muscle in his body was coiled tightly, until the innocent rub of her belly against his erection was sensuous torture.

"I could do this all night, *habiba*," he whispered, his own contrary nature fighting the pull she had on his own control. This was a means to an end—a pleasurable means, though.

"I can't," she threw back at him, her eyes daring him.

Adir laughed and decided to give in.

She groaned into his mouth and he deepened the

pressure, hungrier than he could ever remember being for the taste of a woman's lips.

No, for *this* woman's lips. *This* woman's body, her innocence and the desire she expressed with such fierceness and generosity.

Her hands caught between their bodies while he pressed her against him. When he demanded entry into the sweet cavern of her mouth, she gave it, clinging to him with a deep moan. He licked the inner curve of her lower lip, using every ounce of skill he had at his disposal.

Her hands moved to his shoulders, her breasts pressing into his chest, her mouth so addictively hungry for more. It sealed the night.

He would give her what she desperately needed for one night. She would come with him willingly, he knew that—the fire between them, it was unlike anything he'd ever seen or felt.

"Come away with me, Amira. For one night. A few hours. Steal something for yourself from your own life, *ya habibiti.*"

Her swollen pink lips trembled, her eyes shining with desire along with something else. He didn't have to ask, she was his for the taking—the pulse beating madly at her throat, the hunger in her gaze—and yet Adir wanted her to make the choice.

He would take what he wanted—revenge. He would steal something that belonged to his half brother, just as Zufar had stolen from him. His revenge on Zufar so much fuller if his betrothed came away with him out of her own choice.

If she chose Adir over Zufar even for a few hours…

"A choice, Amira," he said, running his thumbs over her trembling lips, his body primed for possession,

and yet he carefully used the words that would shred
the last bit of her fear and doubts, a ruthless strategy
he had learned from his mother's letters. "You can go
back to your bed and wonder what magic could have
happened between us for the rest of your life. Or..."
He bent his head and licked the pulse throbbing at her
neck and felt her jerk toward him. He smiled wickedly
before sucking the tender skin with his lips before re-
leasing it with a popping sound. This time, she writhed
against him, looking for relief from the ache between
her legs, he knew. She was ready for him, even if she
didn't know it. And the knowledge filled him with a
primal pride, not unlike the rulers before him who had
mastered the harsh desert. "...you can choose me. This.
For a few hours."

When she kissed his knuckles, when she looked up at
him with tears shining in her eyes, as if he was the sun
and moon and stars all combined together, he pushed
away the fragile thread of unease in his gut.

You're a dirty stain.

He would pay Zufar back for those words. He would
take what had been handed to him without guilt.

Victory thrummed through him when she said,
"Yes, I... I would like to spend the...a few hours with
you."

He pressed his mouth against her temple, holding
her tight until the shivers that had overtaken her sub-
sided. She was courageous, this fragile beauty, and he
would make this night worth that courage. He would
show her infinite pleasure.

"I will return you unharmed, yes?"

When she nodded, he took her mouth in a fierce kiss,
forgetting in that instant that she was innocent. He bit
the lush pillow of her lower lip and when she moaned,

tangled his tongue with hers. Heat built inside of him, goaded on and on by a dark need to possess her. To take what should have been Zufar's by right.

His mother's legitimate son, the man who was poised to be King of Khalia, the man who had never doubted his origins or his place in the world, the man who even now denied Adir his rightful place when he himself held Khalia in his palm…

It was a fitting revenge.

His body vibrated with the need to be inside her, here…in the dark stairway. But whatever his half brother thought of him, Adir was no savage.

He pulled the threads of his control together and pulled away from the lush temptation of her mouth. Already, her lips were swollen and her hair mussed with his questing fingers.

And yet Amira didn't back away, her breaths falling and rising rapidly. "Where shall we go?" Her eyes shone with an impish delight, even as she shivered. "I have to return before—"

"I have heard so many tales about her gardens," he said, remembering the beautiful words with which his mother had painted the gardens. "That she toiled hours and hours there, that they were her true love."

"The Queen's Gardens? You know of them?"

He simply nodded.

A wide smile curved Amira's lips. "That's exactly where I wanted to go tonight."

He took her hand in his and led her down the steps. "Then it must be fate that I came upon you tonight, of all nights."

A small frown tied her brows and she halted his steps. Her chin tilted up, a fierce resolve in her eyes. "Not fate, Adir. No. You and I… We ended up in this darkened corridor because we both made choices, yes? Tonight, there is no fate, there is no destiny, there are no forces commanding us. Just you and me."

"You and me," Adir agreed and pulled her on, before she could see the shadow of his dark thoughts in his eyes.

She was his tonight. Not Zufar's. That was all he had to remember.

Amira felt as if she had been floating on clouds for the last two hours. Two whole hours she had spent with Adir by her side, touring Queen Namani's famed gardens. Two hours spent smiling, talking, laughing, teasing.

Two hours in which she had been more herself than she had been her entire life.

Whatever it was Adir did in his real life, it had taken him mere seconds to maneuver them both out of the stairway and through another corridor of the palace manned by armed guards.

Almost as if he had been trained in subterfuge in the military division of Khalia. Or perhaps the map of the Khalian Palace was embedded in his head, because he had known ins and outs through the lit and unlit corridors that wound down to the paths of the garden, routes that even Amira who had visited for years didn't know.

Was that it? Was he a member of the visiting guard called upon as security for the queen's funeral? Someone who traveled all over the region but never stayed still in one place?

Was Amira one of a number of women he did this with?

Seconds after the thought occurred, Amira discarded it. She didn't really care what he did or how he lived. She couldn't afford to. Not if she wanted to steal away this night for herself. Not if she wanted to believe that she deserved a few hours with a man who really saw her. Who admired her and liked her and was attracted to her.

Except for that shock she had glimpsed in his eyes when she had confided to whom she was betrothed, he hadn't mentioned Prince Zufar again. Or the royal family. Only Queen Namani filtered into their conversation once in a while. If she sensed a certain veneration in his tone for the dead queen, Amira ignored it. What she thought of Queen Namani, however contrasting to his view, was irrelevant to tonight.

This night was hers.

So she let herself be Amira and she didn't press him for any answers. Not that she doubted he would give her answers if she demanded them.

For all his charming wit and teasing taunts, there was a remoteness to him. And that was after coming up against that smooth arrogance of a man who knew he was an alpha among men. And also a protector at heart, for she had seen the fierceness of his expression when he saw her bruise.

"Cold?" he asked as she shivered at the thought and Amira nodded.

Instantly, she was surrounded by the warmth of his jacket.

Moonlight carved the deep planes of his face with an even harsher outline. Even with the fragrance of the night-blooming jasmines filling the night breeze with a pungent scent, the scent of him clung to her skin instead. They walked along the walls of the small maze until they reached the famed fountain in the center, lit up by huge brass containers holding lights.

She had visited the palace innumerable times and yet had never seen this cozy spot in the middle of the maze. There was a sense of secrecy about it, amplified by her knowledge that King Tariq had had it built as a present to please his wife Queen Namani.

Galila had never told her if her mother had appreciated it or not.

But it was a beautiful, magical night—as if the universe itself were conspiring to give Amira what she wanted.

The center of the maze felt as if it had been designed for them. The tall hedges provided privacy and the water at the intricately sculpted fountain was a tinkling backdrop that drowned out everything else.

Every sense she possessed tingled with awareness of the man holding her hand.

"Why a nursing degree?" he asked.

Warmth spread through her chest. "When I was a little girl, my mother talked a lot about how she had always dreamed of studying medicine. She bought me this cute doctor's toy set and we used to play… She would be the patient and I the doctor.

"I think she had just as much fun as I did. And then suddenly, she fell ill. I used to sit by her and study and then just like that, it seemed, she was…gone.

"I was a good student, made the top of my grade always. But when I broached the subject of studying medicine with my father, he was dead against it. Said I was destined for better things.

"Soon, Zufar and I were officially betrothed and then…at some royal dinner after our engagement, I told him that I wanted to study nursing. That it would bring a nice background to the various children's charities I would be working with in the future. And that I needed his permission to trump my father's refusal. That if he gave me his accord in that moment, I would never ever ask him for anything else for the rest of our lives. It was the only time I think he really looked at me. Not just this…placeholder of a wife that had been chosen for him, but a real, breathing woman."

"What did he say?"

There was a strange intensity in Adir's voice and Amira smile faltered. "That he…much preferred a wife who knew how to keep herself happy than one who ruined everyone else's life. He…told my father that my education, my future all belonged to him as my future husband. I could have kissed him just for that."

"Did you?"

She shook her head, trying to find again that fun, easy footing between them. An uneasy light came into his eyes whenever she mentioned Zufar. "No…even if I had, it would have been only from gratitude. Nothing like the one we shared." She couldn't imagine ever kissing Zufar like that. Ever sharing this sense of camaraderie with him. Ever feeling a fraction of what she felt with Adir even if she spent a hundred years with him.

Adir turned her toward him, his face wreathed in shadows. "For a woman who recites every inconsequential fact as if her life depends on it, a woman who looks so beguilingly innocent, you're quite cunning."

"You make me sound…wicked."

He laughed, and the sound surrounded her in waves. "You took the situation you were handed and turned it to your advantage to realize your dream. It is a compliment, Amira."

And because the genuineness of his emotion reverberated in his words, Amira went on her toes and pressed her mouth to his. She wanted his laughter and his compliments. But she also wanted to soak in the heat and hardness of his body. To learn what it was to be a woman who desperately desired a man.

She needed to be the woman who reached for what she wanted. This time, she opened up for him, like a sunflower turning toward the sun, trusting him to take her wherever he wanted. This time, when he devoured her, she was ready and more than willing for it.

The male heat of him surrounded her, his fingers moving, touching, digging into her body, waking her up.

She clung to him, to the raw heat he evoked with his wicked mouth, to the rough urgency of his tongue as it slid in a spine-tingling dance against hers.

His fingers buried in her hair, he tugged her face up. "I would love to be there on the day when Amira Ghalib decides to be truly wicked."

She traced the outline of his lips with her thumb, the press of his lengthening erection against her belly searing her skin. "This is the moment, Adir. I want to be wicked. With you."

His dark eyes flared with fire, with need. With deep desire. "Here, with me?"

When he pulled the jacket off her shoulders and laid it on a thick grassy bank, Amira's heart pounded. When he turned her around and undid the zipper holding her long gown together all the way to the curve of her buttocks, her breath grew shallow.

When he pushed the dress off her shoulders and kissed a line down of her spine, all the way to the curves of her buttocks, she thought she would incinerate from the inside out.

And when he fell to his knees, when he turned her around to face him, when he buried his face in the flat curve of her belly, when he gripped her hips and took a deep breath as if to inhale the scent of her arousal, she gasped at the rush of wetness at her core.

When he slid his fingers through the thin strings of

her panties and pulled them down, when he delved into the folds of her sex while his dark eyes held hers captive, when he licked the wetness on his finger with a wicked, all-consuming smile and asked if it was all for him, her knees refused to hold her up and she fell into his waiting arms.

If she lived a hundred years, Amira wouldn't forget the sounds, the scents, the sights of that night. Of the night-blooming jasmine he had pinched between his fingers and rubbed over her belly as he licked her before declaring that no scent in the world could beat the scent of her arousal.

Of the stars shimmering in the sky overhead because he had taken her nipple in his mouth in such a carnal caress that she had thrown her head back into the grass.

Of the throaty sounds she had made, again and again, unashamed, begging whispers when he penetrated her with two long fingers so gently that she thought she would explode for the want of more.

Of the sensations that poured through her, like buffeting waves of the sea when he thrust into her—the quick, sharp flash of pain, the overwhelming fullness when he was seated all the way in her, the feeling that she would never again be whole without him; the sweat beading on his forehead and the tautness of the lean angles of his face; the flutter of butterfly wings of pleasure in her lower belly when she shifted to relieve the fullness, the tight friction that sent arrows of sensation firing in all directions when he moved, the building vortex of need in her lower belly every time he drove into her...

She wanted to drown in the pleasure their bodies created together. She wanted to give herself over to the moment, let him cast her about as he pleased.

But for the even more desperate need to watch his face.

Silvery moonlight caressed the sharp planes, etched tight with need as he thrust in again. The grunting sound he made in the back of his throat wound around her senses. And then when he looked into her eyes, his amber eyes lit with desire, Amira pushed up onto her elbows and kissed him.

He tasted like sweat and horses and masculinity.

"You want something," he whispered and Amira nodded.

"I want to touch your skin."

He nodded.

Amira sneaked her hands under his buttoned shirt, greedy for more and more of him. Velvet rough, his skin was warm, his heart racing under her fingers. She moved her hands restlessly over his chest, discovering the roped muscles of his abdomen she couldn't see, and lower where he was joined with her.

When she snatched her hands back, he smiled. And kissed her on her mouth.

"You like this?" she asked, desperate for more of him, just as he thrust in again.

He wiggled his hips in some swirly motion and Amira's eyes rolled back. "Do you doubt it still, *habiba*?"

And then his fingers were at the throbbing spot where pressure had been building with his every thrust, and then he was rubbing and pinching in between his smooth thrusts and Amira thought she would die if she didn't...

Finally she released a thready, wicked sound when pleasure beat upon her in waves and waves.

"You're the most beautiful thing I've ever seen," he said in a husky voice and Amira's eyes flew open.

And when he moved faster and rougher inside her,

when he pressed a rough, biting kiss to her mouth, when he gazed into her eyes and whispered her name as his own climax rushed him, when the indescribable pleasure he found with her laid him out in all his vulnerability, stripping from him the arrogance and the command and whatever darkness that dwelled in him, Amira knew she had made the right decision.

This man was hers, in this moment.

And she had chosen it.

CHAPTER THREE

Four months later

AMIRA TURNED SIDEWAYS and stared at her reflection in the gilt-edged, full-length oval mirror standing on clawed feet digging into the lush carpet on the floor. Everywhere around her was gilt furniture and priceless rugs and…it was all a cage.

A golden cage from which she had no freedom, a place where no one even knew the real her.

Her hands went to the swell of her stomach, utterly undetectable in the voluminous folds of her jeweled wedding gown.

Her wedding gown…her wedding day…and she was pregnant with another man's child.

Adir's child.

The thousands of gems sewed onto the tight bodice glinted in the mirror. Under the sun's rays cast into the room through the windows, the glitter of the gems reflected everywhere, even catching her in the eye every time she looked up.

At least they made the tears in her eyes look like an illusion of light. Already, her friend Galila and the maid she'd been assigned had given her strange looks when she had insisted on getting herself into the dress that weighed a ton.

But maybe she should have let them see the evidence of her one night of freedom. Maybe it would have been better if the dress had showed her growing belly.

Her father's rage when she'd told him had known no bounds. Until that moment, she hadn't realized how much the powerful connection, the status of being the queen's father mattered to him. Until that night, when he had roughly pushed her and locked her in her room, she had always made excuses for his autocratic, even sometimes violent behavior.

What did he think Prince Zufar would do when he discovered his wife was pregnant with another man's bastard? A word she hated with every inch of her being, a word her father had used again and again to drill it into her that that was what her child would be called if she didn't marry Zufar.

Ya Allah, she hated deception.

Zufar had never been interested in her, but he didn't deserve this.

Her father meant to force her to give her child away. Like an unwanted package thrown onto the streets. A stain on her reputation to be swept away…

A growl emerged from her throat, startling Galila and the maid.

Despite her father's threats, she had made every effort to see Prince Zufar alone last night. Somehow, she would have muddled through the explanation about why the wedding needed to be called off. But her father had caught her two steps away from the prince's private study where he had agreed to see her.

He had dragged her back to her room and back-handed her with such brutal force that she had lost consciousness. And by this morning, it was too late.

Prince Zufar had already left for the parade walk with King Tariq and would meet her at the hall where their wedding ceremony was to be held.

In every guard, in every visiting dignitary, in every man she came across, she had searched for those broad shoulders, that serious face. That wicked, warm smile.

She had searched because she needed a way out of her predicament, she reminded herself. Because she desperately needed to stop this farce her father was bent on having played out. Nothing else.

But there had been no sign of Adir.

"Amira…is everything all right?" asked her childhood friend, Galila—Prince Zufar's sister.

Fear made Amira's mind leap from one useless fact to another. "Did you know that the money that has been spent on the future queen's wedding dress throughout history could have fed and clothed Khalia's poor more than ten times over? That it takes three hundred days and twenty women working from sunup to sundown to create a dress like this?"

Her gaze concerned, Galila took her friend's hands in hers. "My brother might not be…the ideal man. But he's not a monster, Amira." Galila knew of her friend's father's temper and she must think that was why Amira was afraid.

Unable to meet her eyes, Amira pulled away.

Galila sighed. "The maid and I will bring the royal jewelry. Will you be all right for a few moments?"

"Yes, of course," Amira answered automatically. But ten minutes later, her panic multiplied.

Could she run away before Galila and the maid returned with the jewelry? On the way to that vast throne hall, could she claim to be sick and then steal away somehow from the palace?

The gems on the dress itself would probably pay for a few months of food and shelter. Although how far would she go weighing a ton and seriously lacking in energy? For almost a week now, she had barely kept down anything she ate in the morning.

Also, the extravagantly expensive dress would be a dead giveaway. Which meant she would have to get rid of it if she meant to escape without being seen. And to shed the dress, she needed to...

Hysteria bubbled up in her chest as she dipped her head between her knees.

She would keep her baby somehow, no matter what. She wouldn't let anyone separate them.

Just that promise to herself gave her a renewed purpose.

She was gulping down a glass of water when the catch on the huge window rattled. She frowned. It was not a windy day. In fact, Galila and the maid had both noted what a gloriously beautiful day it was to get married and she had snorted...

Her breath hitched as the top of a dark-haired head appeared outside the window. And then a hard, striking face—a face that had haunted her dreams for four months.

The intricately carved silver tumbler slipped from her hand, the loud clang of it softer than her thudding heart.

Broad shoulders. Tapered waist. Hard, powerful thighs that had straddled her hips when he had stroked himself into her, causing such indescribable pleasure that Amira was swamped with heat even now.

Amber eyes. A cruel slash of a mouth that was incapable of infinite tenderness. Adir landed on the floor with sure-footed grace.

"*Salaam-alaikum*, Amira."

She reached for the back of an armchair, blinking rapidly to clear the fast approaching tears. It was only relief. Only relief. She repeated it like a mantra.

Adir's presence meant help. Meant she didn't have to go through with the wedding.

Why he was here didn't matter. He had made no promises and she wouldn't expect anything. But he would help her escape. And then she could make a life for her and the baby, a life that she designed for herself, a life that wasn't ruled by anyone else but her. Once she had settled into a new life, maybe she could tell him. She would not force this on him. She would not change his plans for his own life.

Maybe he would agree to visit her child whenever he was between assignments, or in the country? Maybe they could reach some...

"Amira?"

She startled, her mind a jumble of thoughts. "I'm afraid to blink for fear you'll disappear. It's not rational, I know, because *I see you*. My body remembers your scent—horses and sandalwood and...you. And yet the mind is such a powerful thing, you know? It weaves such illusions. I used to see my mother like that, months after she was gone. Hallucinations are caused by..."

"How much time is left before you marry your prince?"

She flinched at the open rancor in the question. This was not the charming, laid-back man she had given her virginity to. Something was different. Something had altered.

He wasn't smiling. No, it wasn't just the absence of

his smile. He hadn't smiled a lot that night, either. It was the presence of something else in his eyes today.

A dark intensity full of shadows.

A cloud of some intense emotion…resentment? Anger? Why?

He reached her with silent footfalls. His lower lip curled into a sneer as he took in her glittering wedding dress. As if she were nothing but a fake, tawdry imitation of what the future queen should be.

When his gaze returned to her face, that resentment smoothed out for an instant. There was a flash of that tenderness she'd seen that one incredible night.

"My father will arrive to escort me an hour before," she said calmly before the hurt turned into words. "Why do you look at me like that? With such contempt?"

"I do?"

"Yes."

"I'm just wondering if the one night of illicit freedom has scratched the itch for rebellion? You're happy to marry your prince today?"

Her eyes widened, his words landing with a painful punch. "How dare you…?" Looking away from him, she swallowed the anger rising inside her.

Who was this man with such twisted words? How much did she really know about this stranger? How would he react when he learned their one night had resulted in an irrevocable consequence?

"Please… Adir. Do not presume to know what drives my decisions. Everything I do or don't do has consequences." Consequences that she was dreading telling him now. Consequences that were reaching beyond just him and her.

"Where did he strike you this time?" he asked so

smoothly that Amira startled at how easily he made the connection.

Renewed shame filled her. "I was going to tell Prince Zufar that I... I can't marry him. Father...pushed me into the room to stop me. I fell and hit my head against the side table and passed out."

Such savage anger awakened in his expression that she stepped back.

"I will deal with him another time."

"You are not my champion."

"Nevertheless... You have a choice now, Amira. Will you take it?"

She knew nothing about this man except that he had given her a night of incredible pleasure. But right now, he was her only option. To escape, nothing else. And still, her heart raced. "What choice are you giving me, Adir?"

"Do you want to marry him?"

"No."

"Then come away with me."

"Now?"

A shutter flickered in his eyes accompanied by a curt nod.

"I can't tell you how..." She laughed and it was a shaky sound, utterly devoid of mirth. "For once, I don't know what to say. Although I know why I can't. You see, when our brain is hit by—"

He didn't interrupt her like her father. Just moved another step closer. Until she was swimming in that re-membered scent of him.

Feelings of safety and joy and pleasure enveloped her. She looked into those beautiful eyes. He offered no assurances, he made no promises.

Yet Amira trusted this stranger with the intense eyes

and brooding arrogance more than anyone in her life. He was giving her a choice. For the first time in her life, a man was treating her as a person, not a thing to be controlled or molded.

All she wanted right now was to leave this life, this palace, the prince waiting for her. To leave the life of lies that her father was intent on building. What the future held for her—and whether it involved this man— she would figure out later.

"Yes, I'll leave with you, Adir."

A vicious kind of satisfaction filled the planes of his face bringing Amira's frantic breath to a halt. Fingers clamped around her upper arm, and he was already pulling her toward the window even as his gaze scanned the room with a military precision she had noticed in Prince Zufar's bodyguards.

Then suddenly he stopped and took in her elaborate wedding dress. "Take that thing off."

Her breath stilled at the vehemence in that order. "Galila and the maid will be back—"

"You will not come away with me wearing anything that belongs to Prince Zufar. You leave everything behind, Amira...this entire life, do you understand?"

Amira frowned at his autocratic tone. "I do but—"

He simply shook his head and Amira realized he wasn't going to budge on this. A dark light shone in his eyes as he folded his arms and waited.

Her heart thudded. She couldn't change in front of him. Not when it would reveal her belly. She wasn't ready to have that discussion with him. Not yet. Not here where Galila and the maid could walk in any minute.

"I'll change into another gown," she said into the silence, sweat beading on her forehead. "But you have to undo the zipper for me in the back."

He beckoned her with a finger.

Breath held, Amira presented her back to him. The sound of the zipper filled the silence. Her skin burned where the pads of his fingers touched her. His breath feathered over her neck, sending a shiver down her spine.

The reality of standing in front of him in daylight while she could hear the gay sounds of the parade where her betrothed was...

No! She couldn't second-guess herself now.

She held the edges of the peeling dress and sneaked behind the partition she had asked for earlier because she didn't want Galila to know the truth of her condition.

With trembling fingers, she pulled her wedding gown off, hung it up and pulled on another silky one. Just taking off the heavy wedding gown helped her breathe better. Felt like the first step in taking control of her own life. Like she had stepped out of an invisible cage that had stifled her all these years.

She stepped out from behind the partition.

Something flared in Adir's eyes, but when he spoke, he was all business. "Come, I have a Jeep waiting just outside the courtyard."

Amira joined him. As if she were a feather, he lifted her onto the broad windowsill.

Amira swung her legs over and was about to jump when Galila and the maid came back into the room, their hands full of jewelry.

"Amira? What's going on? Where are you—?" And then, "*Adir!* What are you doing here? In Amira's chamber!"

Amira's racing pulse shuddered to a thundering halt

as her mind slowly processed Galila's reaction. And the recognition in her eyes.

Galila knows Adir! How? Who is he?

Adir's rough palm covered her mouth before she could form the question. His arms around her shoulders, he climbed over the windowsill.

Hanging over the ledge, holding Amira with one arm firmly around her, Adir turned to Galila, a grim smile curving his mouth. Darkness shimmered in his eyes, sending a shiver down her spine.

"Tell your brother I've not only seduced his precious bride but that she runs away with me willingly. Tell him I'm stealing away his future queen, just as he stole my birthright."

And before Amira could believe that she'd heard those words fall from his lips, much less understand them, they were both falling.

He had seduced her? To humiliate Prince Zufar?

Suddenly, the night she had spent with him looked twisted, distorted. The solid ground beneath her feet couldn't stop her world collapsing around her.

A sob clawed its way up her throat, swallowing her protest. His fingers clamped around her wrist, Adir pulled her after him.

Heart beating in her throat, Amira watched as Adir maneuvered them around the swarming guards. Sounds and sights came at her like drowning waves. The morning sun throwing off overpowering heat stole her breath. Her throat was parched, her mouth dry.

All the questions Amira wanted to ask of Adir danced on the edge of her tongue as spots swirled around her vision and she sank into the inviting oblivion.

CHAPTER FOUR

ADIR SLID A frowning glance toward Amira's unconscious form while he maneuvered the four-by-four along the rough track slowly transforming into the desert floor.

Her vibrant golden skin looked alarmingly pale, like whisper-thin parchment. Blue shadows hung deep under her eyes. Her lashes, long and thick, feathered toward those sharp cheekbones like the unfurled wings of a falcon soaring against the sky.

Innocent and sophisticated, refined and sensuous, she was truly a prize worthy of a king and he had stolen her away from under Zufar's nose. Now Zufar would face the world and his precious Khalia and its people without a bride, in utter humiliation. Just imagining the thunderous expression on his half brother's face made Adir smile.

Why wasn't she coming around?

His gaze taking in the long column of her throat, he seamlessly took the truck hundreds of feet up a giant ocher sand mound that offered three-hundred-and-sixty-degree views of the desert floor and the border of his own region.

Khalia, Queen Namani's promises, Zufar's arrogance, the turmoil he felt every time he came near his siblings… It was all behind him now.

Here, *he* ruled.

Here, he was the master of the harshest mistress of all—the desert. Here, he had forged an identity from the ashes of the dirty secrets surrounding his birth.

Even though he had lived here for thirty-one years, the sight in front of him, the harsh beauty of it, never failed to steal his breath. Miles and miles of ripples, undulating dunes in all four directions. And against the backdrop of the desolate sight lay his own encampment. A lush mirage against the stark contrast of the stretching emptiness around it.

Here was his destiny, among his people.

Armed guards, trained not to show their obvious curiosity, stood a few feet away as he turned off the ignition. His concern quickly turning to anxiety, he walked around the Jeep and gently picked up Amira. By the time he brought her into his own chamber, water, fruits and several other items he might need to bring her to consciousness were already readied around the expansive room.

Just as he laid her down amidst colorful pillows on the divan, her eyelids fluttered open.

His knee pressing into her hip, his arms around her slender back, he stayed on the divan as she came to slowly.

Eyes so dark that they were almost black were wide in her small-boned face and their intensity pinned him to the spot. Recognition, followed by pleasure and an incandescent joy stared back at him. It was such pure, radiant emotion that it seared him through to his soul. And even as he was staggering under the impact of that, it vanished like the mirage of water under the harsh desert sun.

Wariness and fear dawned in those eyes. A breath

later, she jerked away from him so suddenly that all his fighting instincts came rushing to the fore.

His entire body froze, his heart kicking against his ribcage. He had felt something, mere seconds before she moved back. When his arm had grazed her midriff. When his palm had rested on her stomach.

A slight swell. A bump where she had been flat before. He knew because he had kissed and licked the softness of her belly, tickled it with his breaths...

Was Amira pregnant? With his child?

His knuckles turned white—rage and fear and so many things crowded him, stealing his thoughts. And if he had been an hour late, if he hadn't given in to that primal pull he felt for her against all his rational instincts, against the warnings that he was weakening for a mere woman—an unprecedented thing—Zufar would have married her.

His child would have been Zufar's under the law—to do with what he pleased.

Forever lost to him. And he would never have known.

A growl fell from Adir's mouth. "Amira—"

"No, don't!"

She was half lying down, half sitting up, her hands fisted on both sides into the thick rugs, her breaths shallow and panting. Her eyes were panicked and out of focus. She looked like a deer caught in the sights of the predator. He was the predator she feared.

Reacting to her fear, he put his hands up, showing that he meant her no harm. And still her breathing wouldn't settle. Worse, the more her eyes traveled over him and the tent, the more her agitation increased. The upper curves of her breasts rose and fell. Her cheeks turned an alarmingly pale shade while sweat beaded on her lips.

"I can't…breathe," she whispered.

Adir pulled the knife he always kept against his leg, straddled her hips and with precise movements, cut through the bodice of the dress from the neck to just a little below her navel.

He'd always thought of himself as an educated man, a man dedicated to progress, a man determined to bring as much advancement in technology as possible to his tribes—the man who straddled tradition and progress for the betterment of his people. And yet as he cut away the dress, Adir felt like one of his desert ancestors from the stories he'd been told when he had been a boy. Of warriors capturing cities and claiming prizes and untold treasure.

A treasure was in his hands now.

"No, wait—" she begged in that panicky voice.

He didn't. Holding the knife between his teeth, he grabbed the ripped edges of the dress in his hands and pulled.

And then slowly, with carefully controlled movements that wouldn't tease his control, he got off the bed, re-sheathed his knife and only then did he allow himself to look at her.

Wavy, lustrous strands of hair fell away from the sophisticated hairstyle, falling in wispy curls caressing her face. Some ridiculous, flimsy, sheer thing made out of cream lace covered her from her chest to her thighs. Adir's breath punched up to his throat.

For four months, he had dreamed of her. Of this.

There was nothing else beneath the transparent lace. Nothing but her flesh. Flesh he had held, touched and kissed, cajoled and caressed but not seen, except in flashes and stolen glances under the cover of moonlight.

Every time he went near night-blooming jasmine, he

was reminded of her. Of supple curves and soft cries and skin like silk. Of tight flesh enveloping him so completely. Of dark intimacy and indescribable pleasure.

Now, every X-rated thought and sensation he had enjoyed of that night was finally granted glorious, Technicolor vision. Nothing he had imagined could equal the ripe beauty that was Amira Ghalib.

It was only a few seconds that he took to look—dark red nipples jutting proudly through the cream-colored lace; full, high breasts that had filled his palms so perfectly that he ached to cup them again; the fragile curve of her waist, the lush flare of her hips, with jet black curls at the V of her thighs and…the clear, round swell of her belly.

Ya Allah, she was pregnant!

With a horrified gasp, she pulled the torn edges of the dress together covering it up. But he had already seen it.

A snarl escaped his mouth.

She would have been tied to Zufar irrevocably, owned and possessed, forever out of Adir's reach. *His* child out of his reach.

Another bastard denied his true parentage.

Another thing stolen away from Adir.

"Are you pregnant, Amira?" The question was eating away at him.

Her voice broke into his thoughts with a soft clang, "Is it true? You came to steal me away from Prince Zufar?"

"I said—"

Leaning against the colorful kaleidoscope of vibrant rugs that covered the wall, she looked impossibly lovely and painfully innocent. And stubborn. "Answer my question first," she demanded.

"Yes," he said, indulging her far too much, while his heart beat like a thundering tribal drum in his chest.

Color leached out from her face. "Why?"

Guilt bit into him, and he threw it off.

He had asked her and she had come with him. That his actions had been motivated by something else shouldn't matter to her. "You heard what I said to Princess Galila." It was the moment he had sensed her going utterly still in his arms on that windowsill.

She frowned, and then something dawned in her gaze. "Why did you come for me, Adir? We made no promises to each other. Four months went by after that night. And yet you appear, the morning of my wedding, a mere hour before the ceremony would begin."

"I kept thinking about you. About that night and how incredible it felt. About how I wanted to be inside you again. About how...you were caught in a situation that you didn't want."

With each question she asked, he sensed a wall being erected around her. As if she were calling layer upon layer of composure and self-possession, pushing him out. Removing the Amira of that night out of his reach. "Ah...so you came to be the hero of my story?"

The soft sarcasm jerked his gaze to her. Gone was the sweet, trusting Amira. Instead here was a woman who stared back at him with wariness and mistrust...

No matter, he told himself, as his mind made plans upon plans. What was done was done. If she was going to be in his life in a permanent role, she might as well understand that the Adir she had met that night was only an illusion he had woven to please her.

"Nothing so admirable. I did want to offer you an escape. And indulge in the passion between us a little more, if you were still so inclined."

"So you decided I would be your lover?" Her taunting words couldn't hide the color slowly seeping back into her cheeks.

His concern faded a bit.

"Yes…maybe." He shrugged. "I hadn't exactly worked out the logistics of that. My position does not make it easy for me to have lovers. At least, in a longer time frame. But I knew I wanted you and you needed escape, so it was just a matter of figuring out the optimum timing. I had a guard keep a close ear to the ground in the palace regarding the wedding to relay the news to me as needed."

"You waited, on purpose?" A flash of anger in her eyes. "As if this…as if my life were a chess game? As if I were a pawn?"

"Strategy is my blood, the air I breathe. My libido could wait and so could you if it meant a better result."

"What result?"

"If I were to steal you away on the morning of the wedding, in front of Khalia, in front of the whole world, in front of all of his distinguished guests, Zufar's humiliation would be…complete. My revenge even more fulfilling."

"Why? Why do you hate him so much?"

"Because he continues to deny me what is rightfully mine."

If he thought the sweet Amira he had known would crumble in front of him, he was very much mistaken. "That night when you…" a betraying flash of color seeped up her cheeks, and yet she pushed on bravely, and he couldn't help but admire her composure "…invited me to spend time with you, I had, fortunately for you, confessed who I was. Had you already planned it? To have sex with me?"

Some flicker of emotion in her eyes, desperate and yearning, flashed now. Trained though she might be to weather anything as the future Queen of Khalia, her naïveté and inexperience weren't shed so easily.

Much as she tried to hide it, she was immensely hurt by his actions.

But tenderness was an affection unknown to him. He had neither the intention nor the inclination to soften the truth for her. Nothing—not her wounded big eyes nor her body—would change what he was inside, what had driven him that night to seduce her.

He was a loner. First by fate and later by design. His mother's letters had taught him early on how necessary it was to hold himself apart if he wanted to rise to achieve his destiny.

If not for her, he would have been another goat herder, a small-time rug weaver or any other average tribesman.

But by following her words as tenets, by keeping himself separate from others, by not letting emotions rule his life, he had risen to his current station in life. To heights even she couldn't have imagined for him.

If not for the queen's fiery words, he would have been content to be a simple man, a follower.

But instead, her words had spurred him on, made him a leader. Despite his low beginnings.

Even now, now that he was the sheikh of two tribes, a businessman with interests in multinational corporations, he had no close friends, no family. No women in his life who made him weak or emotional. Only advisors and people who followed his commands. Only people who filled certain roles in his life.

He depended on no one but himself. He let no messy

emotions enter his life except what drove the betterment of his people and his destiny.

Just as a ruler should.

He only knew two things in life: his duty to his people and his destiny as he'd learned from Queen Namani's words for so many years. If Amira needed him to answer a few questions about their short past so that he could move on to planning their future, so that she understood her own station in life now that she was inevitably tied to him, her own part in his life, then so be it.

"Was I standing on that stairway waiting for Zufar's betrothed to fall into my hands?" He let a smile curve his mouth. "No. Did the time I spent with you, doing what we did, add a sweet, exhilarating edge to taking the grand prize that rightly belonged to Zufar? Did I revel in stealing from him as he does from me? Am I, even now, with his runaway bride here in my tent like this, imagining his humiliation, reveling in this moment? Yes, to all."

She sank into the wall behind her as if she meant to burrow inside and disappear, one hand still holding the tattered edges of the dress closed with the other.

He clamped his hands behind him to stop himself from reaching for her. From preventing her retreat.

He wanted to uncurl her fingers gently from that silk and lay her bare to his eyes again. He needed to rip that lace off her body with his teeth and sink into her tight flesh. He desired her arms around his sweaty body, his name on her lips again. Entreating, begging, needing him.

He could banish her fear with his touch, bend her to his will, yes. But he had tasted her willing surrender once and nothing else would do now.

"Does that answer all your questions, Amira?"

There was a faint tremble in her lithe body. Even, white teeth dug hard into her lower lip, sending a shaft of pure sensation to his groin.

"Very clearly, for the moment, yes, thank you."

"Then maybe now you can answer mine—"

And then he saw it. Perversely, it was the sun's rays filtering through the small crease in the tent. He saw the sheen of tears in her eyes. The utter defeat in the bow of her shoulders.

She dragged her breath in through her mouth in a huge, noisy inhale. Bright red painted nails scraped through her lovely hair as if tugging it would give her back her grip on herself.

He lost control of himself then.

He cupped her shoulder, meaning to pull her into his arms. He would just hold her for now. She had been through shock and once she was over it, she would acknowledge that she had chosen to come with him. He would allay all her worries—the fear she must have been living with for four months under the atrocities of her bullying father, knowing she was pregnant and unable to hide it for long.

His motivations didn't change the fact that she had chosen him over Zufar—both that night and today.

That was his true victory—that Zufar had had this woman in his possession and lost her to Adir Al-Zabah. She would again look at him with—

With a soft cry, she jerked away with such force that she almost tripped against the table with refreshments.

"Do not cringe away from me."

Wide eyes pinned him with the regal grace of a queen even as she righted herself. She had been bred to be one—the utter elegance of it was imbued into her every moment. "Do not touch me then."

Even as silent tears poured down her cheeks, she didn't berate him for what he had done to her. Pangs of guilt gripped him.

"You need to calm down. It's not good for you or the baby. Your panic was making you choke—"

"I think I would prefer to choke than endure your touch right now." She whispered the words—almost as if to herself. And it was that more than anything that delivered a punch to his midsection.

He advanced on her, holding onto his control by the skin of his teeth. "Shall I put that to test, *ya habibiti*?"

"It is a test I shall fail and you shall win. As unwilling as my mind is now, there are triggers in my body that sway the brain. It's millions of years of evolutionary instincts firing into action because when it comes down to it, the animal part of my brain recognizes you as the most aggressive male, the best for procreation. Neither does it help that there are other hormones at play that make me even more susceptible to you."

"So you agree that if I touched you now, if I pulled that dress off you and kissed the curve of your breast, licked my way over the satin silk of your belly to the treasure below, I shall not find you unwilling."

"No, you won't. But later, when my brain recovers from the adrenaline injected by the orgasm you give, I shall hate you. Even more than I do now."

I shall hate you...

For four months, all he had done at night was dream of her enthusiastic responses, her soft curves beneath his hard body, the inviting cradle of her thighs. He had spilled himself again and again into his own hand at the remembered memory of her soft cry as she had found her own release.

All he wanted was to reclaim her, to take her on the

night she should have gone to his half brother's bed, to seal his victory. He wanted to make her take those words back.

And yet, one look into her eyes was enough to douse his feverish lust.

He was a man who thrived on control—of himself and his surroundings. This desire he felt for a slip of a girl was nothing. He would have her—again and again until the lust in him was satisfied, yes, but he would not give in to it like a green boy looking at his first nude woman.

He would not touch her until she came to him as his wife. Until she learned her place in his life.

He closed his eyes, took a deep breath and opened them again.

Eyes filled with that nauseating fear met his. He shoved away the dismay that caused inside him. Enough was enough!

It was time to take things in hand. "You are pregnant with my child."

Knuckles white from the tight grip she held on the torn edges of the dress, she stared up at him, innocence and resolve an irresistibly complex combination. "Are you so sure it's yours? What if I had stolen a hundred other nights with a hundred other strangers after you? What if there has been a parade of men in my life and in my body since that night? What if what I shared with you was so good that I didn't wait for—"

He pulled her to him, the pictures she painted making bile rise through his throat. She was his. Only his. "Do not cheapen what happened between us."

Silent tears drew wet paths on her cheeks. She looked so painfully innocent as she dabbed them away with the back of her hand. "*You* did that. Not I."

"Games do not suit you, Amira. That child is mine." His voice shook on those words. Fear clamped his spine. Fear of loss. Of all the things he had never had and now to lose this, too… "If I had been an hour late, if you had become Zufar's wife, that child, my child would have been cast into—"

Whatever she saw in his face clearly startled her. She went to him, a fierceness in her eyes. "Whoever the father of this child is in legal terms, I would never have let him or her go. Never. Adir, I love this child already. I just needed…a way out. I don't want to talk about the past anymore. I…want to look toward the future."

He nodded, seeing the truth shine in her eyes. Whatever her naïveté, Amira would be a good mother. "It is good then that we can agree on what's important."

"Then let this farce end here and allow me to leave."

"We will marry as soon as it can be arranged."

They had both spoken at the same time. Words and eyes collided, the silent room exploding with unspoken emotions.

"No." He had indulged her enough. It was time to set things straight.

Her eyes searched his, wide with shock, seeking the truth. She fell onto her haunches, that stillness turning into shivers. Before he could reach for her, she shrank away from him. Tremors overtook her slender body and she hugged herself.

Adir waited, his patience wearing thin, and yet he felt as if he was on the cusp of something.

When she raised those eyes to him again, terror shone in it. And he felt as if he fell from that cliff into some dark abyss below. Whatever had been between them, that flimsy, intangible thing, he knew it was lost.

Forever.

She looked at him as if he were a stranger, a monster.

Even as he struggled to get a grip on reality, the loss dug into him.

"Amira?"

"A minute ago, you…you were planning logistics and timing to consider me for a temporary lover. Yet now you command that we marry? I didn't want to marry Zufar. I definitely do not want to marry you."

"Neither you nor I have a choice in this matter anymore. Like you said, actions have consequences, yes? My child will not be born a bastard. I don't want a wife that looks at me as if she doesn't know me anymore than you—"

"I don't want a husband whose every word is a lie, who not only is *not* different—as I had foolishly assumed—from all the arrogant, domineering men already pushing me around, but actually hides it beneath a veneer of kindness and charm."

"I'm the same man, Amira." If only his people could hear him now—their sheikh offering an olive branch to this mere slip of a woman, when her fate was all in his hands anyway.

"The man I thought you were that night doesn't exist except in my fantastic imagination. Ordering me or threatening me will not accomplish what you want. I have years…" there was a catch in her tone and she shied her gaze away from him and swallowed "…of experience dealing with men who want to have their way no matter what. You could beat me into a pulp and I would still not surrender my will."

He reached her before he knew he had even moved. "Do not compare me to your father ever again. I'm a man of honor. What I do or don't do has consequences,

Amira. People look to me for guidance. And for the final time, my child will not be born a bastard."

Something in his words pinged inside Amira's head, bringing every panicky thought to a grinding halt. Dread twisted into a tight knot in her chest as she struggled to form the question she should have asked that night.

He had talked of Queen Namani as if he had personal knowledge of her. Of Prince Zufar denying him what was his. Of honor and his station in life and strategy and logistics...

Oh, God, what had she done? Who had she tangled with?

Sweat ran down between her shoulder blades, and an invisible cage began to weave all around her again. "Who are you? Please...the truth this time."

"I didn't lie to you that night. You wanted a night of fantasy and I gave it to you."

She had been so naive, so stupid. Even though her father had prepared her for the reality of royal life from when she had been a little girl, she had still built castles in the air. She had still developed romantic notions. She had believed that fairy tale could be real, if only for one night.

"A night of fantasy, sure. And now it is time to pay the price for that night, yes? My father was right—nothing comes freely in this world. So tell me, who are you?"

"I'm Adir Al-Zabah, the High Sheikh of the Dawab and Peshani tribes. I own three multinational information technology companies. I have a degree in law specializing in international politics and land rights. I have been informed, now and again, that I possess a passably attractive face. And you're carrying my child. I shall protect you, keep you in luxury and more than anything, I would cut my hand off before I would raise it against you. Now, shall we seal the bargain, Amira?"

It felt as if the world under her feet had pulled away.

Shock settled over her skin like a cold chill while Amira stared mutely at the arrogant stranger arranging her life according to his wishes.

Adir Al-Zabah…of course, the renowned High Sheikh of the Dawab and Peshani tribes. His reputation was legendary even among the royals of Khalia and Zyria for he had single-handedly united the Bedouin tribes of this region. Warring among themselves and their way of life dying out, he had breathed new life into them by bridging the gap between tradition and progress.

Powerful, arrogant and educated, there was no equal to him in strategy and in maneuvering the volatile politics of the region. He had brought two IT companies into the cities bordering the tribes' lands in the desert—a move that had been laughed at by political critics, yet in the space of three years had provided his tribesmen with a new mode of living.

A legal dispute had been in court for decades regarding the encroachment of a local government into the lands of the Peshani—he had won the case by bringing the Dawab and Peshani together and driving the incursions out forever.

A mere thirty-one years old, he already was a ruthless leader and a cutting-edge businessman. He was a herald of a new age for the tribes—of not only survival, but economic thriving.

She had thought they were similar souls looking for a connection in their lonely lives. He was no more lost or lonely than the lion was lost in the jungle. No less ruthless than her father or Prince Zufar in how unscrupulous he had used her naïveté and trust.

And they had no more in common than she and Prince Zufar had.

He was another controlling man who thought nothing of her own wishes or dreams.

"No. I will not marry you."

A muscle jumped in his jaw. Clearly, he was not used to being denied anything. "It is high time to let go of your foolish dreams, Amira. Do not make me take away your choices."

"It's not much of a choice if it is the only option, is it?"

She thought he would be furious, he proved she didn't know him.

He stared at her for so long that Amira wondered if the loud thunder of her heart echoed in the room.

And then he smiled. It was the smile of a predator. Of a man who always got what he wanted. Of a man who had ruthlessly seduced her while he had planned her betrothed's humiliation.

"I thought you would be happy to be free of your golden cage. Free of all the expectations and burdens that were thrust on you. Free of Zufar's indifference and your father's brutality. This is the result of a choice you made. So live with it."

"No! You—"

"Enough!" Adir said, losing his control.

Her rebellion was of the insidious kind. It was there in the defiance in her eyes, the upward tilt of her chin as her slender body cringed away from him.

It was the impression she gave. She was small and slender with exquisite curves in all the right places and yet if he closed his eyes now, all he would see would be the bright shining light of her will. Of her determination.

But much as he tried to suppress it, he had to admit there was a niggle of shame. A looming sense of… something he couldn't even recognize. And the unknown quality of it made his voice harsh, his words cruel.

"Will you now act as if I forced you into it all, Amira? You proved that you have no loyalty toward Zufar when you slept with me. You were more than desperate to—"

"You would shame what I gave you honestly? I don't care what you or my father or the entire damned world thinks. I *gave* my body to you. You think I was overcome by fear, that I wanted escape—?"

"Why romanticize it when it's exactly that? You used me and I used you," he said bluntly, even knowing that her inexperience, her sheltered worldview would never see it that way. Her father might have reared her to be a queen—to play politics and games—but there wasn't a malicious bone in her body. But she had to learn fast if she wanted to survive life with him. "Wasn't it payback, too, on your father for his cruelty, on Zufar for not giving you enough—?"

"No! Don't you dare tell me why I did it." For the first time that day, he heard pure steel in her voice. In a matter of seconds, she had transformed from a sweet, innocent temptress to a tigress breathing fire. "Your own twisted motivations color mine. I…was attracted to you. Something about you made me realize a woman's desires for the first time. That I wasn't just a pawn to be used. I *chose* to let you kiss me. I *chose* to let you give me pleasure. I *chose* to give myself one night of escape in your arms. All my life, I fought to make choices of my own within the few parameters I was allowed. That night, I chose you. And neither you nor my father nor the world—no accusations, no shame heaped upon me, no force on this earth—could take that away…the choice I made…from me."

"Then now it is time for us both to live with the consequences of that."

She was nothing to him.

No, she was not nothing to Adir.

She was used to being nothing all her life. She had been nothing before—an object of indifference and neglect to Zufar. But his indifference had mostly left her unharmed.

She had been a means of attaining wealth and power for her father. A pawn to be used for gaining advancement. Even as she had hated it, somehow, Amira had used that to her own advantage. She had time and again persuaded her father that her education, her training to be a nurse, the charity work she did with poor women and women without healthcare, all of it increased her worth as a queen.

She had wielded her betrothal to Prince Zufar as a weapon to achieve her biggest dreams, all within the constraints her father had laid down on her.

But not once had either of them been allowed to touch her heart.

She had endured whatever they had thrown her way but hadn't let them touch the core of her.

What Adir had done to her, what he had stolen from her—oh, she had given her virginity happily enough and she still couldn't regret it—but what he had stolen from her was so much worse.

She had allowed him into her heart.

He had been the first man who had ever made her

feel safe, cherished, wanted. And all her life, Amira had never been cherished.

For the first time in her life, she had seen herself as something other than a pawn. He had given her a taste of utter happiness…

Amira sank to the floor when he walked away without another word. Tears filled her eyes and for the first time since she had learned of her pregnancy, she couldn't stem their flow.

She should think of her child, she should think of its future.

And for her child, she would marry him. But she would never again trust him, never again be so naive as to believe that charming facade.

He would be her husband, the father of her child, he would have ownership of her body, her mind, her thoughts, but never her heart.

Never again would she forget that the man she was marrying had no heart.

CHAPTER FIVE

"How are you feeling today?"

Amira jerked up from the bed. Her scrambled movements only made the man staring at her frown.

No, he wasn't just a man.

She needed to see him as he truly was—a powerful man used to getting his own way. She had lived her whole life dealing with such men and yet quietly achieving her own way. She would this time, too.

Now that she had made and accepted her decision, relief filled her. Even being the Queen of Khalia couldn't have done what Adir had done for her. She was free of the controlling grasp of her father and that was a good thing.

Having lived with her father's constant belittling and control, Adir's arrogance and dominance was nothing. If she had learned one thing from her father, it was that every relationship had a power exchange.

And while she had always been the one with less power in all of her relationships, there had almost always been something to bargain with. Leverage.

And she desperately needed to find what that was when it came to Adir.

"Amira?"

An edge of impatience crept into his tone. For three days, he had wisely left her to stew in her own company.

But she had never been alone, for one or another woman had kept showing up. First to look after her health, she had been told. Then the lovely, funny Zara had shown up to keep her company. And lastly, the old woman Humera.

She shoved away the bitter answers that rose to her lips one after the other. "I have made peace with my fate. And nothing is wrong with my health. But I still do not like you," she said, opting for honesty.

"Look at me when I speak to you."

Exhaling a deep breath, she turned. "Yes, Your Highness."

And just like that, all her reassurances and promises fled.

Awareness filled every pore as those amber eyes watched her with that thoroughly possessive leisure.

He was dressed simply in white robes that suited the desert today. His head was covered by a red and white scarf to keep the heat at bay. His face gleamed dark gold after a morning in the sun, his potent masculinity taking over the tent.

Even having spent two days in his luxurious tent, even having spent two restless nights in the vast expanse that was his bed; even after woman after woman bowed, scraped and saw to her every need as if she were indeed a queen; even as she heard the respectful whispers and the widening amazement in her helpers' eyes when they spoke of him, the reality of it all had still eluded her.

Until now.

She looked at the arrogant angles of his face, his air of command, the way his broad shoulders and lean strength filled the very air around her and could not believe she had been so bold as to have kissed him, to have asked him to make love to her, to have seen him in that moment where he had lost all control of himself. An utterly useless rush of power filled her.

His desire hadn't been faked—this realization that had been simmering under all the other overwhelming facts rose to the fore.

Was that her leverage? Did he still want her—or was she simply the spoils of war, a convenient receptacle to carry his future dynasty?

She licked her lips and saw his eyes flare.

A muscle twitched in his jaw. "I have spent all morning resolving ridiculous disputes pertaining to goats and cattle and what not. Do not test my patience, Amira."

"If you have one of your lackeys draw up a list of dos and don'ts dictating my behavior with you, I shall learn it by heart. What is it that you expect me to provide you with?"

"Other than the obvious?" He moved into the tent with an economic grace that meant Amira couldn't help but stare. A dangerous glint appeared in his amber eyes.

He ran a finger over her jaw so gently that Amira instantly closed her eyes to savor the feeling.

Fiery heat claimed her skin though the temperature fell rapidly with the sun setting outside. Because even with the chaos he had brought to her life, not one single night had passed when Amira had not wished for him beside her on the bed.

Instead, she moved away from him. "I see the speculation in the maids' eyes. Move me to a different tent."

"You give orders like a queen. And they only look at you that way because I haven't yet declared that you're their future sheikha."

She tilted her chin up. "Believe me, that's the last thing I want to be. If I had known who you were that night, I would've screamed the palace down to get away from you. I would have—"

"You're telling yourself lies. But since it probably makes you feel better, I shall leave it so."

The infuriating, arrogant beast! Was he right? Would she have been attracted to him even if she had known what a powerful man he was?

When she had learned the truth three days ago about his identity, she had been in shock, disbelief. But now she wondered how much Adir had really wanted her that night? And how much had been the need to humiliate Zufar?

She sighed, realizing even now that she was looking to put a romantic spin on that night.

"I ran away with you because I needed a way out. But now that the wedding day has passed—"

"He will not take you back, Amira. I have received news."

Amira thought it was a throwaway comment, meant to shame her again. Meant to remind her that she had turned her back on Prince Zufar and that life.

But beneath his penetrating look, something else lingered.

Where was the man who had been so kind and approachable that night? Whose eyes had been full of pleasure and warmth?

"From…the palace? From Khalia?"

"Yes."

For two days, all she had seen of Adir was in discussions outside her elaborate tent. Two women had always been with her and a battalion of guards outside the tent. And as of an hour ago, ten men had been whittled down to one.

That same look—a sense of victory—gleamed in Adir's eyes.

He had been guarding her, she realized now, against Prince Zufar. Assuming he would come to take her back. He hadn't been willing to take the chance of her returning to Prince Zufar and Khalia.

What did that mean? Did he truly want her? Or was she still only a prize he had stolen from Zufar?

"Is there any word from my...my father?" she asked, even knowing that he must loathe her by now for everything she had thrown away, for what she had cost him.

"No. It seems he has washed his hands of you." If there was any tenderness in his tone, she didn't let it move her. Pity was not a good substitute for anything genuine like respect or affection.

"Prince Zufar...is he...?"

"He has replaced you with, of all women, a maid. The man who called me a dirty stain on the name of his house, the King of Khalia, is now married to a palace maid."

Zufar had been forced to marry the maid to save face? What had he thought of her running away with Adir? Had Galila worried for her?

Amira plopped down onto the divan, her knees giving out. For so long, her every breathing moment had been to prepare to be queen. Her fate had been tied to Zufar's.

Of course her disappearance mere hours before a dynastic wedding would have repercussions. At least Adir had made it clear that she was leaving of her own accord.

The connection had been severed the moment she had decided to jump out of the window with Adir, yes, but now...it was as if a crushing weight had been lifted.

Amber eyes locked with hers and any relief she felt was forced out of her.

Arms at his sides, powerful legs sprawled in front of him, he was very much king of the desert.

Heavy, sluggish warmth pooled low in her belly.

Waiting. Watching for every nuance on her face. In that penetrating stare, Amira saw that he wasn't sure of her. His question next confirmed it.

"Are you regretting running away with me? Giving up the queen's life?"

For three days, she had contemplated the question and come up with an answer: no.

The scales had fallen from her eyes but she still couldn't regret running away with him. Couldn't regret that night. Maybe she was as foolish and useless as her father had always called her.

She sighed. "Prince Zufar replacing me with any woman is not a surprise. I'm just…relieved that my foolishness didn't cause him unfixable damage. His indifference toward me did not deserve the humiliation I helped you wreak on him."

"It is a little late to show loyalty toward him."

His fingers closed over the engraved handle of a knife and slowly he peeled off the skin of a piece of fruit. When he sliced a small section and handed it to her, Amira shook her head.

"You chose me. Over him."

"Haven't you crowed about it enough?" She rolled her eyes and the beastly man simply smiled.

Amira breathed harder, faster as he pushed off the chair, another piece of apple held in his hands.

He smiled and in that pure devilish movement, she could see her downfall.

He lifted the piece to her mouth, slow desire making his eyes shine with a brilliant glow.

Here was the answer to her question.

Mesmerized, Amira opened her mouth. He slid the piece between her lips. The pads of his fingers lingered over her lips. She licked his fingers. The sweet and tart taste of him flew like liquid lightning to the place between her thighs. The spot he had touched that night, the spot she had tried to find to relieve the ache he caused…the spot that was throbbing now.

Trembling with need, she sank her teeth into the pad of his thumb.

His chest fell and rose as she sucked the tip into her mouth. His eyes darkened. And when she sucked it between her lips, a sound escaped his mouth—the same low, throaty growl he had made when he had spent himself inside her that night.

Amira jerked away from him, her heart racing. Her breath still uneven.

He wasn't gloating when she looked at him.

She stood at the window, looking out into the red expanse of the gorge and valley beside her when he started talking again.

"See what happens when I simply come near you. You forget all your objections. You look at me as if you're desperate for my touch, eager for me to be inside you."

He said it in such a matter-of-fact voice. As if they hadn't been ready to tear each other's clothes off.

While she…she was still shaking from the depth of her need.

Of course, she and Galila had talked about sex—without mentioning her brother specifically because that made the both of them nauseous—and how a woman's libido could be just as strong as a man's. But it all had been a theory.

She hadn't ever thought that those urges would overwhelm even her mind.

"This attraction between us…it is an added bonus," he said almost thoughtfully.

"An added bonus?"

"I like sex and I like to have a lot of it. But I also intend to remain faithful to my wife. From what I remember of that night, and from the way there's a spark in the air every time I come near you, you're explosively responsive, and like everything else, you're extremely curious about this. The things I could teach you, the things we could do together… The kind of chemistry we share would last a long time. Enough to keep me interested."

She turned instantly, disbelief skating through her.

He looked back at her steadily, his lean face a study in beauty.

If her heart beat any faster, it would jump right out of her chest. "What are you saying?"

"That we could have a more than satisfactory marriage. Zara and Nusrat couldn't stop singing your praises, even though they're prejudiced about any woman that is not from the tribes. Even Humera is impressed by you and she has never given her approval to a single woman in the tribe."

"Humera is the old woman—the midwife who came to see me?"

"Yes."

"Zara told me she never ventures out of the camp. Why did she come here?"

"I asked her to take a look at you."

"Why?"

"Because you look pale and unwell." His gaze swept

over her, but this time there was no mocking smile or taunting desire. A flash of concern shone in it. "You have dark shadows underneath your eyes, and I could break you with one hand."

When he raised a brow, she hurried to reply, "I do not want to be seen as a victim. Whatever my father did, I never let it change me. It shouldn't change how you see me."

He nodded, granting her a privilege. "After two minutes with you, no one could think you were a victim. Amira, I would have you enter this marriage with an open mind. You wield your silence like a weapon, your hurt like a…shield for all the world to see. Vulnerability like yours…"

Longing ripped through her. Here was a man who saw her, who…understood her. An urgency like she never knew gripped her. As if she had to grab onto something before it disappeared.

"I thought you were no different from Zufar or my father. I was wrong."

The hesitation in his gaze made her cover the distance between them, a glimpse of the vulnerability she'd seen that day pulling her like a rope. "How am I different?"

"Zufar couldn't care less whether I was happy or sad. As long as I did my duty and didn't cause scandal, I could do whatever I pleased. My father, as long as I presented myself befitting the status of the prince's betrothed, he could not have cared less if I was rotting with misery on the inside. But you…you care that I am happy about this. Admit it, Adir, you feel guilty for deceiving me. Admit that you felt something that night."

"You're determined to see me as a knight in shining armor. I'm not."

"And you're determined that you will kill whatever you felt for me."

"Enough, Amira! Stop wearing your heart on your sleeve. Your vulnerability is a weakness. A naive, trusting sheikha is a dangerous thing. There will be many who will court your goodwill, who will use that against you. For a woman who has been brought up by a beast of a father intended for a royal life, you're far too innocent. That is the only downside I see in this."

Her heart sank. "The only downside?"

"In marrying you."

If he had slapped her, she would probably have been hurt less. "Then don't. Don't marry me. You can still see our child. I'm sure there is no shortage of women queuing up to be your bride. In fact, I'm surprised. Doesn't a powerful man like you have a girlfriend or two tucked away?"

"I thought it was tacky to mention my past relationships."

"You're the one who keeps reminding me to leave fantasy behind and live in the real world. I have accepted that you're a flesh and blood man with clay feet like the rest of us. So tell me, Adir, how many mistresses will I have to deal with?"

His jaw tightened, and anger flashed in his gaze for the first time. Only then did Amira realize how flat and unemotional he had been so far. "I told you I intend to be faithful to my wife. And I will expect the same, Amira."

When she didn't answer, he tilted her chin up. "I will not tolerate even the thought of you straying."

Even as he commanded her, vulnerability shone in his eyes. This was important to him. This was personal. Amira met his eyes, searching for that man who had laughed with her. Wondering what lay beneath that command and duty. "Do you really believe I'm the sort of woman who would cheat on her husband? One who would bring such…discord, and invite such pain into so many lives?"

Her breath hung serrated in her chest while he studied her. "You spent a night with me while betrothed to him."

Amira felt as if he had slapped her. Tears rose to her eyes and she struggled to blink them away. "Wow. You will use that against me again and again, won't you? For the last time, Zufar was chosen for me. Zufar didn't even know me. He had no right to my feelings."

"And I do?"

She nodded. As much as she didn't want to. "More fool me, but yes. Even before I learned that there was to be a baby. I don't think you'll ever realize what you meant to me that night. *Just* that night."

His hands fell on her shoulders, his gaze so serious. "Amira, all I mean is that you could fall in love with some man later and justify your affair. Love makes people weak, it makes them hurt others. With no thought to consequences. It's the same for men and women."

"You speak as if you have seen this."

He shrugged and looked away. Amira had the eerie sense that she had been close to learning what made him so…remote. So cynical. So alone, even. As if a bright glittering star had been within her reach and she had let it slip without even knowing.

"As little experience as I have with it, that is not love," she said. "That is…selfish indulgence."

"For someone so young and untested and so…innocent…" his knuckles ran down her cheeks, sending a thread of warmth through her "…you have very decided opinions."

"I just know there are some lines I wouldn't cross. Things that I could never live with. And since you insist on this wedding between us, it would be nice if you knew that, too."

"No, you would not be a wife who would cheat on me. You might, however, twist a knife in my gut if I did."

It looked like he knew her well enough after all. Amira laughed and automatically leaned toward him to kiss that sexy mouth.

When he stilled as she leaned toward him, she caught herself. And looked away.

And because she didn't want this awkward moment stretching any longer, she said, "So what about your history of lovers?"

He cleared his throat even as his eyes danced. "The tribes are very conservative socially. The last thing I could do is import a girlfriend from the city just to satisfy my…needs. Neither could I carry on with a woman from the tribes because that's a blatant abuse of power. So I have always kept my…associations short and unmessy. A man like me has no allowance to be emotional in his personal life anyway."

And with that pithy sentence, he revealed so much of how he saw himself. Amira frowned. He made it sound as if it were a necessity to be alone to be a ruler. As if relationships were nothing but weaknesses. "You mean you have never had a girlfriend?"

"No. And since I'm thirty-one years old, my council has been encouraging me to marry for years to establish my line. But until now, I never met the right woman that made it a worthwhile proposition. A woman I could tolerate."

Every word out of his mouth was a tempting pitfall. Every look he cast her a tug on her senses. Her heart should not race like one of her father's thoroughbreds at the thought of being his wife. At the thought of spending all her nights in his beds. But the foolish muscle did.

One. Two. Three. Four. Five.

"And I make it a worthwhile...proposition? Is this your way of wooing me?"

He shrugged, putting paid to any such notions. "You were bred to be a queen. You're beautiful, sophisticated, a consummate asset to a businessman in the outside world. Education, polish, your charity work, even your career, everything about you is an asset to a man in a powerful position. Especially me."

"Especially you? Why?"

"I'm forever caught between progress and tradition and you understand both. You're manipulative, just like me, maybe just subtler in the way you go about it. You're a survivor, Amira."

He didn't even see his actions toward her as wrong. He thought she would be an asset. As if she were a piece of equipment or an accessory.

"I will be an asset as a sheikha. I will give you a good time in bed. I will be a good wife. And what is it that you give me, Adir?"

His usually cynical gaze was filled with confusion and a bitter laugh fell from her mouth.

"It seems all the benefits are yours. What do I gain of this marriage?" Chin tilted up, shoulders square, she faced him. "Why would I exchange one ruthless man for another? One prison for another? Tell me why you would make a good bargain for me. Why I should throw myself into this?"

A dark smile shone in his eyes. He seemed to admire her show of backbone, her clinical reduction of this thing between them into a transaction. He took her hand in his and before she could think to object, pressed a soft kiss to the underside of her wrist. Sensations sparked inside her. "I should not forget one fact."

"What?"

"That you're a fast learner." The wealth of meaning in those words sent her hurtling into a rush of remembered sensations and words so intense that she burned all over.

Widen your legs, Amira... Tilt your hips up when I push in... Hold on, habiba.

He had been a consummate teacher and she an eager pupil.

Could she teach him some things, too? Could there be more to this marriage?

Not love, no. Maybe they were both far too realistic, but perhaps they could have a good marriage.

Her straightforwardness made Adir smile. She was a lioness, slowly coming into her own. Suddenly, the prospect of Amira as his sheikha, of having her in his bed for the rest of his life, seemed less like duty and more a thing to look forward to.

She would be such a challenge—everything she gave would have to be earned. And when her surrender came, it would be so much sweeter.

And when she did give her all to this marriage, there would be no turning back. He would have a true partner, a woman he could share so much with.

For the first time in his life, he could have an actual relationship.

"With me, you could have a marriage of respect and desire. With me, you would be free of even the shadow of your father, forever. With me, you could have a position of power as the sheikha, you could make a true difference in women's lives. With me, you will have a place to belong, Amira. If only you can summon the courage to grab it with both hands."

"Will you give me the freedom to make my own choices?"

"Within reason, yes."

"Our child," she began, "if it's a girl—she will be allowed to study, pursue a career of her own choice and will not be used as a bartering tool to move up in the world."

He raised a brow, the very picture of masculine arrogance. "What will you do if I promise all this and don't keep my word?"

"That you ask that question instead of giving me a blind promise is enough, Adir." His smile told Amira she was right.

What Adir thought of himself and what she thought of him were eons apart. Yes, he had deceived her. But from what she was learning of him, honor was important to him, too. And this child was important.

And any man who wanted to be a good father had something to recommend for himself, didn't he?

"All I ask is that anything that concerns our life, we decide together," she said. "And that you don't force me into any other role except a wife and a mother."

"The tribes will call you their sheikha."

"I can live with an honorary title. Because I already have a career, Adir."

His jaw took on a resolute tilt, his eyes gleaming. "That, *ya habibiti*, is not negotiable. You will be my sheikha, my wife, the mother of my children, and anything else I decide you should be."

He turned to leave and then stopped. "And if it's a boy, Amira?" Something shimmered in his eyes and in that wealth of emotion, Amira knew she had made the right choice even then.

The Adir she had trusted that night was a part of the sheikh, too. And that made her non-choice feel like a very real one.

"If it's a boy, I hope you will help me in raising him to be a good man, Adir. A man who is secure in who he is, a man who knows his roots, a man who understands that his life is full of love," she said on a wild risk. Her heart felt as if it had clawed into her throat as he stared at her. "Yes?"

It was not a trick of light, she knew. It was emotion that glittered in his beautiful eyes.

He nodded, perhaps because his throat was full of emotion just as hers was. At least, Amira wanted to believe so.

"And Adir?"

"Yes, Amira?"

"If it's a boy, I hope he would be as handsome as his *abba*."

The smile he left with dug grooves in his cheeks and Amira went to bed with a smile on her own. For the first time since the night she had met and chosen the man who was to be her husband.

She had thought him hardhearted, remote, a monster. But neither was she simply naive or any of those things he thought her.

She was a lot of things made up together—apparently, even a little bit foolish.

Nothing in life was simple. Not the least of which was Adir Al-Zabah.

CHAPTER SIX

THEIR WEDDING TWO weeks later was a small, private affair—a fact that Amira ended up loving—attended by councilmen from the tribes that Adir was sheikh of, her father and a handful of Adir's close friends and business associates.

He hadn't asked her what kind of a wedding she wanted. Amira had even been surprised that he'd told her that it was to be a rather simple affair since the tribes' elders didn't believing in stepping foot in the city—even for their sheikh's wedding.

"It wouldn't be the elaborate affair that you were expecting with Zufar," he taunted her.

"I would be more than glad to stand in front of the imam with you, just the two of us, and get it done."

A devilish brow arched, he said, "Neither do they want to miss my wedding. It is an occasion they've been waiting years to celebrate."

Amira sighed. Did he think she missed all the fripperies and extravaganza of her royal wedding? Nothing had been her choice—not even the dress. "Even as a young girl, I knew my wedding would never be about what I wanted. Please don't feel the satisfaction of thinking you're taking away something I long for, Adir."

The man never did what she expected. Instead of

anger, he laughed, the pad of his thumb tracing the line of her jaw. "You're developing quite the tart tongue, hmm?"

And then, before she could respond to that, he pressed that sinful mouth to hers.

Fingers crawled into her hair, tilted her head up for his pleasure. The taste and scent of him rushed over her, her body rocking into his.

Such pure sensation. Such naked heat. His lips firm and soft, brushing over and over against hers; his chest crushing her breasts. Her belly bearing the press of his arousal.

Hard. Fast. No gentling, no giving, it was a furious, carnal taking. The skillful pressure of his lips pushed her lips against her teeth until she had to open for him, until tasting him was the only thought in her head.

How had she forgotten how seductively he kissed? His kiss betrayed the urgency of his desire—for days after that agreement, he had not visited her again.

Even when he had driven her to the city for a checkup and the doctor had congratulated them both, he had been thoughtful, his gaze lingering again and again on her face. His fingertips had barely brushed her skin, and that only when necessary. As if he couldn't tolerate being near her.

Finally, Amira couldn't bear it any longer. "What have I done now? You have become remote again."

"Did you send Zufar a letter?"

"Did you intercept it?" she countered, suddenly his attitude making all the sense in the world.

His nostrils flared, a tic throbbing in his jaw. Amira would have laughed if she could corral the disconnect between her mind and body. Whatever his birth, Adir Al-Zabah was every inch a royal who could command as easily as breathe.

Every time she mentioned her own mistrust for him, a certain aloofness descended in his eyes. She could almost hear the command he stifled by sheer self-control. *You can't mistrust me, Amira. As your husband and your overlord, I command you to like me.*

If she weren't so sure of his arrogance, she would have thought that instant reserve hid his dislike of remembering his twisted motivations, even his own confusion that he had behaved less than honorably toward her.

She killed the thought as soon as it was born. One mistake in thinking she understood him and his motivations and his feelings was allowed. Doing it again was sheer stupidity.

"My guard asked me if I wanted it intercepted."

"I merely sent my apologies, Adir. He deserves more from me. After what I did."

His jaw tightened. "And is that it?"

"I wrote to Galila, too. She must be worried about me. I have heard news that she, too, is to be engaged soon."

Just as she assumed, those shutters came down in his eyes. "No note for Prince Malak?"

"Will you always mistrust me like this? Should I question where you have been for a whole week? Should I question why you are keeping your distance from me?" But it was only after she asked the question did she realize that maybe it had nothing to do with her. It had to do with the royal family.

But every time she tried to bring up this…feud between him and Zufar, he tuned her out.

"You will cease your communication with the royal family."

"Galila is my friend. My only friend for a long time."

When it didn't look like he would relent, she took his hands in hers, even if he was unwilling. "Adir, what is the harm in my asking after her? I promise there is nothing about you in those letters. Except a small reassurance that I am safe and happy, given the circumstances."

After what felt like an eternity, he nodded. This time, Amira couldn't catch her impulse in time. She pressed her mouth to his. And with a growl, he took the kiss over until she couldn't even breathe.

His touch, his kisses were fire. It was as if he forgot the resentment, the polite courtesy, it was as if he reveled in her surrender. Like he had done the first evening when they had met.

The hunger he felt for her—the reluctant slide of her tongue against his as he plundered her mouth, his powerful body shaking around her. To keep from pooling into a puddle at his feet, she grasped his shoulders. And the tight clench of his muscles under her hands as she dueled her tongue with his, as she sucked on the tip the way he did with hers brought shallow breaths and thundering hearts. Amira gasped for breath.

He placed a palm over her throat and chest, the heat from it searing her bare skin. Her breasts ached with a languid heaviness that reached right to the tips of her nipples—so close to his fingertips. Her fingers dug into his shoulder muscles. Pleading, almost begging.

"Is this what you're missing?" He didn't move his hand, didn't give her what she needed. Only watched her with a hooded gaze.

"Yes," she admitted, heat streaking her cheeks.

He roughly thrust his fingers through his hair. To stop himself from grabbing her, she knew. A thread of feminine power whispered through her at how easily this…thing between them teased his control.

A harsh smile bared his white teeth. His thumb traced her lower lip. "I want you just as much as you want me." With precise movements, he pushed her away.

"I have been alone for a long time, Amira. I cannot and will not account for my whereabouts to you on every hour at the top of the hour." That he had even answered her question took the bite out of his flippant answer. "And as to why the distance...if I come into that tent, I will be inside you within minutes. Damn it, I cannot sleep for wanting you. But you're to be my wife, the sheikha, and I can't dishonor you and myself by flouting the tribe's traditions so openly."

This was what he had meant by straddling tradition and progress. Amira gazed at him, her heart full of admiration. It took a truly complex man to respect something he clearly didn't agree with.

"I never want the tribes to question your honor. To disrespect you. And if that means a cold dip in the oasis that turns my balls blue until the wedding, then so be it."

Amira didn't know whether to laugh or cry. For she, too, missed him—missed the warmth of his kisses with an increasing ache. She went to him and buried her face in his chest, willing him to hold her. Just for a minute.

To let her pretend, even as she knew she shouldn't, that he was the Adir of that night.

"The more I learn of you from the camp and its people, from Zara and Nusrat and Humera, the more my respect for you grows. As a sheikh, as a leader, as a man who straddles past and future and owns the present...you're exemplary. But I guess it is too much to ask that a man be a paragon, an expert in all walks of life."

His fingers sneaked into her hair and he tugged at it sharply. "And what do you mean by that?"

She gasped and looked into his eyes. The eyes that

she could drown in when they were smiling like now. "You could have simply informed me of your decision. But then I learned that you have shouldered responsibility since a very young age and it's clear your personal life—your interpersonal skills with women—have suffered for that."

"You're the first woman to have complaints, *ya habibiti*."

"Cheap shot, Your Highness. But if it's true, it's because I'm the first woman who dares be honest with you."

Humor twinkled in his eyes, his fingers cradling his jaw. Another tell—she was learning. He did that when he was amused despite himself. "I don't think I've ever been so thoroughly insulted and complimented in the same sentence."

Should it be another victory for her—small though it was—that even amidst the bitterest argument with her, Adir laughed? That she saw a glimpse of the man who had held her so tenderly?

If she wasn't careful, her entire identity would be constructed on what he thought of her.

"You will laugh and cry and do whatever emotionally overcome brides do at our wedding, Amira. I will not have Humera demanding of me again why my betrothed writes secretly to a man I loathe, and why she is not filled with joy at our upcoming nuptials." The arrogant lord that he was, he completely ignored her outraged gasp with a flick of his hand.

"The last thing I need is for the tribeswomen to complain to their husbands that I am forcing you into this and sullying my reputation. And yours in that process."

Of course, that was why he had come to inform her about the wedding. Not because he wanted to. Not because he considered her his partner in this, whatever his proclamations about her being his sheikha. Just like every other man she had dealt with, he meant to give her freedom only within the parameters he set for her. "And if they complained to their husbands, would it have any effect?"

He frowned. And then released a breath. "I forget how little of the world you have seen. The tribes are based on a very clear hierarchy, but women have their own power. Your father...has twisted your views of men."

He was right. The tribes' way of living—hard and with little comfort to the naked eye—was strange in her eyes. But already she had seen the close-knit community it was.

"Why does Humera have such...sway with you?" The old midwife had no family to speak of, was a font of knowledge on old medicinal remedies and the desert tribes and commanded the sheikh with the lift of a single brow. Amira had spied the genuine affection in Adir's eyes when he spoke to Humera.

"She raised me."

"And your parents?"

"My mother and Humera came from the same city. She trusted Humera to raise me when she had to give me up. As a days-old infant. So she sent me to the tribes here where Humera had settled."

To be sent away as a little infant to this harsh landscape...not to know where one had come from.

Amira wanted to ask more. It was all tied to what he had demanded from Zufar, she knew. Whatever Adir's past was, it had shaped him in life. And it was her child's legacy and a part of her life, too, now.

"Who...who was your mother?"

But she knew the answer before he gave it. In fragments and pieces from their conversations, the truth had sunk in, without her even realizing it.

The way he had tilted his chin, something in the way he had trained those eyes on her—a glimpse of Galila that caught her breath. The veneration in his tone that night and every time he spoke of her.

"Queen Namani. I was born of an affair. King Tariq quietly arranged to send me away to Humera."

Zufar, Malak and Galila…he was their half brother! That was why Galila had known him. "And your father?"

His features tightened. "Queen Namani wrote to me every year on my birthday. But she never mentioned his identity."

"So you have no idea who he…is."

A queen's illegitimate son, sent away like a disgrace and he had risen to be the sheikh.

Suddenly, his anger, the fear in his eyes when he had thought of her marrying Zufar after learning of their child's existence—everything fell into place.

He had grown up among strangers, sent away by his mother. He had no idea who his father was. And if she had married Zufar, the entire wretched history would have been repeated with their own child.

"Adir, I'm truly sorry. But you cannot hold me responsible for something I didn't cause willingly. You didn't come back until you had decided that your revenge could have even worse consequences for Zufar."

"It matters not whether I was born a bastard out of wedlock, Amira. I would never agree for a child of mine not to know me." But it did matter because he hadn't known his parents. "It is a truth only Humera and I know."

Amir nodded automatically, her mind whirling.

So why had he come to the palace of Khalia? What had he wanted of Zufar?

Had he told her more truth than even he realized that night?

Had he come looking for family?

Would he tell her truth if she asked?

Just as she turned away from him, his fingers on her wrist pulled her back. His face was so close to hers that his breath caressed her cheek. "I will not have you play the martyr at our wedding."

She laughed. What did the insufferable man want? Even he didn't seem to know. "Believe me, Adir. I hate even aspiring to that role. Passivity has never been my favorite. Anything else Your Highness wishes to command?"

"No, you're not passive, whatever else you are." And then something almost tender glinted in his eyes. Something she wanted to burrow into. "Pick one thing. One thing, one element in this wedding will be as you want it. What do you want, Amira?"

The words hung between them as Amira stared at him with wide eyes. The arrogant tilt of his chin couldn't erase the significance of what he offered.

And suddenly, a small flicker of joy lit up in her chest.

However he coated it, this was personal. This was a small brick he had laid on the foundation of their life.

"Any chance that one element could be the groom?" Amira taunted, hiding the longing inside of her. "I saw this young man the other day—a poet that all the women are mad about, Zara said." Adir's brows tied into a thunderous frown and she gave into the laughter bubbling up through her. "He has the most wonderful smile, I think he's the glaring one—your friend Wasim's younger brother—"

The rest of her words were swallowed up by his warm mouth. A swift, hard kiss of possession. Of utter masculine claim. A reminder that she belonged only to him. Heart thudding, Amira clung to him as he devoured her mouth.

"Do not push me, *habiba*. I already hang on a knife edge of balance."

Amira didn't misunderstand the dark glitter of desire in his eyes.

"My wedding dress… Galila and I once went shopping at this designer boutique in Abu Dhabi. This dress…it was the most gorgeous thing I'd ever seen."

"Why didn't you buy it?"

She shrugged. "My father wouldn't pay for such an expensive dress and for Zufar to pay for it, I would have had to jump through ten hoops. It was probably sold years ago but I remember the design very well. Nusrat is a dab hand at sewing and the women here, Zara says, they do such intricate work. Of course, the fabric would have to be fetched from one of the royal couture houses and we would have to pay the women because I really don't want to presume on my future—"

He nodded, pride shining in his eyes. "It will be done."

"Thank you."

On an impulse, Amira touched her mouth to his cheek. And held onto him when he would have left.

She could have left their meeting on that peaceful note.

He had granted her more than she had ever hoped from him in that small gesture about the dress. And yet something in her couldn't forget the enormity of what he had told her about his mother, couldn't stop thinking of what had brought him into her life.

"Adir…this thing with Prince Zufar…what did you ask of him?"

"That I be acknowledged as Queen Namani's son, as part of the Khalian lineage."

"What did he say?"

"He called me a dirty stain on the royal house."

And so he had not only seduced her but stolen her away on the morning of her wedding to Zufar. Amira struggled to keep her distress out of her face. Their truce was tentative, fragile. For all his kisses and generosity, she was aware of the fragile position he gave her in his life. In his personal one, at least. But she couldn't leave it alone. She couldn't shelve it when it was the basis of their entire relationship.

"It is done now, though, right? I mean, you have taken something away from Zufar, because he took something that was yours. Isn't that what you said?"

"Have I been granted my rightful place, Amira?"

And just like that, Amira's heart sank. She shook her head, no words coming to her lips.

His hand behind him, his face stony, he said, "Then no. It is not done. I will not rest until I have what is mine."

Amira sank to her bed, knowing that while everything had changed for her, nothing had changed for him in the last few weeks.

And nothing—not their child, not this wedding—would change Adir's mind.

She could not forget that. She could not forget that if she let it, Adir's inability and unwillingness to see her as anything more than a convenient wife could hurt her far more than Zufar's indifference could have done.

In fact, if she let it, it would shred her into pieces.

Their wedding day dawned with an explosion of oranges and pinks over the gorge and the valley.

Amira had bathed in a huge tub of water placed next to a roaring fire pit, her thick, long hair scented with rose attar; her skin massaged and scrubbed and polished until it gleamed golden.

On the women's side of the tent, Amira—having been attended and dressed just as elaborately as she had been on her wedding day to Zufar by no fewer than twelve women, all of whom Zara had informed her with a reverent tone considered it a privilege and honor to ready the bride of their ruling sheikh—was joined by at least twenty women, all dressed in simple, yet elegant silk dresses.

For once, she'd been grateful for Humera's authority, for the old midwife had ushered everyone out—even Zara—while Amira donned the lace petticoats that had to go under the dress. Amira didn't even question how Humera knew. The old woman knew everything.

Her slender stature meant she wasn't quite showing in cleverly cut clothes, though naked, the swell of her belly was becoming more and more noticeable.

It was something that made her nervous about her wedding night.

Amidst the colorful rugs that adorned the floor and the walls and the fluttering of bright emerald and deep reds of the women's dresses, Amira's breath had been stuck in her throat when she had been brought to the "bridal tent" as Humera had called it.

All these women and their families were so utterly loyal to Adir, so delighted to welcome Amira into their small sphere of lives. Their respect was so automatically given because they trusted Adir's choice, because they thought she had captured their lonely sheikh's heart after all these years.

Three women played local tunes amidst laughter and

a lot of oohing and aahing over each other's jewelry and clothes.

Her hands and feet had been decorated with henna in intricate swirls. Since Amira had literally run away with him with empty hands, Zara, who Amira had learned to her surprise rode the bus every day to work at Adir's IT company, had been dispatched to buy makeup from one of the luxurious high-end malls that had been built in the nearest city.

After an initial protest, Amira had given in while Zara wielded the makeup brushes with infinite delight.

Every new face that greeted her and congratulated her, every teasing glance from unmarried women like Zara and Nusrat and hushed whispers followed by a blush from one of the married women, every warm hug and genuine smile that was bestowed on her slowly released the grip of the worry that had her in its hold.

Except for Galila's friendship, which had possessed its own restrictions since Amira had been betrothed to her brother, she had been deprived of any woman's company since her mother's death.

Suddenly, it felt like she had been dropped in the middle of a warm, albeit noisy family, full of sisters and cousins and friends as she'd always hoped for. As their sheikha, she knew she couldn't share her doubts about her and Adir, but it was nice to be seen, to have the warmth that had always been lacking in her life before.

When a pregnant woman had complained about being afraid of waiting for the mobile clinic to arrive when she got close to her due date, Amira, to Humera's disapproving glance, had immediately offered to deliver the baby.

Between tears and smiles, the woman had thanked and hugged Amira and soon word spread that she was a registered obstetric nurse. It had taken a strict command from Humera asking the women not to forget that this was their future sheikha and not just any tribeswoman and that it was uncertain if their sheikh would give his wife permission to attend to the tribeswomen like a normal employee.

There had been no censure but a warning in Humera's gaze as she had looked at Amira. A gentle reminder perhaps that she had a ruthless overlord and she wasn't free to give her word in this matter.

But even Humera's warning couldn't douse her enthusiasm. There was a need here and she would do everything to see that she filled that need. This was the whole reason she had studied nursing against all odds. This was what she had envisioned her future to be in her wildest dreams.

Amira winked at one of the women who caught her gaze. If she could help out when she was needed, if she could carve a place for herself and her work amongst the tribes… For the first time in months, Amira felt hope for the future.

She could have a fulfilling life here. She would have Adir's respect, she would have her baby and she would have her work. This new life could be better than anything she'd ever hoped for.

No need for love and all the foolishness and trouble it brought.

No need to worry about keeping her emotional distance from a man who could touch her soul with one searing kiss.

Soon it was time to don her wedding dress.

A slithery gold silk—a color that was cause for celebration—with simple beading and embroidery work that the tribeswomen had toiled over during long cold nights around a huge fire pit in one of the tents that had been arranged just for the purpose.

Time to walk, flanked by all the women, toward the huge tent that had been set up with large fire pits warming it in all four corners.

Time to meet the eyes of the man waiting for her.

Dressed in traditional robes, his dark eyes rimmed with the slightest kohl, he was every forbidden dream Amira had ever had. The slight flare of his nostrils, the wicked gleam in his eyes that she was sure only she saw, told Amira what he thought of her dress. What he thought of her as she looked back at him with a suddenly bashful smile.

Right or wrong, foolish or smart, her own choices had brought her to this point in life, to this man.

And now it was truly up to her to make the best of this marriage.

She would, she promised herself fiercely. She would prove to him that she was the best thing that had happened to him. She would make their home a loving place for this child and any more they might have.

Outwardly, she bowed her head in prayer and promised obedience and love to her husband.

CHAPTER SEVEN

IT TOOK ADIR the better part of the night to extricate himself from the celebrations that continued after the wedding ceremony. He rarely, if ever, drank when he was around the encampment, respecting the elders' tradition of abstaining from alcohol, but tonight he needed a stiff drink.

Tonight, he would give anything to forget the long series of duties that rested on his shoulders, this constant… need he felt to prove himself over and over again, to the tribes, to the world. And more than anything, to himself.

It wasn't confidence he lacked. The quarterlies from his company were enough to proclaim his material wealth in his own mind.

No, it was the void he felt inside himself. A void he had felt all his life. A void that had been dug deeper and deeper by his mother's letters, instead of giving him solace.

A void that he fueled his ambition, his need for power and for something even more intangible.

At least the wedding had been a happy celebration for his own tribes and the choice of his sheikha lauded again and again.

It seemed in that matter no one could find fault with him.

Heads from four different tribes had attended the wedding, had come to give their blessing to his marriage—to openly show their support to him and maybe to thumb their nose at governments that were always trying to absorb their lands by way of some treaty or such.

His reputation and the results he had achieved with Dawab and Peshani were also constant draws. And that he had petitioned the sheikh of their neighboring country, Zyria, to enter the council of local governments had already reached certain ears.

Whether he could draw Sheikh Karim of Zyria into the council and convince him to sign the treaty that Adir had so far negotiated for two countries to sign about not encroaching the tribes' land—land that had been claimed for centuries—was another matter. Yet every tribal chief at his table wanted to know the outcome.

Every tribal chief was vested in that outcome.

They thought Adir meant to amass more power, more connections. As a businessman, it was partly that. But he also wanted peace for the land that had reared him. He wanted to put a stop to the constant skirmishes between the countries that bordered the desert land. He wanted the tribes to thrive.

Is it a legacy that you want to create? Amira had asked him when he had explained his reason for starting the council almost a decade ago. They had been having dinner together because he had wanted to see her before he was denied the sight of her for three whole days before the wedding, according to tradition. He had wanted to lose himself in the languid heat of her mouth, to feel her lithe body in his hands before he went to his bed alone and finished himself off.

But of course, nothing was uneventful or simply relaxing when it came to Amira.

She prodded at him, poked at him until he answered. And his answers when she pushed him, he was beginning to realize, contained truths even he wasn't even aware of.

Like her perceptive question three nights ago.

Why couldn't the blasted woman just accept his answer when he had said that peace in the area was good for his business? That it invited foreign investors, that it brought money into the area—money and wealth that the tribes could really use?

But she wouldn't. When he had glared at her, she had ignored his dictates and come up with her own conclusion.

That it went beyond being a good ruler. That he wanted to make his name, that he wanted to leave a legacy.

And since he had had no good rebuttal for her infuriatingly close-to-truth conclusions, he had simply walked out on her and the dinner. Like a schoolboy who couldn't control his temper.

Why he wanted to leave a legacy had become more than evident today. It was a hard truth he still couldn't swallow.

Suddenly, the path he had set himself felt less like victory and more an eternally unreachable conclusion. When his mother had fueled his fire, had Queen Namani thought of the toll it would take on him, or what it would cost him? Had she ever considered that her words could become an unbearable burden?

Quite without a conscious decision, he had become the figurehead of the movement to keep the tribes separate from state, to preserve their way of living. So other tribes were now curious to see the impact on living and work opportunities brought by the bridges he had built between the traditionally nomadic peoples.

The chiefs of three tribes that Adir didn't rule over had a hundred questions for him. They were testing him, he knew, wondering if he truly believed in their way of life or if he was a sellout.

There had been questions about the eco-adventure tourism company he had built, loud assent when he had said that if the whole world wanted to experience the Bedouin way of life, then the tribes should at least get paid for it. They hadn't even touched the topic of oil rights in tracts of land that the tribes had lived on for several centuries.

It would mean more responsibility for him. Two other tribes ready to pick him to represent their rights when he met government officials in the neighboring countries the following year.

Except one tribal sheikh.

One tribal sheikh who had raised the question to which Adir didn't have the answer. Would never have.

And who reminded Adir that however far he came, there was something he would never have.

"You didn't come to bed."

Adir looked up from his rumination at the husky voice. His bride stood at the partition between the lounging area and the huge bed, her golden-brown hair a mass of silky tangles around her small face.

The light golden hue of the dress—so close to her own skin color that it looked like the material had been poured over her curves—had stolen his breath when she had appeared in front of him earlier that evening.

It did so again.

How had he forgotten what had been awaiting him?

The silk whispered sinuously as she moved—hovering on the edge of the space he occupied—the fabric just as expensive and lush as the wedding dress she had worn for Zufar.

But where that dress had been designed very clearly to draw attention, to advertise and court publicity, this was so simplistic in design that it showed off to perfection the beautiful woman who wore it.

More than ten women from the tribes had worked on the bodice's intricate threadwork for seven days, and Adir had seen the privilege and satisfaction in their eyes as Amira had walked in tonight.

She fought him on what she called his highhanded manner of assigning roles to her, but being a sheikha came to her naturally. Even before the wedding, she had found a way to include the women in the celebration. He had seen it during and after the ceremony— gathering people to her, getting to know them—it was in her very blood.

No training could have created that genuine interest in her eyes as she asked Humera about the tribes or one of the women about her job in his IT company. About mobile medical clinics and goat herding in the same question.

Even he hadn't realized what an absolute gem he had been stealing from Zufar. Had Zufar? Clearly not or his half brother would have treated her with more than indifference.

The dark shadows under those big eyes pricked his guilt. Was Adir doing any better, though? "I didn't realize you'd still be awake. You were weaving by the time we went in to eat."

Surprise lit up her eyes. Did she think him such a

beast that he wouldn't notice his pregnant bride struggling to keep a smile but valiantly trying to greet each and every member attending the wedding? How she'd complimented the cooks who'd prepared the food; how she'd drawn her chin up and proudly answered the wife of one of the tribal chiefs about her knowledge of old traditions?

If he was a man constantly straddling tradition and progress, she was a woman who seamlessly resided in both with her education and her respect for the old. It was a remarkably complex feat that she achieved with a very simple approach—by being open and nonjudgmental of the people he ruled, whatever her personal views.

Not that she was a doormat of any kind.

All he'd heard toward the end of the celebration had been what a lovely and kind woman their sheikha was.

"I didn't wait up for you so much as I fretted over whether you would come to bed and what you would want if you came. And what I would do if you did what you want to do." Pink stole into her cheeks at this, rendering her utterly beautiful and lovely. Of course, she didn't give him a chance to interject a compliment. "Then I fretted some more over what to do if you didn't do what I thought you would do. I think I hurt my brain with a thousand thoughts running in a million directions and just fell asleep."

"Your brain must hurt a lot more frequently then," he said automatically and her face broke into a brilliant smile. That tentative quality that had remained all the last two weeks faded, the imp from their first meeting emerging. It stole his breath, which was a curiosity since his libido was already growling and nothing else should have mattered.

"May I join you, Adir?"

He didn't quite frown but couldn't manage a smile. He had a lot on his mind tonight—about his mother, about a lot of things he couldn't control and he didn't want her intruding on that. He didn't want her innocence and her probing questions. He had always dealt with this alone.

What he did want from her tonight he couldn't take, because he wouldn't be gentle. Not tonight when he was feeling this…turmoil. When he was already on edge after the uncharacteristic celibacy he had forced on himself for the last four long months.

Something he still didn't understand even now.

"I will not be much company tonight, which is what you seem to be looking for. Go back to bed."

"Will you…join me tonight?" she asked, the wariness back.

A more patient man would have taunted her back, asked if she wanted him to join her. A man who hadn't already been through an emotional whirl thanks to her unwanted, unsolicited opinions.

"Do I need to inform you of my intentions, Amira? Give you a schedule every evening as to whether I want to have marital relations or not?"

She paled. "No… I just thought we could wait—"

"No, we shall not wait to consummate this marriage. You're my wife." It was the wrong thing to say to a man whose identity had already been challenged once that night, whose very rule over the tribes was being called into question based on a fact he had no control over. "It is my wedding night, isn't it? I think I shall do as I please at the moment. If I find you're asleep when I come to bed, I will wake you to accommodate me."

He sounded like a man of a different century—a husband before women's lib. He had always considered himself an educated and enlightened man, but Amira drove him to regress to Neanderthal behavior.

She didn't flinch and yet what color had been in her cheeks receded at his snarl. She would leave him alone now, he was sure.

And once he had gotten over his black mood, he would join her in bed and she would welcome him.

Because the one thing Amira wasn't good at was playing games. Beneath the elaborate, roundabout clamor of her thoughts was plain desire. Desire that enflamed him despite his dark mood.

She wanted him next to her in that bed, above her, moving inside her. But she hadn't yet quite come to terms with her desire, nor did she know how to express it without feeling mortified. The realization that his wife needed his touch, the release he could bring, as desperately as he needed hers, went a little way to assuage his own turmoil.

But if he thought his innocent wife would retreat to lick her wounds, he was wrong. Invalidating her own question, she walked into the lounging area, as if propelled by his refusal of company. In defiance of his surly mood?

It never amazed him how much strength she possessed beneath that outward fragility.

"Even Humera avoids me when I'm in this mood," he added as a warning, unable to look away from the ravishing picture she made.

She shrugged and gracefully sank down onto the divan, on the other end. "Then Humera is fortunate. Since I'm your wife, I have no such escape route available."

"I'm giving you one."

"No, you're dictating what kind of marriage we will

have. And I told you that is one place where I shall not bow to you. If you're…upset…" she looked him square in the eye, her eyes widened, and then she started again "…if you're angry and want to fume in silence, then I shall simply sit with you, in silence. Since we're married, it would be nice if you shared your thoughts with me. But if you don't want to, that is fine, too. What I will not tolerate is being completely shut out of your day just because you're in a sulky and snarly mood and then for you to visit me only when you're in the—" whatever she saw in his eyes, she licked her lower lip and Adir's blood fled south "—in the…in the mood for…sex. When I gave my promise today, I meant it. I meant that I would share your life and I mean to share everything. Not just your bed."

Having finished her little speech, she leaned back and scooted upward on the divan. Legs tucked under her, the dress spread around her reclining form, her long neck bared to his hungry gaze, her breasts rising and falling… It was like dangling meat in front of a hungry predator.

"Are you saying I'm not allowed to touch you, Amira?" he asked, half shocked, half taunting.

Her eyes remained closed, the sweep of her lashes casting shadows against her cheekbones. "I'm saying you can have more than my body, Adir. I'm not asking you to pour out your heart. But you also don't have to protect me from your…mood swings. Believe me, I'm not going to protect you from mine."

He laughed then, a sound that rushed up from his belly, a sound that surprised himself. Even in his foul mood, she somehow made him laugh. "Mood swings and tart words…hmm. I thought I was getting a sweet-tempered wife."

"For a man who managed to unite two warring tribes, you're quite dense, aren't you? Use honey rather than vinegar if you want a sweet wife, Adir."

The minx's mouth twitched and Adir lost his hold on his control. On his hunger. "I know what to use to make you sweet, *ya habibiti*. My fingers, my mouth, my tongue."

Her breasts rose and fell rapidly. Lust came at Adir like a punch to his middle, all consuming. Suddenly, he wanted her bared to him.

Those dark pink nipples, the sharp curve of her waist, the jet black curls at the juncture of her thighs.

Sweat beaded over his forehead.

He moved toward her slowly, gently, afraid of spooking her. The tense line of her shoulders said she was aware of his proximity. But she lay there like a queen, supine, a ripe temptation.

Small beads of moisture collected on her upper lip, such plump, pink lips that they reminded him of raspberries. Tart, too.

He moved closer until his thigh touched hers, until he was leaning back beside her.

Her breaths sped up, her fingers on her stomach fluttering, like the wings of a butterfly. And suddenly, from one breath to the next, everything shifted.

She was so slender that it was barely noticeable in her normal clothes, but this close, with her reclining back, he could see the curve of her belly.

He swallowed and placed his face above hers. When she didn't jump away, even as she tensed like a taut bow, he slid his hand in under hers.

There.

Stillness came over him, all his earlier turmoil grinding to a halt.

A life they had created together.

A tiny, tiny being that he was responsible for. A child that would look to him for guidance, protection and...love.

Since he'd learned the truth, all his thoughts had been on legitimizing his child, on Amira and all the strange new things she made him feel. Fatherhood hadn't even been on his mind.

Only now did he realize what a tremendous thing had come into his life. A strange shiver gripped him.

Amira's gaze flicked open, alarm dancing in it. She covered his hand with hers, tangling her fingers with his. "Adir? What is it?"

"Would you give up this baby for anything, Amira?"

She jerked away from him, pure aggression coiling her movements. Her glare could burn him into ashes. "How dare you even ask such a question?"

And yet the same question coiled around him, twisting and turning, choking him. "What about if I offered you the freedom you covet so much in exchange? A fresh start somewhere in the world where no man would ever rule you again? A place in a coveted university to study to your heart's content? What then?"

"No. No. No. Not for anything in this world."

A shaft of pain pinched his heart. Sharp and so incredibly real, more than anything he had ever experienced.

"Adir, you're frightening me. What...what have I done?"

He'd been an innocent babe like this when they had cast him off. His mother had professed her love in all her letters, for the man she had had to cut out of her life, for Adir. She had urged him to make something of himself. There had been an almost mad fervor to her letters in which she had poured out all the injustices done to her as she was forced to give him up and described all her festering resentment for her other children—for Zufar, Malak and even Galila.

But in the end, she had given him away. She had never tried to see him again, had forbidden him from seeing her—only directing his destiny from afar.

And as for his father… "Why is the baby so important to you? It's unexpected and…by your own admission, it ties you to a man who deceived you, yes?"

"Adir—"

"Let's not pretend that if not for the baby, you would have run away before I could catch you, Amira."

"Fine. It is important because it stemmed out of a choice I made. My very own. It grew out of a good thing."

"You still think it's a good thing that you spent the night with me even though you hate me?"

"I do not hate you. I…that night was… Let's just say, a fairy-tale night. That night and this baby are tied together now. I can't claim to love the night but hate the repercussions. How could I hate you or that night when it brought me this tiny creature?"

But unlike Amira, his mother and his father had enjoyed their affair, their love for each other—just not the result, which was him.

He took Amira's unwilling hand in his, lacing their fingers like she had done before. When he tugged her, she came, until she was sitting between his legs, her back resting against his chest, her hips grazing his thighs.

Something inside him calmed. This child of theirs she carried, this woman—they belonged to him. His own. It was atavistic, this thinking, but he couldn't help it. In a life where he had called no one his, *they* were his.

"Adir, please…tell me what brought this on. Tell me—"

"Hush, *habiba*," he said, holding her close, regretting the fact that he had scared her. It was hard to stay mad at her, he was realizing. And even worse, indifferent. "It is nothing to do with you. Or even me. The meeting with the chiefs just brought on questions."

"What kind of questions? Adir, you can't expect me to be your sheikha and not share anything of what makes you *you*."

"What is it you want to learn, Amira?"

"How did you become the sheikh? I mean, after you were sent away like that."

He buried his face in her hair, the scent of her encircling him. "When I united the Dawab and Peshani tribes, I did it unknowingly. They had been warring with each other for years, and the local governments provided just enough fuel to keep them going at each other's throats. Because as long as they were fighting—and trying to make deals to cheat each other—the oil rights on the land they occupied, vast tracts of land, was up for grabs."

Slowly, she relaxed against him. His breath stuttered when she pulled his arms around her middle, a pillow for her soft breasts. He wasn't even sure she was aware of the move. Of how she constantly tempted him, of how innately sensuous she was.

"You pointed out the obvious," she said, and he smiled.

"Yes. When I was at university in Zyria, I met an investor who saw merit in my ideas for an eco-adventure tourism company. Then from there, I went on to buy an arm of an IT company since it was clear that even the Bedouin way of living wasn't going to escape modernization completely."

"I know. I was so amazed to learn that Zara works for you."

The pride in her words made him feel a thousand feet tall—even though he'd never needed validation before. "It took Zara and me and Humera months to convince her parents that it was a good idea for her to use her brains to support the family's meager income. That they were not selling out their daughter to the modern world.

"Once we provided the bus service and they met a recruiter—another woman who works for me—they were convinced."

"And from there, everything took off." She looked over her shoulder at him as if he had achieved the impossible. As if he were truly a hero. "You have done so much for them, Adir. You're a natural leader. Every day, I see their pride in you, their trust that you would always do the right thing for them. It is a trust you have earned."

"Today, two other tribal chiefs attended our wedding."

He could almost see her frown. "And?"

"They were testing the waters, so to speak. That the Dawab and Peshani have given up on decades of enmity is a powerful draw. That they're thriving under my leadership, finding new sources of income and livelihoods while the most traditional of them continue the old ways of goat herding has brought another tribe to be ready to grant me permission to represent them. It is a double-edged sword, a privilege to be given power to rule them. And the second chief…he questioned my birth, about my right to rule over the tribes. He asked about my parentage. About where I had sprung from. He was clearly trying to provoke me into a fight and…"

Adir would have no answer to give, Amira realized.

Even the part he knew of his parentage, he could not proclaim it to the world. He could not say he was of royal lineage, that ruling was in his bones and in his blood.

He couldn't say anything. He would have to take any insults offered him.

Suddenly, Amira wanted to call Zufar out on his pride.

And Queen Namani, what had she bred into Adir through those letters? What had she given him? Not pride, not love, whatever Adir chose to call it. But a festering resentment for his half brothers and sister.

And all this he had borne alone, until now.

"And it made you think of Queen Namani?"

"It made me think of my father, the man she had the affair with. The man she said she loved with all her heart and who in turn adored her." He ran his fingers through his hair. "Queen Namani's letters have been the driving force in my life for as long as I remember."

Curiosity about the old queen ate through Amira. She couldn't even believe it was the same woman that had been her best friend's temperamental mother. "When did she send them?"

"One letter every birthday." The monotony of his voice tore at her for it completely belied the emotion in his eyes. "By the time I began to understand who she was to me, I waited for that day every year. It was a prize, a gift."

"What…what were those letters about?"

"A piece of her heart, just for me, she said. Her true legacy, she called me. She urged me to study, to take control of my life, every letter on every birthday reminding me that I was destined for great things. That I was not to neglect my education at any cost. That I was to rise through the world. That I was not to grow weak in the face of any hurdle. That my path would always be that of a loner, if I wanted to reach my true destiny. Not to trust anyone, not to give into the whims of my heart. That I was to make an advantageous match with a powerful bride when it was time to wed."

The path of a loner... Destiny before heart... *Ya Allah*, was it any wonder he was so remote, so isolated from everyone? The rage Amira felt for the dead queen choked her.

She swallowed it away, for she didn't want to disturb the small intimacy. "Did you tell her that you achieved even more than she could predict? That you had been chosen to rule the tribes?"

"No."

Amira's heart ached for the pain contained in that single word. She forced herself not to look at him for the fear of seeing that pain in his eyes. Because if she did, then she wouldn't be able to control the outrage that filled her. She couldn't arrest the words that needed to be said. "Why...why not?"

"The condition of receiving her letters was that I was never to contact her. Never to betray her confidence. Never to let another soul learn who she was to me."

"But you went to see them after her funeral."

"On her orders. She urged me to claim my place in that last letter."

After there was no harm to her own reputation. When she was no longer in this world to deal with her mistakes. What a coward Queen Namani had been!

"When the old sheikh told me he had chosen me as his successor, it was her words that filled me with confidence. I never gave the identity of my father another thought...until today."

"And today, that man made you wonder about your father. About what kind of a man would not even look up the child he had fathered on the woman he supposedly adored and loved. About the woman who gave you a dream, lured you with it but kept it out of your reach. A woman who only bred anger toward—"

He jerked her up so fast that she would have fallen off the divan if it weren't for his tight grip. "She was forced to give me up. Queen Namani loved me."

"And yet you asked me if I would give this baby up for anything. I wouldn't, Adir. Even if I could understand how she had to, I don't understand her. With Zufar and Galila, she—"

"Enough, Amira! You, with your naive outlook of the world and your loyalty still tied to Zufar, you wouldn't understand. She loved my father and she hated parting with me. I will not hear a word about this from you, ever again. Do you understand?"

Amira wanted to say no, but that she was finally beginning to understand him.

To understand the hold Queen Namani's words still had over him.

She was a perfect woman in his mind—his mother who had spurred him on and on to better things in life. Filled his mind with useless words about destiny and loneliness. And who had made him blind to everything else.

She wanted to argue that the queen had done him more harm than good. She wanted to tell him what she knew of Galila's childhood and how uncaring and neglectful she had been of Zufar, Malak and Galila.

That Zufar, who represented everything Adir did not have, for all his legitimacy hadn't even had what Adir had received from their mother. That Adir's arrival, the knowledge of the letters she had written him, would have been punishment enough to all three of his siblings.

But she could say none of it.

Because Adir was not prepared to hear her.

He wouldn't see the truth. Maybe Queen Namani had truly loved this son she'd been forced to give up, had been weak and selfish, and he had become an outlet for her to thumb her nose at her husband and even her other children.

He wouldn't see that he had become a silent rebellion for a weak woman.

The very thought made Amira want to growl in pain. That she had cast this honorable man in such hard words made her want to rage.

Queen Namani had not only given him up, but also used him for her own agenda.

He would never be prepared to hear the truth. He would never realize that, for all he was in the dark about his father's identity, he didn't need it.

Adir Al-Zabah was a man to be reckoned with, a natural leader, a born king.

This husband of hers, who was noble and thought of his tribes and their needs, was still haunted by a past he couldn't fix. And he couldn't see that Queen Namani had stolen more from him than he could ever imagine— the chance of having a relationship with his siblings, the chance to let the past be left in the past.

The chance of ever inviting more into his life.

And while he was mired in the complex truths of the past, while he was still under the hold of his mother's ghost, there would be room for nothing else in his life.

Or his heart.

It would only ever be a marriage of convenience.

He would only ever be her husband by law. He could never own a place in her heart. He could never hurt her, for she knew what not to expect from him.

And the strange realization gave her the courage to give comfort. The guts to simply offer what he needed from her tonight.

She offered the only thing she knew he would allow her to do. Her legs shook as she let her body sway toward him, giving herself over.

She went to her knees between his thighs, her own need drowning out other cries. His fingers manacled her wrists, his anger vibrating in the air around them.

Amber eyes darkened to a burnished copper, his mouth set into a flat uncompromising line, he held her gaze.

Breath punched up through her throat as her breasts pressed against his hard chest, her soft belly sinking against his abdomen, the press of his arousal a brand against her skin.

"I'm sorry," she said, leaning her forehead against his. "You're right. I don't understand. I can't imagine the…frustration you must feel. I can't imagine the strength it takes for you to be who you are."

She pressed her lips to his and whispered her apology. Again and again. Between soft kisses and hurried breaths. Between the raspy purr of her lips against his and the enticing swirl of her tongue inviting him.

She couldn't bear it if he told her it meant nothing to him except that it would ensure her obedience. If he said it was his due in that arrogant way of his.

If he said she was weak for still living in her naive world.

She still had a life with him, with their baby. She had a family of her own—the three of them and more, in the coming years. She had a taste of his reluctant respect, she had his name and she had his desire. That had to be enough.

That would be enough.

She clasped his cheeks, the bristle of his beard rasping against her palms in sensuous torture. His nostrils flared, his hips pressing roughly against hers, even as he sought to control his anger. And his lust. This relentless need she could see in his eyes. Because it was the same for her.

Another wet, warm kiss against his mouth, the scent of him coiling lazily in her limbs. She dragged the tips of her teeth against his hard jaw. Felt the reward of his fingers roughly tangling in her hair.

She thrust her tongue into his unwilling mouth when he growled. Stroked it against his tongue, like he had done to her just a few days ago. The length and breadth of her pressed into him, she made love to his mouth with hers, willing his control to shatter. Willing him to take over.

And when, with a growl that reverberated up through his chest, he claimed ownership of the kiss, she shivered all over. In relief, in desire.

When he thrust his tongue into her mouth roughly, hungrily, she welcomed him. She welcomed the tips of his fingers digging into her hips, she reveled in how his chest crushed her sensitive breasts. She gloried in the evidence of his hard arousal against her lower belly, in the molten warmth he created at her sex.

His fingers crawled into her hair, pulling and tugging at the pins in it until it fell to her waist. She moaned loudly when he sank his fingers into the thick mass and pulled her closer.

Possessive and rough, his control was in shreds at her

feet. He was shaking with desire and Amira answered in kind. Answered with the only truth he would allow between them.

"I'm glad I met you, Adir. I'm glad you're my husband, that you will be the father to my child. I'm so glad that I chose you that night. And I would gladly do so again and again, given half the chance."

CHAPTER EIGHT

I'M SO GLAD that I chose you that night. And I would gladly do so again and again.

How did such an innocent know what words to say to ensnare such a jaded man as him? To push him to the edge of his control?

How could one surrender and gain victory at the same time? Her words and her eyes, her kisses lit a fire in Adir's blood.

He took her mouth with a feral hunger he could not corral into submission. She melted under his kiss, her lips so sweet yet incinerating, her moans soft but packing a punch, her strokes to keep up with him so inexperienced and yet filled with a ferocious desire that matched his own.

Hands on her back, he crushed her to him while he groped for the zipper of the dress, like a teenage boy touching his first woman. She threw her head back, baring her neck to him—another invitation he could not resist. Her pulse thrummed violently at her neck, the scent of her rose perfume emanating from her soft skin.

While he tugged the hidden zipper down with one hand, he scored the long line of her neck with his teeth. He dug his teeth in at her pulse point and suckled that skin into his mouth, eager for the taste of her to sink into his very marrow.

She tasted of sweat and sweetness, an incredibly erotic combination that only made him hunger for more.

"I will taste you everywhere tonight, *ya habibi*," he promised, his voice gone so deep and husky that even he barely recognized it. That night, he had barely had the time to indulge himself, hardly any time to explore the heady explosion her body promised. "I will lick your flesh, sink my teeth in wherever I please. I will taste the honey between your legs and you will fracture from the unbearable pleasure of it."

He did so, hard and deep, until her pale golden skin bore his mark, like a savage from centuries ago. Lust pounded in his blood as her skin instantly bruised.

She jerked closer to him, her knees trembling, her breath a rough accompaniment to his caresses.

A sob broke out of her as he softly licked the bruise he had given her. When she thrashed against him, searching for more, eager for more, he gave it to her by rocking into the cradle of her thighs. Pressing his erection against the warmth he knew was waiting for him.

She let out another sob as she flung her arms around his shoulders and clung to him.

For every action, there was an equal and opposite reaction—she was Newton's law embodied. He smiled, making a note to tell her of his idiotic comparison. His smart wife would surely get a kick out of that.

"Adir, please… I want more. This dress…it rubs and caresses…"

"Then we will rip it off, *ya habibi*." He grabbed the neckline in his hands when she jerked back from him, her arms protectively held against the bodice of the gown. He had forgotten that he had undone the zipper. A pale golden shoulder peeked at him as the bodice loosened. And the upper curve of one breast was a tantalizing reminder of what awaited him.

Cheeks pink with color, hair a glorious mess around her face, lips swollen with his rough kisses—she was a wet dream come true. A complex, blood-pounding combination of innocence and sensuality.

"No." She settled the fabric over her chest with her palm in a loving caress. Unwittingly making her nipples poke against the slithery silk.

Adir groaned and rubbed his hand against his face. "Come back to me, Amira."

She shook her head, making the long locks cover her face. "I…" She licked her lips and flinched with pain at the indent he had left on her lower lip with his teeth. Instead of feeling guilty for hurting her, lust swirled through him, demanding more. "I will not let you tear this dress. My wedding dress… It's a symbol of so many things to me, so many good things, it's precious to me. I mean to keep it for decades to come."

Decades to come. It was a vow spoken between them, a promise given freely in a relationship he had forced on her.

The rightness of her words soothed a place he didn't realize needed soothing, filled a void he hadn't known existed within him.

He didn't tell her he had no intention of tearing something that was clearly so important to her. Instead, he raised a brow, as if considering her request. For all her innocence and surrender, his wife had a backbone of steel. If she thought he was ordering her around, she would take back that surrender.

And he needed it right now more than he needed air.

"Then you may take it off and put it away."

The fire pit hissed in the silence, while outside the tents, the soft tinkle of instruments permeated the air. They were still celebrating his union with this enchantress. He was a fool to have wasted so many hours roiling in that chief's comments when he should have been here with her.

Enjoying this.

"Take it off? Here?" she asked softly, finally, taking in the light from the solar lanterns around them. Since he hadn't been disturbing her sleep, he hadn't turned any of them down.

A golden glow filled the room, the colorful rugs and throws reflecting a kaleidoscope of colors and shapes onto her form.

Not an inch of her would be hidden from his sight, a realization she seemed to come to at the same moment, for she frowned and looked around again. Her wide eyes filled her face, her cheeks flushing with color.

"But don't you want to go back there?" She pointed behind her to where his vast bed awaited, shrouded in darkness. Another fire pit and the fur rugs provided warmth there.

"No, not today. Some other time, some other night, I will come to that bed, find you in the darkness and be inside you while you slowly surface from sleep, while you're still dreaming of me. Today, I want you here."

Swallowing nervously, she looked at the thin walls reflecting their silhouettes.

"No one would dare wander close to our tent, *ya habibiti*. Nor dare even to glance at even their sheikha's shadow. The night will not carry any of the sounds we make. Now take off that dress and return to me, before I lose the little patience I'm struggling to keep. Come here, Amira," he said, patting the space between his thighs. Slowly, he relaxed into his stance.

Her doe-like gaze went to the place on the divan he pointed to and then to his throbbing erection—pressing upward and blatantly clear against the soft fabric of his robes.

If she stared at him any harder… He laughed, his balls becoming tighter. His blood pounded with such savage hunger that he wondered if he should even be touching her right then. But he let that concern him only for a second longer. The idea of not being inside her within the next few breaths was unendurable.

She would take him and he would ensure she was sobbing with pleasure by the end of it.

"Look at me," he commanded and she obediently did. More out of curiosity than true obedience, he had no doubt. Slowly, he reached for the hem of his robes and pulled them up and over his head.

Leaving himself utterly naked to her roving gaze.

She gasped, a soft, feminine sound that he wanted to hear again and again, and much more loudly. She had made that sound when he had thrust into her—a cross between pain and pleasure, a gasp of wonder.

He needed that in his ears again, he needed her warm breath fluttering the hair on his chest, he needed the silky slide of her thighs against his hair-roughened ones. He needed the soft cries she emitted when he moved inside her, the low keening sound she made in her throat when she climaxed.

He got harder and longer as she studied that part of him, her teeth digging into her lower lip.

"Oh… I… I don't remember you being that…big." Again, a lick of her lower lip. A nervous swallow. But she didn't shy away from studying him greedily. She didn't even do it covertly. No, she looked at him boldly, possessively. "You will hurt me."

"Not today, not ever again. You're a nurse, remember your studies, Amira. You were a virgin last time. The queen's famed gardens are not the most conducive place to making a woman's first time great and—"

"It *was* great. It was…" She closed her eyes and swayed and the bodice of her dress slipped a little further, showing him the thin strap of her slip. A bold red strap.

His blood heated a little more. But he waited and watched, the thrust of her breasts, the small smile playing around her lips a reward in itself.

"So good." She opened her eyes and a fierce blush moved up her chest and neck to her cheeks. "I touched myself after…a few times. Between my legs," she clarified, as if he couldn't understand. As if he wasn't stopping himself from pouncing on her by the skin of her teeth.

The image of her touching herself, her fingers delving between those folds, the wetness that had soaked his fingers that night coating her own, the bundle of nerves at the top throbbing for his touch…

"And?" A word that reverberated with rough need.

"And it was not the same. I… I was able to arouse myself… I closed my eyes and thought of you…your weight on me, your hard thighs, the muscles in your back flexing under my touch, the way you moved in and out… I couldn't breathe for wanting you back inside me again, but whatever I did with my fingers, it was not enough. I could not…bring myself to…" and then, in front of his eyes, his shy wife transformed into something else, owned her desire "…to orgasm." She paused. "I… I shouldn't have told you that. I don't want you to think…" Dismay filled her eyes. "Your opinion means a lot to me, Adir."

And just like that, she unmanned him by her candor, by her open vulnerability. In this, he would give her honesty, too. He had the ability to, at least. "You've no idea how arousing it is to know that you get wet just by thinking of me. Knowing that I can bring you to that edge of desire. But what I would not ever tolerate is you thinking of another man like that. Is that understood?"

"Yes. Will you promise not to think of another woman moving forward, too, Adir? I feel such rage if I even think of you touching another woman, looking at another woman."

"You're all I want, *ya habibiti*. For four months, you're all I've thought of as I've brought myself to release. And tonight, it will be pleasure unlike you've ever known before."

"Even more than that night?"

He smiled wickedly, loving that much about her. Her curiosity, her innate zest for more out of life would always win over any other fear, any atrocities she had been dealt. "Yes, much, much more," he promised fiercely.

She nodded, and the line that tied her brows cleared. Slowly, holding his gaze, with utter care for the damned garment, she pushed it off her shoulders and chest.

The soft red…thing she wore underneath was silky, flimsy and so provocative as it bared half her breasts. Which he realized, with an utterly masculine satisfaction, were already fuller and lusher.

The low V neckline barely skated the line over her nipples.

Adir's breath caught in his throat as she wiggled her hips to let the dress pool down at her feet. There was a flash of a sleek thigh as she stepped over the dress. The black lace hem ended miles above her knees, baring all of her toned thighs and barely, just barely hiding her sex from his sight.

She turned and picked up the dress gently, and in the process flashed her buttocks at him. Adir smiled, wondering if he should tell her what he was sure was inadvertent.

The sight of her bare bottom while she bent over the dress… He wanted to crawl to her, push her head down to the rug and bury himself inside her, to take her like that. He was almost off the divan before he countered the urge.

Not tonight. His wife was adventurous, yes, but one step at a time.

Another time, he promised himself, when her belly was big with his child and he could not cover her body like he could now. Then he would take her from behind, in that utterly dominating position, and yet he would have to be gentle, for he could no more bear the thought of hurting her than he could bear the thought of walking away from the desert—the only home he had ever known.

The challenge it would be to his base instincts, the anticipation of it made his blood sing.

As if intent on torturing him, she straightened the dress and let it hang over a reclining chair. And only then did she turn toward him.

He had no idea what he saw in his face but she let out a long exhale. As if to brace herself. Her eyes full of a vulnerability that pierced him, she placed a hand on her belly, as if she could find support from the silk, and asked, "Do you like it? Remember the day you got so angry that I went with Zara and a couple of other women to that luxury mall? Wasim turned red and ran so fast when he saw Zara and me stop in front of the lingerie store. I told him he shouldn't follow us so closely but he wouldn't listen."

"If I had known what you'd had in mind, I would have taken you myself. And your safety is never a thing to be taken lightly, Amira. Promise me you acknowledge that."

"I do," she said so earnestly that he knew he didn't have to worry that she would take foolish risks. He kept forgetting what a levelheaded woman she was for her age. "I didn't ask you because I wanted it to be a surprise. There are certain things that should remain secret between a husband and wife. Even Humera agrees."

He scowled, knowing that she was once again testing the waters between them. Seeing how far she could push him before he pushed back. "In matters of lingerie, keep your secrets, Amira. But only there."

"Only there," she agreed, and then slowly she came to him.

Adir moved to the edge of the divan, until she was standing between his thighs, her breasts near his face.

It wasn't going to work this way. Not in this state. He would hurt her if he didn't find release first. And that was unacceptable.

And even as lust rode him hard, and the need for release clamored in his blood, Adir knew that she had sneaked under his skin. That something inside him was already changing, morphing and reforming to include this woman. That slowly but surely Amira herself was sinking into his blood.

And for a man who had not known love except in words written by a lonely woman years ago, for a man who had conquered the desert and the harsh challenges it presented, the prospect was utterly daunting.

And totally out of his control.

His skin was like hot velvet, rough but smooth at the same time. And the glide of it against her bare skin, the rough rasp of his thighs against her soft ones…they both groaned at that first skin-to-skin contact.

Her nipples, even through the flimsy silk, pebbled against his chest. And his erection…oh, God, it was fire and heat and steel pressing into her soft belly.

Sensations overwhelmed her, clamoring for her attention, and Amira closed her eyes, welcoming the onslaught. His fingers were callused, rough against her soft skin. The bruise he had given her at her neck pulsed, a perfect contrast of pain that made the pleasure coursing through her that much more powerful, that much sharper.

She sank her fingers into his hair, took a deep breath of that masculine scent. He felt like heaven. Like a safe haven. Like an exhilarating place to land.

"You're like pure silk," he said, puncturing the words with a harsh curse she didn't even understand.

He gave her no warning. By word or the flicker of an eyelid.

She gasped as he grabbed the edges of the neckline and pulled until it tore with a loud rasp. Spine arching, she clutched his head as he took her nipple into his mouth.

Teeth and tongue and wet warmth, there was nothing he didn't do to that aching bud.

Raw heat broke over her skin. His tongue licked at the needy tip, flicked at it again and again. When Amira pressed her fingers into his head, he laughed—a faint, wicked sound he buried in her skin before opening his mouth wide and closing it over her breast again.

This time, he did what she was urging him, what she was begging him to do. He suckled with deep, hard pulls. She jerked as wetness rushed over her sex, coating her thighs in a way that felt so wanton, so utterly wicked. Cupping one, he moved his mouth to the other breast, licking a wet path across and causing aching pulls in counter rhythm to his caress as he kissed her.

She rubbed her thighs shamelessly, the wetness between only intensifying the need for pressure.

Amira gasped and sobbed. Needing him inside her so desperately. "Please, Adir, inside me, now."

"No. Not yet... Four months is too long, *habiba*. I'm sorry, Amira, I'm sorry."

She had no idea what he was apologizing for and she didn't care.

He would never hurt her, not willingly, she knew that now. And she would follow him anywhere under the desert sun.

"Whatever you will give, Adir, please hurry. I feel... empty without you inside me."

He groaned, his movements becoming urgent, rough.

His hands moved from her shoulders to her waist and then further down below, to the hem of her negligee. A harsh growl erupted from his mouth, pinging over her nerves as his palms discovered her bare bottom.

"No panties?" he whispered against her wet nipple, followed by a catlike flick over the turgid tip.

"No...the saleswoman assured me it didn't require..."

Her words misted away as he bunched the gown and pulled it up behind her, until her sex was bared to him. She longed for his fingers, his hardness there. She was vibrating with such need, she was ready to take him in hand and push him inside her.

But of course, the beast had other plans. He took her fingers and wrapped them around his hardness. "Stroke me," he commanded with such dark desire that Amira forgot all about her own body's demands. His forehead resting in the valley between her breasts, he seemed to fight his harsh breathing.

Such fervor, such need clamored in those amber eyes that she would have done anything he asked of her to satisfy that need. To be the one who pushed him to the edge. To be the one he shattered for.

"Show me how," she begged. "I want to please you. Show me how to do it right, Adir." Now the command was in her tone. She felt as if she would break if she wasn't the one that brought him the release she could see him craving.

Why was he fighting this? Didn't he know she was putty in his hands?

"If I do," he breathed against her skin, with a self-deprecating smile, "if I put my hand over your soft one and make you grip me, stroke me the way I need it, I will come instantly." She blushed at his blunt language, even as she boldly explored him with her fingers. "Four months is a long time for a man to be celibate. But if I move inside you, it will be too…short."

"You haven't been with anyone," she said, feeling a surge of something in her chest she couldn't even name.

"No."

Just that. One word. No explanation. No concession. Adir in his true form.

She licked her lips and with a groan, he took her mouth in a hard, swift kiss. "If you find…if you come in my hands," she said, refusing to use euphemisms anymore with him, and was reward by his wicked smile, "how long before you will be able to do it again?"

This time, his raucous laughter, she was sure, could be heard all through the encampment. Tight grooves formed in his cheeks and his sweat-sleek chest shook against hers. "Selfish little thing, aren't you?"

She shrugged. "Just making sure you have a little... stamina left for me." She did a put-upon, troubled sigh, fighting the utter joy that wanted to bubble up in laughter. "You know, marriage is all about compromises and a little give-and-take."

When he kissed her again, it was soft, slow, almost reverent. As if he didn't know what to do with her. The expression in his eyes took her breath away. He wasn't a man given to words, she was realizing, but he felt something for her.

Perhaps just a little spark but it was there.

"It will be slow and deep and I can take my time inside you. I would reward you in return multiple times."

"Now you're speaking in my language."

No sooner had she said the words than he wrapped his fingers over hers. She pumped her grip up and down as he showed her. Again and again, while the soft head rubbed and pushed against her belly. While one rough hand cupped one breast, and one cupped her buttock and he took unapologetically what he needed from her.

Just from her. Only her.

Amira wouldn't have closed her eyes if her life had depended on it.

Those penetrating amber eyes closed, he thrust his hips up and forward in a counter rhythm while she worked her fist up and down, his breath shallow and fast, his skin gleaming with sweat, his neck and shoulder muscles corded so tight—he looked as if he was hewn from the rocks that lay over the gorge. It was a sight Amira would never forget.

His thrusts became faster, the angles and grooves of his face harsher, deeper and then he gave a guttural cry against her breast, before he was shuddering in her arms.

And his release coated her belly.

Amira stared in a sort of rapturous wonder. How could his release give her such satisfaction? Why did seeing him in that moment give him such a hint of vulnerability when he was truly anything but?

The intimacy of the moment, the way he held her as he broke apart… Amira felt as if she had been re-formed in his passion.

In that moment, he was hers. Just a little. Only hers.

Not the sheikh of warring tribes. Not a corporate businessman. Not Queen Namani's discarded son. Or Zufar's resented half brother.

He was just her husband, the man she loved with all her heart.

She pushed sweat-streaked hair from his forehead and pressed a tender kiss to his temple. "Is this how it feels when you bring me to release?"

He looked up and that hint of vulnerability—she hadn't imagined it—disappeared when he smiled that masculine, arrogantly devilish smile that melted her heart just a little.

If they had a boy, she hoped he had that smile of his father's. That glimpse of rakishness that Adir wore beneath the mantle of duty and responsibility. That love of the harsh desert land and all its people.

"It feels like I'm on top of the world when you moan through your release, when you fall apart around my fingers. It feels like…" hands on her buttocks, he lifted her, leaving her no choice but to straddle his hips and then before she could blink, he was gliding into her on a smooth stroke, and Amira clung to his shoulders, the velvet heat of him inside sending a rough, guttural sound up through her throat "…I can conquer anything. Have I risen enough to satisfy my sheikha?"

"Oh…" No words came to her for he had impaled her so thoroughly. "It feels too much this way. Like you're…"

He instantly frowned. "Does it hurt?"

When his hands moved to her hips to pull her off, she fought his grip and pushed down. "No, Adir, please don't leave me."

The slide of her body over his made them both groan together.

"I won't." Tenderly, he pushed the hair off her forehead now. His mouth when it met hers was soft, warm, a melding of more than just bodies. He kissed her as if she were precious to him, as if he couldn't bear to part with her. As if his kisses could say things he couldn't himself. "Relax, *habiba*. Listen to your body."

She took a deep inhale and tried the up-and-down motion again. Another groan fell from her mouth, pleasure fluttering awake in her lower belly.

In knots and waves, it inched into her limbs, as if she were made of drugged honey.

"Now?" he asked.

She smiled and arched her spine. The movement sent her breasts rubbing against his chest and a hiss of male pleasure rent the air.

"Now it feels like heaven."

He moved back on the divan until her knees were on either side of his hips, until he was embedded so deeply within her that Amira couldn't breathe for the tight friction of him inside her walls.

She ran her hands all over him—the jutting tautness of his shoulders, his sweat-slicked back, the ropes of lean muscles across his chest, scraping her fingers over flat, brown nipples.

And he submitted to her touch, as if it were her due. And she loved him all the more for it.

"Now, shall I teach you how to touch yourself just as I taught you to touch me?"

Eyes wide, cheeks full of heat, she stared at him. "You want me to touch myself?"

A deliciously wicked smile split his mouth. "Just when I'm there to enjoy it, yes."

She returned his wicked smile but with an added thoughtful smirk. "And you? Will you only...pleasure yourself when I'm around?"

He laughed and the sound was even more arousing than feeling him inside her. "I'm hoping I don't have to since now you're here to do it for me. And before you argue the same point, in this position—" he thrust up as though to remind her "—it would work better."

When she nodded, he took her hand and brought it between their bodies. Heat broke out over every inch of her skin as he guided her fingers to the exact spot where she'd ached for him.

Her spine arched again as he flicked at that sensitive place with his finger. "Keep doing that when I thrust up."

More than happy to be his pupil, Amira shed the last layer of her inhibitions. His honed torso leaning back, he thrust up into her tight heat while watching her fingers move over her clitoris with hooded eyes.

"Move, Amira, as you want to."

That ache was already building in her lower body, deep waves radiating out when he thrust up and she rubbed herself.

Hand on his shoulder, Amira let herself go. Their bodies soon found a rhythm and, as if he knew her body and needs better than she did herself, he increased the pace.

Soon, Amira didn't know if she was earthbound or flying. Her breasts bounced up and down as she undulated over him. When he cupped one and brought it to his mouth just as his body pounded up into her, she fragmented.

His name fell from her lips like a keening cry as bliss suffused her every breath, every limb and joy filled her heart.

He picked her up, while he was still inside her, and brought her to his bed. Hands raising her bottom, he glided in and out of her, in deep, short thrusts.

His own quick release followed soon after and again Amira witnessed the pleasure it wrought on his face, the way he held her when they were both sweat-slicked and the scent of sex permeated the air.

When he rubbed her lower lip with the pad of his thumb as if he couldn't let her go just yet.

When he grabbed a towel from somewhere and gently wiped her between her legs as if he had done it a thousand times and would for thousands more nights to come.

When he pressed a gentle, soft kiss to her cheek and brought her closer to his body. When his palm, as always, settled on her belly and he asked if she was okay.

She was okay. More okay than she had ever been in her life.

Because, for the first time in her life, she felt like she was home. She was where she belonged.

CHAPTER NINE

Two weeks into being married, Adir wondered why he had waited so long to take on a wife. Like Humera and Zara and Wasim—who had become Amira's biggest champions—kept reminding him, it was Amira that made the institution so agreeable.

Apparently, there wasn't a single man or woman in the camp that didn't adore his wife.

Adir couldn't quite find a fault with her, either—not that he'd been looking for one. In two weeks, their desire for each other had only grown and whatever he asked her to do—or whatever he desired to do to her—his wife jumped in with both feet.

The only niggles in his perfect marriage were their constant fights about her health and the one topic he had forbidden her from bringing up—Queen Namani and her other children.

More than once, he had seen the struggle in her eyes—something she wanted to say when he mentioned a letter from his mother or his past. Since everything concerned with his past or his formative years seemed to lead to Queen Namani or the letters, he had forbidden her to ask questions about his past or even mention it.

Dismay filling her eyes, she had said, "We will never

move forward with our life if we don't face your past together."

He didn't agree with it. They had a perfect life together and talking about his dead mother or her other children wasn't going to make it better.

When it came to Amira's health, on the other hand, Adir knew he was being irrational. At least partly.

For every tenet he laid down about her resting during the hot days, her sleep, her food that she only picked at, his wife defied him. She called him a brute, a beast, her jailer, for after learning that she had fainted of heat stroke when she had been visiting Zara, he had forbidden her to leave their tent at all.

He had even broached the topic of sending her away to his residence in the city. But the stubborn woman refused to leave him.

"I plan to have at least three to four children, and what will you do? Send me away and confine me completely for the next decade? Live separately?" Eyes shining with unshed tears, arms locked tight around his waist, she had burrowed into him one evening.

Having never been the recipient of such frequent physical affection—it never struck him to touch her outside bed except when he kissed her—he had stiffened. But even more shocking had been her matter-of-fact statement about having three to four children. Stunned was an understatement of his own reaction.

He had unhooked her arms from around him, trying to wrap his brain around the fact. "Three to four children?"

"Yes. I hated being an only child. And I want a big family." Then she had sobered, noticing his lack of reaction. Or maybe his shock. "Don't you want more than this child?"

"I...haven't thought that far ahead."

"But you want to be a father, yes? We didn't plan this child, but—"

"Of course, I want to be a father. But I would prefer to do the planning of our lives. Not be informed of your own plans."

She had glared at him, the only one who ever dared to do so with such impunity. "And what is my part in all this? To be a willing vessel when you decide you're ready to impregnate me again? I'm not your subject, Adir. I'm your wife."

"And as my wife, you'll obey me. As to four children, I will think about it."

And then of course she had said the one thing he didn't want to hear. "Imagine how different your life would have been if you had grown up with Zufar and Malak and Galila, if you had—"

To which he had walked out with no response.

He hadn't gone back to their tent that evening, choosing to spend it with the Dawab since he'd been visiting them anyway.

But what he'd been doing was avoiding her. Avoiding the same discussion she was hell-bent on having even as he forbade her again.

His stubborn wife was like a dog with a bit in her teeth. Forever bringing up the subject of the queen and her other children. Forever planting doubts in his mind.

Sharing your day with me, your life with me, hasn't made any less of a ruler out of you, has it? They like seeing you happy. They want to see you happy. The queen was wrong in making you think you had to do this alone. I wish you would let me share what I know of them. Of her.

She poked at him relentlessly, to what end he had no idea.

Of course, the idea of growing up with his mother was never far away from his thoughts. Did she think he didn't wonder what it felt like to be with family? To know one's own roots? To share happiness and grief alike with siblings?

But he had never been given the choice. He'd been denied everything that was his due. And when he had asked for it, when he had demanded it, Zufar had called him a dirty stain.

The only thing that had sustained Adir growing up were those letters. But the only person he had ever been able to count on was himself.

No one else.

He had never received anything that he hadn't worked for in life, anything he hadn't planned and achieved himself, and every time Amira got close to him, every time he spied the something he couldn't define in her eyes, it made him want to run far and fast.

It made him want to shut her down.

It made him hurt her. Even when he had promised himself he wouldn't.

And since he had had no solution, he had stayed away.

When he had returned late the previous night, after having been gone for two days, she had been so silent, almost a shadow of herself. When he'd demanded that she be her normal self, she had smiled a brittle smile that made his chest ache.

"Is this what you mean to do? Punish me when I disagree with you by simply leaving me alone for as long as you please? And then returning to command me to be happy and smiling? Demand that I welcome you into my body, too?"

He had had no answer for her except to say that he had had not a single relationship where there were so many expectations on him. Where he was given things he hadn't earned or asked for, like her trust and affection, and he didn't know how to reciprocate.

At twenty-one, he had become the sheikh and that was the role he always played. No one to question him when he was wrong. No one to demand his time or attention.

And since he had known he was in the wrong and he couldn't bear to see that spirit of her bent, much less broken, he had apologized and carried her back to their bed.

It was the first night he had not made love to her. Because as much as he'd been aching to be inside her, he hadn't wanted her to be right. He didn't want to be the man who shut his wife down emotionally but took physical release. As if she were nothing but a conduit.

He wanted to be more to her, he wanted more out of their relationship, but he had no idea how. It was as if there was a wall between him and the rest of the world, a world that had been erected, brick by brick, by his mother's words.

Was Amira right? Had his mother been selfish?

And then he had hated himself for doubting her.

And so, he had just held Amira in his arms while she had clung to him.

Now, as the pink seeping through under the tents said it was dawn, he woke her up with soft kisses. Having woken up fully aroused again, his erection neatly nestled against her soft buttocks as she burrowed into him in search of warmth, he laid a line of soft kisses against the arch of her spine.

Despite his common sense warning him that his fragile wife needed rest, he couldn't help himself. But he had barely rubbed his fingers over those plump nipples and slowly parted her folds to see if she was wet, than with a grumble, she asked him what he was doing.

The deep shadows under her eyes—worse than the past week—chastened him enough. He pulled both his hands to himself, said sorry and asked her to rest.

To which his oh-so-biddable wife said she couldn't go back to sleep now that he had so thoroughly aroused her. And did he mean to step out and leave her to finish herself with her own fingers so that she could go back to sleep?

"Amira, I need you," he whispered, as close to an admission as he could ever come to.

And his generous wife turned to him, her sleep-mussed eyes glowing with affection. With tenderness. "I would never deny you, Adir. I didn't last night, either."

"I know," he whispered, while kissing every inch of her body. He said sorry again and again, for things he couldn't give. For things he didn't want to give her.

He smiled into her hair—a deep vein of fulfillment spreading through his entire body as he thrust lazily into her tight heat.

Even now, while her climax claimed her and her inner muscles clamped and released him with such mind-numbing, spine-tingling rhythm that his own release tingled up through the backs of his thighs and sent pleasure splintering through him, he didn't know how the witch had manipulated him into doing what he hadn't meant to.

His breath burning through his lungs as if he had run

a marathon, he pulled her back to rest against his chest. Like a magnet turning to true north, his palm found the slight swell of her belly and settled there.

"Amira, are we…is everything okay?" he whispered at her ear, combing through the long, silky hair.

When she didn't answer, he turned her onto her back. Cheeks full of color, she would hardly look at him.

His heart threatened to burst out of his chest. Out of fear or happiness, he had no idea. It was a sensation he had never encountered before.

"Amira, what is it? Are you sore? Does it hurt?"

Sleep-mussed eyes stared back at him with such longing that he flinched and sat up. He didn't want to see such naked affection in her eyes. He could not reciprocate it and Amira was fragile enough to be crushed by this.

Already he had made a mess of their first fight. Already he had hurt her with his inability to communicate. He didn't know how to have a relationship where so much was asked of him. No parent, no sibling, no friend had ever been a part of his life.

If he commanded something as sheikh, it was done without question. Even Humera, for all she had raised him, had become distant in the past decade, for she very clearly believed in the respect his position demanded. Even when he'd been a boy, she had only been intent on making him strong.

And Amira… Half the time, he didn't know what to do with her. He wanted to cocoon her, wrap her in safety and only take her off the shelf when he needed her.

Loving her would make him weak, even if he knew how.

What he needed, what they both needed, was a little distance.

* * *

He was not a man who was ever going to admit that he craved a family connection. That even beneath the right he had demanded of Zufar was a desperate need for a place to belong.

"I'm a little embarrassed," Amira said instead, his sudden withdrawal clear in the tense line of her shoulders. It wasn't the complete truth, but she couldn't give him anything more knowing that he was already retreating from her.

Whatever it was he had seen in her face had utterly spoiled the post-coital haze they had been in.

"By what?" he asked, turning away from her to pull on a pair of pajamas that hung low on his sleek hips.

Fortunately, Amira didn't have to come up with a lie since a guard announced himself from outside their tent. Amira instantly pulled up the rug to cover her bare breasts.

Adir shook his head. "He wouldn't dare to come in. But it has to be important if the guard has asked Wasim for permission to disturb me. Stay in bed. And sleep a little. I will see you later."

"Later when?" she asked, the words slipping out before she could curb them.

She frowned as the guard called out again in an urgent voice.

The dialect was different but she caught the gist of it. Adir's softly spoken commands dismissed the guard, and she had no doubt that he had all but forgotten about her.

He was the sheikh now, the man who was responsible for his people.

In her hurry to get to him, she moved too fast and his

arm around her waist was the only thing that stopped her from stumbling.

The impact of his hard chest against her breasts sent shock waves over her skin. Desire unfurled like petals, a sweet, slow ache in the place between her thighs.

The same desire reflected in his eyes. A wicked smile danced around his mouth. "If you want a kiss before I leave, *ya habibiti*, all you have to do is ask for it."

"I want to go."

His hands fell from her, an instant frown on his forehead. "Go where?"

"To the camp. I heard about the pregnant woman. Adir, I saw her at the henna ceremony. She didn't look good even then. I was pretty sure it is twins, but Humera wouldn't let me do a quick checkup on her."

"Humera was right to stop you. You're not their nurse. You're their sheikha."

"I will always be a nurse first, just as you'll always be a leader first. If she's suddenly bleeding, that's not good. For the babies or her."

"The mobile clinic is on its way. And Wasim will bring Humera to look after her in the meantime."

"Humera is a hundred years old and can barely stand as it is. The guard said the mobile clinic was at least five hours away at another remote village. I can be there in a half hour, I know."

"How? How do you know?"

"I know because I asked the woman which tribe she was from and then I asked Zara where they were encamped. I wanted to visit her in a few days just to make sure she was okay. I could see the desperation in her eyes."

"You haven't slept an hour all night and you weave where you stand—"

"And whose fault is it that I didn't sleep? You're the one who decided you'd avoid me for two days and then make up for it by keeping me up all night. Sex is not how we solve our arguments."

His skin stretched taut over those sharp cheekbones, his mouth a straight-pursed line. "Are you saying I kept you up against your will?"

"No. But I didn't want to deny you."

"So you only…participated? Why? Because it is your duty?"

Amira reached for him, her heart thumping against her chest. He looked so remote, so furious, and yet beneath it, it was clear that he needed her. He needed her to need him, to want him.

He couldn't bear that she might stay in this relationship for anything except that she wanted to be with him. Then why couldn't he see that she felt the same way?

That she needed to be more than just a woman carrying his child, a convenient wife, a prized asset.

She wanted to be the person he needed the most, the woman he loved beyond anyone. And anything else.

She wanted to be enough for him. This life with her—she wanted it to be enough for him.

She wasn't allowed to talk about even her feelings for him.

Why couldn't he admit that they were way past a marriage of convenience? That they belonged together—not because of the baby, but because they had chosen each other?

She wrapped her arms around him, laying her cheek on his chest. He was so essential to her and yet he didn't see that she was her own person. "Of course not. I just… It came out the wrong way. Every time we make love, I'm just as desperate as you are. Just as hungry as you are." She looked up, hoping he would see the truth in her eyes. "Adir, please let me go. I can be back by tomorrow morning."

"No. There has to be someone else." He pushed her away, none too gently, his face set in resolute lines that she hated. As if he was distancing himself from her, becoming a man she couldn't reach. "Because I know you, Amira. If I let you this time, there will be no end. Every time someone in some camp has a little ache, you'll go running. You're exhausted, you're pregnant and—"

"Why is that such a horrible situation to be in? I want to help. Even that evening, I saw a need that I could fill. Just as you have a purpose, I want to have one, too."

"Your purpose is to be my wife and the mother to our children. You will not make decisions without consulting me."

"I'm a trained nurse and to keep me locked away here when someone needs help… Don't stop me please." Not even by a flicker of an eyelid, did he relent. "I… I shall never forgive you if you take away the most important thing to me."

He stared at her, stunned, as if he couldn't quite believe her daring in threatening him. "And being a nurse is the most important thing to you?"

"Yes. It is the one thing in life that is mine, that I built, that I value," she croaked out. It was. It always had been. Until she met a stranger in the moonlight and began weaving foolish, impossible dreams. Before she forgot her own promise to herself and fell in love with him all over again.

Adir had been shaped by the harsh desert, by the finicky affections of a weak woman.

"Whether I married Zufar or some other nameless stranger my father arranged for me, whether I was resented or loved, whether I was deceived or wanted, this…this was the one thing no one could take away from me. I thought you of all men would understand how important it is to me. Strip away your leadership of these people and what remains of you, Adir? Do not do this to me."

Adir had never imagined a woman would have this much hold on him—this constant clamor to ensure her well-being and safety all the time, as he maneuvered the four-by-four over the rising and dropping desert floor to where the Peshani encampment had last been seen four days ago.

Four days ago when he had sent off his pregnant, tired and ready-to-break wife to see to another pregnant woman. For the first time in his adult life, he felt a burning resentment toward the tribespeople and their chosen mode of living.

Toward the mantle of duty that had always sat on his shoulders and yet had never felt so heavy and grasping, until today. Until now.

Ya Allah, he had barely slept and he had a hundred other matters to look to. Even this drive was unnecessary since Wasim could have easily collected her and Zara and brought them back safely.

But no, he hadn't been able to deny himself just as he hadn't been able to deny her.

With all his will, he wished he had been able to say no to her request. To tie her down in his own bed until there was no chance of her putting herself in unneeded peril.

To tell her that she had only one role to play—as his wife and as a mother to their child and as his sheikha. Only, and exactly as he dictated.

He should have held out against her demands. Even Humera, he knew, had been surprised by his assent, however grudgingly it had been given.

But one look into those wide, black eyes, the sight of the quiver of her soft mouth and the urgency, anxiety and the helpless rage that had breathed through her slender body as she had paced around him had made him relent. The way she had hugged herself, retreating from his touch, as if she meant to brace herself against the heap of hurt he would rain on her... Even the memory of how she had looked made his chest tighten as if something heavy was pressing away at him.

If he had said no, something indefinable would have been broken between them. Something he hadn't known had already breathed itself into existence.

He would have broken her. And for all his sins, Adir couldn't stand to be another man, another nameless face that controlled and molded Amira, that relentlessly beat at her spirit until it was a withered, dying thing.

He had seen it in her eyes. He would have lost something he hadn't known he had.

So he had said yes. At least, if he had been able to accompany her, it would have been better.

But the very tribal chief that had mocked Adir's parentage—or the lack of it—had sent a message. That he wanted to talk. Adir wanted dearly to punch the man in his craggy, resentful face, but he had to give the starchy, old man credit.

He hadn't liked Adir, whatever his reasons. But for the sake of his tribe, he was coming forward. He was a ruler who understood that personal matters had no weight in a leader's life.

Something Adir seemed to have forgotten in just four days.

Why hadn't the damn woman returned as promised? Why hadn't Wasim dragged her back as he had been instructed to?

And how could he tolerate sending her away to help someone like this the next time?

He couldn't. He couldn't let her weaken him like this.

And if he didn't, she would... Would he lose her?

He could protect Amira from everything. But this urgency, this ache in his chest, what would he do if he ever lost that respect in her eyes, that affection he spied in her gaze?

And if he did somehow keep it, how long before she realized he would never love her as she deserved to be loved?

That he would always remain, at heart, a man isolated from everyone and everything.

A man who was only capable of ruling but not loving.

CHAPTER TEN

AMIRA COULD NOT believe she had succeeded in persuading Adir to let her accompany him to an oil summit he was attending in the neighboring country, the Kingdom of Zyria.

Of course, she was excited to be visiting Zyria which was a beautiful country, but it was her first official trip with Adir and she was determined to enjoy every minute of it.

Even if he had worn the most frightful scowl the whole time, from when he had arrived at the Peshani encampment to pick her up to when she had begged him to let her join him on the trip.

She had braced herself for his refusal—four days of being at the camp dealing with a difficult birth of twins without drugs or sophisticated equipment had truly tired her, a fact she was sure she wore on her face when he had arrived.

The look in his eyes when he had caught sight of her…such fury as his gaze rested on the shadows under her eyes, the sweat on her forehead since it had been her shift to watch Zareena and the babies. Amira had been terrified he would never let her attend anyone ever again in a medical capacity.

But he had ordered her into the Jeep without a word

and for once, she had wisely bit her tongue and stayed silent, which she realized had gone a long way to pacify his raging temper. Not that the remoteness in his eyes had abated one bit.

Once he had agreed to let her come—a grunt from his throat while not even looking at her—he had left her to the not-so-tender mercies of Humera, who had ordered her to rest while overseeing her packing with Zara and one other woman.

Not a single word as he drove them to a private airstrip in the nearest city.

Not a single murmur in response as she had oohed and aaahed, laying it on thick, as they had embarked on the private jet that was to bring them to the capital of Zyria.

Not a single look in her direction in the three hours they had been on the flight. Though to be fair, Amira had napped for the first two, hoping that he would join her.

In the end, she had washed up, changed and joined him in the front cabin, only to be addressed oh so politely by him, told that he was tired and intended to sleep for the remnant of the flight.

Followed by quite a threat about how he would put her under house arrest for the next few months if she didn't take care to eat well and rest enough.

Having finished her salad and cheese—the only thing she could still manage to eat—Amira paved a path through the thick carpet in the main cabin before deciding she'd had enough.

If he meant to ignore her the whole week they were in Zyria, he didn't know her.

Whatever concerns he had, whatever complaints he

had for her, they would have to deal with them openly. For she refused to have a silently dying marriage.

She refused to give up on this just when they were making progress.

The rear cabin was steeped in darkness when Amira entered it a few minutes later. Her breath became shallow as she let her eyes get used to the relative darkness after the blazing lights in the main cabin.

Slowly, she ventured farther in and found the bed. And on it, dressed only in sweatpants, was Adir, his eyes closed and his arm laid carelessly over his head.

What was she going to do if he was sleeping? She would surely lose her mind if she had to go another minute without talking to him. Or being away from him.

Maybe she could get into the bed and just lie close to him. Feel his heart under her palm. Soak in the warmth from his body. Just breathe him in.

She had barely undone the buttons to her jeans—they were uncomfortable enough to sit in, much less to sleep in—when he said, "I was hoping to get some rest. Alone."

She jumped back, startled. He hadn't moved a muscle nor opened his eyes. Only his arm had moved. Now it covered his eyes—a clear sign to ward her off. As if she were a pest bothering him.

She refused to be cowed. Her jeans fell off her hips and legs in a soft whisper and she stepped out of them. "I won't disturb your rest. I just..." She shook off the sleeveless, long cardigan next, leaving the button-down shirt she had chosen for comfort.

Going to him in his bed in a shirt and bra and panties was like tweaking the tail of a tiger but she didn't care. She desperately needed to be close to him.

"You just what, Amira?" His eyes were still closed, his voice resonating in the small cabin. The husky timbre of it stretched her skin tight.

"I just need to be close to you," she said, hurrying through the words before she lost her nerve. "I know you're furious with me and yourself and you will only emerge from it when you have made some sort of decision inside that head of yours. That you will not even acknowledge me until then. But it's been a total of almost six days since you looked at me, or touched me. Or held me." She swallowed the little something that floated in her throat, determined to say her piece. "I miss you, Adir. It was bad enough that I missed you when I was with the Peshani. But to miss you when you're right in front of me is... My chest hurts."

Silence. Utter, deafening silence.

If his shock could be given form, Amira was sure it would be a giant hole in the small room, suffocating the very air out of her.

Did he still not know what was in her heart? That it was all his?

Amira had no idea how long she stood there like that, waiting for him to respond. Wretched and yet still full of hope.

"I do not like what you do to me," he began. "I... I trusted you to take care of yourself. You promised. And yet when I found you, a breeze could have blown you away. It is not just my child's well-being that concerns me. It is... You make me want to lock you up and throw away the key. To never let you out of my sight, to never again let you...attend to another woman in your life. Do not...do not push me to that, Amira."

"I did take care of myself, Adir. Please, you have to believe me. It was a difficult birth. That first night,

I could not rest for fear of her lifeblood slipping away while I slept. It will not be like that always."

"Always? Do you know how tempted I am to say there will never be another occasion?"

"You would not do that to me."

"I wish I could. I don't want you to look at me like you look at your father. With fear and resentment. So the only way to deal with this is to let me get control of myself. To let me treat this marriage as a polite arrangement. To let me treat you as a partner and nothing more."

"That would kill me just the same."

"To care this much for you while you demand to be true to the one important thing in your life..." such resentment filled his words that Amira gasped "...it is unacceptable."

Did he think nursing meant more to her than him? Than their marriage, than this child of theirs she carried?

"I need to learn to undo this...this hold you have on me."

Her courage faltering, Amira took one last step toward him. Without waiting for his permission, she slid into the bed and scooted close to him until their bodies were touching. Until she could breathe him in. Until the beat of his thundering heart was under her palm.

Ya Allah, she loved him so much, and it hurt to know that he would never feel even a fraction of the same for her.

Had she fallen in love with him that same evening that she had met him? To meet a man who saw her as she was, to be cherished by him—to know Adir that night had been to fall in love with him. Why else had she—who had never done anything so brave and bold in her life before—given herself to him so easily? Without a thought to the consequences when they were so horrible for her?

"What you feel, this small fear, the little bit of caring," she said, "I feel that a thousand times over. I love you so much, you own my heart. You had it from that very first time when you asked me if you could touch me. When you looked at me as if I was the most unbelievable thing you had ever seen. When you held me with such tender care that for the first time in my life, I thought, this is how I wish to be held all the time. I thought, this is how I wish to be looked at. Forever. Always. But it was a foolish dream so I grabbed the night instead with both hands.

"Do you not see, Adir? You changed everything. You changed me. You still continue to do so. For years, I lived in the fear that nothing in life would be my choice. Nursing became my identity, my reason to look forward to another day. I spoke in anger, so anxious to let you see how much I needed to help her. So worried that you will also try to mold me into what you want, not accept me for what I am.

"Continuing to be a nurse is important to me, yes, but not more than you or this baby or the family we're creating for ourselves. It is what I have wanted for so long. Somewhere to belong, someone to love with my whole heart. I would never, never put that at risk for anything."

In his silence, she saw the fear—fear for her, fear that she was beginning to mean something to him. And the need to control it. To suppress it.

Her heart seemed to hover in her throat for an eternity, her every hope thrown on a bold risk she had taken in telling him what he meant to her.

If he rejected her admission, if he so much as decided not to look at her, how would she cope?

After what felt like an eon, he turned to his side.

Heat. Hardness. Heart.

He was everything she had always dreamed of. Here in this moment with her. And yet, just a little out of reach.

His beautiful face was wreathed in shadows, hidden from her, while he studied her.

Amira closed her eyes, terrified of what she would find in his. Or what she would not find.

"I want to believe you, Amira. I have never received such a gift. I do not know what to do with it. I do not... I will never know how to return it."

And just like that, Amira's heart broke a little. But she didn't give up. She would never give up on him.

Not when she had finally understood this. Not when the man she loved was so brave, so honorable, so...full of heart, even if he denied it.

How could she love him any less even after that admission?

Her hands moved of their own accord, finding his hot skin. The jut of his taut shoulders. His velvet rough skin. The small raspy hairs on his chest. The line of his strong throat. The bristle on his jaw. The sharp flare of his nose.

Every inch of him was so dear to her. The love she felt for him filling her with courage. To risk her heart, again and again.

"I want to be your sheikha. I already share the love you have for these fierce people, I already feel your passion for the desert that gives back so much. I would be proud to rule them by your side. I choose you, Adir. Again. This time, knowing what a..." her tears blocked her throat "...a complex, stubborn man you are. Knowing the truth of you at the core of my being.

"I choose this life with you, even knowing that it is sometimes hard and sometimes breathtakingly beautiful. All I ask is that you let me have a little of my passion, too. It is not a zero-sum game, you know that, right? Nursing gave me an identity when I had nothing else to hold onto. But now, it's tied to you, Adir, it's all you."

The silent room reverberated with her declaration. The air so heavy with tension that she wondered if she would choke.

And then he reached for her. Slowly. Softly. His breath feathering through her hair. "I missed you when you were gone. I miss you whenever you're not close to me. I wish to make you happy, Amira."

Amira caught the cry that wanted to escape her mouth. The admission seemed wrenched from him, but at least he had made it. To himself and to her. "You do. Even when you make me want to throttle you, you still make me happy."

She waited with bated breath, but he did no more than continue to stroke her cheek in a featherlight caress. Almost reverent.

He said nothing else.

How foolish she was to think he would return her grand admission. When would she realize that her husband would never be a man who admitted that he felt something for her?

Was it even his fault, when he'd been conditioned by his mother's sweetly poisoned words about what her love had done to her and to him in the process? When he saw what love was through the queen's weak mind and weaker actions?

Maybe Amira and her love would never be enough to overcome the shadow his past would always cast over his present and his future. And that was something she wanted to forget right now.

She wanted to live in this moment. The present was the only thing she would always have with him.

"Adir?"

Still another caress. Just the pads of his fingers against her chin, her nose, her eyes, her hair. Almost indifferently. As if he hadn't yet recovered from her admission.

When he ran his fingers down her neck to her breasts, the breath she had been holding rushed out of her in a painful exhale. Tears seeped to the corners, hot and scorching and it was all she could do to contain them. All she could do not to beg him to love her in return.

All of her was laid bare before him.

Did he know what a tremendous risk she had taken? She, who had been terrified of ever finding a man who saw her, much less loved her?

When he dipped his mouth and kissed her, Amira let all the pain go. Let the taste of him wash away her doubts and fears for the moment.

When he pushed her onto her back without a word, without an acknowledgment of what she had shared, she hardened her heart.

This was all he would give. He had said it without saying it.

His desire, his respect, his loyalty...that was all she could ever have. And it was up to her to live with it.

When he ripped open the shirt and palmed her breasts with a rough urgency, she tried to convince herself that the insistent ache he created in her lower belly with such clever caresses was all she needed.

When he drove her to crazy desperation with his mouth at her breasts, she told herself that all she needed was this…this closeness with him.

When he stripped her to her skin and kissed his way down her body; when his breath fluttered over her inner thighs; when he separated her damp folds with his fingers and licked her at the spot throbbing and aching for him; when he sucked her between his lips while she writhed under his knowing touch; when she splintered into a million fragments under indescribable pleasure; when he drove into her while her muscles still contracted and released; when he came inside her with such intensity that his breath was like the bellows of a forge against her chest, Amira tried to tell herself that this was enough.

That he cared for their child was enough.

That he was trying to accept her as she was, that he was trying, despite his own instincts, not to control her was enough.

That he showed her paradise every time he touched her was enough.

She didn't need his love.

Her mind repeated the same thought in circles, round and round while she slipped into exhausted sleep.

CHAPTER ELEVEN

AMIRA HAD NEVER imagined Adir could be such a witty and fun companion as he was when they toured the capital city of Zyria in the hours he was free during the next few days.

The trip was a little surprise, he had said gruffly when she had inquired about the conference, he had planned for her since it didn't begin for three more days. Amira had thrown a pillow at him at the realization that he had always meant to bring her to Zyria with him.

For official reasons, he had said between long, languorous kisses and Amira had bit his lip then.

Of course, there had always been a devilish humor in him beneath the seriousness. But that he had let her see it, that he had dedicated so much time to spending with her, it was exhilarating and utterly joyous to be with a man who treated his wife like a queen.

No wish of hers was to be neglected.

No want of hers was to go unfulfilled.

No desire of hers was to go unmet.

She didn't remember when she could have mentioned that she had always wanted to see the campus of the famous Al-Haidar University where the first woman had trained to be a nurse almost four hundred years ago. He had had an exclusive tour arranged, with accompaniment by the current dean of the university, a strict, no-nonsense professor who very much reminded Amira of Humera.

Even more surprising was when Adir had joined her on the tour—Amira had simply assumed she would be sent off with a guard and collected in the evening while he looked into his business affairs. But he had patiently and with genuine interest sat through her lengthy interview of Mrs. Ahmed about her longstanding career.

He hadn't even frowned when Amira had admitted that she'd always wanted to finish her surgical training, too—something even Zufar couldn't have convinced her father to let her do.

When he had said maybe after the four children she wanted were in school they could talk about it, she had squealed and embarrassed him by hugging him openly in front of his aide and guard.

The next day, it had been shopping. Amira lost count of the number of dresses he had ordered for her at a couture house or the jewelry he had lavished upon her.

The next day, it was a private, enchanted dinner on the one hundred and fortieth floor of a rotating restaurant, the entirety of which had been booked just for them.

And their nights…their nights were spent in the vast luxury bed in their hotel suite overlooking the wondrous lights of the city.

In the three weeks of their marriage so far, Amira had assumed they had pushed each other to the edge of physical desire in every way. He was continuously surprised and more than overjoyed, he had said once, that she was his equal and willing partner in everything sexual.

She was mistaken.

If she had been bold before, Adir had pushed and pushed her until she was completely unashamed to parade around their hotel suite wearing nothing but her skin in front of him.

It was as if nothing could satisfy him except to experiment with debauchery in every way possible.

She hadn't even blushed when he had pushed her onto her hands and knees in front of the fireplace one evening and entered her from behind, one hand in her hair, one tweaking her clitoris, while he whispered that making love to her like that was his every fantasy come true.

How could she feel anything but glorious pleasure when he was so deeply embedded inside her that he felt as if he were a part of her?

She had only pushed back into him when he had stripped her clothes in front of the huge floor to ceiling glass windows that provided a spectacular view of the jewel of a city.

Until she was bare naked. He had cupped her sensitive breasts, driven her to the edge of orgasm with his fingers and when she had begged him to come inside her, he had taken her over the edge. The cold glass pressing into her breasts and the entire world a panorama of lights and sounds in front of her, Amira's climax had rippled through her.

If he made love to her like a man possessed, then he took such tender care of her after. In the languor that came after sex, he held her in the cocoon of his arms. They talked about their future, about the children she wanted to have, where they would live during summer and winter. He even shared his concerns about the tribes, about the political climate.

Except his past.

It stayed like an ocean-wide divide between them, somehow swallowing up every other good thing.

The days and nights he had exclusively dedicated to

her—just the two of them cut off from the tribes, from the outside word—should have been paradise.

They were.

Even as the words rose to her lips again and again, Amira couldn't bring herself to say it. Already, she felt as if she had bared her soul to him. In those breathless moments, when he studied her, she knew he was waiting for her to say it again.

It was as if he was trying to lavish the world and its gifts on her, trying to make up for the one thing he could not give her.

It was not the same. Not at all.

But Amira pretended that it was. With the hope that pretending would make it feel real.

To think otherwise was to torture herself for years to come.

And as a woman who had always counted her blessings rather than drowned in her sorrows, Amira couldn't allow that.

She couldn't let her love for Adir destroy her and their marriage.

The last three days of the conference, Amira had been informed by Adir's secretary, would be the busiest. More than five nations were sitting down to discuss a treaty and oil rights, and Adir had been invited to represent the tribes.

Because of his relentless efforts to protect the tribes from each other and the encroaching governments who would see them stripped of land and settled in huts on small parcels of land they would deign to give, a seat had been created on the council for a representative of the tribes.

"Most of the deals are brokered during those casual

evenings," Adir had informed her one night. Obvious pride filled his voice as he ran his fingers though her hair. "This is the first time I'm attending it with my sheikha. There will be a certain curiosity about you. Since some attending members are aware that you were…his betrothed."

Amira had frowned.

Instantly, he had kissed her temple. "I have no doubt you will be a rousing success."

Amira had waited eagerly the first evening for reports on how it had gone. Each night, there was a casual dinner set up in the reception hall where the guests and their parties were invited to mingle.

Also, because it was the first time she was meeting the world as his sheikha, for the first time in her life, she was grateful for all the hours of rigorous training in protocol and local politics she had endured from her father's aides and teachers.

Because it was going to come in handy in making Adir proud. This time, it was a role she heartily accepted, for being Adir's wife meant being his partner in everything. He had a complex mind and he readily shared his thoughts with her—whether business or politics. And that was, she realized with a quiet joy, because she had his respect.

But tonight, when the world saw her at his side, she wanted them to see her pride in her husband.

She had chosen an elegant, sea green evening gown in a light, shimmering silk that created a long, chic silhouette without overtly hugging her growing belly. Her hair she had the luxury hotel's stylist set into long silky waves, even though she knew her stubborn locks would straighten out in a matter of hours.

Since she had taken extra caution about her food and water, she had already lost the gauntness around her cheeks. She skipped the bronzer and the blush, settling for some powder and a quick swab of pink lipstick.

Her one big ornamentation was, however, the delicate diamond necklace Adir had given her just this morning.

The door to their private bedroom opened just as she had finished the last brush stroke.

Adir stood behind her, his gaze on her neck reflected in the mirror. Full of warmth and wicked humor.

Tonight, he was dressed in a simple black, three-piece suit, the white of his shirt a stark contrast to his dark olive skin.

He looked breathtaking, sophisticated, a man as easy in a suit among this crowd as he was in his robes among the tribespeople.

Even if that tribal chief had expressed doubts about Adir's parentage in the beginning, it was clear that his trust in Adir was absolute.

Whoever his father had been, whatever his blood, he was a born leader.

Why didn't Adir see that?

"You should have let me buy the other necklace."

They had argued for over twenty minutes about a necklace they had seen at a famed jeweler. Glittering and ostentatious, it had not been to Amira's taste at all.

She took his hand and kissed his palm, the aqua scent of his cologne combined with his own making her belly clench with deep longing. "I like this one. I love that you picked this one." She met his gaze in the mirror and smiled. "It shows that you…" She let the words trail off, wary of seeing his retreat.

"What?"

"Nothing."

He pushed her carefully styled hair away from her neck and kissed her nape. His fingers lingered on her midriff. Amira's breath caught in her throat as he trailed soft kisses up her jaw and to her cheek. Yet there was nothing sexual about the kisses or the way he held her.

He didn't know his strength for his grip was tight as he clutched her to his chest. He rubbed his nose against her cheek, and pressed another kiss to his neck. "Tell me anyway."

Amira sank her fingers into his hair and arched into his embrace. "That you picked this particular piece says that you know me, Adir. It means more to me than the biggest diamond in the world."

He didn't exactly startle. But that stillness came upon him.

Amira braced herself.

With another swift kiss against her lips, he straightened and let her hair fall back into place.

Just a nod in her direction in acknowledgment of what she said.

A little smile played around his lips as she turned in his arms. "You have that glow. The one they say pregnant women have." He carefully placed his hands around her belly again, as if to measure her. "You're growing bigger."

Amira scrunched her face and hit him with her clutch.

"Hey, it is not a complaint." When she didn't quite believe him, he pulled her to him, his hands cradled at her back. "Amira...you could get as fat as you possibly could, and I would still think you beautiful."

She tucked her arm through his. "I would say the glow might be from all the orgasms you bestow."

When he laughed again, she hugged the sound to herself. "Then I shall have to keep bestowing them. Are you ready, Sheikha?"

Amira nodded, her heart bursting to full.

* * *

The evening dinner was in the famed courtyard of the luxury hotel. Soft lavender lights illuminated lovely gardens and walkways while a buffet was laid out under a canopy.

Women glittered in long designer gowns and jewelry. While Adir introduced her to a number of people, Amira stood her ground.

More than once, she steered the conversation smoothly away from her husband's involvement in the tribes. It didn't take her more than ten minutes to realize that Adir was looked upon as a fierce, smart leader, a man who had brought warring tribes to form a cohesive faction, at least in terms of facing the neighboring nations that wanted to control them.

Since she had had a heavy snack, she mostly just tried finger food. At Adir's raised brow—the man watched her like a hawk—she sipped on fresh juice.

For almost two and a half hours, he circulated among the guests, and Amira dutifully followed him.

"You're tired," he whispered at her ear during a lull in the conversation around them. When she reluctantly nodded, he added, "Ten minutes. We will take our leave then. Although he was absent from this morning's council, I have heard that Sheikh Karim intends to show his face here. I want to make his acquaintance."

"Of Zyria?" Amira asked.

A smile of full appreciation, he nodded. "Zyria has not been a member of the council before. I have heard that Karim pushed for a seat and made it sweeter by offering to host this year's convention."

Amira nodded and surreptitiously leaned into him for support.

Not a moment later, a uniformed guard neared them.

"His Highness Sheikh Karim wishes to meet you in his private office."

Adir nodded. "Tell him I will walk my wife back to our room and meet him in fifteen minutes."

More than relieved that she wouldn't have to fake a smile anymore—for she was really tired—Amira let Adir guide her through the thinning crowd toward a different bank of lifts.

"You don't have to see me upstairs. I would rather you finish this meeting and come to bed."

She could see his reluctance, but just before he was about to speak, they turned into a vast, gleaming corridor with life-size pictures on each side. At the other end was the lift.

A dated history and timeline of grand events lined the two walls. Amira didn't even realize Adir had stilled until she swayed on her feet and realized he wasn't supporting her.

She turned and whatever she had been about to say floated away.

His skin was pale under the olive tone, a tremendous stillness in him. As if he was standing in a space separated from everything and everyone around him. The strange fear that she could never reach him again skated up and down her spine.

Heart beating a rapid tattoo, Amira studied him. "Adir?"

He didn't even stir.

Fear coating her throat, she turned toward whatever had stunned him so thoroughly.

It was a life-size picture of two men on the wall— one older and one younger, clearly father and son for anyone to see. The late King Jamil Avari of Zyria and his son, the current King Sheikh Karim.

The man Adir had been waiting to meet. Although he was a teenage boy in the picture.

But even then, the resemblance was riveting.

With a gasp, Amira looked at the next picture—this one taken recently of Sheikh Karim. She stared back at Adir and the picture, as if mesmerized.

It wasn't so much that they were alike as that they had the same bearing. The same tilt of their heads. The same arrogant nose. The same penetrating stare.

No one who would see the two men together would fail to make the connection.

The older man…he had to have been Queen Namani's illicit lover. The late King Jamil must have been Adir's father. Sheikh Karim was his half brother. Another sibling Arif didn't know.

Another chance at a family missed.

Another connection lost to him.

Had King Jamil even known that Queen Namani had given birth to his son?

What a twisted, heartbreaking tale…and in all of it, it was Adir who had suffered. Abandoned by both mother and father.

Born to a king and a queen, was it any wonder he was such a natural leader? That even as he had been orphaned and discarded to the vagaries of desert life, he had emerged as a leader who had done the unthinkable.

Amira bit back on the rage that swirled through her on his behalf.

He had been cheated of so much in life. Fear unlike she had ever known gripped her.

What would this do to Adir?

To them? To their marriage?

Panic poured through her and suddenly Amira couldn't breathe.

"Adir! Adir!"

Amira's cry roused Adir from the state of extreme shock he seemed to have fallen into. He caught her mere seconds before she would have hit the marble floor.

Her golden skin was so pale that his heart jumped into his throat. Just as before, a coldness seemed to trickle down his spine as he lifted her in his arms.

If anything happened to her because of his inattention...

He barked out an order to a nearby guard to carry a message to the waiting sheikh. Within minutes, he was laying Amira down on their bed.

But the stubborn woman refused to stay lying down. She scooted up on the bed and drank the water he brought her.

He sat on the edge of the bed, his attention split. And a deafening thunder in his ears. The last piece of the puzzle. The bastard son of a king and a queen—a dirty stain banished to the desert. Prince Zufar couldn't have known how close to the truth he was.

He should have had everything—a mother and a father and siblings—and yet he had nothing, no one to call his own growing up.

And now...now to learn that he had another brother! A man waiting to see him a few floors down. Mere minutes away. A man who would have information about his father. Information he had wanted his entire life.

"Adir?"

The fear in Amira's voice pulled him back to the now again.

Words came and fell away to Amira's lips.

"You…do you hurt anywhere?" he asked. "I will have the doctor summoned."

Amira kept her fingers stapled over her belly, more as an anchor than any real pain. "No. I'm…fine. For a minute there, I just couldn't breathe. I…" Tears fell away onto her cheeks and she couldn't stop them this time.

She took his hand in hers, willing him to lean on her. Willing him to share the tumult she could see in his eyes. "I'm so sorry, Adir."

He ran a hand through his hair, the only sign that betrayed his inner turmoil. "So I'm not the only one who sees it? Who imagines a connection?"

"No. You…you have too many similarities to miss. You have never met him?"

"No." He pushed away from the bed, her outstretched hand left in thin air.

And just like that, Amira knew she was losing him.

"I have to go out. Will you be all right?"

"Will you confront him?"

"Yes. Maybe. I have to talk to him at the least. I owe it to myself."

"Adir, please, all you will do is bring more pain to yourself. And I couldn't bear it. I couldn't bear to see you struggle with this. Let it go, Adir. Let her go. Let the past rest. Let our future have a chance."

A growl fell from his mouth—a sound so utterly wretched that Amira's tears fell away like rivulets. Tight grooves dug near his mouth.

"I can't, Amira. I can't."

Fear gave way to fury and Amira got off the bed. "What has it brought you until now? Except diminishing the value of what you do have. Except making you wonder what could have been when you are already an honorable leader, a wonderful husband.

"Queen Namani would have done better to leave you alone. To let you believe that you had been completely abandoned. To let you think yourself a true orphan than this...this purgatory she left you in."

"How dare you say that? She loved me. How would you feel if you were forced to give up our child?"

"I would not give up this child for anything. Do you hear me? I feel sorry for her, I do. To fall in love with a man so completely unsuitable; to have to give up the child to protect her reputation, her other children. To be filled with such resentment and poison that she hated everyone else around her... I feel pity for her.

"What I would never agree with is this...perception you have that she was a great mother. She was not. When she wrote those letters to you every year, was she truly thinking of you, Adir? When she never took a risk to see you but poured everything she felt into her letters to you? Or was it her own foolish rebellion against her circumstances? She was a weak, selfish woman."

Rage filled his eyes and yet, unlike her father, he only seemed to retreat under it rather than lash out. "I will not hear a word against her."

"And I will not keep quiet anymore. Because I'm afraid that you will hate me for it. Because I'm afraid that you will never love me if I speak ill of her. Have you wondered why Zufar or Malak or Galila were so shocked by your appearance? So ready to reject you, resent you?

"I do not agree with what he said to you. But, Adir, she was not a good mother to any of them. Believe me, I know of Galila's childhood and her growing up. Your mother was at the very least indifferent to Zufar and Malak. But to Galila, as long as Galila was but a girl, the queen was all love and sweetness. But when Galila transformed into a beautiful young woman, a competitor to even your mother in beauty, your mother took away her love just as easily as one would remove food from a child.

"Maybe she loved you, maybe it broke her to be parted from her lover and then you. Maybe she was never right again. But when she wrote those letters to you, when she fired that resentment in you for them and fueled it all these years, stoking the fire at every opportunity, she was not thinking of you.

"She filled you with her own poison, she made you into a hard man and I hate her for it. I hate that if not for her, you would give us a chance. You would give happiness a chance."

Amira had no idea whether anything she said got through to Adir or not.

He stared at her quietly, in shock as if she had transformed into something he couldn't believe right in front of his eyes. As if she had taken a hammer and destroyed the pedestal on which his mother stood.

And Amira lost all hope.

"What will you do if Sheikh Karim refuses to acknowledge the connection between the two of you? Steal another bride? Drag his name through mud? He and Zufar are just as much innocents in this as you are."

He turned away from her and Amira had had enough.

"You have to choose, Adir."

Fury emanated in those amber eyes, turning them to a burnished gold. "Do not dare to give me ultimatums. You're my wife."

"I'm your wife, and I love you, and I cannot bear to play second fiddle to your past. As long as you cling to the past, there's no hope. You will never see everything you already are, as I see you, as the tribes see you, as the world sees you—a magnificent ruler, a loving leader, a

wonderful husband and a kind lover. You have to choose
between your future and your past."

He shook his head and Amira fell to the bed, her
limbs trembling.

"No. I can't. Whether I accept the past or not, I will
not love you, Amira."

"That is where you're mistaken. I'm not demanding
that you love me no matter what. I'm more than prepared to live with what you do give me. But I can't bear
to be shuffled to second place by the past that haunts
you. I can't bear to love a man whose eyes are filled
with shadows of the past. To love a man whose eyes
are filled with pain.

"Tell me, Adir, right this minute, can you look forward to our future, our life with this child, without forever thinking of a life you could have had? A life you
should have had. With your father or your mother?"

He looked as bleak as she felt. "No."

"Then we're at an impasse. Because I will not live
with a man who's stuck in some other place. With a man
who's always looking back."

If she thought he felt nothing, the fury that dawned
in his eyes shut down that assumption. His stillness
was so unnatural given the burn in his amber eyes, the
emotions rousing within.

"You have no choice, Amira. You're pregnant with
my child. You're my wife. And more than anything
else, you love me. You will not leave me. I admit, I'm
angry right now. But when I think this through, when
I'm calm once more, I will return. And our lives will
resume normally."

CHAPTER TWELVE

It was Amira's favorite time of day when the setting sun painted the sky a myriad of pinks and oranges, and the colors were gloriously reflected in the blue waters that surrounded the palatial house.

When she walked around the beautifully manicured gardens or took the car to the evening bazaar in the nearby village to enjoy the lovely profusion of colors and smells or when she packed a small picnic and watched the sunset from the beach, she could almost forget the rest of the world.

And him.

Almost.

She could forget that her father called a hundred times a day, ready to rip her into pieces for daring to leave Adir. She could forget that when night came and she lay in that big bed in that huge bedroom, she cried herself to tears most nights. She could forget that in her waking moments, half the time she doubted herself for leaving a man who treated her with respect, kindness, even affection.

But then there were moments like this when she placed her hands on her belly, and in her heart knew that she had done the right thing.

She couldn't live with a man who didn't understand

her love. Who thought it was a weakness he could use to bind her to him.

Not day in and day out, no.

Not even for her child.

She had nothing to bargain with, either. And yet instead of fear, all she felt was courage. This was what he had given her.

This courage to stand up for herself, this faith in herself and the choices she had made.

He was going to be furious with her for leaving him, but he would not force her to live with him against her wishes. She had that much faith in him. In her love.

She could not lose her self-respect just to be near him. As much as she wanted to.

She had barely put away the dishes from her dinner when she heard a car drive up the winding driveway.

Frowning, she moved to look through the kitchen window. The guard lived in the outbuilding, and the two maids that looked after the house had already retired for the night.

And then she saw him, a tall, dark form in the lights of the portico.

Her husband.

Hands and legs trembling, she made it to the living room just as he walked into the room.

Fury and something else she couldn't read settled into the lines on his face so deep he looked like he was sculpted that way. And when he opened his mouth, closed it, walked around the room like a caged wild animal and then smoothed his fingers through his hair roughly, Amira knew what the other something was.

Fear.

For her? For the baby?

"I informed Wasim where I was going before I left," she said.

The fury didn't abate at all. He stared at her as if he'd even forgotten she was there. As if the emotion was still riding him high. "You informed him?" He roared the words as if they were wrenched from him under the promise of pain.

His fingers grabbed her shoulders, biting into them. He didn't even seem to realize that he was hurting her.

Neither did she care. It was the pure torment in his eyes that swept through her. That held her transfixed.

She had never seen him so out of control. So ragged at the edge that she could almost believe he was falling apart.

"That's what you have to say about this? That you informed your guard that you're leaving me? Leaving our marriage and disappearing to God knows where? That is not how a wife behaves. Given one chance, you'll walk out on me? Is that what I should expect as a pattern for your future behavior, given the fact that you ran out on Zufar with me?"

Amira didn't even know she had swung her arm. Not until her palm met his cheek with a resounding sting that sent shivers up to her elbow.

She hated violence of any sort and this was what he was reducing her to.

Tears pooled in her eyes and she brushed them away angrily. Hurt splintered through her.

"Get out. I don't want to talk to you. If this is what you think of me, there is no need for words. I want a divorce. I never…" her words came out in a broken whisper "…I never want to see you again."

And then, when she thought she would fall apart, he pulled her to him. His arms around her, his mouth pressed against her temple whispering endearments, he held her as he had done that first evening. So tenderly, so gently, as if she were the most precious thing he had ever held. As if he couldn't breathe if he let go of her.

"I hate you," she said. "I hate you for what you said, and I hate you for making me like this. I hate you for twisting my words, for hurting me. I hate you so much that I…sometimes wish I had never met you."

"No, Amira. Don't say that."

"I begged you to let me and this child be but you dragged me into your life. I begged you to stay, I laid my heart at your feet, Adir, and you trampled all over it. Still, I've stayed strong. For this child. But you…you won't let me have even this…little peace."

"I know, *ya habibi*, this is all my fault. Please, Amira, do not cry. Not over me. I couldn't bear that I hurt you. No more."

Amira stayed in that embrace, holding onto him desperately, because she knew it would be gone in a minute. If this was what he thought of her… "She's long gone, Adir. Right or wrong, she is long gone. And you can't hold onto her. And I won't blame her anymore when it is you that refuses happiness."

"I'm so sorry." His words came out broken, stuttered. "I've been out of my mind. I was lashing out, so angry with you. I'm so sorry, *ya habibiti*."

She didn't want that endearment but Amira didn't call him out for it. "I told you, I left a message and made sure you would receive it. I took your bloody plane, demanded keys of your housekeeper and moved into your house. The women here, they're loyal to you. They would have told you what I had for dinner, for God's sake, if you demanded it. I kept myself safe. I'm not a child, Adir. When will you take me seriously?"

"I was not worried about your safety. What I said, it was awful and wrong and only reflects badly on me. I couldn't believe that you could just…"

"Just what?"

"Just leave me like that. When I was desperate to believe that you loved me. Just when I was beginning to fall in love with you, too. Just when I was beginning to understand that it was already too late, that you already owned a piece of my heart."

Shock waves running through her, she stared. Stupidly.

He was apologizing and he looked even worse than when he had walked in. Clearly, what he had said to her hurt him even more than her. But now…this…

Instead of soothing her, it only made her more mad. "Did you take anything I said seriously, ever?"

"Amira—"

She pushed away from him, wanting to look in his eyes. "You think I left just like that? You think I say words like *I love you* because I'm a naive, foolish girl? Make empty promises because I'm all fairy tales and fantasies?

"I waited all night for you to come back. I worried about what you said to Karim, I worried how he might have hurt you. You sent a message saying you were busy in the morning. You were avoiding me. I didn't do anything rash. I cried, I dried my eyes, took a shower. I even dallied over breakfast, waiting for you. And then, when you…you made it impossible for me to stay, I left. I called your pilot and arranged for him to pick me up. He couldn't even reach you. Do you know how worried I was? If I had stayed in that hotel room, I would have…fallen apart."

"You left, Amira."

He kept repeating it slowly. Amira realized he was not just angry.

And that fear she had glimpsed, it was fear that he had lost her.

Lost her forever.

The anger and hurt and fear that had been sitting like a hard lump in her chest all these days slowly began to deflate. He had been worried that he had lost her. Did she mean so much to him? Would they swing back and forth forever like this?

No.

"You declared so arrogantly that I would not think of leaving you because I loved you. Love is not a weakness, Adir. My love for you, it makes me strong."

"No, it's not a weakness, and you were right about my mother. She loved me, yes, but you were right, she was flawed, too. And in her pain, she passed it on to me. Her legacy to me became this bitterness and if not for you, I would have never seen it."

Amira thought her heart would burst out of her chest. "What do you mean?"

"I never went to see Karim that night. I stayed in the bar downstairs, just thinking, of everything you said. Such a fragile woman, such powerful words."

"I… I never want you to think I didn't understand your pain. I just… I wanted you all for myself," she said.

"No, Amira, you shone the light into a lifetime of darkness. Every word you said, as the hours passed me by, I realized all of it was right. I realized suddenly I didn't really care. There's a certain closure in learning who my father was. In knowing that he loved her just as much as she had loved him. That even though she gave me up, I was born out of love. The minute I embraced that, my desperation to see Karim fell off."

When he fell to his knees and buried his face in her belly, fresh tears pooled in her eyes.

"Everything has changed, Amira. And you're the one who has done it. All my life, I longed to be acknowledged, to be given my rightful place. I longed for a place to belong. But you are right. I already have a family. It's you and this child. It's with the tribes. There's nothing in life that I don't have. Except your love, *habibi*. You, your love, that is what completes me. I'm so sorry for hurting you. For making you feel as if you were second in my life. I love you, Amira, with everything that is in me. You're the first, Amira, in my heart. Just you."

Amira dropped to her knees and almost knocked him off his when she fell into his embrace.

She was sobbing and he was laughing, and then he kissed her. But this time, he told her how precious she was to him.

This time, there was no doubt in her mind that she had finally found a place to land.

With the man she loved.

With the man who understood her, accepted her and loved her. Just as she was.

* * * * *

BOUND BY THE BILLIONAIRE'S VOWS

CLARE CONNELLY

For Arlene, who is courage, strength
and resilience personified.

Not to mention a very dear friend.

PROLOGUE

Six years earlier

'CAN YOU SEE IT, Matteo?'

The newspapers loved to say that Matteo Vin Santo didn't have a heart, but they were wrong.

Observing his grandfather lying weak and pale against the ordinary hospital bed-sheets was making that very organ clutch and grip painfully. The certainty that the man had only hours left to live was ripping it apart completely.

'See what, Nonno?'

'Nonno?' Alfonso Vin Santo smiled, but his lips were chapped and the pain turned the instinctive gesture into a wince. 'You haven't called me that in a long time.'

Matteo didn't respond. His eyes fell to his grandfather's hands. Hands that had shaped a corporate empire; hands that had been at the helm during its demise. He looked away, focusing on the uninspiring view of the outskirts of Florence.

'See the water? You always loved the way the sun bounced off it, no?'

Matteo's eyes swept shut. Though they were in a lino-leum-floored hospital room, he pictured exactly what his grandfather was seeing. The view from the terrace of Il Grande Fortuna, the hotel they'd once owned in Rome, overlooking the Tiber in one direction and the Vatican in the other.

Anger—a familiar response when he thought of the hotel—churned his gut. It was fierce in that moment, so fierce it almost took his breath away.

'Yes. It's beautiful.'

'It is more than beautiful. It is perfect.' Alfonso sighed and then a ghost flickered across his face. A moment of clarity that brought with it pain. 'It was my fault.'

'No, Nonno.' Matteo didn't mention that bastard Johnson's name. There was no need to hurt his grandfather further at the end of his life. But *he* was the man who was to blame. He was the cause of Alfonso's sadness now—him and his stubborn refusal to sell the hotel back. A refusal he'd taken with him to the grave.

But Matteo could fix it.

He *would* fix it.

'I will get it back for you,' he said, and the words were spoken with such soft determination that it wasn't clear if Alfonso had even heard. It didn't matter, though.

The promise was one Matteo made to himself as much as the old man.

No matter what, no matter how, he would return the hotel to his family.

At any cost.

CHAPTER ONE

'Do you have an appointment?'

An appointment? With her own husband? Skye clutched her handbag tighter, thinking of the divorce papers contained within the soft kid-leather. A hint of perspiration ran between her breasts and she shifted uncomfortably. Though the luxurious foyer was well air-conditioned, Skye had been sweltering since touching down at Marco Polo airport earlier that day. Travel weariness, and the exhaustion that had dogged her since walking out on her marriage to Matteo, combined to give her a sense of overwhelming desperation at the task ahead.

'Signor Vin Santo has a full afternoon. I'm sorry,' the receptionist murmured, her expression offering no corresponding apology. If anything, it was all manicured smugness.

Skye's voice was soft when she spoke, weakened by the difficulty of what lay ahead. Divorce was essential—and it had to be now. She'd go to almost any lengths to get Matteo to agree easily. She needed his signature on these papers so she could get the hell out of Italy. Before he discovered the truth. 'If you tell Matteo I'm here, I'm sure he'll cancel whatever he has on.'

The receptionist's disdain was barely concealed. '*Signorina...?*'

Skye's own smile reflected the other woman's emotion.

It was a common mistake. Skye was only twenty-two and she was often told she looked younger still. The make-up she'd applied painstakingly that morning had sweated off throughout the day, and she stood in the impossibly glamorous offices feeling as out of place as she had been in their marriage. Nonetheless, she had a right to be there. A reason. She tilted her chin, staring down at the receptionist as though this weren't the culmination of all her nightmares.

'*Signora,*' Skye corrected emphatically. 'Signora Skye Vin Santo.'

Skye had the satisfaction of seeing the other woman's mouth form a perfect red 'o' of surprise, but she recovered swiftly, reaching for the telephone and lifting it to her ear. Her eyes dropped to Skye's finger and Skye was glad she'd slipped the ten-carat solitaire back into place for the day. '*Mi dispiace!* I'm so sorry, Mrs Vin Santo,' the receptionist said, pressing a button and waiting for the phone to connect. 'I had no idea Signor Vin Santo was married.'

Skye's nod was dismissive, but the words cut deeply. Why should this woman have known of her boss's marital status? It wasn't as though they'd been married long. Skye had walked out on him after just over a month. A month too long.

How had she been so fooled by him even for that period of time? Hell, why had she even married him? That was easy. Out of nowhere, an unwelcome image of Matteo flooded her mind's eye, reminding her of how he'd been the evening they'd met. In a cocktail suit, so handsome and charming, so intent on seducing her. She'd been so easy to seduce and he'd been so persistent. Fate, she'd told herself at the time. Lies, she'd later discovered. All of it.

She heard the rapid-fire Italian conversation without comprehending. Her eyes were fixed to the view of Venice, a city she'd once adored with all of herself. A city she'd thought she'd spend the rest of her days in. She hardened her heart to its charms now, ignoring the way the gondolas glided past, full of grace and pride; the way the water formed glistening little sunlit peaks and troughs as it was stirred by the activity. She ignored the way the ancient buildings huddled together, singing the secrets of their souls, the way the bridges seemed to emote wisdom and strength. She ignored the dazzling colour of the sky and the birds she could see but not hear—she didn't need to hear them to remember the way they sounded. The flapping of their wings was the breath sound of Venice.

It was beautiful, but it was no longer for her. Skye spun round, glad to turn her back on the view, even when it meant she was staring at the disdainful receptionist once more. The woman stood—she was taller than Skye had been able to appreciate while seated—and made her way to stand directly in front of Skye.

'Signor Vin Santo will see you now. Is there something you would like? Some water? A soda?'

Vodka, Skye thought with a wry smile. 'Mineral water would be good. Thank you,' she tacked on belatedly. She hadn't meant to sound rude. Her whole mind was now focused on the job ahead. The most important performance of her life. Getting Matteo to sign the damned papers so she could finally move on—far, far away from him.

'Certainly, madam. This way.' The receptionist moved a little ahead of Skye, swishing her hips as she went, and Skye felt a momentary jab of envy for the other woman's curves. Skye had always been slim, but she'd desperately wanted larger breasts and hips when she was younger and had spent much of her teenage years stuffing her bras with tissues.

'Here we are,' the receptionist smiled, noticeably warmer now she knew to whom she was speaking, and stepped aside. 'He's waiting for you.'

Why did that conjure a very strong image of a wolf?

Because Matteo was all predator. All strong, ruthless, heartless predator.

And she'd been his prey.

Well, that was no longer the case.

Skye squared her shoulders defiantly, mentally bracing herself and straightening her spine, sucking in a deep breath which she hoped would bring courage.

Still, nothing could have prepared her for that moment. The moment when the door swung open and Matteo stood just inside it.

Nothing.

The air ceased to exist; it was sucked out and she stood in a vacuum. A space devoid of oxygen, gravity, reason and sense. There was just her and Matteo, her husband. Her beautiful, hyper-masculine, ruggedly handsome, lying, cheating husband.

Her throat was dry, her nerves quivering.

Strength be damned.

She wanted to run at him. But to kiss him? Or claw his eyes out? Probably, she realised with a sinking heart, the former. She wanted to wrap her arms around his neck and pull his head down, pull his mouth to hers, to greet him as though she still believed in love and happily ever after.

He looked good enough to eat. It was pure coincidence that he was wearing the suit she'd always loved—the navy-blue one that drew attention to his broad shoulders and dark tan. Her eyes lifted to his face: his square jawline with the stubble that was nothing to do with fashion and everything to do with his impatience with something as dull as shaving; higher, to his generous lips and patrician nose; to cheekbones that were firm and high, slashed into his face in a sign of his determination; and eyes that were so dark they were almost black but for the flecks of gold that glistened in their depths.

Eyes that were staring at her now, undertaking their

own inspection, running down her body with the kind of passion and possession she had, once upon a time, found mesmerising and addictive. Eyes that missed nothing, that skated over her stiletto-clad feet, higher to her slim, bare legs and the floaty dress she wore that fell to just above her knees and covered her in a mysterious cloud of pale yellow fabric. Her arms were bare; he caught a glimpse of her wedding ring and grimaced.

Good.

Let him feel the awkwardness of this.

His eyes lifted higher to her face, roaming it freely... marking it for changes?

There were not many. In fact, Skye would have said she looked almost exactly as she had five weeks earlier when she'd left their house, their marriage, their life. All of her changes were internal, except for the heavy fringe she'd had cut a week or so earlier, having decided spontaneously that she needed a change. Some outward sign that she was no longer the same woman who'd been caught up in the Matteo Vin Santo Show.

She had grown up—a lot—in the short space of time. She barely recognised the woman she'd been. So naïve, stupid and so damned trusting!

'Thank you for seeing me,' she said, breaking the silence with a businesslike tone, pleased with how crisply she enunciated each syllable. 'I won't take up much of your time.'

Ah, how well she knew him! She saw the glint of sardonic mockery in his eyes and she resented him for that. His ability to make her feel foolish and immature even in this, the most adult of circumstances.

He said nothing, though, simply stepping deeper into the room, making room for her to enter his office. She did so with no degree of pleasure. She'd been in the room before, and her eyes fell to the table, taking in the very spot where she'd sat and started to sign the papers. The papers that had been the beginning of the end.

'*You don't love me, do you?*' *She stared at the documents and then her husband as all the pieces of information came together. 'I asked my lawyer about this. He told me everything. You. My dad. The whole sordid history. This is why you married me!*'

His surprise was obvious and it infuriated Skye.

'*You really didn't think I'd find out? You didn't think I'd ask about this?*' *She waved the contract in the air. 'It's all been about this damned hotel, hasn't it? A hotel my dad bought from your grandfather. A hotel you've been trying to buy back for fifteen years. My God! This is what our marriage is all about!*'

Silence stretched between them. Silence that pulled, pulled and pulled at her nerve-ends until they snapped.

'*We should talk about this later,*' *he said seriously. 'Just sign the papers and we'll go for dinner tonight.*'

'*Don't.*' *She slammed her palm down on the table. 'Don't you dare infantilise me! I deserve to know the truth. I want to hear it from your own mouth. This hotel is why you came to London. Why you met me. Right?*'

His eyes narrowed and for a moment she wondered if he would say something to make this better, to alleviate the pain that was cracking through her soul.

'*Yes.*'

Skye's heart shook in her chest. She gripped the chairback for support. 'And why you married me?'

He was quiet for a long moment; it was a silence that tore her to shreds. And then he gave a simple, decisive nod that was the death knell to the fragile hopes she still held deep inside.

The memories were swirling through her, threatening to suck her back in time, but the door clicking shut jolted her into the present.

They were alone.

'Well, Skye, this is…unexpected.'

Her heart thumped painfully in her chest, ramming against her ribcage. God, his accent. How had she forgotten the sensual appeal of his husky, deep, Italian-edged voice?

Be strong. This will be over soon enough.

'You must have known I'd come back at some point,' she said with a shrug of her slender shoulders, pleased with how confident the words sounded, even as her fingers were shaking a little.

'I knew no such thing,' he countered. His accent was thicker—a sign of his fury, she knew. It was only in moments of deep emotional distress that this happened. 'You disappeared into thin air after you left my office without so much as the courtesy of a goodbye.'

Skye's caramel eyes flew wide. 'Courtesy? You want to talk about courtesy?'

His eyes narrowed warningly. 'I want to talk about where the hell you've been.'

'Like you care,' she said with a roll of her eyes.

'My wife disappeared, leaving no way to contact her. You think I don't care?'

'This is all about acquisition and ownership for you, isn't it? *Your* wife.' She shook her head angrily, realising that she was fighting a losing battle. 'I was in England,' she said on a sigh.

'Not at your house,' he said, and for a second her heart squeezed. Because it was proof he'd looked for her. Proof he'd tried to find her.

'No.' A rejection of that tenderness.

She knew why he'd looked for her and it had nothing to do with their sham marriage. He must have been furious to discover that she'd cancelled his purchase. That she'd found out about the pieces he'd been casually, secretly, manoeuvring through their short, disastrous marriage. Had he thought he could keep her so sensually fogged that she wouldn't wake up and realise what the hell was going on? He had almost been right. He'd come so close to taking the hotel from her without her even realising.

'Where were you?' he pushed, his own words hardened with something she knew to be anger. Because Matteo Vin Santo liked to win. He liked to win at all costs, and she'd found out just in time.

'It's none of your damned business.' She glared at him now, the veneer of civility slipping away. She tried to grab it but being here with him, in this room, overpowered by how damned handsome he was, made something inside her snap.

'You're my wife,' he corrected, moving closer so that she caught a hint of his masculine fragrance. Her knees almost buckled. 'I have every right to know.'

But it was the wrong thing to say. His casual insistence of his rights fired every hint of anger in her body. 'That's outrageous.' Her eyes held the strength of steel when they locked with his. 'You have no rights. Not where I'm concerned.'

A muscle throbbed at the base of his jaw. 'You're my wife.' As though that explained everything!

'That's what I'm here to talk to you about,' Skye asserted forcefully in an attempt to regain control of the situation, reaching for her handbag at the same moment a sharp knock on the door preceded the interruption of the receptionist.

She brought a bottle of mineral water and a glass with ice cubes and a wedge of lemon into the room and placed them on the boardroom table.

'Thank you,' Skye murmured, relieved to have a form of distraction. She hoped it might calm her raging nerves. She twisted the lid, waiting for the hiss of bubbles to silence and the receptionist to leave the room, before tipping half the water into the glass.

'What, exactly, are you here to discuss?' he prompted,

crossing his arms over his chest. She didn't need to look at him to know how broad that chest was. She lifted her mineral water and moved towards the window instead, staring down at Venice without really seeing it.

'Our marriage.' The words were a ghost. They conjured all the memories she wanted to forget.

The love-at-first-sight romance. The wedding itself. The way their marriage had been marked by nights of complete sensual abandon. Long days of waiting for him to come home hadn't mattered. She'd been so exhausted she'd napped and eaten, preparing for his return, and then she'd been his willing sex slave. Self-disgust at her stupidity gnawed at her gut.

She twisted the enormous diamond around her finger before sliding it off one last time. 'And how we're going to end it.' She spun round, her back to the view, her eyes landing squarely on his face, locking to his. She bravely held his gaze as she placed the ring on the boardroom table, then hastily stepped away from it as though it might burn her.

His expression was grim, but he said nothing initially. There was no shock. No outrage. No attempt to argue. To win her back.

Because it had never really been about her.

It had been about him, his grandfather, her father, and some stupid hotel she'd never even heard of. A vendetta that she knew nothing about which seemed to have controlled the lives of all those she'd loved. Her father, her husband...

Skye straightened her back, wounded pride forming the shield she needed.

'I have the divorce papers here,' she said softly. 'You just need to sign them and I'll take care of the rest.'

He expelled a breath; his expression gave little away. 'Show me.'

Skye could scarcely believe how well this was going!

She'd been fretting about meeting Matteo again, yet he was being so reasonable... She told herself she was relieved.

'Here.' She pulled the document out of her handbag. It was only five pages long. She passed it to him, careful not to get too close, careful not to let their fingers touch.

His eyes, when they met hers, were scathing. He knew. He knew she was avoiding him.

He skimmed each sheet of paper, reading the words quickly, then placed them on the edge of his desk.

'And if I don't want to divorce you?'

Skye froze, the success she'd already been inwardly celebrating shattering. Her face drained of all colour. 'Don't be absurd.' The words were whispered from her before she remembered that she needed to be strong. Confident. Matteo preyed on weakness.

'What's absurd about wanting to stay married to you?'

And he strode across the room, closing the distance between them, his eyes locked to hers until she was quivering where she stood. Strength, apparently, deserted her at her moment of need.

'This wasn't a real marriage,' she muttered, standing her ground with effort. 'We both know that.'

His lips flicked with what she took to reflect silent agreement.

'It felt real enough to me.' The words were dangerously silky. His hand snaked around her waist, catching her completely by surprise. He jerked her against him, her softness meeting his hard strength in a way that was instantly familiar. Desire flooded her. Heat scorched her soul and a soft moan escaped her lips unbidden. It was foolish to stay so close to him, yet she did. She had denied herself this contact for long, miserable weeks, and now she wanted to enjoy it. Just for a moment. One last time.

'It wasn't,' she said huskily. 'I know that now.'

'What do you know?' The question was asked quietly. Almost gently.

'I know everything.' She closed her eyes. 'I know about your father and my father. I know they fell in love with the same woman and your father married her. I know that my father was angry. I know that he went out of his way to hurt your family.' Her words cracked as she glossed over the admittance of her father's part in the angst. 'I know he felt hurt and rejected and that he took it out on you financially.'

Matteo's laugh was a grim rejection. 'You make it sound so sterile. Believe me, this was not the case.' He leaned forward, his expression menacing. 'Carey Johnson bankrupted my grandfather. Your father destroyed *everything* my grandfather spent a *lifetime* building.'

His vehement passion paralysed her for a moment, but belatedly she found her voice. 'And so you wanted to punish me?'

Silence fell around them, thick and caustic. She could see him weighing his words, carefully choosing what to say.

'It was never about punishing you,' he said finally.

'Punishing him, then? Punishing my dad?'

What could he say to that? Wasn't it the truth? Hadn't he delighted in the final insult he'd held over that bastard Carey Johnson? Making Skye moan for him, Matteo, in his bed all night long? Yes. He'd wanted to take his revenge, one sweet night at a time, and Skye had been a very obliging pawn in his game.

'You married me because you loved me.' He returned to their original point with apparent ease, the question asked silkily. 'Remember?'

God, she had loved him. She'd fallen for him, but it had all been an act. She noted dispassionately how he hadn't included his own feelings in the neat summation. His feelings were irrelevant; no, his feelings were *non-existent*. 'Love and hate are so close on the emotional spectrum, aren't they? It amazed me, too, how quickly that love morphed into something else.'

'You're saying you hate me?' he prompted, his free hand lifting to her hip, holding her where she was. She felt the stirring of his arousal and her breath snagged in her throat.

Sex.

That was the only truth of their marriage. Even he wasn't that good an actor. The desire had been real. It had controlled him as much as it had her.

'Of course I hate you,' she hissed, knowing she needed to pull away from him—that she would, in a moment. 'How could I feel anything else for you?'

His laugh was pure, sensual cynicism. 'Careful, *cara*. You and I both know how easy it would be for me to prove you a liar.' He rolled his hips, bringing his arousal into intimate contact with her body, and Skye felt a groan tear through her. Need, unmistakable and urgent, grew within her soul.

'That's just physical,' she hissed, her eyes locked to the top button of his crisp, pale blue shirt. 'And I'm sure you've had enough experience to know it doesn't mean a damned thing.'

'But you haven't,' he reminded her mercilessly, his eyes glowing with intensity. 'You were all mine.'

More memories. Their first time together—her first time with any man. She bit down on her lip, hating the way her nerves jerked in response. He'd taken hold of her that night, body and soul. He'd unlocked parts of her she hadn't even been aware of, and it had all been a part of his game. His plan for revenge. How easy she'd been to con into this marriage—into his bed!

'And I think you still are.'

A garbled sound escaped from Skye's throat. But it wasn't a denial. Was it a sound of surrender? Because he was right. She was desperate to feel his body once more. To be with him one last time.

He would probably always have that power over her, but *everything* hinged on her being able to stay strong. To remember the reason she had to get the papers signed and get the heck away from him. There was no future for them. There couldn't be. How could she stay married to a man she loved with all her heart, raise a baby with him, knowing that he'd used her in the most cynical of ways?

Her only hope was never to see him again. To go far from where he could find her. And that was her plan. Once he'd signed the papers she was going to disappear again. She thought of the ticket in her purse, a flight to Australia for later that night, where she planned to find her way to a remote corner of the country, somewhere with a view of the beach, and set about healing her broken heart.

'You're wrong.' She pulled away from him with determination, moving back to the window and staring out at Venice.

'Am I?'

'Oh, fine.' She shrugged her shoulders, not turning around. 'Apparently, I still…desire you. So what? You were my first lover. I dare say my body won't ever completely forget the lessons you taught me.' Fragments of their nights cut through her determination. The way he'd kissed her for hours; the way his mouth had owned her body. The way they'd swum naked in the moonlit ocean off the coast of Sicily or in the rooftop pool at his Venetian mansion. The sensual massages he'd given her. She pushed those thoughts aside. 'But nor will my heart.'

'And what did I teach your heart, *cara*?'

'Not to trust handsome strangers,' she said, the humour of the comment sucked away by the desperation in her voice. 'Sign the papers, Matteo. This marriage is over.'

'And if I won't?' The words were thick with emotion.

And for a second hope scorched her. But it was a foolish hope, the same blind love that had led her into the marriage.

'You wanted revenge. You got it.'

'I wanted the hotel,' he said with a dangerous softness to his voice. 'You were…a silver lining.'

'A silver lining?' she returned angrily. 'For God's sake, Matteo. I *loved* you! Doesn't that mean anything to you?'

He stared at her long and hard. 'That wasn't love you felt. It was infatuation. Sex.'

She swallowed past a lump of bitterness in her throat. He was wrong. She'd loved him with her whole heart. She wouldn't tell him that now, but somehow knowing that their baby had been conceived with goodness in her heart, at least, mattered a whole lot to her.

'Perhaps you're right,' she said with an attempt at a nonchalant shrug. 'It's all academic now. Our marriage is over. There's obviously no way on earth I could ever forget what you've done. Nor forgive you for it.' She sucked in a breath and stared at him headlong. 'You can have the hotel.'

He was instantly still, every nerve ending in his body in a state of stasis. 'You're saying you'll sell me Il Grande Fortuna?'

'On one condition,' she said frostily, devastation at this final, damning proof seeping into her blood, turning it to ice. 'Sign the damned papers and stay the hell out of my life.'

When Skye had walked out on their marriage, having learned the truth behind his motivations for pursuing her, he'd had to reconcile himself to the reality that he might never recover his grandfather's beloved Il Grande Fortuna.

He'd put all his chips on the one square, gambling on marriage to the rich heiress as the best way to get what he wanted. And to have a little fun along the way.

His plan had been simple enough—seduce her and blind

her with the passion they shared, making her willing to do, say or sign anything he asked of her. And he'd come so close. She had been eating out of the palm of his hand. Until she wasn't.

Their marriage had always been about the hotel.

About returning his family's property to its rightful owner—him.

It had been about righting a wrong of the past.

About avenging his *nonno*.

Hell, he'd married her because it had been the only way to get the hotel back into his family's trust. Now she was giving him the thing he'd wanted all his adult life on a silver platter, yet he found himself hesitating.

Why the hell wasn't he just agreeing to her terms?

Because he didn't like to concede defeat. And, even though he'd have the hotel, he didn't like the idea of Skye walking away from him before he was ready.

'Sign the divorce papers, Teo.' She used the diminutive form of his name by mistake. The way her face paled showed her remorse. That wasn't who they were any more. Hell, they'd never been that couple. Not really.

He'd never even wanted a wife. He'd wanted the hotel, and their marriage had been the clearest way to achieve that aim, but Matteo Vin Santo was a bachelor from way back. If he signed this paper, he'd be rid of the wife he'd never really wanted and he'd have the hotel. The only thing to regret was that he wouldn't have the pleasure of his wife's body again. A small price to pay for achieving a decades-old goal, though. 'Fine.' His nod was curt.

Her relief was palpable. He tried not to take it personally. She'd be all kinds of stupid to want anything other than a divorce from him—and Skye Johnson was definitely not stupid.

'But I have a condition of my own.'

Her brows shot up, her lips parted, and he ached to kiss

her. To wipe that look of disdain from her pretty features. To remind her of just how she came apart in his arms. He'd always loved her in yellow. It showed off her flawless honey skin, the darkness of her hair, the innocence of who she was.

'I want one more night with you.'

Skye froze, her eyes sweeping shut, her lips parting wider as she struggled for breath. He watched the words take effect; the way colour spread through her cheeks.

'No.' It was just a whisper. A husky denial. 'Never.'

He laughed, a harsh sound of cynicism and frustration. 'Never say never, *cara.* Not when you fall apart in my arms as you do…'

Skye tilted her chin, her eyes locked defiantly with his.

'Desire is one thing, but I have no intention of acting on it.'

'Then I have no intention of signing those papers,' he threatened silkily.

Panic flooded her. *Fascinating.*

'What's the matter? Is the idea of being Mrs Matteo Vin Santo so abhorrent to you? I remember a time when you couldn't wait to be my wife—and be in my bed.'

'I didn't know who you were then. Nor what you were capable of.'

'And what am I capable of?'

'It doesn't matter.' Haunted, miserable words that slammed against him. Guilt was not something Matteo had much experience of, but he felt a flush of it. He didn't like it.

His obligation was to his family.

Not Skye.

But her hurt was obvious and it was a hurt he had caused.

Yes, he felt guilt. He felt remorse. He wished…what? That he could change it? That he could have procured the hotel without hurting her?

It wasn't possible. He'd tried that. He'd spent years trying to lure her father into selling and the bastard had been determined.

'Over my dead body.' Those were the last words Carey Johnson had said to Matteo. If Carey had only listened to reason, if he hadn't been driven by the stupid grudge that had led to his taking the hotel in the first instance, it would never have come to this.

But, looking across his office at his wife, Matteo wasn't sure he cared about the hotel, his grandfather or her father. None of them mattered. He wasn't foolish enough to think he could salvage their marriage—nor did he believe he wanted to. But he needed, desperately, to kiss her.

To touch her.

To wipe away the grief that was saturating her slender frame.

Like he used to, as though it were his God-given right to hold her in his arms. They were tinder and flame—together the effect had always been extraordinary.

'Don't.' Her eyes held a warning. 'Don't look at me like that.'

'Like what?' He moved closer, just a few steps, and there was still a table between them. Her ring caught his eye and he reached for it without realising, fingering its weight in his hand, remembering the day he'd bought it. He'd deliberately chosen something enormous, thinking it would be exactly what she would want. The heiress of the Johnson fortune surely valued enormity and extravagance over all else?

Only it had never really suited her. Over the weeks of their short marriage, he'd begun to imagine what he should have chosen instead. Something slender with an understated elegance, made of rose-gold and inlaid diamonds. Perhaps onyx, to match her hair.

He swallowed past the thought. It was a distraction, a

red herring. What he needed was to remember the hotel. To remember the reason he'd done all of this.

'Don't look at me like you're actually sorry this is happening. Like you didn't expect it.' She tilted her chin. 'Like this has anything to do with you and me.'

'It *is* our marriage we're discussing ending.'

'Marriage!' She spat the word and his gut rolled. It was as though a blade had been plunged through him. Her anger and disbelief filled the room. 'This was *never* a marriage! It was a damned trick. A machination. Nothing more. You win, okay? You win! Take the hotel! I don't want it. I don't want anything that will ever remind me of you!' Her voice was loud. He'd put bets on his receptionist Anastasia having heard every word but he didn't care.

Skye's pain was palpable and he longed to kiss her to wipe it away. It was the only way he could think of to remove the ache from her eyes; the tears that glistened on her lashes were tiny, moist recriminations that landed squarely in his chest.

'How you must have loved the knowledge that you had such a sweet revenge over my father! How you'd done something he would have hated, something I would *never* have agreed to if I'd known about your feud. How you must have been *laughing* at me! Every night when you came home you found me so happy to see you, and all the while you were lining up the pieces, getting ready to finally swoop.'

A muscle jerked on the hard ridge of his jaw. 'Yes, Skye. I'm only human. Do you want me to lie to you now? To tell you that our marriage had nothing to do with the fact your father was the biggest bastard on earth? That the fact I hated him with every fibre of my being didn't have anything to do with why I married you?'

She held a hand up. Her fingers were shaking and her face was so pale that, momentarily, he felt a clutch of anxiety for her. She looked terrible; ill. Matteo was torn between anger at the situation and a strange concern for his wife.

Tears spilled out of her eyes now, rolling down her cheeks. She was so weary. All the planning and coping had taken its toll, and she was utterly exhausted. It showed in the tremble of her voice and the grey of her cheeks. 'No. There's nothing you can say that I want to hear. In fact, I can't bear to be in the same room as you for a moment longer. Just sign the divorce papers. Please. Take the hotel and leave me alone.' She bit down on her lip as she tried to keep her sobbing at bay.

It was everything he'd wanted. He'd come to accept that he would never get the hotel back—not once Skye had learned the truth. And here she was, offering it to him on a silver platter just to be rid of him.

Was that it? Was his pride wounded by her desperation to be free of their marriage? Was that why he wanted to rail against her insistence? To remind her of what they'd shared—physically—one last time?

His eyes dropped to the divorce papers and then lifted with a heavy grimness towards her face. 'Fine. If that's what you want.'

'I never want to see you again.'

The heat of Venice slapped her in the face as soon as she stepped out of his office. It was early afternoon and the city was packed. Workers were jostling along the street, tourists were busy taking photographs and Skye was in the midst of them, surprise at what she'd just accomplished moving through her.

She took a step towards the crowds, her mind numb. What now?

Her breath was shallow.

Shock, she supposed, reaching for a pillar to support her.

Stars flew in her eyes and heat spread through her body followed by weakness and an odd, soul-deep exhaustion.

It was over.

She was free.

Her hand pressed to her stomach and another wave of tiredness hit her. She didn't want anything to do with Matteo, but she was going to raise their baby. Could she do it and never think of him?

She'd have to. Matteo was in her past and this baby was her future.

The baby was all that mattered.

She sucked in a breath, but it didn't seem to reach her lungs.

'Eh, you okay, miss?'

A kindly gondola operator lifted his brows, waiting for an answer, so she nodded, even though she wasn't sure she was. 'Just hot,' she said, fanning her face.

But the simple, tiny exertion of moving her hand up and down was the straw that broke the camel's back. Darkness enveloped her.

CHAPTER TWO

MATTEO WASN'T LOOKING out of the window in the hope of seeing her. He'd simply been standing and staring in that direction ever since she'd left. Really, he was barely aware of the flow of traffic in and out along the busy tourist strip.

He saw Skye.

The anguish on her features.

The pain of her heart that she wore so visibly.

He'd used her, and that hadn't bothered him. Causing pain to her had been something he'd been more than willing to gamble. It was her own father's fault—if Skye was hurt, it was because of Carey Johnson's intractable bull-headedness.

But he hadn't banked on witnessing her pain. He hadn't enjoyed that. He was a driven businessman, not an out-and-out bastard. Witnessing the tears gliding down her soft, pale cheeks, the accusation in her eyes…he hadn't been prepared for how that would gut him. How it would make him feel unpleasantly remorseful, even when he knew he would make all the same decisions over again, given the chance.

He lifted his fingers to his chin, rubbing the stubble there, before a commotion dragged his attention down to ground level.

It was the pastel yellow of her dress that caught his eye first. The way it seemed to crumple as she fell, her body, slender and unmistakable, toppling backwards. She fell as she did everything—with grace.

It was the work of a moment. Skye was collapsing, then she was dropping over the edge of the railing into the murky, germ-infested waters of Venice. Had he stayed still a little longer, he would have seen the moment her head cracked against the side of a gondola.

But he didn't.

Adrenalin galvanised him.

Matteo ran from his office faster than he'd known was possible, tearing through the foyer and bursting onto the footpath just as a gondola operator in his distinctive black-and-white-striped shirt dived into the water. The dress made her easy to spot. Though Matteo could see the boat-swain had wrapped an arm around her waist, he couldn't stand idly by. Instincts alone drove his actions. A gentle ribbon of blood swirled through the water; he dove through it.

'Is she breathing?' Matteo pulled Skye to him, holding her as he swam to the edge of the canal. A crowd had formed and someone held their hands down, urging Matteo to lift her out. He passed her body up, then climbed out himself.

She was so peaceful. As though she were asleep.

More blood.

It seeped onto the pavement beneath her head and he gently fingered her scalp, a grim line on his mouth. 'Call a water ambulance,' he demanded, used to being obeyed and not doubting for one second that someone would do as he'd commanded.

'One is on its way,' someone replied.

Thank God. He crouched down beside her, running a hand over her face. 'You're okay, *cara*. You're going to be fine.'

He had the vague impression of the gondola operator being helped out of the water, but his entire focus was on

Skye. He spoke to her softly in his own language, urging her to wake up, not to worry, to trust him, knowing that if she'd been awake she'd have thrown that invitation back in his face.

It was only minutes before the scream of a water ambulance heralded its arrival, but it felt like a lot longer as Matteo stared down at her ashen face and wondered just what the hell had happened to make her fall into the filthy waters of Venice. The water ambulance pulled to a hasty stop beside them and two men began to call orders to the crowd. They climbed up nearby steps and ran to Skye, lifting her onto a flimsy backboard.

'You're with her?' one of them asked Matteo.

He nodded. 'I'm her…husband.'

'You can come, then.'

He could have laughed at the medic's apparent belief that he had any say in Matteo Vin Santo's actions. Matteo paused for the briefest moment, just long enough to toss a thick pile of soggy bank notes at the gondola operator with a quick word of thanks, and then he followed behind.

The speedboat, bright yellow and sleek, accommodated Skye on a bed, and he watched her as the boat made its way speedily through Venice.

Only twice during the trip did her eyes open, and both times she looked at him with a mixture of confusion and non-comprehension.

The boat pulled up at the *ospedale* dock and there was a medical team waiting.

It all happened so quickly. She was admitted after a cursory examination, and there was enough concern on the nurse's face to make Matteo wonder if she was gravely ill.

'What's going on?' he asked, once she was ensconced in her own room.

No one answered. They were all busy working, checking her vital signs, rolling her onto her side and inspecting her head, checking for the damage that was causing the bleeding. A nurse drew several vials of blood and raced them from the room.

And then he was waiting, standing beside her bed, wondering what had happened, wondering if she'd be okay.

After an interminable time, a woman in a white coat entered the room and moved towards Matteo, her smile reassuring. 'She is your wife?'

He nodded. 'Yes.' The word was hardened by years of being in command. Of calling the shots and asking the questions. 'How is she?'

'She's had a bump to the head, but it doesn't look too serious. Unfortunately, the tests we'd usually run to be sure are obviously impossible at the moment. She may be a little groggy when she wakes, possibly for a day or so. I don't anticipate any other complications, though.'

None of her words eased Matteo's concern. 'What happened to her?'

'My guess would be that she passed out. It's not unusual, in her condition. The heat of the day wouldn't have helped—'

'Wait a moment,' he said, lifting a hand to stop her. 'What condition?'

The doctor pulled a face. 'You don't know?'

'Know what, *dottore*?'

'About the baby?'

The world stopped spinning. No. It lurched catastrophically off its axis, sucking Matteo with it. He was in freefall as the doctor's words filtered through his mind. 'What baby?' he asked, the question gravelled.

'Your wife is pregnant. It's very early stages—it's quite by accident that the nurse even tested for it. Does she know?'

Hell.

Matteo's eyes were dragged to Skye, still so peaceful-looking. Despite the fact her dark hair was matted around her, her eyes were shut and she looked serene. Had she known?

I never want to see you, ever *again.*

A muscle clenched in his jaw. Had she really been planning to divorce him and keep their child from him?

An ache spread through him, an ache of misery and disbelief. Of anger and rage. Skye wasn't capable of that deception, surely?

She *couldn't* have known.

'She hadn't mentioned it,' he said with a hint of the ruthless determination that had seen him rebuild a once-great empire from its ashes and ruins. But his mind was reeling. Shock was seeping through him.

Skye was pregnant? And she'd come to him, seeking a divorce? A divorce he'd agreed to because he'd known he owed her that much; because he'd wanted her to be happy. And he'd thought he was done making stupid, emotion-driven decisions!

Would Skye have insisted on a divorce if she'd known about the baby? He couldn't believe it of his wife. And yet, she was the daughter of that bastard Johnson. Did he really have any idea what she was capable of?

His brow was fevered as he replayed every detail of their meeting, looking for signs that she knew her condition. Had she touched her stomach at all? What else would a pregnant woman do? He had no clue.

Hell.

The idea of a baby had never even really occurred to him; foolish, given how often they'd come together.

'Perhaps she has not been symptomatic.' The doctor shrugged, as though it didn't matter. As though it weren't the most important news Matteo had received in his life. As though Skye's knowledge or lack thereof wouldn't change *everything.*

How could he forgive her if she'd planned to keep it from him?

His nod was distracted. 'Is the baby okay?'

'So far as I can tell.' The doctor smiled reassuringly.

They'd only ever talked about children briefly. Skye was too young to have been thinking of having babies and Matteo hadn't entered into the marriage with procreation on his mind. But still! She must have known how much this child would mean to him.

And she'd been intending to take the Vin Santo heir away from him. To raise his child as a Johnson!

Fury whipped at the soles of his feet, spurring him forward. 'Did my wife's handbag…?'

'Yes, I believe it was dropped off separately.' The doctor nodded curtly. 'Someone found it on the pavement.'

His expression was grim.

'I'll have it brought in.'

'Thank you.'

He waited impatiently, staring at Skye, trying to make sense of this, trying to hold his temper together. But, the more time that passed, the more he came to suspect the worst.

She'd been so adamant about the divorce—that it had to be right now. She had no time to wait.

And she'd held out the perfect carrot to get him to fit in with her plans! The hotel! The damned hotel. He would have done anything to get it back, even marrying her. And, yes, even divorcing her.

He'd wanted the matter of their marriage and the hotel resolved and she'd given him that on a platter. What a fool he was! He'd almost let go of the most valuable thing in his life.

His child.

How could he have been so stupid? Hadn't he learned his lesson with the whole Maria debacle? He'd just been a boy then. A young, foolish boy. He'd fallen for her lies hook, line and sinker. He'd fallen in love with her too. And learned how stupid a notion love was. He'd sworn he'd never trust a woman again, and here he'd been about to take Skye's request at face value. Damn it! She was a Johnson, first and foremost. When had he forgotten that?

A hospital staffer arrived minutes later, handing the handbag to him in a large plastic bag.

He took it without speaking, reaching for her bag and ripping it open. There were the damned divorce documents, alongside his purchase contract on the hotel. He removed both angrily and stuffed them in the still-damp pocket of his suit.

He was about to drop the bag to the floor when something else caught his eye.

Curiously, he reached for it, and his anger only darkened when he saw that the object was her passport with a ticket folded neatly inside. A quick inspection showed that it was to take her to Sydney, Australia, later that night.

The evidence was truly damning. All doubt evaporated and left inside him a seed of anger so powerful that it ripped his soul in half.

She had been going to take this child from him. His flesh and blood.

Nausea rolled through him, rising in his chest. He gripped his hands together, his eyes resting on his wife's face—so beautiful, even like this.

Had she truly wanted to raise a child away from him? Without him ever even knowing?

The pain at the very idea was sharp.

'Signor Vin Santo? We have spare clothes if you would like to get changed.' A nurse was smiling at him kindly.

He didn't return it. He couldn't. 'I'll stay with my *wife*, thank you.' The words rang with derision, yet the nurse didn't seem to detect the undercurrent of Matteo's tension.

Fury was at war with disbelief.

A machine was rolled through the door, its wheels making a soft squeaking noise as it was brought to rest beside Skye. The doctor he'd been speaking to earlier bustled in and sent him a look of reassurance.

'Try not to be so worried,' she said, pushing Skye's dress up and arranging the blankets around her hips, exposing only her stomach. It was so flat. Was it possible that the doctor had got it wrong? How could a baby be developing inside her tiny frame?

His eyes devoured her body once more, purposefully looking for changes now. Her neat breasts were still small and round, just enough to fill his palms. But perhaps there was a new roundness to them he hadn't appreciated before...

He swallowed past the bitterness. He would process her betrayal later. Once he knew his baby was okay.

The doctor lifted a part of the machine and pressed it to Skye's belly, and Skye made a soft moaning noise.

'Is it painful?' Matteo asked instinctively.

'No, not at all.' The doctor spun the cart around so that Matteo could see the screen. He lifted his eyes to it and frowned.

'What am I looking at?'

'It's too early to see anything clearly. I would say she is perhaps six weeks.' The doctor smiled at him kindly. 'Your baby is around the size of a lentil.'

'A lentil?'

'A legume,' she clarified. 'But I can see good blood-flow generally. There's nothing here that worries me.' She went to lift the wand but Matteo spoke, arresting her movement.

'What is that?' He pointed to a line at the bottom of the screen.

'Ah. That is the heartbeat.'

'The heartbeat?' He closed his eyes as the reality began to thunder through him.

Emotions gripped him, so strong, so raw, and suddenly he wasn't capable of speech. He stepped away from the bed, from his wife, from the doctor, and sucked in a deep breath of air.

'Why don't you get changed, Signor Vin Santo? You'll be no help to her if you've come down with a flu.'

He didn't answer. He was busy analysing the situation, trying to make sense of it.

Skye was pregnant with his child. With the Vin Santo heir. And she'd wanted to keep the information from him.

Unless… He turned slowly, his eyes locked to the doctor's. Hope briefly flared in his chest. 'You asked if she knew. Is there any way she *wouldn't* have known?'

The doctor's empathy was palpable. 'Of course. It is still very early. If she hasn't mentioned it to you, I think it is highly likely that she didn't yet realise. It really depends on whether she had any other symptoms, and if she had a reason to do a pregnancy test. Were you trying to conceive?'

'No.' Their marriage was about one thing, and one thing only. The hotel. A child would just have complicated matters further.

How the hell had this even happened? She'd been on the pill, hadn't she?

'Your wife will be awake soon.' The doctor leaned over and lifted one of Skye's eyelids, then nodded confidently. 'You will be able to ask her.'

It was suddenly imperative for Matteo to know the truth. No, it was imperative for him to know that she *hadn't* known. He couldn't believe that Skye would have planned to keep this information from him. Despite the evidence against her, he still had hope. A part of him believed she would never do something as calculated as taking a baby from its father.

No matter what he'd done, no matter what she believed,

this was *different*. Their baby was not a pawn; it deserved better than to be used by either of them as a bargaining chip.

But worse was the belief she hadn't intended to use it as a bargaining chip at all. Worse was the realisation that she had simply meant to disappear. To get on a plane and fly out of his life, taking his son or daughter with her.

He ground his teeth together and turned back to the bed.

His heart rolled.

It wasn't possible.

'Matteo? Where am I?'

Her thin, raspy voice drew his attention. He stared at her long and hard before speaking. 'You're in the hospital. In Venice.' His expression was guarded, but he felt anger in his every expression, beneath the mask of civility he had donned with effort.

'Hospital?' Her eyes swept shut. 'I fell. No, I fainted. That happens sometimes.'

'Since when?' he demanded icily, moving closer.

Her hands dropped to her stomach and he could see that she was in turmoil, that she was agonising over what to say. But apparently a need for reassurance eclipsed all other concerns. 'Is he okay? Is my baby okay?'

CHAPTER THREE

EVERY SOUND IN the hospital was audible. The beeping of
far-away machines monitoring the life signs of patients.
The low-key chat of staff. The ringing of a phone. The
whir of an overhead fan. Everything was audible in that
way when things take on an almost supersonic quality in
moments of shock and duress. The sounds had a brightness beyond their due.

Skye waited, her breath held, her worry lurching desperately.

'Matteo?' It was a whisper. A strangled, hoarse cry.
'Please tell me…'

'Our baby is fine,' he said with a coldness that perfo-
rated her relief and doused it in ice.

Skye's eyes fell closed. The whole point of coming to
Italy and forcing his hand, of giving him the hotel, had been
to ensure they were divorced before it was too late. Before
her stomach became rounded, before she had given birth
to their child, before he had any concept there even was a
child. But she wasn't sure she could summon the energy
to care in that moment.

None of that mattered.

She felt only relief.

Tears stung her eyes. 'Thank God. Oh, Matteo, I'm so
relieved.'

'They're going to monitor you,' he said, taking a step

back from the bed and crossing his arms. 'For a few more hours.'

'I'm fine.' Skye reached for the IV cable that was attached to her wrist and pulled it out. Matteo winced as the inch-long needle fell from her arm. 'Fainting is one of the symptoms I'm learning to live with.'

She stood, but was so unsteady that Matteo couldn't help but reach for her. His touch was clinical, but he didn't want to see his wife—no, the mother of his child—splayed across the bed, unconscious again.

'I'm fine,' she reiterated snappishly, and her teeth were bared, her body language the definition of defensive. But it was the behaviour of a badly wounded lioness defending her cub.

She was *terrified*.

Of him? Of his anger? Of what she thought he'd do? So she should be! To attempt to conceal the Vin Santo heir from him… Just who did she think he was? 'So you obviously knew you were pregnant.' The words held a latent threat.

She winced and pulled back, moving away from him by skirting the bed.

'When the hell were you planning on telling me?'

'Would you *stop* yelling?' she murmured.

Matteo ran his hand through his hair, pulling at it with barely suppressed frustration. He hadn't intended to yell; only a rage he hadn't felt for many years, since the last time he'd come up against a Johnson in a confrontation, had completely usurped all his other impulses. He spoke more softly, but there was an inherent danger to the silky edges of his words. 'You weren't going to tell me, were you?'

Skye looked at him for a moment and then turned her attention back to the bed. 'I didn't…feel it was any of your business,' she said, and somehow managed to look confidently defiant even as she extolled the absurd explanation.

'My baby is none of my business?' he responded with scathing disbelief. 'How exactly do you figure?'

'You don't want a child. Not with me. I was doing you a favour.' She shook her head. 'I was doing us *all* a favour. I don't want to raise a baby with you any more than you do with me. And the baby deserves to be born into a world that's not…full of bitterness and acrimony.'

'The baby deserves a chance to know both his parents,' Matteo responded sharply. 'You were going to deny both it and me that opportunity. Weren't you?'

She glared at him. 'You went into this marriage wanting one thing, and one thing only. And now you have it. Children were no part of this.'

'*That* is beside the point. You are, in fact, pregnant with my child. This is not in the realms of the hypothetical. I had a right to know.'

Her mouth dropped open and she stared at him, searching for something to say—anything—that might explain her point of view.

The hurt she'd felt at realising that he'd used her. The fact that he'd conned her into falling in love with him, had used her inexperience and desire against her, knowing that he would never be able to give her the only thing she really wanted.

Love.

Matteo wasn't built to love. She knew that now. The newspapers that declared him heartless and ruthless were right.

What a fool she'd been to believe that their similar upbringings had destined them to be together. As though both having suffered the misfortune of being orphaned meant they would live happily ever after.

How could she explain to him that this option had been the best for everyone?

No words came to mind. Nothing. She had thought about

it long and hard, though. She'd agonised over what to do. And this had made complete sense.

It *still* made sense.

'I don't want to raise a child with you,' she said with a determination that was somewhat belied by her quivering lower lip.

'That is not your decision.'

Skye pulled a face. 'We're divorced, remember? Or as good as.'

Matteo's mouth formed a grim line. 'There will be no divorce.' He reached into his pocket and pulled out the papers, tearing them in half with satisfaction, along with the contract for the hotel. The whole deal was off. This baby changed everything.

Skye's eyes followed the soft ripping of the soggy paper then flew to his face. 'You will not be flying out of Italy, taking my child with you.'

'You can't stop me,' she snapped, wrapping her arms around her slender body, holding herself tight.

'Like hell I can't.' He spoke coldly. 'If necessary I will take this matter to the family courts today.'

Skye's mouth dropped open. 'You…can't stop me from leaving. No court would make a mother remain in a country that she's not even a born citizen of.'

He lifted a hand, silencing her with the simple gesture. 'Perhaps not. But you had better believe I will have every reporter available covering the story. Our child will know, from as soon as he can read, that I fought *like a dog* for him. That I wanted him—and you wanted simply to take him from me.' He leaned closer, his face only inches from Skye's. 'I will fight for him with my dying breath. You will long for the days when we were married, rather than being in constant custody disputes in court.'

She shivered, his threat making her stomach roll. 'You wouldn't do it. You're too private.'

'There is *nothing* I wouldn't do for my child.'

'Then let-let me raise him,' Skye stammered. 'Let me raise our baby, because that's best for everyone. And you can be…involved,' she conceded, because she could clearly see she had no other option.

'How involved?' Matteo demanded.

'You can visit. Several times a year. I suppose I can bring him to Italy when he's older. We'll work out a schedule.' She said the word as though it was the miracle cure they desperately needed. 'Christmas, birthdays, just like every other divorced couple.'

'*Your* parents weren't together,' Matteo said with cold disbelief. 'You told me that you hated feeling pulled from one to the other. Yet you'd suggest it for our child?'

Skye froze. He was right, of course. Though Skye hadn't spoken much about her upbringing, she'd obviously given enough indication for him to glean the truth of her loneliness.

'We'll do it better than they did,' she said softly.

'We won't do it that way at all.'

Disbelief scored her heart. 'You can't make me stay married to you. That's insane.'

'Insane is what you planned to do. Insane is planning to hide your pregnancy and baby from me. Hell, Skye, I cannot believe you thought, for one moment, that I wouldn't find out.'

'How would you have?' she snapped. 'This was just bad luck. If I hadn't passed out…'

His eyes glittered with anger. 'Yes?'

Skye's cheeks were pale. 'You would never have known. Ever.'

'Because you were going to disappear into thin air and hide from me?' He moved closer, his expression menacing. 'And what if you met another man? Would you have married him? Raised my child with him? Would you have let my child, the Vin Santo heir, grow up with no idea of who he is? From where he comes?'

Skye was as white as a sheet and, in the part of Matteo's brain that was working, he recognised that he should ease up. That he should give her a moment to breathe and reach her own conclusions. Only, Matteo had rebuilt the family empire by sheer determination alone and easing up on any of his adversaries was not something he believed in doing.

And Skye *was* his adversary—his enemy—not just by blood, but now also by deed. How could she not be, given the deception she'd been willing to practice?

'Answer me, damn it!' he demanded, and when she didn't respond he grabbed her around the waist, pulling her body to his. Her lips parted on a wave of shock and he took advantage of the surprise, driven by a soul-deep instinct. He ground his mouth to hers, lashing her with his tongue, stirring her into the kind of frenzy that had typified their short, super-heated marriage.

It wasn't just about possessing her. He wanted to possess all of her, to mark his claim on her as his wife, and as the mother of his baby. He wanted to claim their child. 'This is my baby.'

Skye was frozen with shock but it didn't last long. The second Matteo's lips touched hers she was flashing back into the past through the days of their marriage, the nights of their passion, the need that had always defined them. She was losing a battle to the only truth she could rely on—sensual need.

'Would you have raised him with another man?' He asked the question straight into her mouth so that she heard the words in the depths of her soul and felt his pain as though he'd touched her there. But he didn't break their kiss, making it difficult for Skye to answer.

'This is my child.' The statement was filled with judgement. 'And you are my wife.'

Skye made another sound, a mix between a groan and a sob, a sound of desperate emotion and pain, of acknowledgement and regret.

'I won't let you go. Not now.'

His hands moved inwards, finding her still-flat stomach. He ran his fingers over her and he ended their kiss, moving away, looking at her with eyes that were cold despite the raging intimacy they'd just shared. Despite the heat in Skye's blood, her cheeks, the awareness that fired in every part of her body.

'Come home with me.'

It was not a question, yet Skye still wanted to fight. 'It won't work.'

Matteo's eyes glittered. 'Of course it will.'

'Because our last attempt at marriage was such a success?' Skye scoffed, turning away from him so that she could take a moment to get her blood pressure under control, so that he wouldn't see the way she was trembling.

'I will not let you take my child from me. I will raise it on my own, or you can choose to be a part of his life.'

'How c-can you even say that?' she stammered, spinning around to face him head on. 'No court would *ever* award you full custody!'

Matteo's eyes narrowed. 'Do you know who I am?'

A shiver ran down her spine; adrenalin pumped in her body.

'Do you know what I will do to get what I want?'

Skye's heart stammered in her chest. He'd married her for a stupid piece of real estate—an ancient hotel long since shut down; a building in the middle of Rome in which she had no interest. Matteo's determination to get what he wanted was indeed a force to be reckoned with.

To underscore his intent, he added, 'I will not rest until my child is in my home, being raised by me. Here. In Venice, where he belongs. For more than a thousand years, Skye,

Vin Santos have lived on this island.' He pointed downwards, as if to indicate the ancient marshes on which the city was built. 'We are as much a part of Venice as Venice is of us. The child you carry in your womb is of me, of Venice, and this is where he should be. I will not let you take him.'

Skye shook her head, but fear was filling her all the way to the top of her heart.

Was he right? Could he, in fact, take their baby?

She needed to speak to a lawyer, and fast.

'If you fight me, I will spare no expense and I will stop at nothing.' His teeth were bared, his expression vibrating with passionate resolve. 'I will make your life hell, and you will wish, one day, that you'd never met me. And that you'd never had my child.'

Skye was shaking. She was furious! She closed the distance between them on autopilot, lifting a hand and cracking it across his cheek.

'How dare you?' she demanded heatedly, watching as red spread across his cheek from where flesh had connected—hard—with flesh.

'I told you,' he said with a look of cold indifference. 'I will stop at *nothing* to get what I want.'

'And you want our child,' she said, turning her face away, looking towards the door of the hospital.

'*Si.*' Silence cracked between them, angry and vicious. Matteo broke it, forcing himself to be completely honest. To lay out for his wife the truth of their situation. 'But I also want you.'

Skye's stomach flopped instinctively—reflexively— against her judgement and certainly without her consent. 'Why?'

'Because you are my wife,' he said with a shrug, as though it made complete sense. 'And I like that you are my wife. I want you back in my bed, like you should have been all along. There is a silver lining to this mess, no?'

'God, Matteo! How can you think about sex right now? How can you think I'd ever climb back into your *bed* after this? You're blackmailing me in the most hateful way! And I hate you! I hate you!'

'Yes,' he said with a decisive nod, his eyes narrowing. 'But are you not the one who said that hate and love are easily interchanged?'

'I will *never* be dumb enough to love you again. You disgust me.'

His laugh was a sharp dismissal. 'You desire me. Hate does not disqualify lust. *Si?*'

Shame flooded Skye. How could it be true? How could she feel such a strong physical attraction to Matteo, even after all that she knew of him? This man was a total bastard—he was nothing like the man she'd thought she'd married. He'd used her then and he was using her now.

She had very little pride left. And suddenly she had very little will to fight. She lifted her eyes to his, but there was a lingering shred of defiance in them from deep within her. 'Hell will freeze over before I sleep with you again.'

His laugh was mocking. 'You'll be begging me to take you in no time.' He dropped his mouth to hers. 'And I'm going to enjoy it, Mrs Vin Santo.'

There was anger in the depths of her toffee-coloured eyes. 'I swear to you, Matteo, I will never beg for you again.'

His laugh was dismissive. 'We'll see.'

Skye toyed with the necklace, pulling it from side to side, sliding the small locket from one slender shoulder to the other as she stared out at the setting sun.

She wondered, absentmindedly, if her flight had already left. Without her on it, taking with it her dreams of escape. Of freedom. Of a whole new world and life far, far away from Matteo Vin Santo and all his lies.

It was strange being back in the villa. Nothing had changed, yet everything was different.

The last time she'd been here, it had been with an air of delight. With pleasure, excitement. adoration and love. With lust, too. She had been a newlywed and life had been so simple. For, what reason could her powerful billionaire husband have for tricking her into marriage? They were both independently wealthy; he was a renowned ladies' man and there had been no advantage to him in marrying someone like her unless he'd fallen as utterly head over heels in love as she had.

And that had been so easy to believe!

He'd played the part perfectly. How could she have been so fooled by him? He had looked at her and everything had made sense. How had he not felt that?

Her stomach lurched as she remembered their wedding night. The beautiful anticipation of that moment of first possession. For the month they'd dated, he'd insisted on waiting, despite the fact she'd begged him to take her night after night after night.

She saw it now for what it was—another part of his callous, calculated plan. He'd manipulated her inexperience and desire. She had been the one who'd pushed for a quick engagement. He'd withheld the sexual satisfaction she'd been desperate for, knowing it would lead to a fast-track wedding.

What was that expression? Marry in haste, repent at leisure…

To be back in his house, pregnant with his baby, still wanting him but so completely out of love… What a nightmare it was.

Worse, he was right. His body still had the power to make all her will-power crumble. How she hated him for that!

A noise behind her had Skye tilting her head, her dark hair falling like a curtain across her shoulder.

'Dinner's ready.'

His voice was unrecognisable. It was so businesslike. So cold.

She turned away, rejecting him and his closeness, her eyes running across the golden sky, seeking warmth from its light. 'I'm not hungry.'

'I don't give a damn.'

Skye swept her eyes shut.

'You are pregnant. You must eat.'

'I'll eat when I want to. When I'm hungry.' She lifted her legs, curling them against her chest, resting her chin on her knees. She heard Matteo draw closer but didn't risk looking at him.

'Are we going to quarrel about everything?'

Skye stared straight ahead. 'I'm not quarrelling with you.'

'If that were the case you'd already be on your way downstairs for dinner.'

Skye didn't respond.

'Melania has prepared your favourite. She will be disappointed if you don't at least make an appearance.'

'That's not fair,' Skye said softly. Using her affection for his housekeeper to push her into doing what he wanted was a low trick. Then again, why would she expect him to play fair? Matteo had proven, again and again, that he would do whatever it took to get his way.

'What isn't fair?'

'You know I'd never disappoint Melania,' Skye said without meeting his eyes.

'You and she seemed to have a special bond.' Speculation stirred in the depths of his eyes.

'I guess she liked having someone in the house who wasn't a psychopath.' The insult came out on a sigh of frustration. She stood, curving her hands over the balustrade, her eyes following a gondola as it moved slowly down the canal beneath them.

Her frustration was largely aimed at herself. How had this happened? She'd come to Venice with a simple plan. And she'd been so close to freedom. If only she hadn't fainted! If only he hadn't seen!

She swept her eyes shut again, inhaling deeply. 'I'll be down soon.'

Apparently satisfied, he stalked out of the room without a backward glance, leaving Skye all alone.

CHAPTER FOUR

'DO YOU SEE these paintings, Matteo?'

Matteo's eight-year-old eyes followed the direction of his nonno's finger, nodding thoughtfully as he studied the curious artwork. 'What are they?'

Nonno's smile was rich with pride. 'They were painted by a student of Modigliani—you can see his style in the faces, no?'

Matteo nodded, though he had no idea who Modigliani was and what about the faces was reminiscent of his work. Nonetheless, he understood that the information was being imparted with gravitas and importance. He also knew that if he nodded, and at least appeared to know, it would impress his grandfather—and impressing the tall, smartly dressed man had become very important to Matteo in the six months since he'd come to live with him.

'He would spend summers here, at this very hotel, every year, and leave a painting as a gift—in lieu of payment. It is how your great-great-great-grandfather managed to collect so many of the pieces.'

'Modigliano?' Matteo prompted.

Nonno hid his smile. 'Modigliani's student,' he corrected.

'Are they valuable, Nonno?'

'Valuable, yes.' Nonno's eyes narrowed. 'But they are not for selling. They are for keeping and remembering.

One day they will be yours, for you to keep and look after, and then to pass on to your son, and his son, and so forth. They are part of our family legacy, Matteo. That is their true value.'

Matteo's thirty-two-year-old eyes fell on the same painting, studying the angular face, the bright colours and the eyes that seemed to follow him about the room. Thank God his grandfather had had the foresight to strip the hotel of its artwork before the bank had claimed them as assets of the hotel and included them in the degrading fire sale.

'Ah, *signora*!' Melania's voice cracked through his reverie. He turned in time to see his wife pulled into an enormous hug by his housekeeper—a woman who had never shown him any degree of warmth or affection but apparently adored Skye. 'I'm so happy you are home!'

Skye's face drained of all colour but she covered it quickly. 'It's lovely to see you again, Melania. How have you been?'

'Busy, busy. Here, come, sit. I make you risotto.' Melania leaned closer so that Matteo had to hold his breath to hear what she said next. 'And canoli for dessert, *si*?'

'Oh, thank you.' Skye nodded, moving towards the table. Matteo watched as she pulled a seat out and arranged a napkin on her lap, all without meeting his eyes.

Her indifference infuriated him.

So too her air of cold detachment, when he knew how heated she was. He'd felt her heat—even in the hospital it had burst between them, flaring up out of nowhere. But now she had her long hair scraped back into a simple braid that ran down her back, the thick fringe sitting in silent judgement of him, and dressed in clothes that had been hers *before*. Clothes that had been left, hanging in her wardrobe, all the weeks that she had been away...

'So, Skye,' he drawled, waiting until she was settled before taking the seat opposite. He kicked back in his chair a little, his eyes unable to hide their mocking as they latched to hers. 'What exactly *was* your plan?'

She didn't pretend to misunderstand. 'It seems irrelevant now.'

His expression was unchanged. 'You were going to fly off into the Australian sunset?'

Her eyes flew to his, shock holding her body rigid. 'How did you—?'

'How did I know?' he interrupted scathingly. 'Your handbag had your ticket. So this was going to be a fly in, fly out divorce?'

She swallowed, the slender column of her throat moving visibly as she tried to keep her calm. 'Was I supposed to spend the weekend?' she fired back sarcastically, reaching for a water glass and sipping from it without shying away from his look. 'Did you want to take me sightseeing? One last ride down the Grand Canal?'

'Given that you're carrying my child, I would have expected a degree of consultation, yes. Of course, knowing your father as I do, I'm not sure why I am so surprised.'

She looked away, his statement instantly chastening her and angering her in equal measure. But she had no reason to be cowered by him. Not after what he'd done. 'That brings us to the important point, doesn't it? If you'd been honest with me from the beginning, we wouldn't be in this situation,' she pointed out.

'And because you think I lied, you felt it appropriate to repay me by keeping my child from me?' he demanded, reaching for the serving spoon and passing it to Skye.

'You did lie.' She took the implement, avoiding an accidental brush with his fingers as though they contained the plague. 'And this wasn't about repaying you.'

'No? So why not tell me about the baby?'

Skye stared at him long and hard, then shook her head.

How could she answer that without admitting how much she'd loved him? Without telling her husband that his betrayal had broken her heart? Not just once, but every morning when she'd had to wake up and remember, anew, that he wasn't in bed beside her.

Pride kept her silent on that score. That he'd hurt her was bad enough—giving him the satisfaction of knowing just how badly was something she wanted to keep all to herself.

'Why not speak to me about the hotel in the first instance?' She pushed back, scooping a moderate amount of risotto onto her plate and sitting back in her chair. 'If you'd told me you wanted it, if you'd offered to buy it, I would have given that thought.'

'And you might have said no,' he responded, the words hardened by the long years he'd spent trying to get the hotel back. 'How did you learn the truth?'

'I asked our family lawyer about it,' she said quietly. 'He told me *all* about the feud with Dad. The fact you'd tried to buy the hotel. That Dad had said no. That you'd threatened to destroy him. That you'd "make him pay".' The threat sent a shiver running down Skye's spine. Marrying her would indeed have been a punishment to her father, had he lived to see it.

'That same lawyer would have stopped you from selling to me.'

Skye swallowed, silently admitting that there was truth in that. Had she not loved Matteo, would she have sold an asset to a man reputed to be ruthless and selfish just because he wanted it? Would she have sold a damned thing to someone who'd been a sworn enemy of her father? She shrugged, feigning uncertainty. 'You don't know that. I certainly didn't.'

'I knew it,' he said, the words hardened like steel.

'So, what? You decided to seduce me, to propose to me, to make me believe I was in love with you? To take my virginity? And all so you could get me to sign some stupid hotel over to you?'

He turned his face away, his profile resolute. 'The hotel that you disdain means the world to me. Losing it was not an option.'

'Oh, go to hell,' she snapped, scraping her chair back and standing jerkily. 'So that makes this okay? Me being collateral damage is something you can make your peace with because you wanted the hotel?'

He compressed his lips, studying the slender silhouette of her figure, backlit by the evening light.

'It should never have been sold. I had to return it to my family. It was my duty.'

Skye's eyes feathered closed, her lashes forming two dark half-crescents against her cheeks. But it was confirmation—confirmation she didn't really need but somehow was useful to have. It was something to hold tight to her chest, to warn her from letting him anywhere near her heart ever again.

'It was all a lie to you. A game.' She bit down on her lip, the reality one that even now she found she couldn't quite face.

He stood and she followed his movements with eyes that were huge with her hurt.

'Not all of it.' The words were deep and sensual and should have been a warning.

But Skye was too upset to use her brain, so she glared at him angrily and prompted, 'No? You're saying you did feel *something* for me?'

'Oh yes, *cara*. I felt something for you. You cannot fake what we shared.'

And the penny dropped with insulting clarity. 'For God's sake, Matteo.' She spun away from him, moving across the room, staring out at the water beneath them. But her heart was beating at triple speed and blood gushed through her body so fast, so loudly, that she could hear its demanding torrent inside her ears.

He came to stand behind her, his words whispered into her ear. 'I hadn't expected you to be innocent.'

Skye's eyes dropped shut. That night—that beautiful night! How tainted it was now by the knowledge she was forced to overlay on the experience. It hadn't been special and wonderful; it had been fraudulent. A deception. A lie.

'Yeah, well, I was. Innocent and stupid.'

'Why were you stupid?'

She swallowed and shook her head. But it was a mistake. He was still so close that the simple gesture brought her cheek against his chest. She moved away, a small sound of protest on her lips.

'I should have seen through you.'

Matteo didn't respond. He watched her from the small distance she'd carved out; saw the way her head was held straight, her shoulders squared, begrudgingly admiring her for the courage she demonstrated again and again.

'I'm so angry with myself. And with you!' She spun around, forgetting how close he was. But there was nowhere else for her to go—her back was against the wall, literally and figuratively. 'Did you really think I'd be so stupid in love with you, or so sex-fogged, that I'd forget to engage my brain when I signed important legal papers?' She rolled her eyes. 'I mightn't be any good at spotting cheating bastards, but I've been taught to read contracts with care before adding my signature. Even contracts prepared by my "loving" husband.' She spat the last words as a final insult. Her breath was tearing from her chest, making her whole body shift with each intake.

'But I will give you the hotel,' she said after a long, tense silence. 'I will give it to you without strings, right now. If you accept this marriage is over.'

His laugh was a dry sound. 'No.'

'You want the hotel…'

'You think I want it more than *my child*?' His eyes narrowed and there was a dangerous anger in them.

'Yes,' she said simply, her expression filled with the sadness of that truth. 'I think you are obsessed with getting the hotel back. To the exclusion of any kind of human decency or behaviour.'

His eyes darkened with intensity. 'The rules of the game have changed now.'

'Game?' she returned with undisguised fury. How could he refer to their marriage in such a cavalier fashion? She had loved him and he'd broken her heart. Anger bubbled through her.

He spoke as though she hadn't. 'My child will inherit the hotel regardless of what happens to you and me. It will be back in the Vin Santo family one way or another. That is, and always has been, my primary concern.' His eyes narrowed. 'And, in the meantime, we are married. What's yours is mine, no?'

She ground her teeth together. 'You've just got everything worked out, haven't you?'

'Not quite everything,' he said thoughtfully, taking a step towards her. A step that spoke of danger, desire and needs that had long been denied. 'I still don't know how we're going to raise a child together when we cannot be in the same room without arguing at the top of our lungs.'

Colour filled Skye's cheeks. 'I'll do whatever I need to make sure my child is happy. Even pretending to put up with you.'

His laugh sent shivers of danger dancing down her spine. 'And will you put up with this…?' he asked, taking another step towards her and brushing his lips over hers so that he felt the shiver that made her whole body tremble.

'Will you make the most of our marriage by enjoying the one thing that is good about it?' he prompted, sliding his fingers under the waistband of her shirt, connecting with the softness of her flesh.

A husky moan dropped from Skye's mouth. She closed her eyes, unwilling to see the triumph in Matteo's expression that she knew would be there. If she were to admit how badly she wanted this, and him, he would have every right to gloat.

How could she still desire him, even after what he'd done? He'd proven himself to be the worst kind of bastard, yet her body, her treacherous, hungry, body was his for a song.

'No,' she heard herself say, and practically groaned at the word. 'And I know you won't force me.'

He froze, every line in his body like iron. 'Force you? *Dio!*' He stepped back and it was as though ice water had doused them both. 'Of course I am not going to *force* you. What the hell do you think I am? A savage?'

She tried to summon her anger. To rally it to her defence. But there was only sadness now. Grief and despondence at how much she had lost—and the minefield that lay before them.

'I think you're a horrible person,' she said softly. 'I think you're capable of anything. And I hate you.'

'You think I'd force you into my bed?'

'You've forced me into this marriage,' she whispered. 'How is it any different?'

He spun away from her, stalking to the table and sipping his wine. She could see from the set of his shoulders, the straightness of his spine, that she had upset him. Good. Let him feel some of the darkness she was contending with.

'You married me of your own free will,' he said, without turning to face her. 'You chose this life. I am simply holding you to that commitment.'

His logic was both undeniable and astounding all at once. 'I chose a life that was based on lies...'

'Yes, yes, so you've said. But when did I lie?' He spun around, his eyes pinning her to the spot, his question raking her heart over steaming hot coals.

'The whole time! You…'

'Yes?' he prompted. 'What did I say to you that wasn't true?'

Skye opened her mouth, staring at her husband, her mind drawing an absolute blank. 'It was nothing you said, not specifically. It was *everything* you pretended to be.'

'And what was that?'

'Someone who loved me.' She whispered the words, the hurt in her heart a weight she couldn't dispense with. She was glad, in that moment, that she'd never told him the true grief of her upbringing, the loneliness that had lived inside her for as long as she could recall. A loneliness borne of being utterly unloved and unwanted that had only finally eased when she'd met Matteo.

For the first time in her life she'd felt special. Cossetted. Adored. Wanted for who she was, for all of herself.

What an easy target she'd been for him!

'Did I say that?' he queried, the words a simple question. He could have no concept of how cutting they were. Of how cold and cruel.

Skye nodded, but her mouth drew downwards.

Had he ever said those three little words? She had said them often, so often, and she had meant them each time. Had she thought she could love him enough for both of them? Had she thought it would mean something if she kept saying it? That it would make it true and right?

'No.' She whispered the word, grief bringing the sting of tears to her throat. 'You never said it. But you must have known that I just presumed…that I thought you loved me.'

'Love is irrelevant,' he snapped impatiently. He'd been in love before and he hadn't enjoyed the experience one bit.

'Not to me! Loving you, wanting you, it was all tied up in one for me.'

He prowled closer, his eyes holding hers. He stopped right in front of her, so close that she could feel the warmth emanating from his body—a warmth that was at complete odds with the coldness of his heart. 'There is no love here, *cara*. It is best that you accept that and take what I'm willing to offer.'

'And what's that?' she muttered, her heart cracking irreparably.

'A place in my bed. And a promise to pleasure you in all the ways I know you love...'

Matteo's words, his stunningly arrogant 'offer', stayed lodged in Skye's head, chasing itself around, burning through her blood, making her body super-charged with a desire that she resented fully.

The problem was that he had always been an incredible lover. Of course, she had no other point of reference, but she'd always found herself tipping over the edge of pleasure, time and time again. He had learned her body's ways so quickly, supplicating her to him with insulting ease. He had been able to touch her breasts and bring her to orgasm; he had kissed her most private, sensitive parts and she'd fallen apart, piece by piece, until she was broken and rebuilt in an image of passion and need.

He had woken her by moving over her, pushing inside her, stirring her to wakefulness from within, his body commanding hers effortlessly. He'd taught her so much about desire, need and sensual heat.

He had been gentle when she'd needed it, and demanding and firm in a way that had raised every single goosebump on her body. He had kissed every square inch of her flesh, branding himself on her in a million different ways.

And she had always wanted him.

But now, with her hormones in a state of rampant disarray, desire was thick in her veins, threatening to weaken her.

Worse, threatening to lead her to him.

Skye flipped over in the bed, staring at the wall across the room with its ornate wallpaper that she could just make out in the moonlit darkness of the room.

Tears that she'd held at bay all night were closer to the surface now, wetting her eyes and thickening her throat. The wall grew fuzzy before her eyes as grief enveloped her. She pressed a hand to her stomach, breathing deeply, imagining their baby inside her.

How she'd wanted this pregnancy! For the most part, they'd taken precautions, but not every time. And, on those occasions, Skye had wanted a baby to be the result more than she could ever have said.

And she'd got her wish, only the joy she'd anticipated was nowhere to be seen.

The discovery, after leaving Matteo, that they'd created a baby together had presented a whole new world of problems. For, almost immediately after, reality had descended on her like a hurricane. It might have taken two of them to create a baby, but there wouldn't be two of them raising it.

She'd be alone.

Again.

Like always.

Yet not alone, because there would be a baby to care for. A baby she would love with all her heart. She'd love it enough for both of them, and she'd make sure the baby grew up to be kind and smart, adored and loved.

And her child would never be capable of acting like Matteo had!

Skye was determined that she would do everything right and give the baby all the love she'd never known. As well as stability and adoration, support and acceptance. She'd only known the baby to be inside her for days before she'd begun to make wholesale changes to her life and lifestyle.

She didn't want to raise her child as the heir or heiress to a billion-pound fortune—let alone two! She didn't want them to equate wealth with luck or success. While she wanted her child to have everything it needed in life, Skye knew first-hand that true needs weren't based on financial wealth. Not beyond the immediate concerns, in any event. A roof over one's head, a bed, enough food not to feel hungry... Once these things were taken care of, what more did one need?

She'd always had more than she needed, materially. But when it came to love?

She had been starved in the cruellest of ways.

A tear slid out of one eye, landing with a thud onto the silk pillow beneath her.

She'd been such a perfect target for Matteo's plans—what an easy deception it had been for him to weave. He had lied to her but, oh, she'd been begging for the lie.

For the love.

She'd been so desperate for anyone to love her that she hadn't stopped for a moment to question a single, damned thing. She'd learned, years earlier, that fairy tales didn't exist...so why had she let herself forget that so easily?

CHAPTER FIVE

Two years earlier

HE WAS, WITHOUT a doubt, the most stunning man Skye had ever seen. Her eyes kept seeking him out, even when she knew she should have been paying better attention to the people she was locked in conversation with. After all, this party was for her family's charity, and she was the sole surviving member of the Johnson fortune.

How their ranks had dwindled! From her great-grandfather who'd had six children, to her grandfather who had raised four, and then to her father, who had come along with his inability to commit, his incessant cheating, his determination not to settle.

Skye had been the result of an affair with an air hostess and, had her grandfather never intervened, she doubted her father would have known she existed, far less taken an interest in her upbringing.

She had cousins, of course. But, while they'd inherited million-pound fortunes, it was Skye alone who'd been left the reins of the business empire.

Undoubtedly because no one had realised how quickly her father would die—his skiing accident had been a completely unexpected death. Weeks later, her grandfather had died. The rumours spoke of a broken heart—but Skye suspected it had more to do with his daily habit of over-indulgence in whisky.

She'd become a billion-pound heiress at nine years of age, and a childhood always marred by neglect and disinterest had descended into a barren wasteland devoid of human contact. Boarding school, where she'd found it hard to fit in; a great-aunt who'd tolerated Skye for the briefest stints possible during school holidays, and generally only when a nanny couldn't be found to care for her.

Her eyes flicked sideways and landed straight on his face. He was watching her. A *frisson* of something new and intriguing glanced across her spine.

'We're on track to open the children's hospice by Christmas,' the charity's chairman Mr Wu said, his round face beaming.

'That's very good.' Skye nodded. Generally, she was passionate about the children's foundation. It had been one of the initiatives she'd launched when she'd turned twenty-one and had taken control of her family's assets. It was then that she'd begun to attend the board meetings—despite her CEO's misgivings. Gradually, she'd taken more and more of an interest in the running of the business, and had even planned to enrol in law school at some point to augment the corporate education she was gaining through her involvement with the company. The children's work had long been at the fore of her mind, yet she found it almost impossible to focus on the discussions in that moment.

His eyes were so dark they were like granite. She'd never seen anything quite like it. His dark hair, thick and raven's black, was brushed back from his brow, and his face was strong and angular. Handsome? She couldn't have said. Striking, definitely, and utterly breath-taking. It wasn't that he was good-looking as much as he had an indefinable appeal. An attraction that slammed into her from the other side of the room.

Then, there was his body. Broad-shouldered, tall, he looked like an ancient warrior. She could easily imagine him in metal armour, running into battle, his autocratic face determined, his mouth set in a grim line of reckoning.

A shiver ran all the way down her spine and her nipples peaked against the gauze fabric of her gown.

Her cheeks had a guilty, self-conscious flush as she trained her attention back on Mr Wu, listening with determination now, forcing herself to nod and comprehend even when her brain was trying to record if his hands were as large and dominant as the rest of his body. More so, had he been wearing a wedding ring?

The thought came to her out of nowhere. Her blush deepened. Her temperature was skyrocketing—she felt as though she could spontaneously combust at a moment's notice.

Mr Wu made a joke and she laughed, but she couldn't have repeated it for a billion pounds.

It was at least an hour later—an hour filled with meaningless chit chat and forced laughter, an hour in which her eyes had mercilessly followed his progress around the room—when Skye finally found herself face to face with him.

The man who had become rapidly an absolute obsession for her.

'We meet at last.' His voice was better than she could have imagined. The words were husky, thick with a foreign accent. Italian? Greek?

Whatever, they sounded like sunshine and seduction and drove everything but desire from her mind. Skye's lips parted, her eyes flew wide and her mouth was dry—her tongue too thick possibly to admit speech.

It was a completely unfamiliar impulse, but her fingertips tingled with a desire to lift to his chest; to touch him for herself.

Perhaps he felt the same thing because his hand caught hers and lifted it to his lips.

'I'm Matteo Vin Santo,' he said, his eyes probing hers, waiting for a reaction.

There was none—not one of recognition anyway. Skye's father had died before he could tell her the whole sordid history with the Vin Santos, and her grandfather so soon afterwards. Who would have enlightened her about their ancient grudge?

Nobody.

So Skye smiled, a smile of pure, innocent curiosity. A smile that was like a lamb willingly heading towards its own slaughter.

'Skye Johnson.'

'I know.' His wink was slow and deliberate; its effect was marked. Her stomach swooped with instant awareness.

'My reputation precedes me, huh?'

'The place has your name on the door.' His grin was devilish.

'Sorry about that. They insisted.'

'They tend to do that when you donate millions of pounds.' Another wink. Skye's whole body winked back. She felt her insides squeeze with needs she'd never known she possessed and her heart rolled in her chest.

'Ah. Occupational hazard, then,' she managed to murmur, surprised that she could sound normal and calm when her chest was hammering with the force of a very localised typhoon.

'The cost of philanthropy.' His eyes roamed her face thoughtfully, and Skye felt as though he was seeing all manner of secrets and thoughts. All of the things she usually kept wrapped up, tight in her chest.

And she didn't even mind.

'I suppose I'll learn to live with it.' She smiled at him. He smiled back. Her heart clicked into a new gear.

'You know, it's all very refined and elegant,' he said, with obvious disapproval despite the compliment. 'But I'd kill for an actual meal. I don't suppose you'd join me for dinner, Skye Johnson?'

Skye blinked, her expression clouding with doubts for the briefest of moments, and then she nodded. 'I suppose I would,' she murmured, not even questioning the familiarity when he reached down and laced his fingers through hers.

'Let's go, then.'

Perhaps it was her broken sleep the night before. The dreams that had tormented her, shaking her whenever she'd felt close to sleep. Perhaps it was the memories that those dreams had invoked, little shards of the past that had dug painfully into her sides all night, reminding her of what a fool she'd been.

Perhaps it was the way her heart had been tripping back into love in her sleep, against her wishes, reminding her of how she'd felt when first they'd met. Of the way he'd smiled and she'd answered. Of how simple it had all seemed, and of how right it had felt.

Whatever the reason, the second Skye laid eyes on Matteo the next morning she felt as if she'd been pounded by a sledge hammer. He was dressed in a navy-blue suit with a crisp white shirt open at the neck to reveal the thick column of his neck, the dark hairs curling at the base. She had to pause just inside the kitchen door—to brace herself physically before moving deeper into his atmosphere.

How absurd. There was no such thing as 'his' atmosphere. There was only air, and it belonged equally to both of them. Never mind that he changed the feeling of everything simply by being in it—simply by existing.

His eyes lifted to hers, roaming her face, seeing everything she wanted to keep hidden, just as he had that first night they'd met. No doubt he saw the bags under her eyes and the pallor of her skin.

Good.

Let him see how miserable she was!

Let him feel some of the blame for his hand in that. Except he wasn't capable of such an emotion, was he? Since she'd returned to Venice, he'd been unremorseful and unapologetic.

'I wasn't sure what you are eating,' he said conversationally, as though there was nothing awkward about being back in his home more than a month after she'd left, presuming she'd seen the last of him and it for ever. 'I had Melania prepare an assortment of things.' He nodded towards the platter in the centre of the table. Skye's attention drifted to it and her stomach gave a little lurch of nausea.

'Just coffee,' she said, hoping she wasn't about to experience her first bout of morning sickness and vomit all over the tiled floor. Then again, she might get his expensive designer shoes in the process, so there would be some consolation…

'Are you able to drink coffee in your condition?'

Skye's nod was terse. 'A cup a day is fine,' she said. 'Far more risk if I don't have it.'

'To the baby?' he enquired with interest.

'To whomever denies me.' The words were delivered without a hint of humour yet Matteo smiled, dipping his head forward so that she saw only the quickest flicker of amusement on his face before he stood and moved into the kitchen area.

She watched as he retrieved the pot, pouring a good measure into one of the mugs and carrying it over to her. His eyes held hers as he passed it forward but this time, when she tried to carefully manoeuvre her fingers so that she avoided any skin-to-skin contact, he made it impossible. He placed a hand over hers, curving her fingers around the edge of the coffee cup, his eyes locked to hers in a way that made breathing hurt.

'How did you sleep?' The question was asked with a raw intensity. She ignored it, refusing to buy into the cessation of hostilities.

She'd been manipulated by him once before—she was just going to have to work extra hard to avoid it happening again.

'Fine, thank you.'

'I wish I could say the same,' he muttered.

'Bad dreams?' she responded archly.

'Very, very good dreams,' he corrected, the words silky, his implication clear. Still, he added, 'Memories.'

'Ah.' She cleared her throat and took a step away, retrieving her hand still wrapped around the coffee cup, and telling herself that the warmth spreading through her body had to do with the lure of caffeine rather than anything more threatening to her equilibrium.

She lifted the mug upwards, breathing in its tantalising aroma, and fierce, beautiful memories slashed through her. How many coffees had they shared?

Though their marriage had been short, coffee had been a lifeblood of it, and they'd indulged their mutual obsession often. Side by side and, she had thought at the time, in complete harmony. Physically, emotionally and intellectually. How wrong she'd been.

The thoughts weren't helpful. She pushed them aside angrily.

'I have to go into the office today. Just for a few hours.'

Skye didn't turn around. It was a heck of a lot easier to think when she wasn't looking at him. The memories were less forceful. 'Fine,' she said with a nod. 'Why are you telling me?'

Silence.

'I mean, it's not like before, is it?' she asked, the words soft. 'I have no expectation you'll change your schedule for me. In fact, I'd really prefer you wouldn't.'

'It's not like before,' he agreed, coming to stand beside her. 'You are pregnant. The idea of leaving you alone doesn't sit well with me.'

Skye rolled her eyes. 'I'm growing a baby. It's not a particularly high-risk activity.'

'You fell into the canal yesterday,' he reminded her. Unnecessarily. It had taken four showers to wash the smell of Venice out of her hair.

'And I'm still here today,' she said with a shrug. She sipped the coffee, closing her eyes in appreciation as it made its way into her body.

'Does it happen often?'

She shook her head. 'Fainting? That was the fourth time.'

'Why?'

'It's a blood pressure thing,' Skye said, trying to remember the specifics. 'Some women are more prone to it than others. One minute I'm fine, and then I'm all faint, and there are stars in my eyes and the ground rushes up towards me.'

He didn't say anything, which Skye took to mean the conversation was closed. Good. She smiled in his general direction. 'I might drink my coffee in my room,' she said, needing space from him. Distance. Time.

'Aspetti,' he said. 'Wait a moment.' His accent was thicker once more, husky and dark.

She paused, not looking at him. 'Yes?'

'I don't like this.' She heard the frown in his voice. 'I will change my plans. You clearly shouldn't be left alone.'

Panic raced through Skye. 'I'm *fine*!' She spun around to face him, and one look at his expression made her stomach drop. His expression was as determined as she'd ever seen it.

Great.

'Melania is here,' Skye pointed out desperately.

'She has enough to do without playing nursemaid to you.'

'And you don't?' Skye retorted quickly. 'When we were together you were gone twelve hours a day.'

'And you missed me,' he said smoothly.

She rolled her eyes. 'That's not the point I'm making. I only mean that I'm used to you not being here.'

He moved closer. 'It is my baby. And you are my wife. That makes this my responsibility.'

Responsibility. Pain washed over Skye. How long had she felt like a burden? Like she was someone's responsibility and never their joy? How long had she known herself to be cared for out of duty rather than love? The idea that he might be doing so now was galling. And many other things!

She swallowed, but the razor blades in her throat didn't abate.

'You have too much to do. Melania can easily call you if there's a problem.'

'This is not a negotiation,' he said with the ruthless determination she'd come to expect from him. 'I've made up my mind.'

Skye clamped her teeth together, grinding them out of frustration. He obviously wasn't going to listen to reason, but maybe she could use his concern for the baby to get her own way.

'You want to do the right thing? Then go to work. Being around you is definitely no good for my blood pressure.'

He arched a brow and his lips lifted in the hint of a smile. 'I imagine I elevate your blood pressure,' he said silkily. 'And fainting is usually associated with low blood pressure, is it not? So perhaps having me here is going to be just the medicine you need.'

Skye shook her head, but Matteo moved to the table, holding a chair out.

'Sit down, Skye. You're not going to win this, so you

might as well save your breath to argue about something that matters.'

'You don't think my personal freedom matters?' she snapped, staying right where she was.

'I think the baby's safety is our number one priority.'

Chastened, she dipped her head forward. 'I'll be fine.'

'Yes. And I will be here to make sure of it.'

He took his seat at the table and returned his attention to the newspaper, flicking straight to the finance section.

Skye expelled a soft sigh. It was a big house. The fact that he was going to be somewhere in it didn't mean that they'd be falling all over each other. She'd just make a point of staying in her room, or on the rooftop terrace—places where he wouldn't be.

'Okay, whatever.' She shrugged. 'Just remember, there's many months of this to go. That's a long time for you to be out of the office.'

His shrug was pure, sexy indolence. 'I'll be cutting my hours back once the baby is born anyway, so why not start now?'

'Why would you?' Skye demanded, appalled.

'You don't think I will want to spend time with our child? You don't think his or her birth warrants my being here?'

'No!' Too desperate. Too urgent. 'Matteo, this is *my* baby! You agreed to divorce me yesterday. And now you're acting as if we're going to spend every spare moment together for the next eighteen years.'

'At least,' he remarked, his expression droll.

At Skye's obvious panic, he issued a somewhat placatory smile. 'Skye, I had no idea you were pregnant when you came to obtain my signature, as you very well know. Surely you can see that it changes everything?'

'Not for me,' she pointed out caustically. 'I have as little desire to be married to you now as I did then.'

'And I have as much conviction that you are lying now as I did then.'

'Why do you find it so hard to believe that a woman wouldn't want to be married to you? Are you that arrogant, Matteo? Do you really think that after everything you did I'd want to be your wife?'

He sat back in his chair, his eyes resting on her face with curiosity. 'And what did I do?'

Skye's laugh was a hollow intonation. 'Seriously? You want me to catalogue your faults? You've already admitted them.'

A muscle jerked in his jaw. 'I wanted the hotel,' he said with a shrug. 'It changed nothing about our marriage. Nothing about how you felt for me.'

'It changed *everything*! My God, Matteo! You targeted me! I had *no* idea who you were that night but you knew everything about me. I didn't even know about your feud with my family until a little over a month ago. But you did. You knew all about it! You flirted with me and you seduced me, yet it had *nothing* to do with who I am, right? It was all a fake!'

'The passion was not.'

Though it was such a meagre compliment, a tiny crumb of assurance, Skye shook her head dismissively. 'Would you have felt the same way if there was no hotel? Would you have asked me to marry you?'

His eyes gave nothing away. He was all ruthless, dynamic tycoon. The breakfast table might as well have been in a boardroom, for how comfortable he looked behind it.

'What do you want me to say, Skye? We have discussed this. I married you for the hotel. I wish it hadn't been necessary. But this does not mean there weren't certain…benefits to our marriage.'

She dropped her jaw, her eyes clashing with his ruthless gaze. 'I truly can't believe you would stoop so low!'

'I used what means were necessary.' He shrugged his shoulders with apparent unconcern. 'You were all too eager to merge our assets. To give me open slather of your portfolio. That was not my decision, but yours.'

'Yes,' she agreed softly. 'But only because I was in love with you. And I thought you loved me back! Only because I thought our marriage was genuine and your affections were true. If I'd known that the assets were the sole reason you'd proposed then believe me, Matteo, I would have fought you every step of the way.'

'Which is precisely why I had to marry you.' The words were softly voiced.

He stood abruptly, moving around the table. He stopped beside her and crouched down on his powerful haunches so that the fabric of his pants pulled across his strong thighs. She forced herself to look away, but not before the effect of his nearness had imprinted on her consciousness, reminding her of how she had felt pinned beneath those legs, pinned beneath him.

Her mouth was dry, her temperature skyrocketing.

He lifted his fingers to her chin and forced her face back to his, lifting it up so that their faces were level.

'This conversation is redundant. It changes nothing about what we both want now.'

His lips crushed down on hers, shocking her at the same time it answered every single ache that was ripping through her. She surrendered to his kiss even when she knew she ought to fight him. To fight their attraction.

But she was selfish, she was hungry and she had been denied his touch for so long. She needed his touch. It was on the tip of her tongue to whisper the word that was chasing round and round in her mind—*please*—but out of nowhere his words bubbled through her.

'You'll be begging me to take you in no time. And I'm going to enjoy it, Mrs Vin Santo.'

So she said nothing. She kissed him, because she wasn't strong enough not to, but she didn't beg, even when her heart was doing just that.

CHAPTER SIX

SKYE FLIPPED ONTO her back and listened to her meditation even harder, concentrating so much on being relaxed that she became even more agitated when sleep didn't come. And, the more she concentrated on needing to sleep, the harder it became to make peace with the fact that she was still awake, so that she clicked the recording right back to the beginning and focused even harder.

To no avail.

After an hour of breathing deeply, and picturing a still ocean with a single ray of light shimmering across its surface, she was agitated and cranky.

She reached for her phone, silenced the patronising recording and checked the time.

It was just after midnight, and she was wide awake.

With a rustle of the silk sheets, she slipped out of bed, padding across the bedroom to the window. Ancient timber shutters blocked out the noise and lights of Venice. She pushed them outwards—they groaned a little in complaint before opening wide. Just beneath the window was a planter box overflowing with bright red geraniums. They were on almost every window sill in Matteo's villa—though some boasted lavender as well. The fragrance was heady, especially in the spring when an army of bees would swarm across the blossoms, picking them over for sustenance.

Skye reached down and plucked a geranium stalk, twirling it around and then bringing it to her nose. There was an almost metallic fragrance that brought back such memories of her first few weeks in Italy, when she'd picked small bunches and placed them on either side of their bed so that they were the second thing she saw each morning—after Matteo.

He'd teased her for doing it. 'Melania can get you anything you want from the market, you know. Much prettier flowers that will make much bigger arrangements.'

'I like these,' she had insisted with a shrug. 'They're bright and sunny and they grow right outside the window. They're our flowers.'

She had, at the time, liked the way that had sounded. *Ours.* As though the stupid word could infer a degree of seriousness on them that hadn't actually existed.

She tossed the bloom carelessly from the window, leaning forward by a small degree to watch its progress. The air offered little resistance to such a robust bloom. It dragged quickly to the ground, dropping with a soft *thunk* into the water below. It hovered on the surface for a moment, as though looking at her accusingly, before falling further, dropping downwards and disappearing for good.

Even the most beautiful things met their end eventually.

Their marriage should have been one of them.

Their marriage should never have happened, she corrected herself inwardly. That damned hotel! It was one of many properties owned by her family trust. If he hadn't made such an obvious effort to move it to his own possession, she wouldn't have particularly known it existed.

Was there any excuse that could justify what he'd done? Marrying to secure a piece of property?

Sleeping with her—being her first lover as well as her first love?

Could she ever forgive him that duplicity? Did she dare even try?

A warm breeze rustled in the open windows. She angled her face upwards, giving the air full access to her front, letting it loosen her hair, pulling it back from her face. And she breathed in deeply. Geraniums, people, ice-cream, Venice… It was all so familiar.

Her restlessness grew.

She pressed her fingers to her tummy, thinking of their baby. 'Is this your doing?' she whispered. 'Are you making Mummy wake up when it's time to sleep?'

She'd read a book on pregnancy, cover to cover, when she'd first learned of her condition, and it had spoken of pregnancy insomnia—a hormonal condition, not related to the size of the baby so much as the fact it was there, supercharging a woman's blood and body so that sleep became chemically impossible.

She told herself that was the culprit even when she knew, deep down, that it had so much more to do with Matteo's kiss. She sucked in a breath, lifting her fingers to her lips and touching the trembling flesh there.

It had been over in a moment. Just a quick reminder of how he could reduce her to ash and smoke with no effort at all. He had stood afterwards, apparently completely unaffected, and he'd left her alone to eat. To brood. To stew.

And, despite the fact he'd changed his schedule so that he could keep an eye on her throughout the day, she'd barely seen him. He'd been close by at all times, but not in her space.

A fact she should have appreciated…but didn't.

The kiss had stirred something up inside her.

A desire that she had presumed had died with their marriage. A desire that was unwelcome, unwanted and utterly confusing.

Another warm breeze ran across her flesh, spreading goose-bumps with it.

Sleep seemed impossible to grasp and attempting to do

so made no sense. On the spur of the moment, she moved across her room quietly, pulling the door inward gently. She paused, listening for a moment. The house was quiet. Was he asleep?

The image was striking.

He slept naked.

Always naked.

Her heart throbbed inside her chest as her eyes ran down the hallway towards his bedroom—the bedroom they'd shared.

Was he in there now, naked, tanned, virile…? Was he in there, thinking about her?

She forced herself to look away. She had no intention of giving in to her body's physical needs. She wasn't that stupid, or that weak.

She turned in the opposite direction and made her way along the corridor, her eyes skimming over the impressive collection of art—some of it Renaissance, much of it more modern—until she reached the wide stairs inlaid with mosaics. They were as they'd been when the home had first been built, and Skye had always felt a little disrespectful when she'd walked on the practical artwork. She moved upwards with care to the next level of the house, which boasted guest rooms and an impressive library, not stopping to remove a book from the shelves that she'd come to love.

When she'd first arrived in Venice, a newly-wed who'd believed that all the happiness of the world was before her, she'd decided she'd read her way through the books, starting at the top left and moving all the way across, then sliding down a shelf. She'd decided that it didn't matter what she read—history, romance, fiction, non-fiction— they were all stories and she was hungry for them to become a part of her.

She'd read sixteen books. She remembered quite clearly

where she was up to on the shelf. She'd had the last book in her handbag the day she'd gone to Matteo's office. The day she'd read the contracts and started to wonder at the phrasing. The day the penny had finally started to drop.

She'd never finished the story and didn't plan to.

With a determined tilt of her chin, she moved upwards. The staircase narrowed once she turned the corner, and a small window let in a sharp blade of moonlight. She skipped past it quickly, almost surprised that it didn't slice through her with its bright intensity. At the top of the stairs, a narrow door stood closed. She rested her palm against it for a second, steeling herself for what she knew lay beyond.

Even on this side, at the top of the ancient staircase surrounded by darkness, she could picture the rooftop garden. The bougainvillea that seemed to have a life all of its own, clambering across the timber beams, forming a sort of green room. It would be covered in an extravagant blanket of purple flowers, so vibrant that they had always reminded Skye of plums cast from paper. But the bougainvillea didn't have full autonomy amongst the scrambling vines. There was wisteria too, fragrant and heavy with the grape-shaped blooms. They were disarray in the midst of order, greenery and earth in a city shaped by the sea. She had loved the juxtaposition of their wildness against the plain blue sky. She had sat beneath them, reading, sipping iced tea and dreaming of Matteo, feeling the sun on her legs as though it were his hands or his mouth.

There was the plunge pool, tiled and neat, with views over the ocean towards the mainland. She had dipped her body into it whenever the heat had become too much, refreshing herself in its soothing water, propped against the pool coping and staring at the view with a deep sense of gratitude and a very full heart.

It was here that they'd first made love, and it was impossible not to carry that memory with her as she finally pushed the door open and moved onto the terrace. The night had been so perfect; every time she'd been on the terrace its memory had wrapped around her, filling her with a sense of complete disbelief. How had she been so lucky? To have met and fallen in love with a man like Matteo—it was more than she'd ever believed possible. And that had been a good way to feel. It wasn't possible. His love had been a fraud. A fake.

The terrace was dimly lit—only a single lamp now illuminating the ghostly outline of her favourite vines, giving them an ethereal, slightly eerie feel. The stars shone as though heaven had been blanketed by diamonds and there was a splashing noise that drew her reluctant gaze.

Reluctant, because she knew immediately who was creating the noise.

Who else could it be?

This was Matteo's private sanctuary, where he came to escape the hectic speed of the real world. And he'd let her, and no one else, in to enjoy it. At the time, that had flattered her. Now? It was a very cheap price to pay for the hotel he had hoped to steal.

Colour danced along her cheek bones. Angry colour.

How dared he be so beautiful? The moon seemed to caress his flesh, spreading diamond dust over his shoulders and back as he stared out at the view she had loved so much. Droplets of water shivered from his dark pelt of hair, glancing his broad shoulders before slipping lower, over his arms.

Desire swirled in her gut.

Skye ignored it.

This had been a bad idea. A stupid, stupid thought. She took a step backwards, moving towards the open door, needing to put all the distance she could between herself and her husband.

She didn't want to speak to him. She couldn't see any

more of him. Was he wearing bathers? Or swimming naked, as they'd always done in the past?

A husk of breath caught in her throat and she spun, needing distance.

Splashing.

And then his voice, low and commanding. 'Skye.'

She froze, her eyes shut, her lips parted.

Her pulse was a raging torrent of need. Damn it! Why did she feel this for him even when she hated him for what he'd done?

'Turn around.' The words were a command and she wanted to ignore them. She hardened her heart to the power he had over her, or tried to at least. She wanted to run. She wanted to ignore him, to pretend she hadn't heard. But it was obvious she had, and the idea of seeming afraid of him in any way was anathema to Skye.

She turned slowly. She looked around with great care, as one might lift one's eyes to study a solar eclipse, expecting at any moment to be burned by the sight of him.

Only it was less a solar eclipse and more a moonlit fairy tale. The beam of light bounced off him and wisped like a cloud between them, drawing her in, pulling at her as gravity might, if it were silvery and glittered.

She swallowed, taking a step forward without realising it.

He walked through the water in time with her own steps, so that he reached the edge nearest to her at the same time Skye's toes met the grouting. His powerful body ripped him from the water with ease; the water droplets scattered over his flesh, pulling her gaze downward to the chaotic wetness that moved over his chest.

'I couldn't sleep,' she explained, her eyes locked with his even when she knew she needed to look away. The air around them was thick, and it had more to do with their past, their present, than the heat of the balmy summer night.

No, it was the whisperings of their story that was wrapping around them, pulling them back in, and for Skye's part all she could see was the never-ending nature of it all. The love she'd felt for him had turned to hate, but there was still so much love there too. For, having never loved before, not properly, she had given her love to Matteo with no expectation or hope of return.

She had given him her heart for life, and there was no way to take it back.

Despite what he'd done.

And now? A baby that would bind them for ever; the future yawned before her like a minefield of needs she would have to navigate.

She had to do it better.

She had to draw a line in the sand and keep him firmly on one side of it.

But she also needed him. His mouth, his hands, his body. All of him.

Need was all she could hear, and it was tormenting her with the loudness of its demands and the insistence that she indulge it.

With the last shred of will-power she possessed, she smiled—a smile that was sense and reason in the midst of their moonshine madness. 'Are you done?' she asked, unknowingly caustic. 'I thought I'd go for a swim.'

His fingers reached for her, and the second they connected with her she drew a sharp gasp of breath. It didn't help.

'In this?' he asked, reaching for her cotton nightgown, the teasing smile on his lips sucking her further back into the vortex of their past, to a time when that smile had driven her wild. When it had made her feel connected to him and full of pleasure—not just sexual pleasure, but true pleasure at the place she had in his life, and the place he had in hers.

That smile was a dangerous lie. Listening to it would be foolish. And she was no longer foolish. At least, she was no longer so easy to fool.

'No.' A whisper.

'May I?' He held the fabric in his fingers—she held her breath in her lungs. His meaning was impossible to mis-interpret.

Knowing she was playing with fire, that they were on the precipice of a very, very steep ravine, that she was one crazy decision away from falling head-first into it, she nonetheless nodded. Her eyes latched to his as he lifted, so slowly that impatience ran through her, guiding the fabric along her body, brushing it over her flesh as he balled it at her waist, pausing there, his knuckles glancing across her skin. Higher still, he teased the sensitive flesh at the side of her breasts so that she bit down on her lower lip, wondering if he'd touch her and what she'd say if he did.

'Hands up,' he said with a smile that sunk her stomach.

She complied readily, her eyes still clinging to his, as if held there by an invisible magnetic force. She reached for the heavens and he lifted the fabric the rest of the way, leaving her standing before him in just a simple lace thong.

He tossed the fabric aside carelessly, hooking it onto the edge of a sunbed before returning his full attention to Skye.

The moon slid silver across her flesh, across his face, bathing them in the magic of that moment.

'May I?' The same question, but his voice was deeper, huskier, and she wasn't sure what he intended.

She nodded anyway, watching as he pressed his palms to her stomach first, his fingers splayed wide, as if looking for proof of the pregnancy in her abdomen. As if seeking confirmation, his eyes found hers, and she felt the swirl of emotion between them—the hunger, the need, the anger, the betrayal. It was all around her, making it impossible for Skye to know what she felt and what she wanted. Only she knew she shouldn't want this. That she should put an end to what was happening.

His hands moved higher, cupping her breasts, running over her nipples. It was an achingly familiar touch. Though it had been more than a month since she'd been naked with him, she had never forgotten the perfection of this.

It was hard to forget when memories haunted your dreams.

'I want to kiss you,' he murmured, moving his hands back to her hips, holding her still, needing her as much as she needed him. He was wet, his body slick with the pool water. Skye's eyes dropped to his chest. His heart was in there.

The heart that was cold and ruthless and hurtful. The heart she would never hold in her hands, as he held hers in his. She swallowed, danger swirling around her.

Could she sleep with him anyway?

Could she fall back into his bed, knowing that he didn't love her?

Whenever they'd been together in the past she'd truly believed that they'd been making love. That their desire was a physical representation of their emotional commitment. But Matteo had never loved her. She doubted he was even capable of the emotion.

Could she ignore that fact? Could she let sex slowly ease that pain? Wasn't it better than nothing?

'What's stopping you?' she asked softly. But the words were rich with her doubt and uncertainty.

Matteo lifted his thumb, padding it over her lip. 'What do you want?'

Skye's smile was a pale imitation of the real deal. 'You didn't care what I wanted this morning.'

'You wanted me to kiss you then.'

Skye blinked, looking away, swallowing, trying to untangle the knot of her desire and thoughts.

'And now?' she prompted.

His smile was loaded with self-deprecation. 'I can't hear what you want over what I want. I need you to tell me.'

She sliced her eyes back to his face, her breath forced as she struggled to take stock of that moment. 'What do *you* want?' she asked with a quiet intensity.

His face cracked with an unfamiliar emotion. 'I want it to be like it used to be.'

Surprise spread through her, until she realised he was just talking about sex. Again. He wanted her whenever need overtook him. He wanted her willing, compliant body at his command.

Her response was throaty. 'It's not possible.'

He looked as though he was about to say something, but apparently changed his mind. 'Swim with me.'

It wasn't an invitation; it wasn't a command. It was simply an idea, one that moved through her. They'd swum together so often in the past. Was there anything wrong with doing so one last time?

She nodded jerkily, moving closer to the water's edge. Skye dove in with an unconscious grace. The pool wasn't long, only ten metres, but it was very deep. She had always enjoyed trying to swim down and touch the bottom, dragging her fingertips over the smooth tiles, tracing the lines of grout, holding her breath until she'd felt like her lungs might burst. She did so now, gliding right to the base, where it was dark and quiet, and she felt the bottom like it was a touchstone that could take her back.

A touchstone that had the power of rewind. That could slide her through the veils of time into the past. The past where she'd been happy—where she'd believed their marriage to be real.

But it was temporary.

She emerged in the present, the same uncertainty clogging between them, and made her way to the pool edge that overlooked the ocean. It was dark now, only a few cruise ships visible, their bright lights showing the outline of the boats. Matteo swam beside her, bracing himself against the pool, his elbow lightly brushing hers.

Skye didn't move away.

'I've been wondering something,' he said, not looking in her direction.

'Yeah?'

'When did you find out?'

She tilted her head towards his slowly, her eyes running over his autocratic profile, noting the details of his features even as she tried to make sense of the question.

'About the baby,' he clarified, the words deep and husky.

'Oh.' She looked away again. Her face was pale beneath the moon's light. 'A couple of weeks ago.'

He was quiet for a long moment. So long that she wondered if perhaps he hadn't heard or hadn't understood.

'And how did you feel?'

'How did I feel?' she repeated, a frown spreading across her face.

'Yes.' A small sound of impatience coloured the word. 'Were you surprised? Happy? Upset?'

Skye tilted her head back in the water, dipping her hair completely under the surface, brushing her thick fringe back with it. 'All of the above,' she said with a shrug, lifting her head out of the water.

'And when did you decide that you wouldn't tell me?'

Skye pulled a face. 'It's not like I made a decision. I guess…' Her eyes flicked to his for a moment and then instantly jumped away. 'It didn't really occur to me that I *would* tell you.'

'No?' A simple question, but she felt the intensity of feelings that coloured it.

She pushed up straight, staring out at the ocean and wishing she were bobbing on top of it, far from her husband, her marriage, his beautiful home. Far from the desire that lashed her even as she knew she should be more sensible.

'No.'

He said nothing, but she intuited his silent judgement.

'Our marriage was over.'

'Which doesn't change the fact we made a child together.'

Skye nodded softly. 'I was upset.' She returned to the original question. 'That was my first feeling. Devastation. I couldn't believe the timing. If it had been a few weeks earlier…' She shook her head. 'I've always wanted children. Even as a teenager, I imagined myself with a big family. Lots of kids. A loving husband.' She pressed her cheek against her hands, turning to face him. 'A happy family.'

'Like you never had,' he said perceptively.

There was no sense in denying it. She'd told him enough of her upbringing for him to know that she'd been miserable. 'Yes.'

'Are you happy now?'

She shook her head slowly; the tears that sparkled on her eyes were a surprise. 'How can I be?' she whispered. 'I'm trapped. This marriage is everything I don't want. I mean, I can't wait to meet my—our—baby. I know I'm going to love him or her so much. But, Matteo, if you felt *anything* for me at all, ever…if there was anything in your motivation beyond revenge and greed…surely you can see that making me stay married to you is a mistake?'

He made a noise of frustration, closing the distance between them, his hands seeking her hips under water. He pulled her away from the edge of the pool quickly, holding her to his body, his eyes boring down into hers.

'How can you call this a mistake?'

And he kissed her then, hard, desperately, hungrily, with all the need that was thick inside him. He kissed her, and he held her close to him, and then he moved one hand away. She felt his fingers brush against her stomach as he sought the waistband of his swim shorts and pushed them downwards. His legs moved, freeing him of his impediment, and then he was naked against her, his arousal hard to her stomach.

Yearning was like wildfire, advantageous and determined. It flicked over her, demanding her attention and indulgence. It was a force too needy to ignore, and she didn't want to ignore it anyway.

But hurt was too strong to be forgotten, and he had hurt her badly.

'I hate you,' she said seriously, pulling away from him long enough to stare into his eyes, to show him that she meant it. 'This is just physical. It doesn't mean anything.'

A muscle jerked in the base of his jaw. He looked as though he wanted to say something, and for a moment she hoped he would argue; but then he nodded, pulling her to the end of the pool that was shallower so that his feet touched the bottom. And then he brought his mouth back to hers and beneath the water his fingers sought her underwear, pushing them away easily. He had barely removed them before she lifted up, wrapping her legs around his waist so that he could easily slide inside her, deep inside her.

He did so, thrusting slowly at first so that she moaned into his mouth, her fingers lifting of their own accord and tangling in his dark, wet hair.

More tears filled her eyes, thickening in her throat as memories slammed through her. The perfection of this was a cruel irony, given their emotional discordance. Yet she didn't resent it. She was grateful for it. Grateful at least for this connection.

In all her life, it was undoubtedly the most meaningful, even when it meant so very little to him.

She dropped her fingers to his shoulders, digging them

into his smooth, tanned flesh, rolling her hips as he pushed deeper.

He slid his mouth down to her neck, nipping the flesh at its base, moving deeper and faster. She gripped his shoulders as the world began to fade away from her, as pleasure began to eclipse everything else, just as it always had. She tilted her head back, and her breasts surfaced above the water so that he could lean forward and catch one nipple in his mouth, flicking it with his tongue.

Her breasts were so sensitive. It tipped her over the edge. She cried out into the night sky of Venice, the ancient sky with its prehistoric stars; she cried out, she held him and she drifted away on a wave of pleasure, on a moment of perfection. But he didn't let her come back down to earth. Even as she was trembling, he lifted her back, crushing her to his body and moving to the steps; lifting her higher; spinning her so that he could place her bottom on the edge of the pool.

He brought his mouth down to hers, pushing her backwards so that she was lying flat against the tiles that surrounded the pool. His mouth worshipped her, tasting her mouth first, then her breasts, licking the water from them at the same time he layered new needs, wants and memories across her. His tongue teased her stomach and he smiled against her belly, then dragged his mouth lower, to her womanhood, her core of femininity, lashing her once with his tongue so that she moaned and arched her back.

'Tell me what you want,' he invited, the words roughened by emotions she couldn't understand, emotions that did something new to her, something dangerous.

Skye stared upwards, her mind fuzzy, desire thick in her blood.

She wanted her husband. She wanted him kissing her, making love to her; she wanted it all.

You'll be begging me to take you...

'Tell me what *you* want,' she challenged, the words husky, her breath burning in her lungs. She pushed up on her elbows, glaring at him, her cheeks flushed, her eyes sparkling with defiance even as she was riding a wave of pleasure that was robbing her of sanity.

His smile was lightly mocking. 'Isn't it obvious?' And he brought his mouth back to her most sensitive flesh, so that she could no longer think or speak—she could only feel—and she felt *everything*. She felt the cool breeze on her flesh, the night around them; she felt the moon looking down and the stars watching on; she felt his mouth, she felt his hands, she felt her heart, she felt her raging blood.

'Please…' The word escaped her mouth before she could catch it and she bit down on her lip, hating that he had been right. That she had ended up asking him to take her once more. That she was close to begging for him.

He didn't stop.

He didn't gloat, either. And she appreciated that. She arched her back and his hands ran upwards along her sides, holding her steady, and then he pushed away, moving over her, taking her once more, thrusting inside her and answering all the questions she'd hadn't known to ask.

It was perfection, yet it was also so flawed.

As if he could read the thought, even before she knew that she'd had it, he brought his mouth to hers. 'This has always been perfect between us.'

But it wasn't perfect!

It wasn't perfect to want someone so much when it had nothing to do with love.

All the fantasies she'd had about life and relationships and marriage and family and belonging disintegrated. Yet, maybe this was enough.

It felt like enough, being made love to by—no, having sex with—her husband. It was easy to think that everything would be wonderful for ever more.

'It's crazy,' she whispered, but she didn't stop moving beneath him, writhing, feeling, welcoming, needing.

'*Si.*' Speech was impossible as he moved faster, deeper, kissing her in time with his body's movements so that she was dancing to a rhythm all of his making.

She collapsed beneath him at the same moment he exploded and they rode that perfect wave of delight together, neither wanting to contemplate what would come next. Nor what it would mean.

CHAPTER SEVEN

'AND WHAT WE did last night is safe?' His eyes latched to hers over the spread of newspapers, coffee and croissants.

Skye's cheeks flushed at the oblique reference to the way they'd made love by the plunge pool, only metres from where they'd first slept together.

'I think it's a little late to be worrying about unwanted consequences, don't you?'

His smile was just a tight flicker of his lips. 'I mean so far as the baby is concerned.'

She laughed. 'Of course. Do you think sex might pose a threat?'

Dark colour slashed his cheeks. 'I have no clue, *cara*. It is the first time I've slept with a pregnant woman.'

She focused back on the newspaper, the headline swimming before her eyes. 'It's fine,' she said thickly. 'No risk.'

'Good.' He reached across, curving his hands over hers. 'Because I want to do more of that.'

Her pulse thumped heavily in her veins. She kept her attention averted. Didn't she want that too? Well, yes, but there was definitely a risk to *her* if she made a habit of falling into his arms.

'More swimming?' she prompted.

'Not what I meant.'

'I know.' She lifted her face, her eyes locking to his with

a shyness that was at odds with what they'd shared. 'I know what you meant.'

'And I think you want it too.'

She swallowed, focusing on a point over his shoulder. 'I think we have to be careful *not* to do that again.'

His brow furrowed but she didn't see it. 'Why the hell not?'

'You want us to raise this baby together? That's hard enough without bringing sex into it.'

'We're married.' He laughed softly. 'And expecting a baby. Sex is already a part of it.'

She was quiet, uncertain what to say, and he moved the conversation along, his eyes watchful. 'Just think about it.'

She thought about pointing out that she didn't *need* to think about it. That her mind was working this morning, as it hadn't been the night before, and that sex was definitely going to complicate things unbearably.

For her, anyway.

Apparently it had never been an issue for him.

He'd been able to compartmentalise sex from the rest. From the lies. The betrayal.

'It's too complicated.'

He compressed his lips with frustration. 'I think we established last night that *nothing* about that is complicated. It is as easy for us as ever.'

'But your heart's not at risk,' she said pointedly. 'But, for me, having loved you once makes me terrified of being stupid all over again. Of mistaking sex for something else entirely. Especially when you can make my body feel like that.' She stood up uneasily, changing the subject even when her mind was still ticking over the facts, trying to make sense of it. 'It's such a nice day. I'm going to go for a walk.'

He didn't look at her. In fact, he continued to stare straight ahead, almost as though he hadn't heard. She moved towards the door and his voice commanded her to stop.

'Wait a moment.' He stood and she held her breath, wondering if he was going to say something that might change how she felt, while knowing he couldn't. There was nothing. 'I will come with you.'

Exasperation was obvious in Skye's expression. 'That's not necessary.'

'Tell me something, Mrs Vin Santo. Is it only when I kiss you that you listen to reason?' He stood, his intent obvious as he moved towards her. He came so close, and she held her breath, waiting, knowing what was coming. Knowing she could move away, be firm.

She didn't.

She stood her ground and stared right back.

No, she did more than that. She willed him to kiss her. For his kisses didn't only take away her senses and stir her desire. They took away her pain too.

And she longed for that moment of peace. Of clarity and pleasure—of happiness.

'I don't want you trying to swim in the canals again.'

'I'll keep my land legs.'

'Perhaps.' His eyes glinted with determination. 'But I'll be there to make sure of it.'

There really never had been any sense arguing with Matteo. He always got what he wanted. Throughout their marriage, certainly, but even their marriage itself was proof of the lengths to which he'd go to achieve his aims.

She walked beside him, retracing routes that were instantly familiar to her. Paths that she'd travelled often in the past, when she'd been in love and Venice had been the physical representation of that state of mind. When she'd been keen to explore every last crevice of this beautiful city, letting its ancient stories breathe into her.

They passed a *gelateria* and she slowed a little, staring in at the beautifully arranged piles of confectionery, each colourful heap decorated with a piece of fruit or a wedge of chocolate.

'You want some?' he asked, apparently attuned to her every thought.

She bit down on her lip and nodded.

'*Bacio* still your favourite?'

The memory was one of her favourites but the cruel irony of it slapped her in the face.

Kisses.

The *gelato* she'd loved and that he'd teased her with, kissing her as he'd spelled it out, dribbling the ice-cream over her flesh as he'd kissed her everywhere.

'No,' she said quickly, shaking her head to dislodge the recollection. 'Strawberry.'

He arched a brow, perhaps understanding why she was keen to substitute a different flavour. 'If you're sure.'

He approached the vendor and she watched for a moment before turning her attention down the street. It was like so many of the little paths she loved in Venice. The water to one side, the lines of houses built so that they were all attached, though painted in different colours, all shades of yellow and orange, some pale, some bright, with window boxes overflowing with flowers. Some houses had rooftop gardens like Matteo's, and greenery bloomed overhead.

There were not many people in the street, but her eyes landed on a small boy just a little way down. He looked frightened. Her brows drew together as she looked around for an adult who might be accompanying him and saw no one.

She smiled at him encouragingly.

He didn't return it.

He could only stare.

She drew closer on autopilot, and as she got nearer she

noticed new details about him. His clothes were perhaps a size too small. His jeans finished about an inch up from his ankles and his shirt just met his waistband, so that the smallest movement would drive it upwards, separating it and exposing his stomach. His hair was close-cropped.

She paused just in front of him. 'Hi.'

He blinked.

'Are you okay?' she asked in halting Italian. More memories—Matteo in bed, teaching her phrases, laughing at her mispronunciations and penalising her with kisses that made her head spin so that, in the end, she'd longed to say the words incorrectly even when she knew them by heart.

'Yes, madam,' he replied in his own tongue, then said something else. Something too fast and accented for her to understand.

Her smile was apologetic. 'I'm sorry, my Italian is not very good.'

'He said he's never seen anyone like you before.' Matteo's voice came from right behind her. He stood, holding two *gelato* cones. He handed one to her and he passed the other to the child.

Matteo spoke in rapid-fire Italian, but she caught enough of his words to get the gist. 'Eat it. You look hungry.'

The child didn't need to be told twice. He instantly reached for the *gelato*, his grubby fingers wrapping around the cone.

'I wonder what he meant,' Skye said, looking up at Matteo.

Matteo phrased the question to the child, raising his brows at the response.

'He said you are very beautiful, and very fancy.'

Skye's cheeks flushed pink. She stood, giving Matteo her full attention. 'You're making that up.'

'Why on earth would I do that?'

'I don't know. Why do you do anything?'

The little boy's fingers reached out and ran across Skye's forearm, touching her skin gently as he murmured something in Italian. She smiled down at him, not at all concerned by the touch. Matteo, beside her, apparently didn't feel the same. He stiffened noticeably.

'He says you are very soft. Like…'

Skye held her breath. 'Like what?'

'Like a petal.'

She laughed. 'Quite the romantic, huh?' But she sobered at the look of wonderment on the little boy's face. 'Do you think he's okay? Does he need something?'

'He's Romani, most likely,' Matteo said.

'Where are his parents?'

Matteo asked the child, but compressed his lips, apparently disapproving of his wife's involvement in the child's life.

Skye didn't care. As though she could simply leave a young boy—he must have only been six or seven, if that—on the streets!

'His family have a boat near by, he says. He works from here.'

'Works?' Skye's confusion was obvious. 'He's too young to work.'

She crouched down again, dislodging the boy's grip. 'Do you need anything?' she asked in English.

He shook his head, then looked at the ice-cream, and Skye smiled.

But she wasn't convinced. She reached into her bag and pulled out several notes. She handed them to the little boy, making sure his fingers were tight around the paper. 'Take this and go home,' she said softly. 'You should be at school. *Scuola.*'

His eyes were huge. He looked at the amount in his palm and then hugged Skye, so that she laughed. 'Home,' she said gently.

He turned and ran off, his skinny little legs bowed at the knees.

Emotions lurched inside Skye. Damned pregnancy hormones.

'Are you going to rescue every impoverished child you see? If so, might I suggest we avoid St Mark's.'

She threw her husband a look of impatience. 'It's so sad. That poor little boy.'

Matteo shrugged. 'He looked happy enough to me.'

Was it any surprise to Skye that her famously cold-hearted husband hadn't been moved by the sight of the obviously hungry little boy? It was just another mark against him; another proof of his emotional detachment.

They walked in silence for a moment, Skye tasting her ice-cream, enjoying the sweetness and the relief of the cold texture on a very warm summer day. But somewhere near the Rialto Bridge she paused.

'You gave him your *gelato*.'

Matteo nodded slowly. 'So?'

'Because you thought he looked hungry too.' Skye scanned his face. 'Because you *did* care!'

Matteo's expression flashed with emotions Skye didn't recognise.

'And they say you don't have a heart.'

'I have a heart, *cara*,' he promised. And her own stuttered to a stop, thumping hard in her chest. 'And our baby will know that.' He dropped his mouth towards hers and for a second she held her breath, expecting another kiss. *Needing* the gesture that was so simple and so complicated all at once.

But instead he took a bite off the top of her ice-cream, and she laughed instinctively, automatically. 'Hey! I'm eating for two, don't you know?'

He straightened, a smile in his eyes so obvious that her stomach flipped and flopped with warmth and with…*love*. She squashed the feeling.

She didn't want it.

That knowledge sobered her.

'I wonder what our child will be like,' she said distractedly as they moved closer to the Grand Canal.

'Can you imagine him or her?'

'I sometimes have a dream,' she said with a shrug of her slender shoulders. 'I can see a little baby. Chubby with caramel skin like yours—dark eyes, dimples.' She shrugged again. 'But I guess all babies are a bit like that.'

'It is how I picture our child too. A little girl with a fringe like yours.'

'I don't think babies are born with hair styles,' she pointed out. 'You think it will be a girl?'

He pulled a face. 'I don't know. I don't care.'

'Really? And here I had you pegged for one of those patriarchal guys who would be all about the male heir.'

He dug his hands into his pocket. 'I was not close to my father,' he said after a long silence, one that was heavy with his own reflections and memories. 'My grandfather more or less raised me. Perhaps if I had seen a different example of father and son bonding I might yearn more for a son of my own.' His lips twisted into a dismissive smile. 'As it is, I just want our child to be healthy. And to have his mother's heart.'

'Yeah? Why is that?'

'According to you, I don't have one,' he pointed out.

'That's according to everyone,' she corrected, and began walking once more. One foot in front of the other. Trying not to think about his heart and their baby growing inside her. Nor to think about the way *he'd* moved inside her only the night before.

'*Si*. And what do you think, Skye? Am I as heartless as everyone says?'

Her face paled. 'I don't think you should ask me that.'

'Because your answer would hurt my feelings?'

'Perhaps,' she whispered. 'Does it matter what I think?'

He was quiet for a moment, his expression serious, and then he smiled as though physically pushing the conversation aside. 'I'm hungry. Shall we lunch?'

'Didn't we just finish breakfast?'

He made a *tsk*ing noise of disapproval. 'And you say you are eating for two! Breakfast was hours ago.' He reached down and wrapped his fingers around her hand, lifting the ice-cream cone to his lips while his eyes held hers. He took another bite.

Skye's heart throbbed at the simple gesture of intimacy.

Really, in the scheme of things it meant nothing, yet it made her soul soar. Happiness was right in front of her and his smile was telling her to grab it.

But his smile lied.

It always had done.

Maybe he couldn't help it.

She wasn't going to risk being hurt again just to find out.

'Lunch sounds good,' she said, as if pulling a rain cloud over the sunshine of their banter of only seconds ago. The words were cold and damp. Sensible.

Safe.

'Which way?' she asked, swapping her *gelato* to the other hand to prevent any further incursions. Any new suggestions of an intimacy that was fraudulent.

He looked at her for a moment, long and hard, then turned back to the path in front of them. 'Not much further. This way.'

They walked in silence, but it was no longer comfortable. It was thick with the doubts and frustrations that were, undoubtedly, to become the hallmarks of their relationship.

After almost ten minutes, Matteo slowed. 'Here.'

Skye paused, looking in the direction he'd cocked his head, and she expelled a breath of uncertainty. 'Here?'

'Something wrong with it?'

She took in the crisp white table cloths, the small vases with carnations in each one, the enormous chandeliers that looked to line the dining room, the pianist in the corner playing what she thought to be Bach.

'It's just a little more formal than I'd expected.'

'I'm sure they will fix you a sandwich, if you would prefer.'

It was another breath from the past. The memory of how he'd teased her mercilessly about her love for cucumber sandwiches, something he found bland and so quintessentially British.

'Fine,' she said with a furrowed brow, moving ahead of him into the beautiful restaurant.

A man in a tuxedo greeted them, his brows thick and dark, his hair grey. After a short conversation with Matteo in fluent Italian, the waiter directed them into the restaurant. It was so much grander, and more beautiful, from inside.

From this vantage point, Skye could see that the tables were propped beneath windows that looked out over the Grand Canal, and the stately Rialto Bridge as it spanned one side to the other. There were window boxes at each window filled with pretty pink azaleas, and the floor was tiled with shimmering black and white marble. Several waiters and waitresses stood waiting to serve, all in elegant crisp white shirts and black tuxedo jackets, and, like a butler parody brought to life, one stood with a silver tray balanced on top of his white-gloved palm.

'This way, madam,' the waiter said, and Skye realised she'd been frozen in time.

What was wrong with her? It wasn't as though she'd never been in such a beautiful restaurant. She'd grown up with the proverbial silver spoon. She'd had more birthdays in places like this than she could remember.

But being here with Matteo, the strains of world-class

piano music reaching them, the flowers moving gently in the breeze, was all so…*romantic.*

The word whispered itself through her soul and she did her best to push it aside. She kept a neutral expression on her features as she strode through the restaurant, taking the seat opposite Matteo and wishing she'd worn something a little fancier than jeans and a grey T-shirt. At least her jewellery gave the ensemble an air of formality; the clunky gold and green necklace was one of a kind and matched her manicure. A manicure she'd had done when she'd imagined that she'd be flying off to Australia single, pregnant and far away from Matteo and his manipulations. She eyed her nails with a small frown.

'Yes,' he said slowly, as she sat down. 'I've been thinking the same thing.'

Her heartbeat accelerated wildly. 'What's that?'

He reached into the pocket of his jacket and lifted out a small box. She recognised it instantly. Her back was straight but her spine tingled with apprehension and misgivings.

He flicked it open and slid the box across to her, with considerably less fanfare than the last time he'd presented a ring box for her inspection.

'Nothing would make me happier than if you'd agree to marry me, Skye. Say you will.'

The words seemed to glisten in the air around her, dancing and lifting her up. She nodded with all the enthusiasm that her heart gave rise to. 'Of course I will!'

'I don't like seeing you without it on,' he said with a shrug.

Skye reached for the box but made no effort to liberate the ring inside. She ran her finger over the huge diamond, remembering how her first reaction had been one of mixed feelings. Delight, euphoria and bliss at the thought of marrying Matteo Vin Santo, whom she had loved from almost the moment they'd met. But disappointment too that he'd thought her pretentious enough to want a ring such as this. She supposed it was the fact she was a billion-pound heiress, that people presumed she was used to expensive items and only valued those things that had a high material cost.

It wasn't true, though. Skye had always shied away from ostentation and visible signs of wealth.

'You don't like it, do you?' he asked quietly, his eyes reading every nuanced expression that crossed her face.

She lifted startled eyes to his. 'I… It's… It feels a little like a prison sentence now,' she said with a shake of her head. 'That's all.'

'Now who's the liar?' he countered silkily, suspending the conversation when another waiter appeared.

'Good afternoon, madam, sir. I… Oh! *Scusa—mi dispiace!* I'm so sorry! I'm interrupting a special moment. My apologies…'

'It's fine,' Skye hastened to reassure him.

'I go, I go. I give you time.'

Skye watched the man leave, perplexed, and then turned her attention to Matteo. He hadn't moved. His attention was still on Skye's face, watchful and attentive. 'Why didn't you tell me?'

She knew what he meant and didn't bother to obfuscate. 'You chose it,' she said with a shrug. And now she lifted the ring out, holding it between her forefinger and thumb. 'I used to love it for that reason alone.'

'But it's not what you would have chosen?'

'I would never have wanted to choose my own ring.' She fixed him with a determined gaze. 'In hindsight, it should have told me how little you knew me.'

His lips twisted with mockery. Directed at her, or himself?

He reached across, retrieving the ring from her hands and sliding it back onto her ring finger. 'Wear it until I arrange a replacement.'

Her blood bubbled and swirled. A replacement spoke of such permanence. And in the meantime?

She stared down at the enormous diamond—a diamond that had kept her company all the time she'd been married to Matteo, a diamond she had thought she would wear for ever, and felt a hint of disloyalty. 'Perhaps we can have it turned into a pendant. If it's a daughter, she can have it for her sixteenth birthday.'

His eyes held a sparkle she didn't understand. 'Certainly. Or we can sell it for our son's first car.'

'God, this is really happening, isn't it?'

'Yes, *cara*. It is.'

'You seem so glad about that.'

He shrugged. 'Having not planned it does not make the news less welcome.'

'You didn't want children.'

'You are so sure of that?'

She nodded. 'You said so.'

A frown pulled at his features. 'You are twenty-two years old, Skye. I cannot think what I was doing at twenty-two, but it was not raising a child.'

'You were running your business,' she pointed out. 'In fact, you had been doing so for several years.'

'You remember so clearly.'

Her cheeks flooded with peach. Of course she remembered. She remembered everything he'd ever said, as though he'd imprinted his words against the iron of her soul, branding her for all time.

'So it's not like you were out being all irresponsible or anything. You were working hard.'

'I was doing both,' he said seriously. 'I worked hard. Played harder.'

Jealousy fired through her and she hated it. For one thing, she'd still been a child when he had been twenty-two. There was no way she could be threatened by the fact he'd had relationships before her.

The waiter appeared silently, and another waitress behind him who carried a tray with champagne flutes; champagne and a platter of food.

'Compliments of the establishment,' the waiter murmured, placing the food and drinks down, bowing low and then disappearing.

'I suppose it would be rude to tell him we don't want champagne?'

He ignored her question. 'I didn't think having children made sense.' He shrugged. 'But that decision is now out of my hands.'

She tilted her face away, staring out at the Grand Canal and the hustle and bustle of Venice in the afternoon.

It was a city like no other.

Its character changed so completely depending on what time of day it was. Now, in the early afternoon, the *strada* were crowded with tourists, big and happy, wearing hats and cameras and beaming smiles, talking loudly and laughing and eating as they walked, making their way back to the cruise terminal, ready to continue their tour of Europe.

Come night time, the streets would be filled with Venetians, promenading elegantly, speaking quietly, their voices taking on a musical quality as they lulled against the canals.

'Of course it's not…ideal,' she said jerkily. 'I meant what I said when I came to see you. I want a divorce.' Her voice wobbled and she forced herself to be calm, digging her nails into her palms. 'But I can understand why you want to give this a chance.' She swallowed. 'So I think we should try this. Try to make it work. For the baby's sake.'

His eyes held a quality that filled her with something strange. Emotions were rioting beneath her skin. 'A real marriage?'

'No.' Her smile was wistful. 'It will never be that. We'll both know that it's just for our son or daughter. But I'll stop fighting this. I'll try to make a life here. A life outside of you.' She breathed out softly then turned to face him. 'But if I'm miserable, I'll go. And I will trust that deep down, beneath the way you are, beyond being ruthless and determined and cold, there is a good man who will be reasonable and treat me with respect, for the sake of our child.' She tilted her chin at a defiant angle, and Matteo was silent. The champagne bottle sat between them, mocking the seriousness of their discussion with its frothy enthusiasm.

'So pragmatic,' he murmured after a long pause. Was Skye imagining the way his words were deepened by emotion?

'I took a page out of your book,' she volleyed back.

'You perfected it, it would appear.'

Matteo stared out at the canal, his expression sombre.

How could he argue with such impeccable logic? He couldn't. For all his bluster and bravado, had he really expected he'd keep Skye locked up in his house forever? Had he thought he could threaten her with a custody battle and that she'd give up her life and freedom to be in a marriage that made her miserable?

It wasn't as though he could outgun her on the legal side. She had endless resources and a great reputation. If anything, attacking her in the courts would backfire badly, given her age and philanthropic history. And his reputation as a cold, heartless bastard.

'Matteo? You're a thousand miles away.'

He blinked, drawing his attention back to Skye. She was lifting a final spoonful of the dessert to her lips. Lips that were pink and full and that drew his gaze as a flower did a bee.

His stomach lurched. Desire, unfathomable, irrepressible desire, swarmed him.

'I was thinking about the bridge,' he said after a moment's pause.

'The Rialto?'

He nodded, a gruff shift of his head. 'You know, it took a heap of money to build. They had to get funds from lots of different sources. There was even a sort of early iteration of the lottery that raised money for its construction.'

Skye tilted her head to the side. 'I didn't know that.'

'I was thinking that sometimes taking a gamble on something pays off. Sometimes it can lead to something unique and lasting.' He turned his attention back to her. 'Don't you think?'

CHAPTER EIGHT

SKYE SHIFTED UNCOMFORTABLY in her seat, keeping her discomfort hidden from her husband's all-seeing gaze.

Only, Matteo did see the way she winced, and leaned forward. 'What is it?'

'Nothing,' Skye said, a tight smile on her face. 'I just walked too far today, that's all.' This day, and every day for the last week, since they'd taken to strolling around Venice each morning, afterwards stopping somewhere new for lunch.

Conversation was limited to unsensational topics, like the weather or current events or politics; nothing that they disagreed on. Nothing that could remind Skye that they were enemies, really, beneath the romance of Venice and the fact they were going to become parents.

But deep down she knew they were pretending again. At least they both knew the rules this time.

And Matteo seemed determined to stick to them. After the night on the terrace, he hadn't said or done anything out of line. Not a word of seduction, not a hint of flirtation. He'd been the perfect gentleman.

'You're in pain?'

'No, no.' She winced again. 'Just a little. It's my lower back, that's all. It's an occupational hazard of the whole pregnancy thing.'

'We've been pushing it.' His words were tinged with self-recrimination. 'I'm sorry.'

'It's hardly your fault,' Skye said, her brows drawn together. 'I'm the one who keeps suggesting we go out.'

He held his expression neutral but there was a hint of something she didn't understand that danced in the edges of his eyes. 'I was foolish to let you walk so much.'

'*Let* me?' Skye countered. 'Remember that whole "me being an autonomous human being" thing? Remember how I have that small thing called free will?'

Again, his eyes flicked with something she didn't understand and then he stood, moving around the dinner table, extending his hands to her.

'What is it?' She looked at him, lifting her hands into his, the brightness of her diamond glinting in the pale light of the room.

'Let me help you.'

'I'm fine,' she demurred, instantly pushing against whatever help he had in mind.

'What's the matter, Skye? Are you afraid of what might happen if I touch you?'

She swallowed past the lump in her throat, her eyes holding his. She was terrified.

Terrified of how badly she wanted him. The week they'd spent trawling all over Venice, exploring it anew, had been like the honeymoon they'd never had. It was the other piece of the puzzle. After their wedding, they'd had sex. A lot of sex. And she'd thought that was intimacy. But walking side by side, not touching, just talking, had been different.

It had been a form of torturous foreplay and, yes, she was afraid of what would happen if he touched her. But she stood anyway, not blinking, not doing anything to convey that fear.

'Lie down.' He nodded towards one of the long couches

that sat opposite them. She nodded, moving across the room with the grace that was innate to her.

'You don't have to do this…'

'You're uncomfortable because of *my* baby. Of course I have to help you. It is my duty.'

Again, his insistence on his *duty* filled her with a cold ache—it served as a reminder of the fact he viewed her as an obligation. A responsibility. She kept her face averted as she lay down on her stomach, tilting her head to look out towards the view. She could see only the flower pots, an explosion of geraniums in the pale moonlight.

His hands on her back were gentle.

He knelt at her side and ran his fingers over her with just enough pressure to bring a sense of immediate relief.

'May I lift your shirt?' The words were throaty and deep.

Skye's eyes were drawn to his. 'Yes.'

He pushed the fabric up slowly and she held her breath. It was just a few inches, enough for him to be able to massage her naked flesh. But it was skin-to-skin contact and it rocked her world. She bit down on her lower lip and shut her eyes, surrendering to the sensations that were rioting through her.

'What's this from?' He drew his finger over her skin, tracing a very pale imperfection that ran in a semi-circular shape.

'A dog bite,' Skye murmured, sleepy and relaxed. 'When I was twelve.'

She didn't see him frown. 'It only bit you here?'

Skye stifled a yawn. 'Yes. He was old and quite crazy, really. He'd got a fright and I was sitting on the floor, right beside him. He gave me a fright, let me tell you.'

'I didn't know you had a dog.'

'He wasn't mine,' Skye murmured, shifting a little. Her back was feeling much better but she didn't tell Matteo that. He continued to move his palms over her flesh and she didn't want him to stop. Ever. 'He was my great-aunt's.'

Matteo's hands were still for a moment. 'She raised you after your father died?'

'Yeah.' Another yawn. 'She had seven dogs. Apparently she had a penchant for taking in strays. I was her last, though.'

'You were hardly a stray,' Matteo pointed out. 'Are you close to her?'

'She passed away three years ago,' Skye said crisply, closing the conversation out of habit.

'Were you close to her? Before she died,' Matteo pushed, either not comprehending her cues or not caring about them.

Skye tossed the words around in her mind, making sense of them, listening to them as if she were an outsider. 'She raised me,' Skye said after a long pause. 'I'm very grateful to her.'

But Matteo wasn't fooled by Skye's selective choice of language. She was hiding something, and that rankled. More than it should, given their relationship, or lack thereof. What had he expected? That she'd suddenly open up and confide all her deep and dark secrets to him?

She certainly wouldn't now. But how come they'd never discussed this before, when they'd first married? Why hadn't he asked more questions?

Because he hadn't wanted to know.

Skye had simply been a means to an end, not a person with her own thoughts, feelings, history and sadness.

The realisation wasn't new, yet it sat strangely in his chest, like an accusation lined with barbed wire. He'd looked at her and seen the hotel.

He gazed down on his wife and a tight smile cracked his lips as he saw that she had fallen asleep. With her dark hair and pink cheeks and pale skin, her red lips shaped like two perfect rose petals. She was his own Snow White.

Only he was no Prince Charming. Prince Charming would never have married her for a hotel. To avenge a theft that had taken place years earlier. And he certainly wouldn't have blackmailed her into staying married.

His smile faded as he reached for her gently, lifting her as though she weighed nothing, and cradling her to his chest.

She stirred a little, lifting a hand to him, but then she relaxed, a smile on her face.

He lifted his gaze, staring straight ahead as he carried her through the house and up the stairs, to the solitude of her own room.

Skye's dreams were of Matteo. Of the night they'd met— the night she'd fallen in love. Her dreams were of their conversations, the words he'd offered her that had been more special than gold dust. 'I don't believe in fairy tales,' she'd told him the day after they'd met, when the mirage of a fairy tale had hovered on her horizon. She hadn't dared try to grab it. Reaching for perfection resulted in pain.

'Even when you're living one?' he'd pushed, pressing his lips to her cheek so that her stomach had lurched, her heart had thumped and her body had gone into sensory meltdown.

'There's no such thing.' She'd learned that lesson years ago. Her mother had deserted her. Her father had never bothered to get to know her. Her great-aunt had avoided affection as though it were a sign of personal weakness to care for another human. Boarding school had been more a prison than a Hogwarts. 'There's just real life.'

'But sometimes real life can be every bit as perfect as a fairy tale, no?'

Her dreams were of their first kiss, his proposal, their wedding, their first time together. All the times thereafter. The fairy tale she'd thought she was living. A fairy tale that had been a nightmare, in all ways but one. He'd betrayed her and he'd broken her heart, but his body called to hers. Nothing would change that.

She moaned in her bed, arching her back, and she could feel the ghost of his hands on her. A phantom touch that was a torment because it was not real. She stretched her hands out, instinctively seeking him, and not finding him. She reached for him and didn't connect with flesh.

The sense of loss was instant and it was sharp. She stood on autopilot, still groggy from sleep, her body in complete charge. She moved through his home with no idea of the time. It could have been midnight, or it could have been the early hours of the morning. It didn't matter.

She contemplated knocking on his door, but didn't. She pushed it inwards, hovering on the threshold.

There was no such thing as fairy tales. She'd been right. That wasn't what this was. But he was her husband and in that moment she needed him with a ferocity that wouldn't be quelled. He was asleep in bed. She tiptoed across the floorboards and then rolled her eyes.

Was she afraid of waking him? Wasn't that kind of the point?

Still, she crept towards the bed, pausing for a moment to study him.

He was a stunning specimen of masculinity but, asleep like this, she felt all his vulnerabilities as well. She could see the man he was and the boy he'd been. She could see all the parts of him and her heart lurched with recognition of the fact that she loved all those parts. His arrogance. His determination. Even his ruthlessness. For these aspects all made Matteo who he was.

She moved quietly but quickly, shedding her clothes, thinking she should have done it before she made her way to his room, then she pushed the sheet back and straddled him, dropping her mouth to his and kissing him.

He made a low moan from deep in his throat and his hands lifted, catching her face and holding her still so that his eyes could latch to hers. His room was dark but there was enough light cast by the moon and the lights beyond the villa for them to see one another. He stared at her for a moment, at her face, her lips that were parted in expectation, her eyes that were hooded with desire and her body that was naked, needing him.

'I want you,' she said simply and he groaned once more, dropping his hands to her hips and positioning her so that she could slide onto his length and take him deep inside.

She tilted her head to the ceiling at the feeling, so welcome, so familiar, so perfect. Her body was on fire. Every nerve ending was dancing inside her, quivering with the rightness of his touch. She dropped forward, bringing her mouth to his, kissing him hungrily as he moved inside her. She rolled her hips, her rhythm desperate and fast, her needs insatiable, and he laughed softly, nodding against her head.

'I know.'

He caught her at the waist and rolled her easily, breaking their bodies apart. And, though it was a brief separation, it was enough for Skye to issue a sound of complaint that had him laughing once more, softly, a short sound that filled her with impatience. But then he was back, moving into her deeper, harder, his body taking control of hers and commanding their desire; building it up, wrapping it around them, making her tremble and writhe beneath him as pleasure built and built inside her, stretching like a coil that wouldn't be contained.

She cried out as it reached fever pitch and then broke across her. She dug her nails into his shoulders and held on for dear life, hoping it would save her. The galaxy was around her, cosmic and beautiful, and she was flying through it, just a piece of flotsam, a heavenly, bliss, pleasure-filled piece of flotsam.

He dropped his mouth to her breasts and took one into his mouth, rolling his tongue over her nipple as his fingers sought the other, tormenting it between his forefinger and thumb. Her breasts ached for him and he knew that. He pushed deeper inside her and she sobbed—it was a sob of relief. Of joy. Of gratitude.

It was also a sob of fear.

What hope did she have of controlling her emotions when there was this to contend with? It didn't matter if she called it 'having sex' or 'sleeping together' or 'making love'. A rose by any other name…

She was making love. Every touch, every movement, every sensation, was binding her with the emotion and she would never be free of that.

'I loved you so much,' she said, the words not exactly what she wanted to say, yet they were a reflection of what she was thinking, feeling, needing him to know.

Another explosion built, starting deep in her abdomen and spreading to the far reaches of her body, carrying delirium in its wake so that her fingertips tingled and she burst apart with pleasure. He kissed her harder and then he joined her, the rapture holding them both, wrapping around them with the same sense of urgency and euphoric release. Their breathing was in unison. Hard and fast, it filled the room. He pulled away a little, his eyes heavy as they surveyed her.

'That was a nice surprise,' he murmured minutes later, once their breath had slowed and a hint of normality had returned to the room.

She didn't say anything. She was a tangle of feelings that had gone from delight to despair in the space of seconds. The same desire that was beautiful and mesmerising was also a trap. It was a torment.

She looked at him and then turned her face.

'Are you okay?' The question was filled with such tenderness that her heart splintered off, new shards joining the old.

'I am now,' she bluffed, bravado brightening her voice. He rolled off her but pulled her to him, holding her back to his chest, his arm curled around her body in a gesture of intimacy that hadn't even belonged in their marriage. She lay against him, her body curled like a conch shell, her eyes on the moonlit wallpaper opposite, her heart breaking as she felt his beating, hard and resolute.

Determined.

The problem with whatever the hell they'd just done was that everything felt so perfect. In contrast to the reality of their situation, when she was in his arms, when his body was buried in hers, she could believe that they *were* in a fairy tale.

The ending, the inevitable realisation that it *wasn't* perfect, was like being dropped into the middle of a war zone. Remembering that only a week and a half earlier she'd stormed her way into his office demanding a divorce—a divorce he had agreed to!—was like being doused in cold water.

Slowly, once sleep had claimed him firmly in its grasp, she wriggled away from his warmth, moving to the opposite side of the bed at first and flipping on her side to look at him as he slept.

His breathing was even, his expression relaxed. He wasn't tormented by the emotional barrenness of their marriage.

He didn't care about it.

He didn't want anything from her.

Except for the hotel.

And now the baby.

And, yes, sex.

That was what their marriage boiled down to for him.

She had to find a way to remember that. Then, she'd be okay. Wouldn't she?

'I had an incredible dream last night.' The words were drawled and deep, murmured from across the table where they were eating breakfast.

'I think I had the same dream,' she responded without looking at him. It was easier to play it light, to be cool and relaxed when she wasn't looking at him.

She turned her attention back to the paper, skimming the news without really taking any of it in. Silence returned and she was momentarily mollified by it. She sipped her coffee, replacing it carefully on the table. His hand reached out and covered hers, and her pulse kicked up a notch.

'Why did you leave?'

Skye's gaze jolted to his. 'When?'

'Last night.'

She looked down at the paper again. 'Was I meant to stay?'

'It was late. You must have been tired.'

She looked at him briefly, holding his gaze with what she hoped passed as unconcern, then gave the paper her attention once more. As if to underscore that she was in fact reading, and not just staring at a collection of words on the page, she pulled her hand free from his and turned a page. 'I sleep better in my own bed.'

'You never had a problem in my room before...'

Skye swallowed. He wasn't going to let this rest, apparently. She forced herself to meet his eyes and dropped the act. Her face was stern, her voice not a tone that invited argument. 'I don't want that.'

His eyes roamed her face thoughtfully. 'You won't sleep in my bed, but you'll come to my room when you want sex in the middle of the night?'

She nodded slowly. 'Yeah.'

'So I am like…a booty call?' he prompted, wiggling his brows so that she laughed—a laugh borne of relief that he had dropped his inquisition.

'Yep.'

He shook his head. 'Mmm, but then when I wake up wanting you, you are not within reach.'

'And you can't walk down the corridor, as I did?'

'Ah.' His eyes drew together. 'Your advances are always welcome. I cannot be certain that you would feel the same if I were to reciprocate with a midnight intrusion.'

Skye's cheeks flamed. 'I thought you wanted to make me beg for you,' she reminded him, and had the satisfaction of seeing something darken his eyes.

'I haven't done too well at that, have I?'

Skye arched a brow. 'Looking for compliments?'

'No.' He was serious. 'I'm glad you came to me last night, Skye.'

Her throat thickened and she looked away, her eyes suspiciously moist. Stupid pregnancy hormones making her emotions haywire! 'It was the massage,' she said with a shrug.

'Then you shall have massages often.' She turned back to him just in time to see him wink. Her chest compressed as though cement were being pressed against it. 'But today? You are my prisoner in other ways.'

She paused, her expression showing curiosity.

'Today, you rest. You relax and tell me what you need. I will bring you anything your heart desires.'

She nodded, but deep down she knew he could never do that. What her heart desired, really desired, wasn't on offer from Matteo Vin Santo, and never would be.

CHAPTER NINE

SKYE PUSHED THE dress onto the hanger, adding it to the collection she was gathering in one side of the dressing room. She paused, midway through reaching for the next option, staring at her reflection in the mirror. Her stomach, usually so flat, was thicker around the middle. Not round yet.

Just...different.

Her breasts had changed too. They were no longer neat and modest, and her bras had begun to pinch her sides painfully. It was enough to make her feel uncomfortable in her usual wardrobe. She ran her hands down her body, curling her fingertips over her flesh, breathing in deeply as though she could hear the little life inside her, if only she listened hard enough.

This was really happening.

Her smile was bright. She saw the joy in her face and it made her heart lurch.

Be careful, Skye. Don't forget that this isn't perfect. *It's not a fairy tale.*

But the baby was pretty damned close. All her life, she'd never known true love. She thought she'd found it with Matteo, but she'd been wrong there.

The baby would love her, though, and she would love him. With her whole heart. She would never, ever let him be hurt or sad, or feel alone or frightened. She lifted the final dress over her head, pulling it down, studying it from all angles before nodding and removing it.

She pulled her own shirt back on then tossed the new clothes over her arm and shouldered out of the changing room.

Matteo stood out like a sore thumb, waiting in the middle of the boutique, dressed in a dark suit. But he was holding something in his hands. As she got closer, her heart skidded against her rib cage. It was a soft toy.

A toy for their child.

'I thought he would need something,' Matteo said with a shrug and a bemused smile.

Skye smiled back but turned away quickly, feeling the now-familiar prick of tears threatening. She laid the dresses onto the counter in time to see the shop assistant practically wipe her drool from the side of her mouth, staring at Matteo as though he were *gelato* on a hot summer's day.

Skye understood.

She'd felt like that plenty of times.

'All this?' the assistant asked in heavily accented English.

'And the toy,' Skye said with a nod. She waited while the assistant rung the clothes up and bagged them, and then Matteo slid his credit card across, something which both surprised and frustrated Skye.

'You're buying my clothes now?' she enquired silkily as they stepped out of the boutique.

'You only need new clothes because of my baby.' His response was filled with infuriating logic.

'My baby too.'

'Yes, *cara*. I am aware of that. But it helps me feel...involved,' he said with a shrug of his shoulders and a degree of honesty that made her gut clench.

'Do you *not* feel involved otherwise?'

'No, I mean, you get to grow the baby and all the work is yours for now. Delivery, nursing.' He shrugged. 'I want to do something too.'

She would never have thought he would feel that way. She chanced a sidelong glance at his profile and then looked straight ahead as they walked down the busy street. Tourists flocked around them.

'You know, we haven't talked about a nursery,' she said thoughtfully. 'That's something you could help with.'

His whole face lit up. 'Why had I not thought of this?'

Skye burst out laughing. 'Uh-oh. Why do I feel like I've just made a very dangerous suggestion?'

'You think three bedrooms will be enough?'

She shook her head. 'One bedroom is definitely fine. And near mine.'

'Ours,' he said softly. He reached down and captured her hand. 'I would like you to be in my room again, Skye.'

Danger lurked in the softly spoken statement. She made a small gesture of demur, knowing she could never concede that intimacy again. 'Then we'll both be waking up at all hours. Separate rooms are better.' She tried to make the statement as light as possible, so that he wouldn't know how her heart had thundered at the idea of surrendering all of herself to this marriage once again.

'We'll need a room for the nanny,' he murmured, apparently still running a million miles an hour, planning for their baby in a whole new way now. One that Skye found, frankly, a tiny bit scary.

'Hold up.' She lifted a hand, pausing, turning to face him. 'What nanny?'

'You think we'll need two? Perhaps a day nanny and a night nanny. How does this work?'

'No, no, no. No nanny.'

Matteo's expression showed confusion. 'Skye, you don't have to do this without help.'

'You think I *can't* do it?'

His sigh was exasperated. 'That's not what I meant.'

'Because I'm going to be a great mother.' She froze. 'Aren't I?' Suddenly she was dizzy, hot and cold. She moved away from him, towards the wall of a building. She propped herself against it; panic pursued her. 'Oh, God. What if I'm not?' Her eyes were huge when they met his.

'You are going to be an excellent mother,' he said, moving closer, his large body framing hers.

'But you don't know that. I don't know that. I didn't… I never even knew my mother. I had a succession of step-mothers and wasn't close to any of them. I have no idea what being a mother actually means. What if I'm terrible? What if I shout? What if I'm impatient? What if I don't know the rules? Oh, God, Matteo. I'm not going to be any good at this.'

His face showed his confusion, and also a hint of amusement that she deeply resented.

'This isn't funny.' She groaned. 'I got so caught up in how much I'd love this baby that I never really thought about whether or not I'd be able to give our baby what it needs. What if I can't?'

'Skye?'

'I have no clue what time babies should go to sleep. Or kids. What about when he's older and he wants to watch a scary movie?'

'Skye?'

'And food? What do babies eat? What if I poison our child? What if I *choke* our child?'

'How are you going to choke it?' He stifled a laugh.

'I don't know! By feeding it caramel when it's two months old. I don't know!'

He dropped his mouth to hers, suffocating the words that were tumbling out of her on a wave of panic. It was a kiss of reassurance, a kiss of kindness. He kissed her and she responded, her body leaning towards his, her fingers splaying wide across his shirt. His legs, so strong and firm, stood on either side of her body, effectively imprisoning her against the wall.

'We're going to need a nanny,' she said into his mouth, the certainty that she didn't want to do this alone absolute in her mind.

'No.' He shook his head. 'I was wrong. We can get one later, if you feel it is necessary. If you want more freedom. Or if the baby isn't sleeping and you need a rest. But I will be here. I will be holding your hand, just as you will be holding mine. This isn't just your child, your responsibility. It's mine too. We're in it together.'

Slightly reassured, but still not convinced, she nodded. 'Maybe we should just meet with a few agencies. Just in case.'

'If you'd like,' he shrugged. 'Skye?'

She blinked up at him.

'You are going to be a terrific mother. You are already so in love with our baby. That's the most important thing by far.' His eyes scanned her face. 'I am sorry that you never felt that from your own mother.'

His words were precious. They meant the world to Skye. She didn't know if he was right or not, but having his support was so important.

'What if I'm not?'

'You will be.' His confidence did something strange inside of Skye. It tied knots around her heart, knots that made everything seem fine, good and safe. But there was danger in that safety, because it was so like the happiness she'd felt before. The happiness that had filled her heart and made her believe that their marriage was everything she'd been waiting for.

That he was the answer to questions she didn't even know she had.

Her smile was guarded. She nodded slowly, mentally putting essential distance between them. Their past lay before her—quicksand that could devour her at any point if she didn't take care.

'Matteo?'

'*Si?*'

She turned away from the wall, walking once more. Slowly. Thoughtfully. 'Tell me about our families.'

She didn't look up at him, so didn't see the way his expression tightened. The way his lips dragged downwards with sour memories. 'What would you like to know?'

Skye turned her fingers into the handle of the carrier bag. 'I don't know. I guess everything. My dad's lawyer didn't have all the details.'

'What did he say?'

'Only that your mother had been engaged to my father. That she met your dad and it was…love at first sight. That she ran away with him in the middle of the night.' Skye shrugged.

'*Si.*' Matteo nodded warily. 'Your father was young and arrogant. He couldn't accept that your mother preferred my father. So he made her life miserable.'

'Miserable how?' Skye prompted, thinking of her father, and frowning when she could hardly call his face to mind.

'He moved to Italy and turned up everywhere my parents went. When my mother conceived me, and your father began to accept that it was over, he turned to the business. It was a tough time for my grandfather—he had expanded too quickly and the global markets faltered. He was vulnerable and your father acted on that.'

'How?' Skye pushed.

'He actively acquired my grandfather's competitors and then drove my grandfather's businesses into the ground. Nonno borrowed heavily to prop up his failing business interests but it was not enough. Eventually, he had to sell almost everything.'

'Including the hotel,' Skye murmured.

'Your father didn't want my grandfather's businesses.' His tone was grave. 'He wanted simply to destroy them. To take something good and strong and ruin it just because he could.'

Skye's eyes glistened with shame at the description of her father's actions. Actions that made her wish Matteo was wrong. But she knew he wasn't. Strange that she could trust him so implicitly on this matter when he'd proven himself to be just as duplicitous.

Matteo stared at her long and hard for a moment before allowing the conversation to move onwards. 'The bankruptcy broke him. I went to live with him around the time it was happening. I saw a man who was proud and intelligent, who had worked hard all his life, be destroyed by the actions of your father.'

The hatred in the words chilled Skye to the core. But what could she say to refute it?

'My father used to talk about a woman he had loved. I suppose it was your mother. I think losing her destroyed him, in the same way your grandfather's business losses—'

'No.' Matteo's interruption was swift, his rebuke absolute. 'You cannot compare the two. My parents fell in love. There was nothing malicious in what they did. Your father spent a decade tearing my family's wealth apart. It was his sole mission. He was motivated solely by revenge and hatred.'

'Isn't that a little like the pot calling the kettle black?' Skye murmured. The pleasant atmosphere of only moments ago had turned dark and uncomfortable. She felt the animosity of their past, the tension that had dogged her in the first days of their second attempt at marriage, and it was back with a vengeance.

She stopped walking and looked in both directions of the street. 'I'm a little tired,' she said, not completely without truth.

Matteo studied her, as though he could see the truth of what she was saying if he looked hard enough. 'Skye?' He lifted a hand as though to touch her cheek but held it wide of her face, his expression confused. 'What happened between them has no bearing on us.'

'How can you say that?' The words were heavy with feelings. 'Everything we are is because of them. Everything.'

She wouldn't cry.

She wouldn't.

But her hand lifted to her stomach, pressing against it gently. 'This baby deserves better than to be born into so much hate.'

'There is no hate here.'

'Yes, there is.' Her eyes laced to his, and she forced herself to see all angles. To remember everything they were— everything they'd been. 'My father hated your father. Your grandfather hated my father. You hated my father. Everyone hated everyone.'

'I don't hate you,' he said simply.

She looked away from him.

'And you don't hate me.'

That was true. She didn't hate him. She didn't know what she felt for him.

'I hate what you did.' The words were gravelled. 'I hate what you did to me. I hate what you're capable of. I hate what you took away from me. I hate that… I hate that…'

She swept her eyes shut, unable to finish the sentence.

'Go on,' he prompted.

But it was too awful. Even to *think*, let alone to say!

'I hate…'

'Yes?'

'I wish I was having this baby with anyone but you,' she finished finally, thinking it was marginally better than to admit the truth of her thoughts—that she hated that she was having a baby with Matteo. That they were to be bound together for the rest of their days.

He was silent, staring at her for so long that she wondered if he was going to say anything at all. Colour faded from her cheeks and desolation surrounded her.

It was soul-deep and wearying.

'This marriage is crazy,' she whispered.

And it seemed to rouse him. Matteo's eyes sparked with hers, and his jaw clenched, determination vibrating from him to Skye in passion-filled waves. 'Perhaps. But we *are* married, Skye. And I have no intention of letting you go.' He reached for her hand and caught it, bringing it to his lips. 'Come. Let me take you home. You said you are tired.'

She was.

Weary. Tired. Exhausted…but it was not the kind of exhaustion that could be cured with a rest. This state of weariness came from deep within, sapping her of all her strength.

'Yes,' she murmured. 'Fine. Let's go home.'

Matteo stared out at the canal without seeing. The moon was obstructed by thick, silver clouds and the city was almost completely dark. Only the far away glow of cruise ships offered any break in the bleakness of the night.

Skye was asleep upstairs, and Matteo remained where he was, looking out of the window as though answers might leap through it directly at him.

She was miserable, and that was his fault. The whole damned thing.

When had he decided that he would take the hotel? When had their marriage become a part of it?

Why hadn't he spoken to her? For surely, as soon as they'd made love, he had been confident Skye would have done almost anything he'd asked of her. But if she'd said no?

Then she'd have said no, he thought angrily.

When had he picked up the mantle of this feud as though his own life depended on it? Hadn't enough already been sacrificed to its purposeless pursuit? His grandfather had been broken by another man's vengeance.

And now Matteo was breaking Skye.

Had broken her.

Her face, as it had been that afternoon, came to his mind and he felt the sharp, unrelenting point of blame stab him square in the chest. She had looked…

Words flew through his mind. Sad? No, so much worse than sad.

Disappointed? Angry? Bereft?

All of the above. And something else. Something indefinable that sat heavily inside him like an accusation he would never lose.

Loving Maria had been simple. They'd made sense. She was a glamorous actress, albeit not a very good one, with legs that went on for ever. She had a penchant for expensive jewellery and six-star vacations, and he'd been happy to give them to her.

The fact she'd been using him for his social status had never occurred to him until she'd leap-frogged him to sleep with a Swedish duke. It had broken his heart. He'd felt that pain, which was how he recognised it so clearly on Skye's features.

He'd broken her heart. Badly. She had been a means to an end—a pawn in his fight to return Il Grande Fortuna to its rightful owner. He hadn't thought beyond the steps he needed to take to reacquire the property. Marry Skye, make her trust him, take what he wanted.

And her?

Had he really never thought about how his actions might affect her? Or had he simply never cared, because she was the daughter of the only person he'd ever hated? Had he carried his hatred of Carey Johnson onto Skye, almost delighting in the knowledge he was using her?

With an angry sigh, he pushed to standing, moving towards the open doors and breathing in the unique tang of Venice's air.

He had only seen his grandfather cry once.

The sight had dug right into his heart and pressed into his nerves, changing everything he thought he knew about life. Alfonso hadn't known that Matteo had been watching. He'd thought he was alone. And he'd given into the groundswell of emotions without hesitation. They had consumed him, his strong, powerful body racked by sobs as he'd stared at the papers before him. Papers that hadn't made sense to Matteo at the time.

Now he knew what they were.

Overdue notices.

Mortgage payment requests.

Bills that Alfonso couldn't cover.

Matteo gripped the railing hard, remembering more than Alfonso's tears. Now he remembered Skye's father. The smug, condescending glint in his face as he'd refused to deal with Matteo. When he'd refused to see reason and sell the hotel back.

You're going to regret this. That was what Matteo had said.

It had been a prophetic statement, in the end. Only it was Matteo who was full of regrets.

Matteo who had lived to wish things—everything—had been different.

There was only one thing in the midst of this that made sense. There was one way Matteo had to erase Skye's hurts—and mitigate his own. There was one thing he could remind her of that would bring happiness to both of them.

His face was set in a grim line as he moved back into the villa, walking with a slow determination to her bedroom.

She was his wife. And, when she was in his arms, nothing else seemed to matter a damn.

CHAPTER TEN

IT WAS THE lawyer's office, right beside the doctor's, that made her think of it. Skye stared at her bruschetta without attempting to bite into it.

'Matteo?'

He, apparently, was suffering from no such lack of appetite. Skye watched as he forked a scoop of spaghetti into his mouth, savouring the flavours with obvious pleasure. 'Do you think perhaps we should speak to a lawyer?'

He froze, his eyes haunted as they met hers. *'Che?'*

'Everything between us is so complicated.' A line formed between her brows as she frowned, and anxiety swirled through her. Her pregnancy was still in its infancy, but before they knew it the baby would be with them. They'd be parents. 'Don't you think we should make arrangements now? Before we get too caught up in the whole "being a family" thing?'

'What kind of arrangements?' Neither his voice nor his expression gave anything away.

'Oh.' Skye waved a hand through the air and her selection of colourful bangles made a tingling noise as they knocked together. 'Everything.' Her frown deepened. 'I suppose a proper pre-nuptial agreement.'

Matteo returned his attention to the spaghetti, forking another generous portion into his mouth. 'We are married. A pre-nuptial agreement now would seem irrelevant.'

Skye nodded slowly, but her frame of mind didn't shift. 'I think we need to be pragmatic.' She swallowed. 'Do you remember what you said?'

He pulled a face, one of amusement and mockery. 'When?'

'You told me that you never lied to me.' She stared down at her plate, the past swirling like angry floodwaters. 'And you did. Not directly, but by omission. You knew how I felt, and how I believed you felt, and you didn't tell me the truth about any of this. But you never claimed to love me. You don't love me.' She paused, just long enough for him to interject. To say something that would ease the pain in her splintered heart.

He didn't.

She swallowed and pushed on. 'And I don't love you.' The words tasted bitter in her mouth. 'We need to remember that. Once the baby comes along and we love our child to the ends of the earth, I don't want to make the mistake of feeling like this is a real relationship.'

'It *is* a real relationship,' he said with exasperation. 'You are my wife in every way.'

'No.' Her eyes were enormous as they lifted to his. 'And it's not your fault that you don't realise that. You and I just have very different ideas of what a marriage is.' Her smile was lopsided. 'Ironic, really, given that you were the one who taught me to believe in fairy tales. Perhaps the reason you believe in them is that you expect so little of them.'

His eyes narrowed.

'I want it all. I want love and happiness and a true meeting of the minds. That will never be us.' She expelled a soft sigh. 'But we both want this baby, and so we'll raise it together. But I think it's very important that we don't lose sight of the truth of what we are.'

'And what's that, *bella*?'

'Well…' She pressed a single finger into the table top,

tilting her head to the side as she examined her words carefully. 'We're two people who are going to have a baby. And we happen to be sleeping together.'

'Oh, good. I'm glad that's part of your contract.' He winked, his light-heartedness annoying her.

'I'm serious, Teo.' She tapped her finger once more. 'We both have considerable assets. I think we should get everything ordered. And I think we should have a custody arrangement drawn up. Just in case.'

'Hell, Skye. A *custody* arrangement? You're pregnant with my child and you're already planning for a divorce?'

'Not necessarily,' she responded softly. 'But if we find this impossible, I don't want to have to go through all that then. I think we should rationally make a plan now, knowing that there's a good chance this won't work out. I think we should agree now, while we are level-headed and still... like one another enough to speak fairly.'

Matteo shook his head. 'No.'

'It makes sense.' She leaned forward. 'You know that. You're thinking with your heart, not your head.'

'I thought I didn't have a heart?'

'You do where our baby is concerned. You do where your *nonno* was concerned.' *It's only me you don't love*, Skye thought bitterly, reaching for her mineral water and sipping it to bring relief to her dry mouth. 'You told me yourself that you would fight for this baby. That you would stop at nothing to raise it. Well, I don't want to fight you later.'

'You'd rather fight me now?'

A muscle jerked in Skye's jaw as she clenched her teeth together. 'I'd rather not fight you at all. It's not ideal that we're going to be raising this child together, but I think we can make it work so long as we're reasonable. *I'm* prepared to be reasonable.'

'How so?' he prompted, dark colour staining his cheeks.

Fascinated at why he was so angry, Skye continued, 'Well, I'll stay in Venice. Near you. My business interests are well looked after. I don't need to be in London. And I can skip over when I do have to be on hand.' Emboldened by his silence, she continued, 'But I don't think we should share custody equally. I think the baby should have a home, somewhere they spend most of their time…'

'I agree completely.'

'And that it should be with his mother. With me.'

'Ah.' He shook his head. 'No. My child is being raised in my home.'

'Damn it, Matteo.' Skye leaned forward. 'I'm not saying we're going to get divorced. I'm just saying we should have a plan in place *in case*.'

'And I am saying I'm not prepared to discuss it,' he dismissed. 'Not now. Not ever. You are my wife. This is my child. We are a family.'

A family.

Skye froze, her face paling visibly.

A family?

All her life, it was the one thing she'd ever wanted, and this was not what she had expected it to look like. Nothing about what they were was what she'd imagined.

She swept her eyes closed, rejecting the description instantly.

'We're not family. We're just two people stupid enough to get pregnant when they should have known better.' She pushed her plate away. 'I'm not hungry.'

'Hey, hey.' He reached for her hand, curving his fingers over it. His surprise was obvious. Skye felt it too. She wasn't sure where her feelings were coming from, only that they were strong and they were real. 'This is good news. We both want this baby, don't we?'

She nodded, but her heart was heavy. She did, she wanted this baby so badly, but not like this. It was at such odds with how she'd imagined it would be. She pulled her hand away, clasping it in her lap, withdrawing from him in every way.

'But wanting the baby isn't the same as being a family. We're not a family. We're not even really a couple.' She swallowed. 'We both need to remember that.'

Matteo stared at her long and hard, his expression inscrutable.

A chasm of loss was swarming through him. But what could he say? How could he dispute her words? He had agreed to divorce her, when she'd come to Venice. Had he really been prepared to let her walk away?

Never to see her again?

The idea sat inside him like a strange kind of blade, running the sharpness of its edge through his body, his organs; tormenting him and wounding him in ways he was unable to appraise. But what could he say to her?

The reassurances he wanted to offer were buried deep inside him. It was only in bed that things made sense. There he could make her understand.

Unless...

The idea came to him out of nowhere, but instantly it was perfect.

'Skye? There is something I would like you to see.'

It was only once they'd boarded the flight to Rome that Skye twigged as to where he was taking her.

And what to see.

The hotel.

Anxiety had met tension in her gut, but now she felt an overwhelming sense of fascination. This was the building, after all, that had formed battle lines between her husband and her father.

And it was a beautiful building. At least, it would have been at one time. Now it was in a state of complete disrepair, the once-grand foyer boarded over so that even the high ceilings and marbled floor couldn't counteract the doom and gloom. But she knew what it was, even without his explanation. There were no signs out the front, there was no name on the door, but there was an air of importance that shrouded them as Matteo inserted a thick bronze key into the door and then scraped it inwards.

Pigeons had at some point taken up residence above, so that the step was covered in white splodges of poop, and there were empty soda cans discarded to the side of the door.

Matteo turned to face Skye with a raised brow. 'Your father never bothered to change the locks.' It was an indictment, as though the oversight was evidence that Carey hadn't cared about the building at all.

Inside, it was dark and enormous, and there was a lingering odour of dust and disuse.

'The last time I was here,' Matteo said thickly, 'It was just before Christmas. A tree stood over there.' He nodded towards the stairs, which were wide and sweeping, moving in a large, wide circle upwards to the mezzanine above. 'It had the most beautiful decorations, fine gold and a dark red, made of glass from Murano. It was a real tree, and enormous, so that the whole room smelled of pine. There were lights, twinkling little fairy lights that shimmered in the tree and across the ceiling. And there was a pianist in the corner, playing old-fashioned Christmas carols.' His eyes held some of the magic of the scene when they dropped to Skye's face. 'It was a special place, Skye.'

She nodded, perfectly able to envisage the beauty he had seen. The spectre of what he'd described. He crouched down, his trousers straining across his powerful haunches as he ran his fingertips over the floor. Snakes appeared in the thick coating of dust, revealing the grain of the marble beneath. 'This was quarried from the south and it took six months to ship it all up.' He stood, wiping his hands together, his eyes simply skimming over hers as he moved deeper into the hotel.

He moved to what Skye presumed would have been the reception area. A tall, dark wood bench with a marble top, the same as the floor. There were old-fashioned lights above it, as she'd imagined might have been used in banks in the twenties and thirties. Matteo pressed one of the gold switches on the wall but it did nothing.

Of course, there was no power.

'My great-great-great-grandfather built this hotel.' His voice carried an emotional note. 'He built it, and then each generation added to it. Yes, we created an empire, and yes, we have money, but this hotel—' He broke off, looking around the room with such helplessness that Skye's heart thudded inside her and pain gulfed in her belly. 'My family lives in these walls.'

She nodded and turned away from Matteo, unable and unwilling to expose herself to him in that moment, as realisation after realisation dropped through her. This place meant everything to Matteo, and her father had taken it and refused to sell it back.

'Your father didn't want it.' Matteo echoed her thoughts unconsciously. 'In fact, letting it fall into disrepair pleased him.' The words were uttered grimly.

'I don't believe it,' Skye said quietly. 'What reason could he have for buying something and then destroying it?'

'You know the answer to that.'

'Revenge,' she muttered, the word coursing through her venomously. 'Damned revenge.'

'Yes. He closed the hotel and had it boarded up as soon as it had been transferred to him. He told me he would have torn it down if the place weren't protected by historical covenants.'

'God, Matteo.' Skye squeezed her eyes shut, guilt filling her. 'I'm sorry.'

'This was not your doing, *cara*.'

'But he hurt you and I wish… I wish…'

'Hush.' Matteo came around from behind the reception desk, staring down at his wife and fighting every urge he had to touch her, knowing that it would solve nothing. 'You and I wish the same thing,' he said with frustration and urgency. 'We both wish it hadn't happened. But then…' He dropped his hands to her stomach, pressing his fingers into her, imagining the baby that was coming to life with every day that passed. 'We wouldn't have this gift. And I believe our baby is a gift, *cara*. I married you for the hotel, and it no longer matters. Not compared to the baby that grows within your body.' He dropped his mouth to hers, kissing her lightly. 'It means everything to me.'

Skye's heart trembled in her chest. His love for their unborn child filled her with happiness, but there was envy too, for the way he was able to be so lavish in his praise for the baby and remain as closed off to her as ever before.

'I know this is not as either of us would have wanted,' he continued thickly. 'But you are pregnant, and we need to focus on making this work. We do not know what will happen tomorrow, or next week, or in a month. But I am committed to this baby. With all that I am.'

Skye couldn't answer. Tears were clogged in her throat. She was a tangle of emotions; they were running through her, violent and insistent. She did her best to blank them. To be calm.

'I'm just trying to be smart.'

Matteo grinned. A grin that made her tummy flop and her own lips twist in an answering smile.

'You're already smart.' He shrugged. 'Why don't we try to be happy now?'

Happy. The word lodged inside her as he moved away

once more, deeper into the hotel, towards the stairs. The smell was stronger there, and she realised that the carpet had been saturated over time. With a frown, she looked up and saw that the roof had a hole in it. It had been patched at some point, but a hint of the sky was visible through it.

Matteo was looking at it too, his expression impossible to read. Then he roused himself and took a step upwards, placing a hand in the small of her back. It was just a tiny gesture; it meant nothing. And, in terms of their intimacy, it was nothing like what they'd shared.

And yet it set Skye's pulse racing.

'How many rooms are there?' she asked, the question a little breathy as she tried to control her raging emotions.

If he noticed, he was sympathetic enough to respond in kind. 'There were fifty.'

'An even fifty?' she responded.

'Originally only twenty,' he said with a nod. 'When the trend was for accommodation to feature apartments rather than rooms. But over the time each lodging was downsized, to make more accommodation. Though, compared to a lot of hotels I've stayed in, they're still pretty spacious.'

'It's in a great location,' she murmured, moving up the stairs beside him. The hotel was just past The Vatican, overlooking the river Tiber.

'Yes.' Pride coloured the word. 'Once upon a time, this was the premier hotel in Rome. Royalty stayed here. Celebrities. Film stars. Musicians. Even a magician, for a time, who took to making red roses appear throughout the restaurant.' He was back in time, Skye could tell. The look on his face was one of nostalgia and grief. 'But it was more than that. The same families would come and stay at the same times each year. Groups would visit for Christmas, and again in the spring. It was a community. The breakfast room was alive each morning, and we always had the most incredible chefs. The food was truly *Romano*. Seasonal, fresh, exquisite.'

He expelled an angry breath, at odds with the wonderment his words were painting around them.

'Did you spend much time here?'

'As a child, *si*. My parents would bring us here every Christmas. We would sing carols in the foyer, and my *nonno* arranged a gift for every child in the hotel. I got to dress up as an elf and hand them out when I was very young.'

'You? An elf?' She looked at him quizzically, trying to imagine this specimen of pure masculinity as something so cute and harmless.

'Yes. What's wrong with that?'

'I'm just finding it hard to picture,' she said with a teasing smile. 'And after your parents died?' she pushed, wanting to know more, suddenly needing to understand her husband. So much of him was a mystery to her, and she didn't want that.

'Yes. For the few years my grandfather continued to hold the hotel. It was one of his last assets to go. Its loss destroyed him.'

She shook her head from side to side. 'And you were so young.'

'I swore that day that I would get the hotel back.' He stared around the foyer. 'I know it is just a building to you, but to our family, to me, this hotel is redemption.'

She nodded slowly, tears close to the surface.

'Let me show you the terrace.'

Skye went with him even though a part of her was dreading what was to follow.

The hotel was beautiful.

She got it.

Her family had taken it from his, and he had been angry about it. So angry that he'd married her to get it back.

The truth of that was appalling and yet, walking beside

him through the hotel that her father had vandalised with his neglect, a hotel that her father had let fall into a state of complete abandon and disgrace, churned her up with anger.

She could imagine her husband's emotions. The strength of despair that must have filled him.

'He should have sold it back to you.'

'*Si, certamente,*' Matteo agreed. 'But he felt my father had taken everything from him. This was the perfect recompense for that.'

'People aren't objects,' Skye said with a shake of her head. 'Your mother chose to be with your father. If she'd loved my dad then she would have married him.' She paused, lifting a hand to her temple as a sharp pain burst through her.

Matteo noticed instantly. 'You are okay?'

'Yes, I'm fine.' She nodded. The pain passed and she continued upwards. 'These are bedrooms?'

'Now they are simply empty rooms.' The joke fell flat as remorse overrode humour. His eyes met hers for a moment before continuing an inspection of the run-down visage. 'The furniture was sold by the bank at auction to cover my grandfather's business debts.'

Skye nodded, pausing near one of the doorways. She lifted a hand to it, surprised when it pushed inwards. The room was large and spacious, open-plan, so that she could see the view of Rome from the grimy windows, and a bathroom that, at one time, would have been palatial.

A movement in the corner startled her and she squealed, but Matteo was right there, a strong arm around her waist. His smile was teasing. 'It is just a bat.'

'How do you know?'

His eyes scanned the room. 'They are everywhere in here. The security team I employ keeps drifters and vandals from setting up in the hotel, but bats we are powerless to prevent.'

Skye's heart turned over. 'You have security looking after the place? Even when it's no longer yours?'

'It will always be mine, in my heart,' he said seriously. 'If no one else is to look after it, then I will.' His smile was tight and didn't reach his eyes. 'I'm sure your father would have had me arrested for trespassing, if he were still alive.'

Skye said nothing. How could she deny it? It was obvious that the depth of her father's animosity had run deeper than she'd appreciated.

'I trust you will be kinder?' He winked, the smile on his face making her stomach flip and flop.

She nodded, distracted, and stepped out of the room, moving beside him back towards the stairs. Her headache had disappeared and now her head was throbbing instead, a low, dull pain. She pressed her fingers to her hair, loosening it and hoping the discomfort would pass.

She didn't want to cut their tour short.

'What is it?'

His solicitous question had Skye's head lifting towards his, and he was closer than she'd expected, so that she could have lifted up on tiptoes and kissed him. And she wanted to. She really wanted to.

Maybe it was the magic of the place but suddenly, though she was surrounded by the past, it no longer seemed to matter.

Let's be happy.

He was her happy.

But he was also her pain, her head pointed out.

'Skye?'

'Oh.' She nodded. 'Just a headache. I get them when I fly, sometimes.'

'Are you sure?'

'Yeah.' She nodded. 'I'll be fine. What next?'

CHAPTER ELEVEN

'I THINK WE should fix it.'

Matteo stared at Skye, pulling his attention away from the view of Rome to look at his wife. Here, finally, there was light. The rest of the hotel had fallen into a state of dinge and disrepair, but on the rooftop terrace he could imagine the hotel as it had once been.

Of course, back in its heyday, the terrace always had been full of Rome's elite sipping cocktails, overlooking the city, listening to the music that was playing.

'Fix what?'

'The hotel,' she murmured slowly. 'It's too beautiful, too grand, to be left like this.'

Matteo was very still, his eyes holding his wife's as though nothing made sense. 'You want to fix the hotel?'

'Yeah.' But his muted response made her doubt, made her pause. 'Don't you think it's a good idea?'

He pulled a face. 'Of course I do. It is what I intended to do when I…'

'When you stole it back from me, your unwitting wife?' She arched a brow meaningfully.

'As soon as I could,' he corrected. 'Skye…'

'It's okay.' Her response was soft. 'I get it. I understand why this place means so much to you.'

'Si?'

She nodded. ' I'll never forgive you for what you did.

But I think my dad raised the stakes. I think he should have sold this place back to you. No, I think he should never have bought it.'

'We had to sell,' he said softly.

'But he bought it just to ruin it,' Skye murmured, shaking her head. 'Such needless destruction. I want to undo that.'

Matteo's eyes met hers and it was a moment that was perfect and poignant all at once. Because his eyes locked with Skye's and she felt, for the first time, as though maybe he did love her. And it wasn't about her at all. It was about the hotel. The damned hotel.

She looked away awkwardly. 'I know it will take time. And a lot of money. But can you imagine?'

'I don't need to imagine. I can remember.'

Skye nodded. 'I presume you have an idea as to where to start?'

His nod was brusque. 'Let's discuss it over dinner.'

Skye rolled her eyes. 'We ate on the plane.'

'Is our marriage going to consist of me suggesting food and you insisting you are not hungry? I do not seem to remember this being the case before.'

'Before, you found a way to deplete my energy and increase my appetite constantly.'

'Ah. Something I am happy to do now, believe me.'

Her stomach swooped and a wave of nausea buffered her. Suddenly, the idea of something like hot chips or focaccia was infinitely appealing. 'I could eat,' she said, changing the subject onto safer ground.

'And we will talk about Il Grande Fortuna.' His eyes glittered and her heart stuttered. He loved this place, and she owned it. He loved the baby she was growing. Suddenly, the fact he didn't love her seemed less important. Perhaps she could make do with these small crumbs?

She studied the hotel with renewed interest as they

moved inside and down the stairs. While it was dark and dilapidated, so much of it was still glorious. The spine of the place was unmistakably perfect. The wide staircase, the chandeliers, the high ceilings and the skylights that were frosted over now with smog and dust but that had been, at one point, crystal-clear and had permitted light from the sun and the stars to filter into the hotel.

'It's beautiful,' she said as they reached the foyer, her eyes chasing the potential through the present.

'It was,' he agreed.

'And it will be again.' They walked towards the door in silence, but once there Skye paused. 'Thank you for showing it to me. It's helped me understand, I guess.'

'Understand?' he prompted.

'I understand why it means so much to you. If it had been less special…' She didn't finish the thought. She wasn't even sure of what she'd wanted to say.

Matteo pushed the door open and Skye stepped onto the street, looking left and right and imagining how they would rejuvenate even this aspect. She crossed to the other side as Matteo locked the door and stood with her hands on her hips, staring up at the façade, imagining it once it had been cleaned and had flags hanging from the brass poles that were languishing in neglect. She imagined it with window boxes that would be full of geraniums, all bright red, greeting the day as it rose overhead and offering their guests a hint of wild flora in the middle of Rome.

'What are you thinking of?' he asked as he came to stand beside her.

She smiled wistfully. 'Of the geraniums we'll have planted. On every window sill, just like at your villa.' She sighed. 'I loved waking up to them. Before. Before I left,' she clarified, colour darkening her cheeks at the oblique reference to their first attempt at married life. 'I used to pick them and place them in a vase—'

'I remember.' A gravelled interruption.

'I mean they're such an ordinary flower, I suppose, yet they're beautiful and resilient and so willing to grow,' she said with a shrug. 'I can see them here.'

'So can I,' he agreed, without taking his eyes from her face.

Discussing the hotel with Matteo over dinner brought the project more to life for Skye, so that by the time they boarded the flight home late that night, and then arrived back in Venice, Skye was full of excitement.

'I don't think I'm going to be able to sleep,' she murmured as they walked in the door of the villa. It was almost midnight, and she should have been exhausted, but a strange feeling was flooding her body.

The nausea was back, and she knew why. It was the sheer thrill of what they were going to do. Not just the baby, but everything else.

The hotel—something she'd viewed as an intense negative—was now something she contemplated with enthusiasm. And she was also utterly in love with it. Yes, she could admit her love for the hotel. It was simple. It was impossible *not* to love it. Or perhaps that was the baby in her stomach, willing her to connect with the ancestry that meant so much to the Vin Santos.

'We could swim instead,' he suggested with a sensual look that flopped Skye's stomach.

'Maybe a quick swim.' She nodded.

He reached down and held her hand, pulling her with him towards the stairs. She went willingly until they reached the terrace where they had first made love. The night of their wedding. And suddenly Skye didn't want to remember that. She didn't want to remember anything about their first attempt at marriage.

She wanted to write over the memories with new ones.

Memories that were full of who she was now, the truth of their relationship something they both held in the palms of their hands. This was no love story, but there was enough between them to make this work. So long as she didn't forget. So long as she didn't lose her heart to him again.

'Matteo,' she murmured, and he stopped walking near the edge of the pool, pausing to look down at her. 'I want...'

She didn't finish the sentence. There was no need. He understood what his wife needed and wanted; it was the same desire that was heavy in his body. He dropped his mouth to hers, kissing her, holding her; bending her towards the ground and running his hands over her body at the same time, discarding her clothes, teasing her with the lightness of his touch while his mouth was ravaging hers.

He grabbed her hands and lifted them, pulling them behind his neck, and plying her body to his so there was barely even air between them. His dominance of her was almost as complete as hers of him. The moon shone overhead and the night was warm, yet Skye shivered in his arms, her body covered in a fine film of goose-bumps. He ran his hands down her back, finding the curve of her rear and lifting her effortlessly; wrapping her naked legs around his waist and holding her to his hard, confident body.

He turned slowly, kissing her neck, moving her to one of the sun lounges and laying her down with the kind of reverence that could make her forget everything.

Wasn't that what she'd wanted? To forget their first marriage and enter into this relationship as if it were new and fresh, and they were two different people?

And weren't they? She'd never again be the innocent, naïve woman who had believed herself swept off her feet.

Matteo didn't love her.

He never had.

Perhaps there was something smart in seeing their relationship as a transaction. Taking what was good from it and not lamenting what was missing.

There *was* so much good between them.

But could she ever really forgive him?

Did she want to?

His mouth drove into hers, sending all thoughts from her mind. But Skye was afraid. Afraid of how easily he could make her body sing. Afraid of how much she wanted him. Afraid of how she was going to cope in the years that would follow.

'This is just sex,' she whispered as he dragged his mouth to her breasts.

'Perfect can't-get-enough sex,' he agreed, with a smile that said nothing of the emotional torment she was feeling.

Would she never get enough? Was this a life sentence?

Her heart skidded inside her.

And it was joy that made her smile.

She'd never be able to resist him, and maybe that was okay. In that moment, everything was perfect. But it was a perfection that couldn't and wouldn't last. If only Skye had known to make the most of it while she could...

'Matteo?'

It was the middle of the night. No, it was past that. They'd made love somewhere in the early hours of the morning and then he'd carried Skye to his bed, insisting that she spend the night beside him. He couldn't have said why it mattered so much to him, only that he liked the way it felt to have her body curled back against his, for his arm to be wrapped around her stomach. To know that their baby was there, safe and loved.

He groaned, smiling as he pressed a kiss into Skye's warm, smooth shoulder. But it was damp, covered in salty perspiration, and the taste on his lips had him blinking his eyes open.

'Something's wrong,' she said with more urgency, and he focused on her face. She was sweating all over: her hair was wet, and she was pale and shaking.

'*Bella*, what is it?' He pushed out of bed and was reaching for his jeans in one movement. 'Skye?'

She pressed the palm of her hand to her stomach and tears filled her eyes. 'Something's *wrong*!' She said it with more urgency. 'I'm scared.'

It was awful.

Awful for him, but so much worse for his wife. All he could do was hold her hand and whisper to her in Italian as the proof of their loss slowly left her body. He kissed her and he held her, but Skye wasn't really in the room with him. She was stoic and brave, but she had obviously divorced her mind from the horror of what they were experiencing.

Her eyes were empty, just like her womb, just like her soul and her hopes for the future. The future they had both imagined and hoped for.

She listened to the doctor, who came to assure Skye that sometimes these things 'just happened'. She listened to the nurses as they kindly explained that lots of women miscarried early on in their pregnancies and later went on to have healthy babies. That she had an eighty percent likelihood of carrying to term 'next time'. She listened as her heart was breaking and her body was emptying itself of the life that she had loved with all her heart.

And only when they were alone, and an unappetising dinner had been brought with a sweet cup of tea, did tears moisten her eyes.

'*Cara...*' Matteo crouched beside her, trying to draw her eyes in his direction. But she stared at the wall with eyes that were wet and distraught. 'Talk to me.'

She couldn't.

There were no words.

She reached for her tea and sipped it, happy when the boiling water scalded her tongue. Pleased that the pain meant she was alive again. That she could feel.

Because inside she was numb.

She was cold, she was empty and she was alone in a way that was so much worse than any other form of loneliness she'd ever known.

The fluorescent light overhead flickered, and with each dimming it made a crackling sound. Just a low, muted buzzing. Skye heard it as though she were in a void.

A silent sob racked her body, lifting it off the bed and dropping it back down again. She turned away from him then, not wanting him to see the anguish that contorted her features.

'Bella, per favore...' He groaned, reaching a hand up and laying it on her thigh. She didn't pull away from him physically, but emotionally she was cutting every cord that had ever joined her to him. She was rejecting the intimacy and rejecting him, relegating him to a portion of her mind that was never to be looked at again.

'I want to go home,' she said after several long moments.

'Of course. I'm sure that will happen soon. They probably just want to observe you a little longer, to be sure you are okay.'

'Okay?' she repeated with soft disbelief. Then, she nodded. Because he seemed to expect it. 'I'm okay.' She placed the plastic tea cup onto the table beside her, staring at the ripples in the drink's surface.

Matteo's frown was infinitesimal and he smothered it quickly before she could see it. Not that she was looking in his direction. Her face was averted with unwavering determination.

God, her face.

She was so pale. He pushed up and sat on the bed beside her, wincing as she flinched away from him.

'Please.' It was just a whisper. Her fingers caught at the blanket, pulling at it awkwardly. 'I want to leave here.'

'Lo so, lo so.' He reached up and ran a hand gently over her hair; it was matted and still damp from the perspiration. 'I am sure it won't be long.'

She spun round to face him, dislodging his touch. 'I need you to get me out of here. Now.'

The urgency of her heart communicated itself through her words. He stood immediately. There was nothing he wouldn't do for her in that moment. 'I'm so sorry, Skye.'

'Sorry?' she whispered, her eyes enormous. 'Why are you sorry? This was my fault, not yours.'

He shook his head slowly. 'No. It wasn't anyone's fault. They told you that…'

'I want to go home,' she said with more urgency. 'Please.'

He nodded, a single, terse movement. 'I'll speak to someone.' His eyes clung to her as he moved to the door. 'Just wait. A moment.'

She didn't respond. What was she meant to do?

Did he expect her to get up and try to make a bid for freedom out of the air-conditioning vent?

There were no windows in the room.

No view of the outside. And somehow that felt appropriate, as though even the beauty of Venice had turned its back on her.

When Matteo came back a few minutes later, it was with a doctor clutching a chart. Her smile was sympathetic as she studied Skye.

'I'm happy to let you go home,' the doctor said without preamble. 'So long as you'll come back in a week, or at the first sign of any complications.'

'What kind of complications?' Matteo responded.

'Oh, infection. Raised temperature. Anything out of the ordinary. Okay?'

Skye bit down on her lip and nodded, though she was barely comprehending. 'Fine. Of course. Thank you.' The words sounded so normal, but *nothing* was normal. The whole world was off its axis.

'You will take care of her?'

'*Si.*' Matteo's single-word answer was gruff. Skye squeezed her eyes shut against it. One syllable, so full of falsity. So unnecessary.

'I'll be fine,' Skye murmured, attempting a smile. It felt awful on her lips, heavy and sodden all at once. She let it fall almost instantly.

The images she had allowed to populate her mind were disintegrating, like puffs of cloud she couldn't reach out and grab. She squeezed her eyes shut and tried to picture the baby she'd imagined them having. But he was gone. That chubby face wouldn't come to mind. She couldn't remember the dimples she'd seen there, nor the curls of dark hair.

She couldn't see him! She couldn't feel him!

Panic rose inside her, and then nausea, and she reached out instinctively. Matteo was there, his arms wrapping around her, holding her. He smelled so good, so strong, and he felt so right. But he was wrong. This was all wrong.

She stiffened and pushed away from him, swallowing away the pain in her throat. There would be a time to process this. For now, Skye was in survival mode.

A water taxi was waiting to take them home, and the boat operator was far cheerier than either Skye or Matteo had tolerance for. They sat in silence, shocked and uncomprehending as the boat steered them towards Matteo's home.

It was a clear, sunshine-filled morning.

Skye's heart felt only coldness.

When the boat came to a stop near Matteo's, he held a

hand out for her, to help her step out. Only the fact she was still in pain and discomfort implored her to take it. Just for the briefest possible moment.

She didn't want to touch him.

She didn't want to *feel* his touch.

'Thank you,' she murmured, staring up at the villa. The geraniums were smiling down at her, encouraging her.

She blinked away from them. She did her best to blot out the sunshine too.

'Come, *cara*.' He put a hand in the small of her back. She stepped forward, shaking him free, moving as quickly as she could towards his front door.

Everything was different.

Not like before, when she'd returned to their marriage and she'd thought herself miserable.

She was truly miserable now, and she viewed everything through the veil of that misery and despair.

It was still only early in the day, and they'd hardly slept. The last twenty-four hours passed before her eyes like some kind of movie. They'd been in Rome and she'd been so happy, looking at the hotel and imagining the way they could heal the wounds that had caused its demise. Had she hoped it might lead him to love her?

Yes.

She had felt that it was a beginning, when really it had been an end.

For what purpose did their marriage serve now? There was no love. And no baby.

And no point in her staying in Venice with Matteo.

CHAPTER TWELVE

'You must eat something.'

Skye didn't smile, though a part of her remembered the number of times he'd said just that to her. But then she'd been pregnant, and his concern had made sense. He'd been worried for their baby.

Now?

She shook her head. It wasn't his place to worry about her.

In the three days since the miscarriage, she'd survived on tea and dry biscuits, and she'd barely moved from her spot on the sofa. She stared out at Venice, but she wasn't really looking. She was simply existing.

'I'm not hungry,' she said, because Matteo seemed to be waiting for her to say something.

'But your body is recovering. You must be strong and well, Skye.'

'Why?' she asked, though it wasn't really a question, so much as a word that was breathed out by her sigh.

'Because. I need you to be well.'

Skye didn't look at him. She couldn't. 'Why?'

He crouched beside her and pressed a hand into her thigh. 'Because you are my wife.'

She flinched, as though he'd threatened her. 'No.'

Matteo was very quiet, watching her for several long

seconds, and then he abandoned the conversation. Not out of a desire to avoid it, but out of a need to avoid upsetting her further. He could see her breath becoming rushed and her cheeks flushing pink. He let it go, for the moment. 'Would you like a tea?'

'No.' She turned to face him now. There was nothing familiar in Skye's face. She was altered and broken, completely different. He could hardly recognise the woman he'd married. Her face was pale and her hair was heavy and lank. Her eyes, though, were so full of darkness and aching sadness.

His chest squeezed, as though it had been weighed down with something heavy.

'If you have the papers redrawn, I'll sign the hotel over to you before I leave.'

Matteo froze, his body tense, his expression incomprehensible. 'Before you leave? Where are you planning to go, Skye?'

She turned away from him again, staring out at Venice. It was annoyingly perfect beyond the window. Sunny and bright, with blue skies as far as she could see. 'Home. I want to go home.'

His tone had urgency. 'You *are* home.'

She swallowed, her throat moving visibly. 'No.'

'We're married and we live—'

She spoke over him. 'Without the baby, there's no point to my being here.'

'Yes, there is!' He was emphatic. 'My God, Skye. This doesn't change anything. It's…it is all the more reason for you to stay. I want to… You can't leave. I want us to be together. I want to have a family with you, Skye, one day. This wasn't the right time. This wasn't meant to be. But that doesn't mean we can't have other babies one day—'

'Don't!' The word was a sharp hiss and she recoiled as

she said it. Recoiled from him and his words, from each and every platitude designed to make her feel better but which had the exact opposite effect. 'God, just don't.'

'Cara,' he said softly. 'You are hurting. So am I. It will take time before we feel like ourselves again...'

'You have no idea what I'm feeling,' she said, tilting her head to his. 'So don't tell me how I'm supposed to act. Don't tell me I'm going to be like myself again.'

He nodded sympathetically, but when he spoke it was with grim determination. 'This was my baby too. Do you think you are the only one who is grieving?'

She sucked in a deep breath. 'Are you trying to make me feel guilty now?'

He sighed. 'No, nothing like that. But you are not alone in this.'

'Yes, I am.' She squeezed her eyes shut against all the pain and sadness that was choking her. 'And I *want* to be alone.' She lay back against the sofa, turning her back on him and closing her eyes.

She breathed in and out and now, with her eyes shut, and sadness filling her up; she could finally see their baby again. She could see his little face and the dimples she'd imagined he'd have; she sobbed freely, believing herself to be alone. She sobbed with all the grief in her heart. And she wasn't just grieving their baby. It was everything. The loss of hope. Of love. Of her belief that she had found her own *happily ever after*.

'You're not alone,' he said finally, after so long that she'd presumed he'd left. 'I'm here with you.'

She sobbed harder, grieving their baby as well as their love. Grieving the life she'd imagined before her.

It was all a lie, just like everything about them.

'I wish I'd never met you. I wish you'd never spoken to me.'

'Hush, hush,' he murmured, patting her back.

'I hate you,' she sobbed into the pillow. 'I hate you so much.'

Skye wasn't sleeping, so much as dozing fitfully. She was exhausted, yet the second she closed her eyes and drifted off she awoke in a panic, feeling as though she were drowning and there was nothing she could do to stop the water that was gushing into her lungs.

She woke in such a manner early the next day, and she noticed three things.

A small water glass had been filled with geraniums at some point and placed on the occasional table beside her. And she knew who had done it. The gesture iced her heart, for it was at once both so sweet and meaningless.

Matteo was asleep across the room, sitting in an armchair dressed in day clothes, looking as exhausted as she felt.

And she was hungry.

It was just a kernel of need, but it was unmistakable. She pushed off the sofa quietly, careful not to wake Matteo, and padded into the kitchen. There was no Melania, no one. Skye wondered, vaguely, if Matteo had told Melania. Had even asked her to give them space.

The fridge was full, as always, but when Skye opened it and looked inside she couldn't make up her mind as to what she felt like.

She opted for a small croissant, simply because she could eat it without any preparation or fuss. She took it with her onto the terrace and stared out at the city, her stomach dropping with grief at this place that would never be her home.

'Cara.' The word was gravelled. She spun around, her cheeks flushing with something like guilt. Matteo looked... terrible and delicious all at once. She tamped down on the stirring of primal needs.

She wouldn't answer their call ever again.

'I thought you were gone.'

She blinked, turning away from him, facing out towards Venice. 'No.'

She felt him move behind her and braced for the inevitable physical contact. Perhaps understanding what she needed most of all, he stayed a little distance away, giving her space.

'How are you feeling today?'

She shrugged. What words were there for how she felt?

'Come and rest some more,' he said softly. 'It's early.'

She nodded, but didn't move. 'I don't understand,' she said finally. 'I don't understand what happened.'

His throat moved as he swallowed. She caught the action and wondered at his own emotions. 'The doctor said that, more than likely, there was a genetic abnormality within the baby. An "incompatibility with life", she called it.'

Skye squeezed her eyes shut, the detail layering more guilt onto her wounded heart.

'There was nothing you could have done differently.'

'Of course there is. It was my baby. My body. I should have…'

'There was nothing you could have done.' He was insistent.

'Do you know what I thought? Only a week or so ago? I told you that I wished I was having the baby with anyone but you.' Her voice cracked. 'What I meant was that I wished I wasn't pregnant with your baby.'

She let the words hit their mark, strangely pleased when his face paled beneath his tan and his eyes squeezed shut for a moment.

'I wished I wasn't pregnant, and now I'm not.'

'One thing has nothing to do with the other,' he said after a moment, the words gentle.

'I didn't deserve the baby.' A hollow whisper. 'That's why I lost it.'

'No, stop. You must stop.' He drew his brows together, his expression sombre. 'Do not torment yourself with what you should and could have done differently.' His mouth was a grim slash. 'If either of us was at fault here, if either of us should have behaved differently, it was not you.'

He turned his attention back to the canal. 'I am sorry, Skye. For everything I've done to you.' She jerked her head around to face him, shock making the details of his appearance somehow brighter than they should have been. The grey flesh beneath his eyes; the stubble on his chin that spoke of a lack of interest in grooming, the way his mouth was drawn downward.

Her heart ached for him.

And for herself.

And for their baby.

'I'm going inside,' she murmured, turning and moving back into the villa.

A week after the loss, Skye was no longer in any physical discomfort. Her body was itself again. But her mind and heart would never be the same. She woke early one morning and went to the terrace, diving into the water of the pool wearing only her underwear. She swum for an hour, up and back, up and back, hoping that she would exhaust herself to the point of sleep finally. Real sleep, not sleep tormented by dreams of what their baby might have been like, and the certainty that she'd lost something she'd never replace.

A week after that, and she had learned to numb herself to the grief. At least, some of the time.

And she had accepted that she had to move on.

All the while, Matteo had watched her, had been close to her without invading her space, had accepted her state of non-communication and had waited for the time when she would open up to him again.

His waiting was futile, though, because she never would.

Later that night, once Melania had set the table for dinner, Skye poured herself a large glass of Pinot Grigio. She sipped almost half of it, placed it at her setting at the table, and went in search of Matteo.

When she found him, her heart almost cracked open once more.

He was in his study, holding the stupid stuffed toy he'd bought for the baby.

The ground lurched beneath Skye and it took every ounce of strength she had been trying to rediscover not to break down in tears.

'I've booked a taxi,' she murmured. 'It will be here soon. I thought we could discuss the logistics of our divorce before I go.'

God, the words had sounded so clinical and professional when she'd rehearsed them, but now they just seemed discordant and wrong.

His eyes, hollow and almost looking suspiciously moist, lifted to hers. 'Why?'

Skye didn't know if he was talking about the baby, or about her, or any of it. She shook her head, staring across at him, the cavern of the room opening before her.

She smiled, a weak smile that was almost impossible to unearth. 'I don't belong here. I want to go home.'

'You're my wife.'

Skye ignored the statement. He'd said it often enough, and she knew that the words meant nothing. 'Only until our divorce is processed.' She swallowed past the pain in her throat. 'We lost the baby, Teo.' She said it as though perhaps he hadn't realised. 'There is nothing left here.'

He moved quickly, sweeping across the room, dropping

the toy as he went. 'Yes, there is!' He spoke with urgency. 'There's us. You and me.'

She shook her head. 'No.'

'I don't want you to go. I need you…'

Skye swept her eyes shut; her heart was twisting painfully in her chest, despite her certainty that she had no more grief left to feel. 'Why? Why do you need me?'

'Why do you need me?' he pushed, lifting a hand to her chest, feeling her heart beating, feeling her goodness.

Because she loved him.

Because he was a part of her.

She stiffened her spine, mentally holding herself at a distance from him. 'I don't.' And she didn't want to. 'I need to start forgetting.'

'Please, don't.' He lifted his hands to cup her face, and she saw all the grief he was feeling. She felt guilt for it. For the baby she'd offered him and then lost. 'Don't forget.'

'Why not?' She sniffed, focusing on a point over his shoulder. 'I look at you and I just remember…everything. I don't want to remember.' She cleared her throat. 'I don't want any payment for the hotel. It should never have been taken from you.' She reached up and cupped her hand over his, allowing herself to be weak for a moment. She closed her eyes and breathed him in. 'When it's finished, I might come back and stay in it for a night.'

It was something she had no intention of doing, though. When she left, she would never again set foot in Italy.

'This is madness. You are grieving now, we both are, but that doesn't change anything about our marriage. Even before I knew about the baby I didn't want you to go. You are my wife and you love me.'

Skye shivered softly. Was there any point in denying it? To him, to herself? She did love him. It was an incontrovertible fact. 'You don't love me, though.' She looked up at him. 'Do you?'

He stared down at her, and for a moment she thought he was actually going to say it. She wondered how it would sound, to hear those words on his lips and know they were meant for her. But then he turned away from her and scooped the toy up off the floor.

'You mean more to me than any other woman ever has.'

Skye's lips twisted at the faint praise. 'Let's talk in the dining room,' she said quietly.

'A last supper?' he queried, turning around to pin her with his gaze.

'It is better that we sort out the logistics now. So that we don't need…'

'To speak again?' He swore under his breath. 'I don't want that! I don't want you to go!'

'I can't stay.' She spun away from him and stalked down the corridor away from him, her heart breaking, her anger rising, her feelings rioting. He was just behind her, reaching for her, pulling at her hand so that she stopped and collided with him.

'Why not?' He was right there, his chest moving hard and fast as he sucked in air and expelled it angrily.

'Because there's no baby! And no love. This marriage is just a cruel joke.'

'I know nothing of love,' he said, the words rasping inside him. 'The one time I thought I felt it I was so wrong. I know nothing about how hearts are meant to feel. And I am so sick of hearing people talk about a heart as though it is the beginning and end of what a man is supposed to give to a woman! Do I love you? Do you have my *heart*?' He stared at her and she held her breath, her eyes clinging to his.

'No, *cara*. You have *all* of me. My blood. My body. My mind. All of me is yours, and has been since the moment I met you. When I tell you I need you, I do not mean it in the way you think. It is not sex that I am referring to. I *need*

you as I *need* air, and I *need* water. You are no less important to me and my survival than these things. I thought I
married you for the hotel.' He lifted a finger to her lips,
silencing anything she might be going to say. 'But somewhere in those early days, while you were falling in love
with me, I was doing the exact same thing.'

His words ripped through her; they were everything
she'd needed to hear a fortnight earlier. Now, they only
compounded her grief. 'Don't say that! You don't need to
lie to me, Matteo! You can have the hotel. You can let me
go. You can get on with your own life…'

'*You* are my life! Yes, I wanted the hotel. I spent so much
of my life wanting it that I did whatever I could to finally
have it. But that changes *niente* about what I want now.'
He cupped her face, holding her still so that he could stare
down at her, his eyes boring into hers.

'How can you not see what you are to me? Why do you
need me to define how I feel about you by the way other
people feel? Nothing about what we are has ever been experienced before. Do you truly believe this is just love?
Such an insipid, boring, common description for what I
feel! I despise that word, as though saying it changes a
damned thing! Love is a feeling that can be transient and
cheap, that many claim to have felt. The word is thrown
about like emotional confetti. That's not what we are! No
one has felt this! Ever! I have told another woman that I
loved her, and yet I never felt for her what I do for you! It
cheapens what we are, to use that same word. You are my
everything. You are like a universe that lives in my chest.
Is this what you need to hear?'

She stared at him and could scarcely breathe for the
flood of feelings rioting inside of her. 'You have never,
not once, told me any of that. How can I believe you truly
mean it? I'd be stupid to trust you again.'

'Believe me, *cara*, I would have told you sooner if I

ad understood my own feelings.' His face was pale, and she didn't doubt the truth of what he was saying. 'I did marry you for the hotel. I didn't care about you, or what you wanted. Not at first. I can't tell you when that changed. I only know that, now? Now you are *all* I care about.' He shook his head angrily. '*Dio*, when you talked about a pre-emptive custody arrangement the other day, I felt like you were bludgeoning me. Even then, I didn't understand why I should have such an irrational response to your very logi-cal suggestion. But I see now, Skye. I have been so in love with you this whole damned time that the idea of losing you again was impossible. Impossible.'

He stared at her for a long moment. 'The first time you left, I was so angry. I was angry because I didn't want to feel anything else. And when you came back, you wanted a divorce, and I thought I should give it to you. I see now that I signed the papers out of shame and guilt, out of a wish to undo the pain I had caused you. Out of a need for you to be happy, because I loved you. Because I loved you with all my heart.'

Skye shook her head, instinctively railing against his version of events that didn't fit with how she'd felt.

His voice became more urgent, as he felt her pulling away from him despite everything he was offering. 'And we were given a baby. A reason to *fight*. To fight for what we have.'

'But the baby is gone…'

'Yes.' Emotions passed over his face. 'And we will grieve that loss for ever. For the rest of our lives. But we will grieve *together*, because we are meant to be so.'

Oh, but her heart. The heart he held, the heart he'd bro-ken, the heart that was now ripped into tiny pieces, the heart that was empty. It rejected everything he said. It had learned, at last.

'You were right,' she whispered, pulling back, away

from his touch, standing straight. 'Love is a lie. It's all a lie.' She forced herself to meet his eyes. 'I can't stay.'

He squared his strong jaw, his eyes warring with hers, his natural tendency to overrule and dominate combated by his newly discovered need to comfort his wife. 'This isn't...'

She bit down on her lip. 'There's too much pain here.'

'But so much good,' he murmured.

'Not enough.' She blinked, stepping away from him. 'I have wanted love all my life, and I fell in love with someone who doesn't even know what it means.'

'I told you...'

She swallowed, trying to make sense of her thoughts. 'I know it wasn't just about the hotel. And I know it wasn't just about the baby.' Her voice cracked on the single word as her dreams and hopes sped away from her. 'You don't like losing, Matteo. And if I walk out that door, you've lost.'

'I don't care about losing. I care about losing *you*!'

The distinction was an important one, but Skye was becoming more convinced of what she needed to do with every painful moment that passed.

'You've already lost me.' She blinked, but tears still filled her eyes. 'You lost me the day you proposed, knowing it was just for the hotel.' She lifted a hand, her trembling fingers running over his cheek. 'You lost me the day you stood in front of me and vowed to love me for the rest of your life, knowing you didn't feel that way. You lost me all the times you've told me that all we have is sex. You lost me a long time ago. I'm just making it official now.' She pulled away from him, her heart no longer breaking. It simply ceased to exist. 'I have to go.'

There was disbelief and desperation etched on his face. 'Give me a chance. Another week...'

'You need to understand, Matteo.' The words echoed with the strength of her intent. 'I don't *want* to give you a chance. I don't want you to change my mind. I don't ever want to trust you not to hurt me, because I know that you will. You're incapable of love, and love is all I really want.' She cleared her throat and rallied her emotions as best she could. 'I'd appreciate it if you'd pass my best onto Melania. Explain that I couldn't stay.'

Matteo's skin was pale beneath his tan. 'Skye, I do love you. With all that I am…'

Her eyes were defiant but her voice was soft. Gentle. 'It's okay. No more lies. You can let me go. Let's both pretend this never happened.'

CHAPTER THIRTEEN

SKYE STARED AT the flowers. She admired the lilies with their pristine white petals. *He says you are very soft. Like a petal.*

Instinctively, she looked away. Towards the daffodils with their bright-yellow colour so like the sunlight of Venice. Her heart lurched and her eyes skidded onwards.

'What'll it be, miss?'

She blinked at the man standing like a flower-worshipping troll deep in the cave of his floristry van and tried to smile. She suspected it came off as more of a wince, as most of her smiles had done for a while.

Her eyes dropped back to the collection of blooms.

The red gerberas were beautiful, but the second she looked at them she saw only the geraniums that had grown rampant at Matteo's villa, and she couldn't bear to have a substitute for the flower.

'Miss?'

She nodded and reached for a thick collection of gladioli, choosing them at random.

But, as she walked home and held them in the palm of her hands, she had to acknowledge that their long, spiked stems somewhat matched her current mood. They were still barely budding. Just a streak of colour along the length indicated that, one day soon, they would be bright and glorious. For the moment, they were simply a beginning.

She moved through the streets of Fulham, weaving through people, breathing in as she past her favourite dim sum house, enjoying the intoxicating combination of soy sauce and spices that permeated the air.

It was a nice day, given that autumn was now upon them, and the local pub had people spilling out onto the footpath. Their noise was loud. She kept her head averted, refusing to look at the flower pots that had, yes, geraniums, but also pansies and stocks. But in twisting her face away, she looked across the street and saw...

Her heart thumped. She froze.

Matteo?

His back was to her, but he wore the navy suit she loved and his dark hair was brushing against its collar. Her tongue felt heavy in her mouth. Sweat beaded across her upper lip and she held her breath.

A woman emerged from the bakery, her smile wide. God, she was pregnant, her stomach rounded as though she were due to have the baby any moment. Skye's gut twisted. The man turned to embrace her and Skye saw his pale skin and slightly tipped nose.

It was not Matteo. She pushed her head down and hurried onwards, turning off the main road after a block and moving down the little side street on which her townhouse stood.

'Hi!' One of the little boys from the house next door called to her, his public school uniform in a state of disarray that Skye suspected would earn him a talking to when his mother and father got home. His tie was wonky and his shirt pocket was almost completely torn loose.

'Rugby,' he explained with a shrug, and she nodded, turning away and moving quickly towards her gate. She unclipped it and pushed up the stairs, unlocking her door and heaving it open as though it weighed a ton.

Simple tasks such as opening a door had become oner-

ous since leaving Italy, but she knew that wouldn't last
One day she would feel like herself again.

Flowers would help.

Her house was dark and cold, despite the mildness of
the day. She frowned as she moved deeper into it, stepping
over the mail on the floor, resolving to tend to it later, as
she had done for the last week or so.

She arranged the gladioli in a slender vase and turned
the television on, raising the volume until noise and conversation filled much of the downstairs of her home. She
liked the company.

She liked that the television expected nothing of her.

The afternoon dragged.

She made a cup of tea at some point around dark.

And then a piece of toast nearer to nine.

And, finally, she decided she'd done enough. She'd made
it through the day. She could sleep, and start all over again
in the morning.

Her expression was grim, her skin pale like moonlight
as she moved back through the house. Her eyes caught
the stack of mail on the floor as she turned to move up
the stairs.

With a resigned sigh, she changed course, crouching
down and scooping it up.

It would make for bedtime reading at least, she thought,
wishing she'd thought to pick up some new books while
she'd been out. Maybe other people's lives would provide
the distraction she needed.

She tossed it unceremoniously on the bed and began to
undress for the shower.

The water was warm. She luxuriated beneath it, wiping
her mind clean, refusing to think about Italy, about Matteo
and about their baby. She refused to think about the things
he'd said to her on her last afternoon in Venice.

But none the less, his words rolled through her, spinning around her and making her gasp.

'You are my everything. You are like a universe that lives in my chest.'

She moaned softly, reaching for the loofah and running it over her body.

'When I tell you I need you, I do not mean it in the way you think. It is not sex that I am referring to. I need you as I need air, and I need water.'

She had been right to leave him. She could never trust him, and what was love without trust?

Memories of their days walking through Venice flooded her—of his sharing his *gelato* with the little Romani boy, of the way he'd held her hand and talked about the history of the city and his time growing up in it—and she sobbed, unable to hold her heartache at bay a moment longer.

It was here, in the night time, alone in her enormous house, that she finally allowed herself to admit that the pain wasn't easing. That the ache inside her chest was growing wider with each day that passed. With each day she spent away from Matteo.

It was here that she always came to question her decision, even though she was certain, really, that she'd been right to leave him. To protect herself from the dangers of loving a man like Matteo and living in fear of when his favour would cease to exist.

She closed her eyes; she saw him and her heart lurched.

She banged her palm against the shower then dropped her hand to the taps, turning them slowly, easing the water. But she didn't get out. She stood there immobile for a time. Broken. Her head bent, her back bowed, her body emptying of any hope, happiness and light.

She would gain control of this, though.

She'd known loss and loneliness all her life, and she'd

always found ways to cope. She would do so again. Wouldn't she?

In the end, she pushed the mail to one side of the bed and fell asleep naked, with no energy to so much as find a nightgown. Exhaustion was the saving grace of her current emotional state, but it was followed reliably by insomnia, so that somewhere before dawn she woke, bright and early, and she knew she wouldn't find the relief offered by sleep again.

She sat up in her bed and reached for the stack of mail, contemplating making a cup of coffee, and decided she'd reward herself with a mug only when she'd successfully made her way through at least five of the envelopes.

The first three were invitations to parties and events. She pushed them to one side, knowing she needed to engage some kind of assistant to deal with this stuff. Usually, she was able to keep on top of it, but since Venice she'd been…well…a mess. Besides, she wasn't in a particularly festive mood.

The fourth item was an advertising flyer. She pushed it away without looking and reached for the fifth. It was a little thicker than the rest. She slid her finger under the glued back, already fantasising about the coffee she was going to be enjoying within minutes.

She unfolded the paper and instantly caught her breath.

Her fingertips shook as she straightened the page properly.

The Vin Santo business emblem was unmistakable. A powerful VS embossed in black. She ran her fingertip over it even as her eyes fled to the words.

They were handwritten.

It means nothing without you.

Her heart raced hard and fast against her chest. And, for the first time since leaving Venice, colour was in her cheeks and something like hope and joy filled her. She flipped the page and saw what was behind it.

The contracts she'd had sent for the transfer of the hotel.

Exactly as she'd sent them, except for one vital detail.

He'd put a large, black cross through each page. And had failed to add his signature.

She shuddered, falling back against the pillows, her eyes shut, the letter clutched to her chest.

It means nothing without you.

She groaned, pushing the bed linen off her and standing, reaching for her robe. She wrapped it around her body, cinching it at the waist, and brought the letter with her as she moved back downstairs into the kitchen.

She slid a pod into her coffee machine, pressing the button distractedly as she read his words for the tenth time.

It means nothing without you.

The hotel was all he'd wanted.

It was why he'd married her.

And she was offering it to him now with no strings, no regrets.

Did he really mean this? Why not just take the damned hotel and be done with it?

It means nothing without you.

She closed her eyes and she was back in Rome, staring at the building, admiring its beauty, imagining it for its potential. Seeing it as they would have made it, with its flowers, its flags and its doormen.

She breathed in and tasted the history of the hotel, the past that lived within its walls. She saw it as Matteo had described, full of people and music, atmosphere and pleasure. She saw the terrace with elegant cocktails and guests milling about.

And she forced her eyes open.

For the first time in a month, she knew what she had to do.

This hotel had to be returned to its rightful owner. Matteo *had* to fix the damage her father's vengeance had done. From this pile of sadness, something good could come.

And she'd just have to make him see sense.

Matteo stared at the email with a strange sense of non-comprehension. Skye's lawyer was requesting a meeting, in person, with him.

And he knew what it was about.

The damned divorce.

In the five weeks since she'd left, he'd begun to hope that perhaps silence was golden. That she'd changed her mind. That perhaps she needed space to grieve, to come to terms with their loss, but she would see he'd meant every word he'd said.

He'd given her the breathing space to do what she needed; he owed her that much. And every day that had passed he'd hoped meant she would change her mind. That her certainty was fading.

But now?

He shook his head, reaching for his phone and dialling the number on the top of the page.

'Matteo Vin Santo. I need to make an appointment with Charles Younger.'

Skye stared at the view of London, wondering at her own treachery. She had always loved this city, yet now she found herself seeing only its grey sky and bleak steel monoliths. She didn't see the way the sun glinted off the side of the buildings, nor the way the Thames glistened through its heart like a powerful lifeblood.

She flicked her gaze down to her wristwatch and her pulse ran faster.

He was late.

Or was it possible that he wasn't coming?

She gnawed at her lip and moved away from the window, towards the table at the side of the meeting room. It had a selection of Danish pastries, a jug of fruit juice and bottles of cold water.

Skye opted for coffee, pouring a large measure into a fine bone-china cup and clasping it between her hands. It was reassuring to feel its warmth and smell its comforting aroma. Somehow, it grounded her.

A noise outside the door sounded and she froze, bracing herself for what was to come, knowing she would need all her wits about her to get through the next portion of her day.

The door pushed open and Charles Younger stood on the other side, incredibly handsome for a man in his sixties, with a kindly smile.

'Skye.' He nodded as he moved into the room.

But she wasn't looking at Charles.

Her eyes were greedy and they moved past the lawyer instantly, seeking the man she had been denied for so long. Matteo stepped into the room and everything froze. Time and physical existence.

It was all completely wrong. Being here with him yet not being able to touch him. Knowing she couldn't smile at him, even when she wanted so badly to pretend everything was as she'd thought—as she'd hoped.

Her own feelings overtook every other sense, but then, after only seconds, her eyes began to work properly, to see more than her own grief and heartache.

Her eyes saw him.

They saw the pallor of his skin and the grey beneath his eyes. The way his five o'clock shadow was more pronounced than ever, and the way his suit, which usually looked as though it had been lovingly stitched to his body, seemed loose and ill-fitting. She saw the way his eyes held hers for only a brief moment before moving away.

She saw in him something she recognised instantly, for it moved inside her.

She saw how he was broken.

And a sob filled her chest. She bit it back with effort, knowing she had to be strong.

'I'll be outside,' Charles said quietly. 'Just holler when you need me.'

Skye nodded curtly, a little more able to handle the situation given that she'd called the meeting and it was, more or less, on her home turf.

Charles left and silence fell. It sucked the air from the room and replaced it with something else altogether.

'Skye,' Matteo murmured, taking a step towards her and then pausing, his expression shifting. 'How are you?'

The question was her undoing, because he'd asked it in a way that had gone beyond civility. He asked as though knowing how she was meant everything to him.

'I'm...' She frowned. How could she respond? He looked as though he hadn't slept in weeks. Possibly hadn't eaten in that time either. 'Would you like something?' She grimaced as she heard the vague question leave her mouth. 'Croissant? Danish?'

His eyes glittered with a hint of the ruthlessness that was his stock in trade. She was glad to see it. She would take his ruthlessness over the sense of brokenness any day. 'Neither of those things.'

Her heart kerthunked.

'I'm glad you came,' she said softly, then cleared her throat and tried again. 'Please, take a seat.'

He arched a brow but did as she said, moving to one side of the table and sitting in a chair as though he owned it. That was an innate skill he possessed, she thought as she took the seat opposite. He commanded furniture, rooms, people, all effortlessly.

She cupped her coffee in front of herself and saw the moment his eyes dropped to her hands. Was he noticing that she didn't wear the wedding ring? Did he care?

Yes.

He cared. She couldn't deny that he was in pain, as she was.

The information felt strange inside her. Like a weight she didn't know how to carry.

'Well, Skye,' he drawled, his accent thick. 'Why am I here?'

She nodded, understanding that he wanted this over as quickly as she did. Pain lodged in her chest.

'I got your letter.'

'What letter?' he prompted, his brow furrowed.

'The hotel.' She didn't meet his eyes. 'The returned contracts.'

Silence prickled around the room. 'I sent that a long time ago.'

She shrugged. 'I just got it.' She thought of the pile of mail she'd been stepping over and wondered when, exactly, the contracts had arrived. Charles had sent them almost as soon as she'd returned, with much disapproval and uncertainty about what Skye was proposing.

'I see.' He reclined back in his chair and she chanced a look at his face, then instantly wished she hadn't when her whole body seemed to catch fire. Her arms flecked with goose-bumps and desire slammed through her.

'I want you to have the hotel.' She leaned forward. 'It deserves to be what it used to be.'

His eyes narrowed. 'Then you are certainly able to renovate it.'

She recoiled as if he'd slapped her. How could she? How could she walk into the place that was like a living testament to Matteo? How could she oversee its renovations knowing that every colour scheme she chose or fitting she selected would be like touching Matteo all over again?

'No.' A terse word full of fear and meaning. 'I don't want it.'

'Nor do I,' he said softly. 'Unless you are part of the deal.'

'No more deals,' she whispered. 'Just common sense.'

'Common sense?' He arched a brow and then stood, moving towards the window. Skye's eyes captured every detail of him, greedily devouring him under the cover of his back being turned. She saw that he was, indeed, slimmer than he had been. That his hair was longer. That he was altered physically by what they'd experienced.

And guilt waved through her. Losing the baby had been a nightmare for her. But what about Matteo? She couldn't deny that he'd wanted their child. She didn't doubt that for a moment.

'How are you?' She whispered the question, the words full of haunted agony.

'How am I?' He spun around, pinning her with eyes that were full of Matteo, yet were not. Eyes that glowed with arrogance and pain. Eyes that were miserable.

'How am I?' he repeated, moving across the room towards her so that she held her breath and felt like she was being whipped with every step he took. His proximity was danger and delight.

'I am ruined, Skye.'

She couldn't hold her sob this time. It burst out of her but she said nothing. She could only stare and *feel*. Feel *everything*, all at once. All her hopes and loves and needs and wants, all her soul and her body and her heart.

'I am ruined.' He crouched before her and stared at her without touching. 'I am a half-man since you left. I have spent these weeks needing you, needing to hear your voice, to know that you are okay. Worrying for you, wishing for you. I have lived and breathed every day full of anger at my own stupidity. And the worst part of it is that you're right. You were right to walk out on me. After what I did to you, how can I hope you would love me still? You offered me your heart once and I was not man enough to understand what a gift it was. A stupid hotel! For a stupid hotel, I gambled you.'

Skye stared at him, her skin pricking with goose-bumps.

'I spent my life wanting that damned building, to the point I was blind to the truth of what we had. I hated your father, and I thought I was getting some petty kind of revenge in marrying you. And yet he has the last laugh, because I ruined even this. I fell in love with you and seem to have done everything I could to push you away.'

He dragged a hand through his hair. 'I have tormented myself with memories of all that I have said to you. Done to you. Of the way I have made it seem as though it's only your body I value, because I was too proud to admit how utterly you have all of me. How I rejected your love even when it was all I wanted.'

Skye bit back another sob, the grief of their situation permeating her body.

'I don't deserve you. I know that. But, even now, I need to know that you understand. That this is your decision. If you want me, I am yours. I don't expect you to be stupid enough to give me another chance, Skye, but if you were… If you did…'

'Don't!' she cried, squeezing her eyes shut. 'This is hard enough…'

He reached for her hand and pressed it to his chest, and then he held his other palm flat against hers. 'Feel how we beat in unison. How our hearts know what we are too stupid to comprehend.'

She shook her head, tears stinging her eyes. 'Teo…'

He moved his hand from her chest and reached into the breast pocket of his suit. He pulled out a small velvet box and Skye froze, staring at her husband and then the little cube.

Before she could say anything, he popped the lid open and Skye's gaze fell to the ring.

And her chest rolled.

It was perfect.

Of their own volition, her fingertips moved to the ring and lifted it, staring at the details with a sense of awe. It was rose-gold with intricate patterns carved into the narrow band, and there were small diamonds set the whole way around. They were not of huge value, nor size, but they were beautiful.

'It's...very nice,' she said softly, sliding it back into the box.

Matteo's smile was just a quick twist of his lips. 'It is what I should have chosen the first time around. I knew, as soon as you wore the other, that I had been wrong. That you are someone who prefers beauty over cost.'

She swallowed and looked away. 'The hotel...'

He shook his head, interrupting her with urgency. 'Do you remember what you said about love and hate? About how close they are on the emotional spectrum?'

Skye turned to face him, her eyes huge.

'I hated your father, Skye. I hated him practically my whole life, to an almost mythical proportion. I came here, to London, wanting the hotel more than anything in my life. I expected to hate you. I thought I could use you without experiencing even a hint of remorse over it.'

She hardened her heart and tilted her chin, telling herself to be strong even when she was grieving anew, like barely healed wounds were being sliced open.

'But I met you and everything changed. The world began to spin in entirely the wrong direction. Hate became love, but I didn't want to believe it. My idiocy makes it no less true, my darling, my love. Can you not see that I have loved you all along?'

Her expression was mutinous but hope flared large in her chest. 'You still tried to take the hotel.'

'Something I will always regret,' he murmured. 'Something I am trying to fix now, if you will let me. I want it out of our lives. It meant everything to me because it was such a big part of my family's history. But I will not jeopardise our future for my past.'

Skye swallowed, his words turning something around inside her. She remembered something else he'd said to her, what felt like a lifetime ago. *You are already smart. Why not be happy?*

'I don't know what to think. I don't know what to say. I feel one thing and I think another.'

'I know, I know.' He nodded gently, kneeling and pressing his forehead to hers. 'And you are right to question me. I *know* I will never hurt you again, but that it will take time to show you. So I ask you the same question I did in Venice on your last day. I know I have no right to even hope; that you have no reason to trust me. But, Skye, I ask only… Will you simply give me a chance to show you, *cara*?'

Her heart was trembling. 'I just… I don't think I can.' At his look of anguish, certainty filled her. 'The thing is, a chance isn't good enough.'

He nodded, putting some space between them.

'Then tell me what you need, *bella*. Tell me what will make you happy and I will do it.'

'Even if that means leaving? And never seeing me again?'

A muscle jerked in his cheek but he nodded. 'Yes, Skye.' She saw him swallow and brace himself, and she understood the emotions that were spreading through him. The pain and fear and miserable acceptance. But he continued bravely. 'I will never *not* love you. I will never not need you. But I will leave you alone…if this is what you want.'

And, finally, she smiled.

A smile that spread over her face and through her body. A smile that was definitely not matched by Matteo's expression.

'Why would I want you to leave me alone?'

He frowned, his confusion understandable.

'Oh, Matteo.' His name quivered against her mouth. 'I wish everything between us had been different.' She chewed on her lower lip thoughtfully. 'I wish there was no family feud, no hotel. No anger and hatred. But, even with things the way they were, I still loved you.'

His lips were grim. 'Because you are all that is kind and good. Only you could love a man like me…'

She held a hand up to silence him, pressing her fingertip to his lips. 'I married you because I loved you. I left you because I loved you too much to live with you, when you didn't feel the same way about me.'

'Only I did, *cara*. I've been such a damned fool.'

'Yes,' Skye murmured, narrowing her eyes thoughtfully. 'But, seeing as you've seen the light and are prepared to spend the rest of your life showing me each and every day just how much I mean to you, it would be rather foolish for me to make either of us suffer a moment longer. Right?' She lifted a hand to his cheek. 'We *are* both miserable, aren't we?'

His eyes swept over her face and he nodded, a grim gesture of agreement.

'So let's not be.' She lifted her hands and held his face, then moved her own closer.

'What exactly do you mean?' He was cautious, his expression guarded.

'You're my husband,' she said with an impish grin, mirroring a phrase he used often. She leaned her face forward, so their lips were only an inch apart. 'And I love you. As much now…no, more…than the day we married.'

His groan was heavy with emotion; his eyes swept shut. When he opened them again, Skye was staring at him, a smile on her sweet, pink lips.

'Do not kiss me,' he warned throatily. 'Or I will ravage you here and now.'

Skye's eyes twinkled. 'Then how about we go back to my place?'

'Right now?'

'Right now.'

They didn't make it upstairs.

They barely made it to her sofa. Skye welcomed her husband back into her home and her arms, needing to feel him more than she'd ever felt anyone or anything. He kissed her, he held her and he made love to her in a way that showed her what he'd been showing her all along.

There was no way their chemistry was just a physical thing.

It was all of them. It was everything.

She lay on his chest afterwards, her head pressed to his toned body, listening to the strong beating of his heart and knowing he was right—that it did indeed beat in unison with hers.

'Well, *cara*, what do you say?' he murmured against her hair, adjusting himself slightly as he reached to their pile of rumpled clothes on the floor beside them.

'About what?' The words were heavy with satisfaction and completion. She was energised and exhausted all at once.

He brought his hand close to her face and she blinked her eyes towards him, moving so that she could see him more clearly. She stared at the ring box, and her heart ker-thunked against her ribcage.

'Would you consider wearing this ring? Will you be my wife?'

She wrinkled her nose. 'I *am* your wife.'

'Yes, you are,' he agreed, pulling the ring from its position and holding it towards her. Skye pushed up higher and held out her hand. Her fingertips were quivering.

'But I want the world to know it.' His eyes glittered with her possessively. 'With this ring, in this moment, with all my heart…' the words were gravelled '… I thee wed.'

She stared down at it and smiled, meeting his eyes and nodding. She wasn't even sure he'd asked a question, but she knew she needed to reassure him. To promise him that she had meant what she'd said in her lawyer's office.

'I had it inscribed,' he said huskily, holding the ring out to her.

She took it and lifted it closer to her eyes, peering into the fine gold band and reading the elegant scrawl.

Tu sei il mio sangue.

'You are my *sangue*?' she asked, repeating the final word aloud.

'You are my blood,' he said with a nod. 'And everything else of me. Always.'

A shiver of delight ran down her spine and she handed the ring back to him then extended her hand.

She watched as her husband slid the ring onto her finger—it fitted exactly. As though it had been designed for her.

'It's perfect.'

'As are you.' He pushed up and kissed her with a drugging, sensual need. 'It is very old. One of six that were made in the middle ages by a famous Venetian designer.'

She nodded, but she was moving over him already, her hands and her wedding ring tangling in his thick hair. Over his shoulder, her eyes caught sight of the gladioli she'd purchased over a week earlier. They had begun to bloom without her noticing and they stood now, proud and confident, filled with colour and light, the promise of all that they were fulfilled.

'You are as much a part of Venetian history as I am,' he murmured and she nodded, tears sparkling in her eyes.

'And I always will be.'

EPILOGUE

Two years later

'ARE YOU READY?' Skye asked her husband, smiling at him. She had expected to be nervous, given what they were about to do. But it was Matteo who showed all the signs of being on the brink of a breakdown.

Well, that was only fair.

This baby belonged to both of them, after all. They'd both helped make it, over long, exhausting months.

And now it was time.

Finally.

To show the world what the Vin Santos had achieved, side by side.

'As I'll ever be.' He squeezed her hand and his eyes roamed her face. *'Ti amo.'*

'Lo so.'

'Let's go.' The door to the car was opened and Matteo stepped out, standing aside to make room for his wife.

She was resplendent in a black ballgown. Cameras flashed everywhere, perfectly catching the bright red of the geraniums that tumbled in the moonlight from every window of the hotel.

'Have you heard news of the twins?' he asked, tucking a hand into the small of her back.

Skye's gaze drifted up past the brass flagpoles towards the perfectly restored windows that overlooked the river Tiber.

'The nanny texted just before. They have been asleep for over an hour.' She nodded. 'They're waiting for us in the penthouse.'

'Ah! I thought Francesca was going to give us some difficulties there,' he said.

'She never does travel well,' Skye agreed. 'Then again, she's only twelve months old. That's normal for this age, I believe.'

'And she is very cute.' He winked. 'Like her mother.'

Skye felt colour flush along to the roots of her hair, amazed at how his compliments could still turn her insides to mush.

'And Alfonso is just like you.'

'Yes.' Matteo grimaced. 'I'm sorry about that. His determination is a force to be reckoned with.'

Skye nodded. 'But we'll reckon with it together.'

The crowds parted to allow them entry into the hotel. Christmas Eve at Il Grande Fortuna for the first time in decades was just as magical as Skye had hoped—it was everything she'd imagined from Matteo's stories and the photographs she'd seen. It was sublime.

'Shall we dance?'

Skye nodded, catching the classical Christmas carols and smiling. *'Si.'*

She put her hand in his and he held her tight, and with his body he promised everything she already knew to be true.

She was safe with him and she was loved by him.

They were a family.

And she'd never feel loneliness again.

* * * * *

COMING SOON!

We really hope you enjoyed reading this book. If you're looking for more romance, be sure to head to the shops when new books are available on

Thursday
23rd August

To see which titles are coming soon, please visit **millsandboon.co.uk**

MILLS & BOON

Coming next month

THE HEIR THE PRINCE SECURES
Jennie Lucas

He eyed the baby in the stroller, who looked back at him with dark eyes exactly like his own. He said simply, 'I need you and Esme with me.'

'In London?'

Leaning forward, he whispered, 'Everywhere.'

She felt the warmth of his breath against her skin, and her heartbeat quickened. For so long, Tess would have done anything to hear Stefano speak those words.

But she'd suffered too much shock and grief today. He couldn't tempt her to forget so easily how badly he'd treated her. She pulled away.

'Why would I come with you?'

Stefano's eyes widened. She saw she'd surprised him.

Giving her a crooked grin, he said, 'I can think of a few reasons.'

'If you want to spend time with Esme, I will be happy to arrange that. But if you think I'll give up my family and friends and home—' she lifted her chin '—and come with you to Europe as some kind of paid nanny—'

'No. Not my nanny.' Stefano's thumb lightly traced her tender lower lip. 'I have something else in mind.'

Unwilling desire shot down her body, making her nipples taut as tension coiled low in her belly. Her pride was screaming for her to push him away but it was difficult to hear her pride over the rising pleas of her body.

'I—I won't be your mistress, either,' she stammered, shivering, searching his gaze.

'No.' With a smile that made his dark eyes gleam, Stefano shook his head. 'Not my mistress.'

'Then…then what?' Tess stammered, feeling foolish for even suggesting a handsome billionaire prince like Stefano would want a regular girl like her as his mistress. Her cheeks were hot. 'You don't want me as your nanny, not as your mistress, so—what? You just want me to come to London as someone who watches your baby for free?' Her voice shook. 'Some kind of…p-poor relation?'

'No.' Taking her in his arms, Stefano said quietly, 'Tess. Look at me.'

Although she didn't want to obey, she could not resist. She opened her eyes, and the intensity of his glittering eyes scared her.

'I don't want you to be my mistress, Tess. I don't want you to be my nanny.' His dark eyes burned through her. 'I want you to be my wife.'

Continue reading
THE HEIR THE PRINCE SECURES
Jennie Lucas

Available next month
www.millsandboon.co.uk

LET'S TALK
Romance

For exclusive extracts, competitions
and special offers, find us online:

f facebook.com/millsandboon

◉ @millsandboonuk

🐦 @millsandboon

Or get in touch on 0844 844 1351*

For all the latest titles coming soon, visit
millsandboon.co.uk/nextmonth